There was a rattle and a c

Cindy Ann turned and saw Chester hunched over the padlock of the tool chest with a rusted ball-peen hammer in hand. With a grimace of stubborn determination, the boy began to assault the lock with a number of sharp, well-placed blows.

I've got to get out of here, she told herself. *Get out before it's too late.*

As Cindy reached the loose board in the wall, she caught sight of something out of the corner of her eye. It was a dark object tucked away in the dank shadows near an old plow.

It was a hat —a grey fedora long since misshapen and water-

logged by dampness. Curiously, she picked up the hat and turned it over in her hands.

"Gotcha . . . Johnny!" rasped a gravelly voice in her mind, followed by the deafening and deadly discharge of a twelve-gauge shotgun.

Cindy whirled, her heart pounding and tears welling in her eyes, just as the padlock burst apart under a mighty swing of the hammer. Chester grinned, freed the clasp from the rest of the broken lock, and began to lift the lid.

The girl screamed shrilly, full of terror and dread.

"DON'T OPEN THAT BOX!"

Copyright ©1990 by Ronald Kelly
ISBN 978-1-63789-815-4
Macabre Ink is an imprint of Crossroad Press Publishing
All rights reserved. No part of this book may be used or reproduced in any manner
whatsoever without written permission except in the case of
brief quotations embodied in critical articles and reviews
For information address Crossroad Press at 141 Brayden Dr., Hertford, NC 27944
www.crossroadpress.com

Ctrossroad Press Trade Edition

To Jason,
Sometimes true evil can only be seen through the eyes of a child.

RONALD KELLY

HINDSIGHT

BONUS NOVELLA:

POTTER'S FIELD

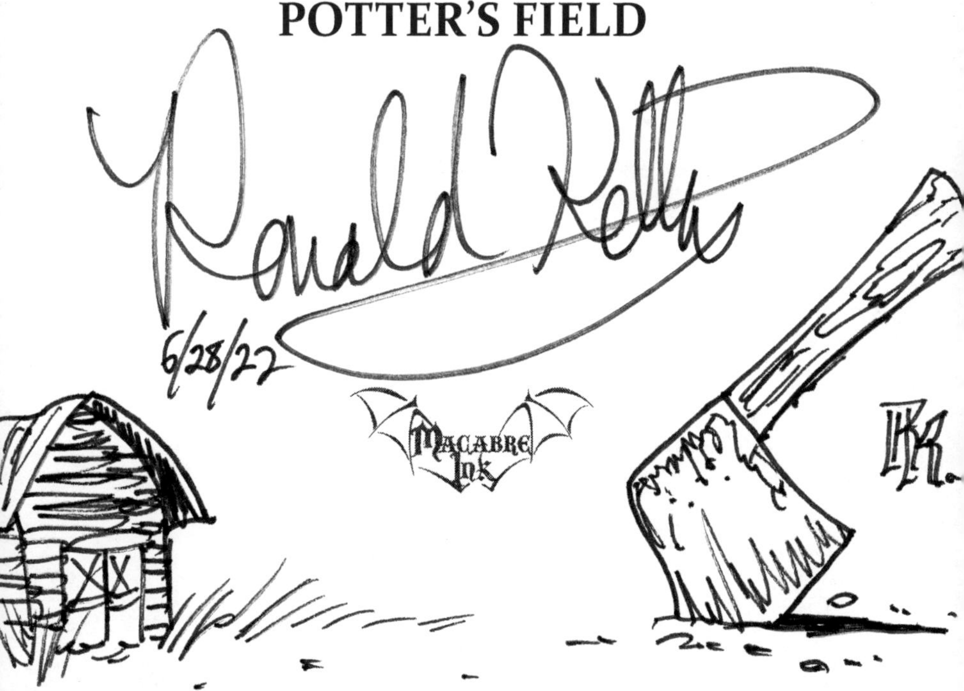

To Mama and the little girl who knew things.

Prologue

1936 was a bad year for the tobacco farmer in Tennessee.

There had been rough times before; failed crops due to circumstances beyond human control. Weather, insects, and disease . . . all had a hand in doing their fair share of damage in the past. But now they faced a new menace, one that the common dirt farmer could not fight using horse sense and elbow grease. The Depression had its thorny claws in Bedloe County. And, Lord help them, money was one thing they could not cultivate from a mixture of sweat and precious earth.

Men, rawboned and aged from long years of laboring in sun and snow, now stood silently at the break of day. They listened to the distant crowing of the rooster and stared forlornly, some bitterly, at land that no longer belonged to them. The rich, fertile tobacco land that had provided for their fathers and their grandfathers before them was now in the hands of the banker. Deeds had been signed over, heritages traded in for a handful of greenbacks — money to pay bills and buy food, with barely enough left over to buy the children their winter shoes come September. Many had moved northward to the pressing crowds and vague promises of factories and mills. Those who chose to remain hunted steady work at poor wages or sought out odd jobs wherever they might be found.

Land stretched barren across the county; unplowed, empty, and useless. On some of the acreage stood the tobacco barns — huge hulking structures once used to fire-cure the leaves before grading and marketing. One such structure, the largest in Bedloe County, stood alone amid the neglected acres of one Harvey Brewer. It had not been used since the day Harvey's wife,

Norma, died of a stroke back in the summer of 1928. On that day, the old man had given up all interests, farming included. He had chained and padlocked the huge, double doors of the barn, left his entire tobacco crop to rot and wither in the field, and confined himself to the house he and Norma had shared for fifty-seven years. There he remained, unwilling to leave its darkened rooms, except for an occasional stroll into town for a few meager supplies.

Meanwhile, the tobacco barn stood sentry at the edge of the Brewer property, seemingly impervious to the effects of time. Built of sturdy lumber and capped with eaves of corrugated tin, the structure observed the events of passing years. It witnessed the crashing fall of the economy and the hardship that followed. There had been prosperity and happiness in the past, but those memories had now lost their luster. Times were hard and full of hopelessness. Bitterness, anger, and grief spread across the southern land, all born from one sorry state of widespread misfortune . . . poverty.

Perhaps it was the old gray-wood barn's detachment from hard times that made it a secret haven for a select few,; a cool oasis amid a burning desert of utter despair. Loose boarding gave access to the dark interior where solitude reigned. Inhibitions were left outside, and therefore, sin was spawned. Oh, it began with small, insignificant transgressions at first: the smoking of an adolescent's first hand-rolled cigarette or the passionate petting of two love-struck teenagers.

But it would not end there, for small sins would surely blossom into those of a darker and more unsavory nature. In the murky confines of the old barn they would be nurtured. The rafters would echo with the rasp of dirty laughter, and the air would grow tainted with the stench of cheap liquor, until, one night, a great evil would be committed in the belly of that abandoned structure… a terrible and unspeakable evil.

And there it would be concealed, buried and forgotten, until the prying eyes of a single child revealed the very nature of its horror.

Part One

Bloody Spring

Chapter One

"Now, ain't that just the cutest thing?" said Vera Mae Holt. The perky mother-to-be peeled back the brown wrapping paper and held up her third and final gift, a tiny nightshirt of blue cotton flannel.

"I used the same pattern for little Jason's first nightie," Clara Jones smiled proudly. She bounced her ten-month-old son playfully on her knee. Clara's prowess as a seamstress was well known throughout Bedloe County. Between four children of her own and those of neighboring families, her old Singer foot-pedal sewing machine had no chance whatsoever of gathering dust.

"Well, Clara, I surely appreciate it." Vera Mae beamed. She delicately folded the tiny garment and placed it beside her rocking chair, along with the other gifts.

It was the twelfth day of May, a bright and balmy day painted brilliant with wild flowers, greenery, and a cloudless blue sky. A light breeze drifted through the peeling posts of the Holts' front porch and swept comfortably around the women sitting there. The warm current was as gentle and fresh as the wakening breath of a newborn infant, which was appropriate, for the gathering on the porch was a baby shower for the expectant Vera Mae.

The group was a small, close-knit one, just a few of the neighboring ladies who lived along the rutted dirt stretch of Old Newsome Road. Accompanying them was a scattering of fidgety youngsters, all of whom would much rather be out playing than standing idly about on the porch of the Holts' small, three-room farmhouse.

Vera Mae sat in the straight-backed rocker, her freckled face glowing with maternal anticipation and her belly just as prominent. The girl was barely eighteen, and this was her first child. She and Winston Holt had married less than a year ago, but her sudden pregnancy had not really shocked the ladies of Bedloe County. Since the age of fourteen, Vera Mae had developed something of a reputation in the town of Coleman, Tennessee. She had been pegged as a brassy girl, a loose young woman who enjoyed strong drink and dancing. Why, she had even been seen on several occasions, staggering drunk at the Bloody Bucket, a local beer joint. But then she had met Winston at a church supper, and he seemed to be able to keep a handle on her. Since marrying, she had tamed most of her improper behavior, but still possessed a fair amount of sassiness. That morning she seemed to flaunt her pregnancy as much as she had once flaunted her questionable morals.

The others on the porch were all good neighbors. Behind Vera Mae stood her mother, Eliza Reeves, a frail woman with silver hair and thick spectacles. Nearby sat Stella Longcreek, a petite woman in her forties, and of course Clara and her bouncing boy Jason. On the porch swing sat Maudie Biggs. Maudie was a hefty woman in her late thirties. Her round face was pretty, but drably plain, her dark red hair showing streaks of premature grayness. Beside her on the pinewood swing sat four-year-old Sammy, a dark-haired child rather tall and gangling for a boy his age. To Maudie's left, leaning with her back to the tarpaper wall, stood Cindy Ann.

Cindy was the sort of child some folks noticed right off, while others neglected to notice at all. She was an overly shy girl, small for going on ten, and frail to the point of boniness. The two things that made her stand out the most were her hazel green eyes and her orange-red hair, both undoubtedly inherited from her mother's side of the family.

After the gifts had been opened and the small talk had dwindled, the women sat in the shade and grew silent. The pause in conversation was awkward, but understandable, for further talk and gossip would only bring up the inevitable subject of hard times. All five women were the wives of farmers, mostly of tobacco. Their men had all suffered the plight of the Depression; all had had to give up farming temporarily until better times made the growing of their particular crop profitable again. Winston Holt and his father-in-law, Jasper, worked at a sawmill over in Galbreth County. Stella Longcreek worked at the post office in town, her no-account, drifting husband having left her years ago. Norman Jones had bid farewell to Clara and her children last March to find a .steady job up north in Michigan, hoping to settle there and send for them later. As for the Biggs family, Maudie's husband, Clayburn, made a few dollars weekly doing odd jobs and mechanic work for some of the more fortunate citizens in Coleman.

Vera Mae started to break the silence by commenting on Stella's prized flower garden, when she felt a strange sensation. Her words faded, and her eyes widened slightly.

"What's the matter, Vera darling?" asked her mother.

The young woman smiled with a mixture of wonderment and pride. "The baby just kicked," Vera said, toying with a strand of curly blond hair. "I do believe the little fella's gonna be some square dancer, the way he's been carrying on this morning."

"They really let you know they're there the last few days," Clara volunteered, putting her two-cents' worth in as far as child bearing was concerned. "I'd say you'll be due before the end of the week."

"Yes, ma'am," agreed Vera Mae. "Shouldn't be long." The blonde turned her eyes to the red-haired child who stood near the porch swing. "You sure have been awful quiet this morning, Cynthia Ann."

The nine-year-old nodded and offered a polite smile.

Maudie Biggs glanced apologetically at the other women. "Cindy just ain't had much of anything to say since her bout with the fever."

Stella leaned forward and talked in a low, confidential tone of voice. "Well now, that's perfectly understandable, Maudie. I mean, a child her age shut up in the hospital with typhoid for nearly six months, well, it must've been quite a fright. She'll get her spunk back now that she's out of that awful place and back home with her family."

Maudie Biggs wasn't sure. Cynthia Ann had always been a shy, introverted girl, one who was more content with listening than talking. Maudie's older daughter, Polly, was just the opposite. The feisty twelve-year-old could talk the ears off a corn stalk.

Vera Mae Holt placed her hand on her bloated stomach and blushed. "My, the little booger's sure giving me a time of it today." She stretched her free hand out toward Cindy. "Child, do you want to feel my baby kick?"

Cindy took a reluctant step, then turned her eyes to Maudie. "Mama?"

"Go ahead if you want to," Maudie said with a wink. She had never believed in keeping the subject of sex and the miracle of birth a mysterious taboo as far as their five children were concerned. No confusing tales of midwives toting infants in satchels or babies discovered beneath cabbage leaves; just straight forward answers whenever that delicate curiosity arose.

Cindy walked timidly across the dusty boards of the porch until she came within a few feet of Vera Mae. She gave the woman her right hand. As Vera lowered the girl's open palm to the bulge of her midsection, Cindy felt her nervousness rise to a heart-thumping crescendo. Her young mind reeled, her senses seeming to tingle with excitement. But it was not the mystery of pregnancy that scared Cynthia Ann. No, it was something else... something extremely difficult to explain. She was frightened of what she might think or, rather, *feel* when her hand made contact with the young woman's belly.

Vera Mae laughed incredulously as the red-haired girl resisted her grasp. "Don't be frightened now, Cindy Ann. It ain't gonna jump out and bite you!"

The blonde pulled her hand a few inches closer, and suddenly the flat of her palm was there, pressed against the curvature of her abdomen. Just as abruptly, Cindy felt a peculiar warmth engulf her. It was a safe, unthreatening warmth, not a burning, dry heat like the fevers she had run for days during her long stay in the Nashville hospital. The warmth that engulfed her now was soothing, a liquid sensation almost like that of lying in a tub of warm water.

"You just wait a second and you'll feel it. You'll feel him kick."

Cindy did not answer. The feeling of warmth was spreading past her physical being, washing across her thoughts, dominating them like the coming of a deep slumber. She knew she should be frightened, terribly frightened, for what she now experienced was far from normal. But the sensation felt all too pleasurable, too *safe* to pull away from. She let her mind drift, let her senses focus solely on the life within Vera Mae.

She sensed darkness around her. Her mortal eyes still saw Vera Mae's glowing face and the pretty flower print of her dress, but her inner senses, the *stronger* senses, saw nothing but dull blackness. The absence of light did not frighten her. There was still the warmth, the sensation of floating safely in bodily fluid. It was a feeling that echoed strangely from Cindy's own past, years and years ago. Although the child could not pinpoint the elusive memory, it was deeply rooted, forever imprinted upon her subconscious. What she now experienced was the security of fetal existence, the dark liquid warmth of the womb.

"Do you feel it kicking?"

Vera Mae's voice came to her from a hundred miles away. She felt the kick, but it was as if it were her own and not that of the unborn infant. The jerk was involuntary, the unconscious impulse of newly developed muscle and bone. Her bare foot struck out, but instead of hitting the wooden boards of the porch floor, it seemed to strike a cushiony wall. A living wall of soft membrane.

"There, did you feel it just then?"

Cindy didn't answer. She could not. She was so involved with her strange experience that nothing else mattered, nothing but the surge of warmth and darkness that engulfed her.

"Cynthia Ann . . . what's wrong?" Her mother's voice, muffled and distant.

Abruptly, the pleasant state of contentment vanished. An electric jolt of alarm rushed through her as something brushed her face, something unseen in the darkness. It was long and pliant, weaving like a snake around her head and shoulders. She began to jerk spasmodically as the length of cord slipped around her throat. Cindy felt the elastic rope close tighter and tighter, choking, strangling the very life from her.

"What's wrong, girl?"

"For heaven's sake, Cynthia Ann, what's the matter?"

Tighter the cord bunched, constricting the tender muscles of her throat, cutting off the precious supply of blood and oxygen from her brain. She felt dizzy, as if she were about to pass out or . . . die. The sudden realization snapped Cindy out of her panic, and she knew at once what she must do. Pull away, screamed her thoughts. *Pull away now . . . before it's too late!*

And just as the last spasm of life seemed to shudder through her being, she pulled her hand away from Vera's stomach and found herself back in the world she knew —a world of light and color and concerned hands reaching out to grasp her.

"Cindy . . . what happened?" demanded Maudie, her voice upset. "What in tarnation is the matter with you?"

Cindy ignored her mother's flustered questions. Her bright hazel eyes were glazed as she stared blankly at Vera Mae's puzzled face.

"It's dead," she told her.

Vera Mae Holt leaned forward, her confusion now edged with cold fear. "What did you say, child?"

"The baby . . . it's dead."

Maudie Biggs was shocked into dumb silence, as were the others present. Her hands closed firmly, almost angrily, upon the girl's narrow shoulders. "Now, that's pure nonsense, Cindy. Why would you want to say such a terrible thing?"

The numbness had worn off now, and the redheaded girl stared at her mother, tears welling in her eyes. "It's true, Mama," she choked hoarsely. "I swear it's true. It is dead. It is!"

Maudie glared hard at her daughter and then glanced up at the other ladies. Clara and Stella both eyed the child coldly, as if they thought her outburst to be some awfully distasteful joke. Vera Mae and her mother were just the opposite. They seemed truly affected by Cindy's exclamation. Vera Mae sat back in her rocking chair, her pretty face pale and sick with worry.

"That's a mighty hateful thing to say to someone in Vera Mae's delicate condition!" Maudie said heatedly. She steered Cindy toward the edge of the porch and swatted her sharply on the bottom. "Now, you take your brother and wait for me out by the gate. I'll be there directly."

Cindy cast a quick glance at Vera Mae, a glance full of pity and sorrow, then took little Sammy's hand and descended the wooden steps. Old Tippy, the Biggs' bluetick hound, poked his head from where he had been dozing beneath the porch and reluctantly followed the two children. As the trio crossed the ankle-deep grass of the yard, Cindy heard the young mother-to-be speak in a trembling voice.

"Mama ... I don't feel so good. I want to lie down for a while."

Then Cindy was running. She reached the chicken wire fence and its open gate, its metal strands rusted orange from years of neglect and harsh weather. She released Sammy's hand and hugged the hinged post, her eyes streaming with bitter tears and her breath hitching in shuddering sobs. What she had just experienced on the front porch of the Holt house was something she could not even begin to comprehend. It had all happened in her mind, yet it had been so *real*. The entire episode had horrified her, as did the knowledge that Vera Mae's unborn baby had died only a few short moments before.

She listened as her mother apologized for her unusual behavior, then saw Maudie's blurry form through the prism of her tears. A moment later the woman's powerful hand had closed around Cindy's upper arm, hustling her down the dirt road toward home.

"How dare you embarrass me like that in front of Vera Mae and the others!" grated Maudie, dragging her daughter to the side of the road. She pulled a slender switch from a hickory tree and stripped the leaves from its length with one sweep of her hand. "You just wait till we get home, young lady! I'll give you a whipping you won't soon forget!"

Cindy Ann stared at the wicked switch through her tears, her bare legs almost stinging at the mere thought of the punishment to come. She cried mournfully all the way home, but it was not for her own sake. Her tears came because of something she had seen just before pulling her hand from Vera's bulging waist.

A fleeting glimpse of a small, white casket being lowered into a gaping maw of Tennessee red clay.

Chapter Two

They buried Vera Mae's stillborn child the following Sunday. The cause of death became apparent at the end of her torturous labor. The umbilical cord, the life link between mother and child, had entwined itself around the delicate neck and strangled the infant boy.

Only a few neighbors and close friends accompanied the Holts and their kin to the little cemetery near the Coleman Church of Christ. The day was identical to the one on which the baby shower took place. The sky was clear, the sloping hillside with its scattering of tombstones blanketed with a carpet of young clover and buttercups. Women in dark dresses and veils and rawboned men in ill-fitting suits stood out conspicuously against the sunny, spring afternoon. In everyone's mind, there was something basically wrong about the day's cheerfulness. It just did not seem like a day for burying.

Vera Mae stood beside the tiny grave with her new husband and their kin. She looked much different than she had a few days earlier. The glow of motherly expectation had been replaced by grim depression, and she looked as if she had aged twenty years overnight. She stared across the small hole in the earth, her glazed eyes settling on familiar faces. The recognition seemed to fire an ugly emotion deep in Vera Mae, and she glared at the gathering of concerned country folk with the deepest of hatred.

Most of the blonde's hard feelings were directed at the Biggs family, who stood foremost at the grave's edge. Maudie was there, along with her husband. Clayburn Biggs was a lanky, dark-haired man of forty; a man bronzed Indian red from a life of back-breaking work in the harshest of elements. His face was long and homely and hangdog sad. At the urging of his wife, Clay had abandoned his faded Duckhead overalls and dusty brown hat for his best Sunday-go-to-meeting duds. Patent leather shoes and a touch of Wildroot Creme Oil had transformed Clayburn Biggs from a grease monkey of a tobacco farmer into a rather impressive figure of a man.

Vera Mae's hate raked the faces of the couple and then moved on to the Biggs children. Polly stood beside her mother, while Josh, a sheepish youth of fourteen, took his place beside his pa. Next to him stood Johnny, the eldest. Vera had gone to school with Johnny, but did not know him as well as the other boys in her class. Whereas all the other boys could not keep their eyes, or their hands, off the spicy blonde, Johnny Biggs had never flirted or come on to her in any way. He had always been the perfect gentleman, much to the disgust of Vera Mae's ego.

Her eyes left Johnny and centered on Cynthia Ann. Cindy caught Vera's burning gaze on her. She sensed the hatred directed at her and averted her own eyes to the exposed earth of the gravesite. There it was, the same as in her fleeting vision a few days before. A gaping black hole tunneled by spade and hoe from the rich Tennessee clay. And, within, a perfectly constructed coffin in miniature. Someone had been thoughtful enough to put a thin coat of white paint upon the pine boards, again turning Cindy's strange prophecy into stark reality.

The preacher, Brother Stan Powell, began to read from the Twenty-third Psalm as men respectfully removed their hats and women began to sob softly into lace handkerchiefs. His words were comforting to them all. He told of Vera Mae's tragic loss and gave it a blessed meaning, assuring that God had chosen in His divine wisdom to recall the unborn angel back into His heavenly fold.

Everyone seemed to take solace in the good reverend's soothing words. All except Vera Mae. Her eyes continued to glare at the little white casket as if her very will might raise the precious baby from its eternal rest. The young woman's emotions were understandable to them all, especially the ladies, for Vera Mae had lived a miraculous dream for nine long months.

A dream that had abruptly plunged into the depths of nightmare because of the single touch of a child.

After the preacher had said all there was to say, folks began to express their heartfelt condolences and file down the rocky pathway to the churchyard. Winston and Vera Mae seemed far away, unreceptive to the constant barrage of sympathy. However, when Clay and his family walked over, the young blonde's eyes grew livid with sudden fury. She pushed past Clay and Maudie, searching out the source of all her grief, all her lost hopes and dreams. Finally, she found it. As Winston took his wife gently by the shoulders, Vera extended a trembling finger at the cowering Cindy Ann.

"You!" she cried. "You're the one who did this! You're the one who hexed my baby!" The grieving woman's words came at a rapid pace, slurred, but clearly heard by everyone there, even those on their way down the pathway.

Cindy stared up at Vera Mae, frightened at the spectacle she was making of herself. Everyone within arm's length could smell the liquor on Vera's breath. Obviously, the girl had gotten hold of a bottle shortly before the funeral. Cindy knew much of the woman's anger was just a mixture of grief and cheap whiskey, but a good portion of it was out of genuine loathing for the girl with the fiery red hair.

"Come on now, Vera Mae," Winston told her softly. "There ain't no call to blame the child. What happened to the baby was the Lord's doing, not Cindy's."

"Hah!" laughed Vera Mae. The sound came out humorless, a harsh and balking noise. "What happened to my baby was more the devil's deed than God's. She's a damned witch, I'm telling you. Laid her evil hands upon me and struck my baby dead!"

Cindy backed away from the raving woman, aware that she had met up with someone's legs. She looked up to see her big brother Johnny there. Johnny's nearness had always made her feel safe, for she had a special fondness for him above the others. But this time she could find no comfort from Vera's withering glare or the haunting truth of her hard words.

As the sobbing woman was led away by her mother and

father, Winston Holt, haggard and unshaven, crouched before Cindy and smiled. "I don't want you worrying none about Vera Mae. She didn't mean it. Just her grief talking, is all." He put his calloused hand on her shoulder. "Nary one of us blame you for what happened."

But what he said was not true. Winston's concern was false. Cindy sensed that strongly as she looked into his handsome face. The hate that seethed beyond those sunken, blue eyes was every bit as real as his wife's. *How could you have done such a thing, you little bitch!* his thoughts screamed at her. *How could you do that to our baby?* She felt the heat well up inside him, felt the rage threaten to break from its restraint. She knew he wanted to grab her shoulders roughly and shake her, strike her savagely across the face. But the facade remained intact. Winston Holt walked away, that smile of innocent reassurance held rigidly on his face.

The tears came then, uncontrollable tears spilling down her freckled cheeks. She broke away from her family and ran blindly down the worn pathway, weaving through the departing crowd. Spotting her daddy's old Ford pickup, Cindy climbed into the bed and found a safe corner near the rear of the cab, next to the spare tire. There she wept, long and hard. She wept for Winston and Vera Mae, and for the baby that now lay forever beneath dark red soil; but most of all, she wept for herself. Why had she been cursed with such a horrible power, Cindy wondered. Why did she have to conjure so much misery, so much heartache and suffering, for herself as well as others?

Her sobbing had reached its peak by the time her family got to the truck. Clay, Maudie, and Sammy climbed into the front, while the others piled into the back. She sensed someone settle beside her and felt the comforting caress of a strong but gentle hand on the back of her neck.

"It's gonna be all right, pumpkin. Everything's gonna turn out just fine."

It was Johnny of course. Always Johnny who came to her aid. During her long stay in the hospital, he had been the only one, other than Mama and Pappy, to visit her regularly. She remembered those days best of all, him reading her books like

Swiss Family Robinson and the *Wizard of Oz*, making her laugh no matter how sick she felt. What she would ever do without him, now that he was about to leave home for the steady work of the CCC camps, she could hardly imagine.

At that moment, she did not even want to. Cindy buried her face against Johnny's shirtfront and continued her soft weeping, reveling in the nearness of him, wanting never to let go.

Chapter Three

The amber light of the setting sun peeked through the broadcloth curtains of the back bedroom when Cindy finally lay, exhausted and cried out, on the big, feather bed that she and her sister Polly shared. The rest of the family sat around the kitchen table, eating supper. Their quiet voices filtered through the bedroom door along with the clatter of old china dishes and silverware.

Cindy had half expected her father to make an appearance in the doorway, telling her to quit feeling sorry for herself and join the others for supper. But he hadn't and for that she was grateful. In the hour she had lain on the quilted bed, the nine-year-old had mulled things over in her mind, sorting out confusion and unsettling questions, trying desperately to find the right answers. She found herself thinking about her life, how it had become so very miserable in the past year—the confining year of her illness.

It began last June, on a hot noonday trip to the branch. While the other children played in the near-dry creek bed, she had found a spot all her own. She had stripped down to her undergarments, intending to wade through a still pool of murky water. The summer had been sweltering so far, and there had been no rain for weeks; so only a few puddles of stagnant water could be found in the stony bed of Green Creek.

Watching for snakes, she started across the ankle-deep pool. Halfway there she felt a pin prick at the back of her neck. She swatted at the sudden sting and found it to be a large mosquito. Cindy forgot the bothersome insect and continued on, but then another one bit her and another, stinging her on the bare arms and legs. Suddenly, a living cloud engulfed her. The swarming parasites covered her body, stinging, bringing huge, ugly welts. The maddening buzz of the insects filled her ears, turning fear into panic. Cindy ran screaming up the hollow, away from the harrowing mist of disease-infested mosquitoes.

A week or so later, Cindy was put to bed with a high fever. When her temperature reached a dangerous level, one that could not be controlled with cold compresses and home remedies, the Biggs family knew that their folk medicine was losing out. Clay drove the girl to Nashville one stormy night and checked her into a hospital there. The doctor informed Clay and Maudie that their reluctance to hospitalize their daughter had only worsened her condition.

For two months she lay in burning fever, her young mind drifting in and out of consciousness. Ice packs and various medicines only seemed to hold the illness at bay. Cindy remembered very little about those days. The fiery fever had cut her recollections into confusing fragments. She faintly remembered the faces of doctors and nurses, and the faces of her parents visiting her every weekend. Her fever also brought hallucinations, such as the trunk overflowing with pretty, china dolls that sat at the foot of her hospital bed. The one she had wanted to reach for so many times, yet knew didn't actually exist.

And there was the rooster. That seemed to be the most vivid concoction of her delirium.

There had been a cafe across the street from her hospital room, a greasy spoon whose name she had forgotten. But its sign, which she could plainly see from the window, sported a large depiction of a strutting bantam rooster, the outline laced in neon. During the daylight hours the sign was blandly unimpressive. But at night, the sign was lit up and, oh, what a sight it was. The rooster itself came alive, its magnificent plumage glowing in neon iridescence of yellow, red, and green. In burning fits of fever, Cindy would sometimes imagine the great bird strutting proudly along her windowsill, the hissing and popping of old neon bulbs transforming into an echoing cock crow. The sights and sounds of the hallucination seemed starkly real to the little girl. They almost seemed to transcend the barriers of her weakened mind and awaken something hidden dormant, in the far reaches of her soul.

After a stay of six months, due to complications of pneumonia and mild meningitis, she was finally released in late November. She was still sick, but on a steady road to recovery. Most of her hair had fallen out, she weighed a good twenty pounds lighter, and her legs were so weakened from the illness that folks wondered if she would ever walk again. But the love and guidance of her family had made her slow recovery easier and less painful. By the spring of the following year she was nearly back to normal.

Cindy was concerned however with her father's staunch attitude toward her. Since her return home, Clayburn had had very little to say to his daughter, his eyes noticeably cold toward her. Although she did not know it then, Clay Biggs had sold a good portion of his precious tobacco land to Ransom Potts, the local banker, just to pay off Cindy's expensive hospital bills.

It was during her recovery that Cynthia Ann began to notice that things about her had changed. It was her thoughts and feelings that seemed strangely alien, a disturbing knowledge of things unknown to others. She began to sense things, to know about events that were to take place in the near future. The episodes were insignificant at first, little things, like what her mother would be fixing for supper that night or what song her brother Johnny planned to sing before he even picked up his guitar. But then the power had grown more frightening in nature. Like with Vera Mae Holt and her baby.

Cindy was jolted from her disturbing memories as her mother entered the bedroom and, shutting the door behind her, walked to the bed.

"You feeling any better, Cynthia Ann? I fixed you up a plate." Maudie Biggs held out a plate of white beans and a slab of yellow cornbread, as well as a glass of cold buttermilk. "It ain't much, I'm afraid, but you know how times are."

"Yeah, I know," said Cindy. Suddenly her problems were secondary, her ravenous appetite taking their place.

Maudie sat beside her daughter as the child ate. She watched her, concern etched in the lines of her plain face. Hesitantly,

Maudie reached out and brushed the bangs from Cindy's eyes. The nine-year-old looked up to see tears welling in her mother's eyes.

"Mama . . . what's wrong?"

"I'm sorry," she whispered. "I'm so sorry I whipped you the other day."

"That's all right, Mama," Cindy began, even as she remembered the stinging lashes of the hickory switch on the backs of her legs.

Maudie dried her eyes with the end of her apron. "No, it wasn't all right. I should've known what you said about Vera Mae's baby was true. I reckon I just didn't want to admit to myself that you really had the gift."

Cindy eyed her mother curiously. "The *gift*?"

Maudie took the supper plate from Cindy's hands and set it on the nightstand beside the bed. "Yes, honey, the gift of second sight. Your grandma Darrow had the gift. She got the power right after she laid up sick in the bed with the flu when she was but thirteen. That's why I started looking for the signs right after you came back from the hospital. Grandma always told me that most girls who received the gift got it right after a bad sickness."

The sudden information explained some things to Cindy, but still it did nothing to ease her fears. "Mama, this gift ... is it something bad?"

"No, baby," assured Maudie. "It's a gift from God."

"Then why did Vera Mae's baby die? Did I hex it or something?" Thoughts of that tiny, white casket under the church cemetery kept haunting her.

"No, that wasn't your fault. You've got to make yourself believe that. Predicting that baby's death, well, that was just something that came to you. There's no need for you to feel guilty over it. And like the times when you get a feeling about things that are going to happen, you're just foreseeing the future. You don't really have any hand in making it all come to pass."

"You mean like the fortune teller at the county fair?"

"Sort of like that, but it's different. They used to call them prophets or soothsayers in the Bible."

The girl's thoughts turned inward as she considered what her newfound gift might mean in the future. Would she touch her mother or father one day and foresee their deaths, know the hour and circumstances of their passing? Would she see her own death? The questions that ran through her mind were enough to chill her to the bone.

"Now, I don't want you to pay no attention to what folks might say about you," Maudie told her flatly. "After what Vera Mae accused you of, some might call you a witch or a jinx or such. But you won't pay no never mind to any of them, 'cause you know they're all wrong. It's just the gift, that's all. The Lord has seen fit to bless you with it, child, so it's something you need to learn to cherish, not to curse."

"I'll sure try, Mama." In a way, Cindy felt much better, but in another sense, she felt a creeping apprehension about the subject they had just discussed.

"One more thing," Maudie pointed out. "It'd be best if you'd not mention our little talk to your pappy. He's a good, hardworking man, but he understands only what he can see or touch. He holds no faith in such things as foresight. Most hereabout don't. That's why we'll just keep it among ourselves. No need to anger your pappy none."

"It'll just be our secret, Mama." Cindy Ann smiled. Her mother suddenly gathered her in a smothering hug, a rare show of affection from a woman who usually regarded her young'uns with a stern eye and an iron rule.

"Well, you finish up your supper and, if you feel like it, join us on the porch. Your pappy's got the radio warmed up for Edgar Bergen and Charlie McCarthy."

"I'll be out directly," promised Cindy. As her mother left, she took the plate and dug in. The food was welcomed, for she was hungry. But her thoughts, however, lingered on things other than nourishment. There was still that underlying feeling of guilt — guilt for the misfortune brought upon the Holts and their stillborn baby. And accompanying that guilt was a nagging uneasiness.

She could not help but wonder just who was going to suffer next.

Chapter Four

It was a Friday and the last day of school when Johnny left the Biggs household, anxious to spend the coming year working for the Civilian Conservation Corps at Cherokee National Forest.

The children sat sullenly around the kitchen table awaiting breakfast, their school books and lunch pails beside their plates. The old German cuckoo clock in the hallway sang the arrival of six o'clock. They all turned their heads solemnly when their brother Johnny appeared in the doorway. He toted a bedroll packed with his few personal belongings in one hand, while the other clutched the fretted neck of his ever present flat-top guitar.

All eyes followed Johnny as he unburdened himself and pulled out a chair to sit down. Johnny Biggs was a handsome, young man, as tall and lanky as his father, but whose features were devoid of Clay's grim homeliness. Johnny's thin brows always seemed to be cocked in an expression of mild amusement, his lips forever curled in a wry grin. There was a maturity to him that transcended his eighteen years, yet he still managed to maintain an air of reckless boyishness. That morning he was decked out in his traveling clothes and his charcoal gray fedora, the brim pulled low. The hat had been an heirloom given to him by Grandpa Biggs, who had presented it to Clay's firstborn just before his death. Johnny had not spent a waking hour without it since.

The Civilian Conservation Corps had been formed a few years before; one of Roosevelt's New Deal programs established to relieve unemployment in such impoverished rural areas as central Tennessee. The CCC was intended for young, unmarried men, providing them with steady work and a much needed thirty dollars a month. The job consisted of working the national parks, planting trees, fighting forest fires, and maintaining roads and trails.

Johnny and his two best friends, C.J. Potts and Billy Longcreek, had applied for CCC work upon turning eighteen. They had only recently received their letters from the government informing them of their acceptance. Johnny had wanted the job for the steady thirty a month, most of which he intended on sending back home to his folks. Billy Longcreek's intentions were to get away from his overbearing mother, as well as his dark resentment for his father, who had deserted them when he was an infant. C.J., well, old C.J. was going for several reasons. First of all, he wanted to put the little farming community behind him, as well as his pompous, greedy father, Ransom Potts, the president of the Coleman Citizens Bank. But mostly, C.J. wanted something to brag about when he returned. It was just his crude way of showing his self-importance to a county that held as much ill regard for him as it did for his selfish, foreclosing father.

Maudie set a platter of steaming hot biscuits in the center of the table. She expected some degree of praise from her brood, but received only an appreciative grin from Johnny. The others—Polly, Josh, Cindy and Sammy — sat there glumly, staring forlornly at their older brother.

"You young'uns keep sporting those long faces and Johnny might get it in his head to stay up there in them mountains," Maudie told them all.

Johnny agreed. "Y'all look like you're at a wake. Well, I'm far from kicking the bucket, so there ain't nothing for no one to be grieving about."

"But, we'll miss you something awful, Johnny." Polly pouted; she who usually spent the breakfast hour pestering her siblings and making a general nuisance of herself.

"The only thing you're gonna miss is having one less body to pick on, Miss Prissy-Pants." Johnny grinned slyly. "Why, it'll be a doozie of a job just trying to bail you outta all the trouble you'll cause whilst I'm gone. Might even find that Sheriff Taylor White has had enough of your shenanigans and locked you up in the Bedloe County jailhouse."

"Now I am glad you're going!" said Polly, wagging her coal-black pigtails and sticking her tongue out. She received a scolding look from her mother, who told her straight out, "You stick your ugly tongue out over the eating table again, young lady, and I'll lay a hot fork across it." To illustrate the point, Maudie lifted a cooking fork dripping with bacon grease from a cast-iron skillet.

The twelve-year-old clammed up immediately, unable to determine whether her mother was serious or just joking. Johnny chuckled heartily and commenced to eating. He started by filling his blue china plate to the rim with brown molasses.. Taking a good-sized pat of fresh country butter from a saucer, he mashed it thoroughly into the syrupy sorghum. He then procured one of the big cat-head biscuits and went at it.

It was nearing six-thirty when the children left the table to get ready for school. "I'm sure gonna miss your home cooking, Mama," Johnny told her. He pushed his chair back from the kitchen table, yawning and stretching like an old, yellow cat in the sun. "Where's Pappy? I want to say good-bye before I go."

"Last I saw, your daddy was out back working on Clint Devane's Chevrolet. Been at it since daybreak."

Johnny nodded and took off out the back door, letting the screen door slam loudly behind him. He stood on the back porch for a moment and looked over to where the black, Chevy sedan was parked beneath a spreading chestnut tree. He started through the dewy grass. The hood was open, greasy tools laid out haphazardly on the left front fender. Clay Biggs was nowhere to be seen.

"Pappy?" he called out.

"Back here, son," answered Clay's baritone voice.

He found his father at the fence row behind the smokehouse. Clay stood there, his grease-blackened hands crossed over a weathered post, his blue eyes staring blankly to the north. He often found his papa that way, mostly in the morning or at sundown, surveying the vast tract of land that no longer belonged to him. The earth which had once born row upon row of brilliant green tobacco now lay empty and unplowed. Unsightly weeds sprouted high like an obscene gesture in Clay's eyes, as did a hand-painted sign near the edge of the road. It proclaimed PROPERTY OF THE COLEMAN CITIZENS BANK. As far as Clay Biggs was concerned it might as well have read PROPERTY OF RANSOM POTTS, for it was the rotund banker who had taken the acreage in exchange for the amount that had paid off Cindy's hospital bills in full.

"You'll get it back someday, Pappy," Johnny assured him.

"I keep hoping that, son, but every month we just get deeper in debt and that land seems even farther out of reach."

Johnny Biggs stooped by the fence row where Tippy lay on his back, sunning his belly. He ran a hand absently over the hound's speckled chest, his eyes on his father. "Now that I'm gonna be working, I'll be able to send most of that money home. Kinda help out some."

Clay continued to stare out over the pasture. "And we'd surely appreciate it, son," he replied. "Though you needn't do it if you don't want to."

"I want to, Pappy." Johnny stood up and spotted C.J. and Billy sauntering down the road to the house. "There's the boys. I reckon I'd better be going."

Clay stood like a statue by the fence, saying nothing.

"Well, take care," Johnny said with a big lump in his throat. He adjusted the brim of the gray fedora and turned to go.

"Johnny?"

The boy turned back and saw his daddy start toward him, hand outstretched. Johnny took it with a big grin. "I'm damned proud of you, boy," Clay told him. "All grown up and going off to work. You're finally a man. You stick to your own mind and walk straight and you'll make a damned fine one."

"Thank you," Johnny said, voice cracking. He walked back to the house, tears threatening to come, but he steeled his backbone and ducked back into the kitchen, the coonhound at his heels.

Maudie overlooked the dog's entrance. All her attention was focused on Johnny. "So you're leaving now," she breathed. Tears collected on her lower lashes, then trickled down her round cheeks. "Would you do me a favor before you go?"

"I surely will."

"Sing me a song."

Johnny grinned. "Let's go out on the front porch."

He picked up his bindle and guitar, and they made their way through the house to the front porch. The rest of the Biggs clan was there, holding their school books and wearing sullen frowns.

As Maudie sat on the porch swing, Johnny shook a tortoise-shell pick from the hollow of his guitar and began playing. Much to his mother's delight, he sang "Will the Circle be Unbroken," one of Maudie's favorites. His voice, rich and fluid, sang the verses much as an expert woodcrafter might caress and carve a stick of coarse walnut into a thing of beauty. He sang it with such depth and emotion that had the Carter Family been there, the gospel trio would have surely been put to shame.

After the last chord had been played, Johnny received a round of applause. "Thank y'all very much" he smiled, sweeping off his hat in an exaggerated bow.

"Come on, Johnny," yelled C.J. Potts from the road. He stood there at the gate with Billy Longcreek. "We ain't got all day!"

"Keep your suspenders buckled, C.J.," Johnny bellowed back. "I'm a-coming!" He turned to the children, and they rushed him, clutching him in one massive hug. "You young'uns behave yourselves and mind your folks, and I'll send you a souvenir from the mountains."

The three stepped away reluctantly, and Johnny regarded his brother Josh, who stood against a porch post. "Don't you dig all the sang outta them woods or hunt down all the ripe coons, cause I'm gonna want my fair share when I get back."

Josh grinned slow-wittedly and shook his older brother's hand. "Heck, Johnny, you know I ain't that good a hunter."

"Johnny!" whined C.J. impatiently from the road.

"Coming!" Johnny picked up his gear and guitar and eyed his mother as she sat in the swing. "Good-bye, Mama."

"You write me," Maudie told him.

"You bet. Just as soon as I get there."

Then he was walking down the crude two-by-four steps of the porch, strolling through the abundance of Johnson grass and new clover, past Maudie's patch of marigolds and purple irises.

Cindy stood by the porch railing and sadly watched her brother's departure. As she stooped to retrieve her books, something came over her. It hit with the force and fury of a physical blow, yet it struck inside her young mind. There was some confusion at first, then a horrible realization of great danger. Abruptly, a chill gripped her frail body, and a sensation ran along her skin like the pattering of a cold rain. But that was not what frightened her the most. It was the undeniable fear of pursuit that caused her heart to pound, almost as though someone were coming for her from behind.

Cindy Ann broke away from the disturbing sensation. Her eyes focused on the departing back of Johnny. Did her feeling have anything to do with him? She had no idea, but could not let him go without saying something. She ran down the steps and out into the yard, intent on warning him.

"Johnny!"

The lanky, young man stopped and grinned quizzically as the girl paused breathlessly, in the frame of the open gate. "What's the matter, Cindy Ann?"

Cindy opened her mouth, but only stammered, for she did not know exactly what to say to him. "Johnny," she finally managed. "Be careful."

"I will, pumpkin," he promised. "And don't you worry none. I'll be back in a year and a day." Johnny ran his hand playfully through her orange-red hair. "A year and a day." Then Johnny joined his buddies and the three started down the dusty dirt road, laughing and horsing around.

"You young' uns get on to school now," Maudie commanded from the porch. "Wouldn't want to be late for your last day."

Cindy, however, paid her no mind. She continued to stand there by the front gate, her hands clutching her school books absently to her chest. Her hazel eyes watched as the three boys headed north for town, their feet scuffling clouds of powdery dust from the roadbed. And the feeling, that cold, overbearing sensation that had gripped her moments before, remained there in the back of her mind, as it would for the remainder of that hazy, spring day.

Chapter Five

"Witch, Witch, the red-haired bitch! Set her on fire and roll her in a ditch!"

The degrading chant assaulted Cindy from all directions as she sat motionlessly on one of the playground swings. The girl's eyes were diverted from the gloating children and their playful accusation. She stared at the earth at her feet, ground scrubbed bare by generations of scuffling feet, and tried hard to hold back angry tears.

It was one o'clock, the time of afternoon recess, when Chester Martin and his cronies once again descended upon the quiet Biggs girl, their minds brimming with mischief and their grins with pure meanness. The others were just followers, looking for approval from the school bully, perhaps agreeing to his every whim in order to escape ridicule themselves. They were merely pawns, of course, an army of gutless children that Chester used to amplify his strength and his amusement at humiliating those weaker than he.

And today Cindy Ann was the victim. Ever since the tale of Vera Mae's hexed baby had swept the little farming community, Cindy had experienced a strange interest directed toward her, from adults as well as children. It was much more tolerable with the grown-ups, for they silently appraised her with solemn stares and no harsh words. Women in a family way crossed the road to avoid her, and the old men playing checkers on the porch of Woody's General Store refused to make their move until the "jinx" had passed. Such responses were easy for a child to ignore. It was when those her own age, her classmates and friends, turned on her that the new attention became downright painful.

Chester Martin had been the first to jump on the superstitious bandwagon and had begun his scathing remarks and taunting the day after the infant's burial. Chester was an ugly boy, tall for his age and fat. His hair was greasy black, and his dark eyes possessed the same oily quality. His father, Sonny Martin, owned Coleman's only gas station, and folks swore his scrappy ten-year-old was every bit as pushy and mean as he was.

It was on that final day of school that Chester invented the sneering chant that he relished so. He and the others repeated it over and over again, their ugly words assaulting the little girl from all sides. Cindy had attempted to pay them no attention at first, but her resistance began to dissolve as more of her classmates joined in.

"Witch, Witch, the red-haired bitch! Set her on fire and roll her in a ditch!"

Cindy Ann felt the tears come; welling in her hazel eyes, but tried to hide them from the others. She wondered where Polly or Josh were, why they had not intervened and stopped Chester's hateful assault. But then she remembered. The older kids were limited to the far side of the playground during recess. If they had heard the commotion, there was a chance they would not have known who it was being directed at.

As the taunting grew louder and the circle closed in around her, Cindy could take it no longer. She glared tearfully at Chester Martin. "Stop it!" she yelled at them all. "Why don't you just leave me alone?"

"You gonna make us stop, crybaby?" snarled Chester. He moved in closer, hands on chubby hips. "Huh? You gonna make us?"

Beneath the girl's latent panic, defiance exploded. She returned Chester's sneer with one of her own. "I'll go tell Mrs. Harris!" she retorted. "I swear I'll tell her!"

Chester's round face flashed crimson with rage. He grabbed a fistful of Cindy's flower print dress and shoved. The girl lost her balance on the seat of the swing and fell backward. Cindy hit the ground hard. For a dizzying moment, she simply laid there, the breath knocked from her lungs.

"You wanna fight me, witch?" The Martin boy laughed. "Naw, that ain't yer way, is it? You'd just as soon hex me, like you did that Holt baby. Come on and hex me if you can! I dare you to try!"

Chester's followers had backed away now, having lost their stomach for the cruel game. They fidgeted on the carpet of new spring grass, staring at the two in silence. They all knew what would happen then, for they had experienced enough of Chester's bullying to predict the outcome. The boy would push her around some more, perhaps even hit her, then laugh as she ran crying for the teacher.

But that was not what happened at all.

Cindy Ann Biggs sat up from the dust of the playground, her breath heaving raggedly from her chest and tears coursing down her freckled face. But something was missing. All her fear, her cowardice at the threat of the looming bully, had dissipated like smoke in a swift breeze. In its place lurked a peculiar feeling, knowledge of things she should not have known. She stared at Chester Martin, and she instantly knew the boy, knew all his dislikes, his hates, all his ugly emotion. And she also knew his fears.

Mrs. Harris's fourth-grade class watched intently as the girl stood and faced the schoolyard pest. There was something disturbing in her expression, a calmness that should have been sniveling fear. Her green eyes held none of the shy detachment that usually occupied them. Now they possessed a cold, unnerving boldness that could only be described as a shade short of sinister.

Chester stepped toward her menacingly, his meaty fist reared back for a blow. "You'd best run, witch, or I'll give you a shiner that'll last you the summer!"

Cindy only stared at him. Then, in a voice as clipped and cool as frost on a pump handle, she said, "I'd watch where I stepped if I was you, Chester."

The pudgy boy puzzled over her warning for a second, then directed his eyes downward. There, entwined around his ankles, was the writhing length of a copperhead snake.

With a squeal of fright, Chester leaped from the spot, his

huge face paling at the sight of the auburn serpent. He sprinted a couple of yards, and then turned to look. The place he had stood only a moment before was now vacant. No coiled copperhead, just trampled grass. "Where'd it go?" he yelped, his voice an octave higher than before.

The other children stared at him in confusion. The bully's actions were totally unlike him. All regarded Chester with puzzlement, some even giggling halfheartedly, thinking that maybe it was one of Chester's weird jokes. The only child that did not seem in the dark was Cindy Ann.

"Behind you," she hissed with a thin smile that did not match the look in her eyes.

Chester whirled in time to see the snake again, this time much larger than before, coiled a foot to his right. He jumped away just as the copperhead struck out. He screamed as the snake's fangs snagged the cuff of his faded overalls.

The next few moments were pure confusion for the gathering of school kids, but pure hell for the swaggering bully. Chester would run a few feet and again encounter another serpent. Sometimes it would be the copperhead waiting there, coiled and on the verge of striking. Other times it would be a rattler or a cottonmouth. No matter how fast he ran to elude the snakes, he would always step into another's path.

Soon his screams of "Snake! Snake! Snake!" reached the teacher's ears. Mrs. Harris came running, along with Mr. Foster, the school's black custodian. He carried a coal shovel in his dark hands, ready to dispatch the invading reptile.

By the time they reached the playground, Chester was hurting himself trying to escape the multitude of snakes. He ran head on into several trees, blackening his eyes and bloodying his nose in his blind panic. The spectacle was horrifying to behold, and soon, other grades and their teachers ran to see what was happening.

"For heaven's sake, Mr. Foster, kill it!" Mrs. Harris yelled. She stared in bewilderment as Chester staggered from tree to tree, screaming his head off, his puffy features bloody and bruised.

The Negro ran into the grass, the shovel held ready for a

swing that would cleave the snake in half. However, search as he may, Foster saw only crab grass and wild flowers. "I don't see no snake, Mrs. Harris."

The teacher watched as Chester continued to collide with trees, crying and screaming as he went. "Well, keep on looking. It must be around here somewhere."

The janitor shrugged and kept up his search, however futile. The man would step back whenever the hysterical youngster ran near, eyeing him like someone possessed by the devil.

Mrs. Harris turned when one of her students tugged on her sleeve. "It's Cindy Biggs," piped Eddie Forbes, a towheaded boy with a chipped front tooth. "She's done put a hex on him."

At the explanation, she regarded Cindy Ann. The red-haired girl stood serenely beside the swings, watching Chester tear wildly from one tree to the next, to the seesaw and back again.

Reluctantly, the teacher laid a hand on the girl's shoulder, "Cindy Ann?"

The girl pulled her attention from the boy long enough to look up at her teacher. The woman was struck speechless by the change in the shy, little girl. A strange satisfaction filled Cindy's freckled face; a smugness born of some underlying emotion that Mrs. Harris could not quite place. It almost seemed as if Cindy was causing the source of the boy's frightful agitation.

"Stop it, Cindy," she told the child sharply, feeling foolish for actually believing that the girl had anything to do with Chester's erratic behavior.

Cindy ignored her. She continued to watch as the custodian finally grabbed the screaming boy and held his flailing arms.

"What's going on here?" asked Ralph Davis, the bespectacled principal of Bedloe County's only public school.

"I'm not exactly sure," the teacher admitted. Her eyes swept the neighboring class and spotted Cindy's pigtailed sister. "Polly Biggs, come here a minute."

Polly went to where Mrs. Harris crouched by her little sister. "Yes, ma'am? What's wrong?"

"You've got to make her stop, Polly."

The twelve-year-old eyed the teacher skeptically. "Stop her from doing what? She's just standing there."

The woman was irritated by Polly's impudence. "I don't know. She's done something to Chester. I don't know how, but she has!"

Mr. Foster yelped in pain as Chester sank his teeth into the man's forearm. Struggling from his grasp, Chester ran a few paces and then tripped. The boy fell sprawling into a mud puddle. Chester Martin screamed bloody murder, a dozen imaginary water moccasins squirming around his thrashing body.

Polly knelt before Cindy. She placed her hands on her sister's rigid shoulders and shook her gently. "Come on, Cindy Ann, snap out of it." Polly's usually spunky voice now stammered with a cold, inexplicable fear. "Please, Cindy, you've got to!"

Then, as Polly began to shake her roughly, Cindy's eyes lost their glazed look, and she peered around in frightened confusion. "What's wrong?" she breathed. "What'd I do?"

"Nothing, Cindy," assured Polly, pulling her baby sister close to her side. The older girl gave Mrs. Harris a withering glare. "You didn't do nothing a'tall."

The teacher turned her eyes from the two, a deep blush reddening her cheeks. She walked to where the janitor was helping Chester Martin out of the puddle. The squalling boy stood there, mud-splattered and trembling, the profusion of serpents completely stricken from his mind.

Cindy's tears soaked through Polly's drab pink dress as she sobbed. "I wanna go home!"

The principal glanced at his pocket watch and then nodded to Polly. "Go ahead and take her on home," he allowed. Mr. Davis stared at Cindy, looked over at Chester, then walked back to his office, shaking his head.

For the Biggs children, the last day of school had not turned out to be the time of rejoicing that usually preceded summer vacation. They all walked home quietly; Polly, Cindy, and Josh, all bewildered at what had taken place. Before they reached Old Newsome Road, the three agreed to say nothing about the incident to their parents. It was safe to say that Maudie and Clay would hear about it soon enough, from the wagging tongues of Coleman's town gossips.

Chapter Six

After leaving the Biggs house that morning, Johnny and his buddies neglected to hitch a ride to Nashville and take the afternoon bus like they had first planned to do. "Let's play hooky one last time," insisted C.J. with a sparkle of sly mischief in his beady eyes. Not wanting to put Potts into one of his cranky moods, Johnny and Billy conceded. The remainder of that breezy spring day was spent doing the things they had enjoyed as kids: swiping apples, skinny-dipping in Weaver's Pond, and teasing the girls outside Jenson's Drugstore in town.

As the evening drew on and storm clouds darkened the vast Tennessee sky, C.J.'s cravings turned to more adult pleasures. Reluctant to refuse their cocky friend's request, Johnny and Billy agreed to accompany him to Coleman's only beer joint.

The Bloody Bucket was located across the railroad tracks from the town square. After passing the water tower and a gathering of shabby tin and tarpaper shacks, the tavern sat back from the roadway. It was a low, seedy building, its windows flashing brilliant with neon beer signs and its interior constantly thrumming with the feisty beat of honky-tonk music. The Bloody Bucket had been named such for its violent reputation. Numerous fistfights and knifings had tarnished the saloon's history, as had the shady dealings of its owner, Otis Schofield. Vices such as illegal whiskey, prostitution, and backroom gambling had plagued Schofield's reputation with the local townsfolk. During the long stretch of Prohibition, the roadhouse had been forced to close its doors, but Schofield had remained busy. He faded from public life, manufacturing and transporting bootleg whiskey under the noses of federal agents.

When the 18th amendment was repealed in '33, Otis reopened the Bloody Bucket and had enjoyed a brisk business ever since.

It was because of the joint's sleazy reputation that Johnny Biggs and Billy Longcreek were reluctant to set foot inside the Bloody Bucket. Neither had ever darkened its doorway, having the good sense to avoid its seamy temptations. C.J. Potts, however, claimed to be a regular patron of the establishment. He led the way boldly as the three walked inside and strolled up to the long bar lined with padded stools.

It was a Friday night and the joint was jumping. The tavern was packed, echoing with the clink of beer bottles, the dry shuffle of playing cards, and the fast-paced picking and singing of hillbilly music. The lighting was muted a murky, golden orange by the heavy pall of cigarette smoke that lingered among the tables. A gathering of poker players guffawed loudly about something that had happened at the school that day. Something about snakes that weren't really there, from what Johnny could make out. The four ceased their laughter after receiving a cold glare from Sonny Martin, who stood over his fifth beer at the end of the bar.

"Bartender, three beers for my pals and I," demanded C.J. with a flourish of bogus authority. His flat cap was perched at a cocky angle, and his scruffy, pencil-thin mustache suggested a hint of Douglas Fairbanks, despite his weasely features.

Otis Schofield regarded the boy wearily, a bit ruffled by his brashness. "You boys think you're old enough to set foot in here? I mean you hardly look like you've been weaned from your mama's teat, let alone deserving of strong drink."

C.J. was indignant at Schofield's insinuation. "Why, I'll have you know we're on our way to Cherokee National Forest. We're gonna be working the CCC there for the next year."

Otis raised his bushy brows in mock respect. "Why, that's mighty commendable, boys! In fact, that surely deserves a drink on the house. Jasper, bring out three mugs of that special beer."

"Special beer?" C.J. asked curiously.

"A special German blend imported from overseas," boasted the burly saloon owner. Jasper Berle, Schofield's bartender and right-hand man, slid three mugs of foamy, golden brew down the polished length of the bar. "Enjoy, boys!" Otis grinned, his massive, tattooed forearms crossed before his barrel chest.

"Much obliged." C.J. grabbed the mug and took a big swig. Billy was about to drink his, when he noticed that Johnny was making no move toward the beer. Johnny could see something awful untrustworthy in Schofield's gold-crowned grin.

"Gaggh!" sputtered C. J., dropping his mug on the sawdust floor. He hacked and gasped until he was red in the face. "What the hell is this stuff? It tastes like horse piss!"

Otis and his cronies cackled wildly. "I reckon that's because that's what it is! I wasn't lying to you, though. It did come from a German horse!" Laughter erupted down the bar, soon joined by those at the surrounding tables.

C.J. choked angrily and shook a fist over the bar. "Why, you dumb bastard! I oughta whip your fat ass for that!"

Schofield suddenly produced a Louisville Slugger from under the counter. He waved the baseball bat at C.J., the humor now absent from his hard eyes. "You'd best skedaddle outta here, boy, before I lay this upside your ugly head!"

Johnny and Billy pulled their buddy away from the bar, despite his eagerness to fight. Johnny noticed that the heavy wood column of Schofield's bat was dark at its widest point and realized that the stains were blood.

"Come on, C.J., cool down. It was just a stupid joke. No need to get yourself killed over it."

As the three ducked through the tavern door, Otis rapped his bat loudly on the bar top. "I don't wanna see you young'uns back in here tonight, you hear me?"

The fresh night air hit their senses as they walked across the congested parking lot, away from the stifling pall of tobacco smoke and the sweet-sour stench of hard liquor. Johnny and Billy were relieved to be away from the place, but C.J. still fumed over the incident. He acted as if his manhood had been questioned just because of his inability to get them all a snootful of good drinking liquor.

They went to the tree they had stashed their gear under, then started through the crowded parking lot toward the main highway. "I think we'd better find us a ride to Nashville tonight," suggested Johnny. "Maybe catch a bus tomorrow morning to the mountains."

Billy agreed wholeheartedly. "Yeah, we're supposed to report for work on Monday. That doesn't leave us much time to get settled once we get there."

C.J. seemed disgusted by their sensible talk. "Hey, you clowns sound like a couple of shawl-knitting grannies. We're finally free, boys. Free from eighteen years of being bossed around. Let's celebrate! Find us a shot of booze and then get on to Nashville."

"I believe we might be able to help you fellas out on both them counts."

The voice came from a beat-up truck parked in the inky shadows of a black walnut tree. From the darkness emerged two men. Something about the pair bothered Johnny, almost frightened him. It was almost like having a couple of fiddle-back spiders crawl up your arm while rummaging through a woodpile.

"Do we know you?" asked C.J., shifting his bedroll to his shoulder.

"Maybe . . . maybe not," said the larger of the two. He was a hulking bear of a man with sandy blond hair and a chaw of tobacco stuck in one side of his jaw. "Who we are ain't all that important anyway, is it? All that matters to you is a drink of top-grade hooch."

"You're on the right track . . . if you ain't pulling our legs."

The big man nodded to his sidekick, a lanky individual with goofy, rodent like features. The other produced a silver flask from his back pocket and tossed it to Potts. "Try a swig of that. Genuine white mule."

C.J. uncapped the flask and took a swallow. He stood there, unaffected for a moment. Then the alcohol hit him like a slap in the face. "Whoeee!" the boy exclaimed. "That's prime stuff! Where'd you get it?"

"Made it ourselves," bragged the big man leaning back on the grill of his rattletrap pickup. "For a dollar apiece you boys can drink your fill."

"Hot dog!" whooped C.J. He fumbled in his pocket and

produced a sizable money roll. He peeled off a single bill. "You just hand that jug right over."

The man laughed. His eyes ignored the dollar and settled on the wad of greenbacks instead. "Now, you don't think I'd be fool enough to tote it around in the truck with me, do ya? I ain't that daring!"

"We can take you to where it is, though," said the skinny fellow. His oily hair hung lankily over his forehead, and he had crooked buckteeth. "Ain't too far from here and it'd be well worth the ride."

"Well, what're we waiting for? Let's go!" C.J. exclaimed.

Johnny grabbed his friend's elbow. "I don't know if we should or not. We really need to get to Nashville tonight."

"Well, you're in luck then." The big fellow beamed. "We were planning on heading up there for the weekend. You're welcome to ride along if you want."

Johnny was not a bit fooled by the man's sudden friendliness. He had noticed the way he had eyed C.J.'s bankroll. He did not trust the two strangers and their harmless proposition. He and Billy both carried a few dollars each, but C.J. had close to forty dollars on him. If the two men got them drunk with poison rotgut, there was more than a good chance they would wake up in a ditch the next morning, their pockets emptied and their heads aching like rotten teeth.

But Potts would have no part of Johnny's hesitation. "What in tarnation is the matter with you, Biggs? You're acting like a damned sissy. We got us a chance at some gut-burning moonshine and at a dollar a head. Hell, man, we can't pass that up!"

Thick clouds rumbled with thunder overhead. "You fellas better make your minds up fast. Looks like it might pour down rain any minute now."

Johnny cussed himself for giving in, but he had known C.J. since the first grade and knew there would be no living with him if he didn't get his way. "All right, but just one drink. Then we head for Nashville."

"You boys won't regret it." The lanky fellow with the Mortimer Snerd face winked. "Best damned shine in the whole county."

As the two men climbed into the cab of their primer-gray Ford, Billy took Johnny aside. "Who are these guys? Seems like I've seen them around town before." The half-breed boy's dark, Cherokee eyes were bright with concern and mistrust.

It was only when they began to climb into the bed of the truck with C.J. that Johnny had a vague idea who the men were. The back was piled with gardening and carpentry tools, the materials of traveling handymen. The two had been hanging around Coleman for about a month now, doing odd jobs for some of the richer folks in town. He knew the big fellow was named Bully, while the other one, lanky of build and gawky of looks, was known as Claude. Johnny had no idea what their last names were. As far as he knew, no one in town did either.

"Nice guitar you got there," complimented the one called Bully. "How's about playing something for us on the way?""

Johnny agreed. As the truck pulled away from the Bloody Bucket and headed southward, the music of the flat-top guitar and Johnny's fluid voice lit the crisp country air, singing "Cotton-Eyed Joe," "T for Texas," and the "Salty Dog Blues."

Chapter Seven

"Hey, I know where we're headed now," said C.J. Potts as the pickup moved off the main highway onto a stretch of dirt road.

Johnny and Billy exchanged knowing glances. They also knew where the rutted track led to. "The old Brewer place," breathed Johnny.

C.J. grinned slyly, the promise of freshly distilled corn liquor foremost in his mind. "Why, Old Brewer's barn is the perfect place to hide a still. Nobody ever goes near that old tobacco shed anymore ... not even old Harvey."

He was right. As Bully's truck drove past the dark farmhouse and moved slowly down a rutted dirt path that cut across the old man's property, they could see the decay and overgrowth of years of flagrant neglect. Harvey Brewer had once been the most prosperous tobacco farmer in Bedloe County. He owned two hundred acres of prime tobacco land which had annually yielded a crop that most dirt farmers only dreamed about. His smoking barn was the largest in the county, and after his own leaves had been cut and cured, he had loaned out the great structure to his neighbors for their own use. The huge gray-wood barn could smoke as many as four crops' worth at one curing.

Then in the summer of '28, Harvey came in from the fields for dinner one day and found no meal cooking on the stove. He searched the house for his beloved Norma. Harvey finally discovered his wife lying in her flower garden, having died of a stroke while weeding her precious flowers. Harvey had never been the same man after that. After Norma's funeral, he had left acre upon acre of young tobacco to insects and root rot, chained the double doors of the old curing barn, and become a lonely recluse, leaving the little, clapboard house only for mail and groceries.

The Ford's headlights splashed over the choking growth of thicket that grew heavy on both sides of the cramped pathway. Pink-headed thistle, honeysuckle, and blackberry bramble, along with the occasional growth of wild tobacco, choked the rich earth that had once boasted a lush sea of dark green Burley and Pryor.

"We're here, boys," called out Bully as he braked his gray truck to a jolting halt. The three young men in the bed craned their necks, and all eyes appraised the massive hulk of the old tobacco barn.

It had the same weathered appearance of a multitude of other barns and shacks in the rural, farming community. Its walls were constructed of rough boarding long since washed a dull gray by decades of merciless Tennessee weather. The sheets of corrugated tin that made up the sloping roof were flaked dark orange with rust. A mass of inflamed storm clouds, threatening heavy rainfall before the night was out, wreathed the sharp lines of the barn's eaves, giving it a strangely ominous appearance, almost demonic in nature. There in the gathering darkness of the turbulent spring night, Harvey Brewer's curing barn resembled some unholy shrine, rather than an empty structure of timber and tin. It appeared as some ancient temple, coldly reverent, yet somehow terribly sinister.

"Well, come on, you guys!" C.J. grinned enthusiastically. "You'd better move your butts if you want your share of the hooch!"

Almost reluctantly, Johnny Biggs and Billy Longcreek accompanied Potts as he climbed from the truck bed. Bully and Claude talked quietly in the cab for a moment, then joined them. Bully lingered long enough to pull a long object wrapped in burlap from beneath the truck seat.

"Just a little protection, boys," Bully assured them. "Never know when revenuers might be lurking about."

Bully and Claude ignored the huge, double doors forever

sealed with a thick length of heavy logging chain and a large padlock. They walked around the far corner of the building, maybe to some hidden entrance concealed from prying eyes. "Well, are you boys gonna stand there all night or are you gonna come drink your fill?"

"We're a-coming!" C.J. grinned. He motioned for his two buddies to follow.

Johnny and Billy exchanged worried glances, then headed around the side of the building, leaving their gear in the truck. Bully waited there, holding a loose board ajar for the boys to squeeze through. Claude stood to one side, a kerosene lantern dangling from one hand. He grinned almost ghoulishly, his wild eyes and protruding teeth giving him the appearance of a sideshow geek.

Thunder rolled loudly overhead, and they all knew that rain would soon come down in drenching sheets, soaking the rich, Tennessee topsoil. C.J. ducked through the wall's narrow opening first, followed by Johnny and Billy and Bully. The last one through was Claude. He let the board fall back into place with a rasping scrape of ancient wood.

The kerosene lamp cast an eerie glow upon the spacious interior of the old barn. The floor was packed earth, furrowed in places by long beds of singed charcoal once used to fire the tobacco leaves. A single ladder led up one wall to the loft. There sturdy rafters stretched the width of the barn. It was there that the tobacco had been split, secured to long poles, and hung across the beams for the curing process.

Johnny's sharp blue eyes surveyed the earthen floor. Except for a few empty whiskey bottles, a scattering of water-logged pinochle cards, and a long, casket-like tool chest at one side, the place was empty.

"There's no still in here," he told his buddies.

And he was right. Even if he had not had the advantage of the coal oil lamp, he could have determined its absence by the smell alone. There was no acrid odor of a wood fire, no scent of hot copper tubing and tin vats. No smell of corn mash, malt, or the sour stench of the finished product. None of those scents dominated the cavernous interior of the old curing barn, only the musky smell of raw earth and the faint trace of long forgotten tobacco leaves.

C.J. Potts whirled like an irate monkey in a cage. "What the hell is going on here?"

"You've been suckered, that's what," Bully told him in a cold, matter-of-fact voice. He let the burlap slide from the length of his sawed-off shotgun.

"Now, just wait a minute —" began Billy, taking a step forward.

"Shut up, injun," sneered Claude. The gangly man had moved to the wooden tool box, setting his lantern on the dusty lid where an assortment of rusty tools lay. "My partner's the only one who does the talking now."

A heavy silence filled the barn... a silence thick with tension and underlying fear. Thunder crashed overhead, past the cobwebbed rafters, past the rusted sheets of tin. No one paid the storm any attention. Three minds raced in cold anxiety, desperately searching for some way out of the mess they were in. The other two minds, the thoughts of the perpetrators, regarded the situation calmly, well aware of the final outcome.

"What're you bastards up to?" spat C. J. indignantly. "What about our liquor?"

Bully laughed. "You're a real dumb-ass, ain't you, boy? Ain't you got it through your thick skull that there ain't no shine here? Do I have to spell it out for you?"

Potts grew silent. He swallowed dryly and eyed the sawed-down barrels of the twelve gauge. The twin muzzles looked like the bores of cannons.

"What do you want from us?" Johnny asked dully.

"We want the money you're carrying." Bully directed his gun at C. J.'s scrawny form. "Especially that wad of dough your partner flashed back at the beer joint. Boy, that money roll could choke a Missouri mule."

Potts' inherent greed for money smothered his apparent fear, and defiance flared in his eyes. "Well, you can just go straight to hell, mister! Both of you can, if you think I'll give up my traveling money to the likes of you!"

Bully held his scattergun steadily at the hip, the twin

hammers cocked back and ready. "You're making things awful hard for you and your friends," the big man said. "What's a few bucks to you anyhow? I hear your daddy owns half the county already."

C J.'s face burned a crimson red in the soft glow of the lantern. "I'm getting outta here! I ain't gonna take this anymore!"

"No," replied Bully. "Not anymore."

The deafening bellow of the shotgun's twin barrels exploded throughout the old barn, rattling the weathered structure. The force of the loads hit C. J. full in the stomach, knocking him ten feet from where he had been standing. As the echo of the blast died and the sulfurous pall of gun smoke dissipated to the rafters, all eyes were on the cocky teenager. C. J. sat on the earthen floor, an ugly hole torn through his midsection from belly to back.

Johnny watched numbly as C. J.'s hands moved sluggishly to the wound, as if trying to hold in the gory mess of blood and chewed entrails. C.J. stared dumbly at his friends, then fell backward with a gurgle. A crimson froth shot from his nose and mouth, staining the front of his blue chambray shirt.

Billy began to scream. Uncontrollable wails as shrill as those of a woman tore from his throat, piercing the musky air and reverberating off the shadowy walls. The half-breed began to back away, staring in terror at C.J.'s blood-splattered body, then at Bully and Claude.

He screamed once more, then dove for the ladder that rose upward to the loft.

"Stop him," Bully said, spitting a stream of tobacco juice at the barn floor.

Claude nodded and absently grabbed up a rusty hatchet from atop the old tool chest. He raised it overhead as he approached the frightened boy, a gleam of pure meanness in his eyes. He swung down forcefully just as Billy Longcreek grasped the first rung. The hatchet struck Billy across the left wrist, cleanly cleaving his hand from his arm.

Billy's screams increased tenfold as he dropped from the ladder, landing with a thud in a bed of ashen charcoal. The boy thrashed in agony, the stump of his wrist spouting a grisly fountain of life's blood.

Claude stared in disgust at the hysterical man at his feet. He cast an uncertain glance at his partner. "What should I do?"

"Finish him."

A crooked grin split Claude's homely face, and he let the hatchet drop once again. The rusty edge buried itself in Billy's skull, ending his terror forever.

Johnny began to back away from the two murderers, away from the lifeless bodies of his best friends. The numb state of shock suddenly vanished, as if he had been doused with ice water, and the horror of what was happening hit him full force. His mind raced, desperately seeking some small chance for survival.

He looked to Bully. The big man snapped open the breech of his shotgun and fumbled in his pants pocket for fresh shells. Claude was attempting to pry his hatchet from Billy's scalp.

Now, Johnny's thoughts screamed. *You've gotta get out of here right now!*

Johnny Biggs turned and ran, his scuffed work boots pounding on the hard-packed earth and scatterings of burnt charcoal and ashes. He reached the wall where they had made their entrance. He grasped frantically at boards, finding only secure lumber. *Where? Where the hell is the loose one?*

"You've got no place to run to, boy." Bully's statement was emphasized by the crisp clack of the shotgun's breech snapping shut.

Oh, dear Lord, please. . . please, let me out of this place! Then a board slid open on a loose nail, and the exit was there. The cool night air washed over Johnny, heightening his senses, increasing his fear. He ducked through the narrow portal, knocking the dark gray fedora from his head in his haste. His face met the inky twilight, then his arms and torso. But as he dragged his left leg through, a rusty nail snagged his trouser leg. He heard the two men coming for him on the other side of the gray-wood barn.

Close! His mind whirled as he felt for the source of his entrapment. *Oh, Lord, I was so blasted close!*

The roar of Bully's shotgun made his heart skip a beat in sheer horror. The load of double-aught hit him in the left buttock. Johnny was propelled into the darkness, the force of the shot knocking him clear of the wall's narrow passageway. He hit the ground hard, then rolled a couple of feet. He ended up on his back in the heavy thicket. Frightened to even move, he lay perfectly still and listened for the shot that would end his life.

"Where the hell is he?" growled Claude, no more than a dozen feet away. There was the sound of the loose board scraping on its nail and the swish of footsteps in high grass.

"Must be out here somewhere," said Bully. "I put a load of buckshot in his tail end; there's no mistaking that."

Johnny reached down to his left thigh. His denim trousers were saturated with warm blood. His trembling fingers traced the erratic pattern of his injury, feeling the neatly punched holes in his flesh. *I'm shot! God help me, I've been shot!*

"Let's split up," Bully suggested. "We gotta find that boy. If he gets away, we're done for."

Johnny waited for a long moment before moving. The thrashing of searching men dominated the underbrush, along with the soft patter of the starting rainfall. Johnny raised his lean face toward the heavens, letting drops of cool water wash his brow and cheekbones, clearing his mind of the slaughter witnessed mere seconds before.

All right, just get a hold of yourself, he told himself. *You can get out of this alive if you just keep your wits about you.*

There were two acres of heavy thicket between him and the woods that bordered the Brewer property. If he could just make it that far and claim the dark cover of the forest, then he would make it. He had grown up in those woods between the Brewer place and Old Newsome Road. He had hunted coon for miles on a moonlit night, had fished for crawdads and minnows in the clearwater creek. Despite his disabling injury, Johnny was certain he could make it the quarter mile to the safety of the Biggs house.

The boy waited until both men were out of earshot, then carefully got to his feet. Agony lanced like hot knives through the muscle of his gunshot leg. Johnny gritted his teeth, attempting to bear the pain without sound. Slowly, he began the long journey through the tangle of underbrush.

The thicket that was once Harvey Brewer's prime tobacco land was now a nearly impenetrable wall of blackberry bush, thistle, and milkweed. Great masses of newly bloomed honeysuckle blocked his way at every turn, as did scrubby trees and brush. It was pure hell getting through the thorny bramble without making enough noise to wake the dead.

The rain increased its tempo, changing from a gentle spring rain into a pounding downpour. Johnny's hair was soon plastered to his head, his clothing clinging wetly to him like a second skin. Several times a mighty boom would assault his ears, and he would duck. But it was only the roll of thunder or the brittle whip crack of lightning.

It took Johnny ten minutes to cross a hundred yards of heavy thicket, but soon the brush began to thin out. Through the rain he could see the dark woods nearby. *I'm gonna make it,* he thought wearily.

He had taken a couple of steps into the open when he spotted a dark form only a few yards away, its back to the wounded boy. Johnny dropped to the ground. He landed wrong on his hurt leg, and the sudden pain forced a low groan from his lips. He lay there, shivering, beneath a scraggly growth of wild tobacco, one of the plants left to rot in the field by a morose Harvey Brewer.

The form turned its head, staring hard at the spot where Johnny had stood a second before. Then it started toward the spot to investigate, the length of the sawed-off shotgun resting easily on one broad shoulder.

Johnny Biggs lay there, eyes screwed shut, lips mouthing a silent prayer. He tried to picture his father and mother, but the horror within blocked their faces from his mind. The only thing that stuck with him in that awful moment was the image of little Cindy Ann standing in the gateway, an expression of awful sadness creasing her freckled face. *Be careful, Johnny.* The words assaulted him again and again, and he bitterly wished he had turned around that very moment and stayed safely in the bosom of his family, instead of gallivanting off with C. J. and Billy, the promise of a year's freedom foremost in their youthful minds.

Footsteps thrashed the thick overgrowth, walking closer, moving dangerously near the spot where Johnny crouched. He heard the man cough, and a glob of warm saliva hit the boy on the nape of the neck. Johnny braced himself, awaiting an indication of discovery, but none came. The hunter continued through the choking brush, his eyes intent, his meaty finger lightly caressing the trigger of his gun.

Johnny waited for what seemed an eternity. His ears strained as the big man's rustling progress faded and safety once again presented itself. *Just a few more feet. Then I'll be home free.*

The lanky son of Clayburn Biggs felt the driving rain on his back as he struggled to his feet and faced the woods.

"Gotcha, Johnny," rasped Bully from behind.

Then came the thunder.

Chapter Eight

Maudie Biggs put her children to bed that Friday night and then returned to the front porch. Clay had been out there since after suppertime, just sitting in an old cane-backed chair, staring grimly into the darkness. Her husband had been spending most of his evenings like that lately, and it worried her to no end. More than once she had seen the look of a desperate man in his eyes.

The black sky rumbled. A steady rain fell earthward, giving sustenance to the spring vegetation, pattering noisily on the leathery leaves of the big magnolia near the road. Maudie closed the screen door quietly and stood behind her man. Her thick hands rested comfortingly on his lean shoulders. Clay acknowledged her touch with a faint grunt of approval.

She watched silently as he fished a sack of Bull Durham from his shirt pocket and began to hand-roll himself a smoke. His method of constructing a cigarette had always been a source of wonder and envy to most men in Bedloe County, for Clayburn Biggs could roll a perfect smoke using only one hand, without spilling a single grain of tobacco. Once, back in his wilder days, the feat had earned him fame at some of the local honky-tonks, and had net him a few spare bucks nightly, betting against unsuspecting drunks. But those times had long since passed, and now he performed the stunt purely for the entertainment of his five young'uns.

Maudie thought back twenty years, when Clay had first started courting her. She had been sixteen then, the shy daughter of a minister, and Clay had been the rawboned son of a poor tobacco farmer. He had been quite a hell-raiser in those days,

Clay had. But Maudie had seen something basically good in the man, some underlying decency that others had failed to notice. His days had been spent in the fields, working hard with his father and brothers on a patch of land hardly big enough for tobacco growing, but his youthful nights had been devoted to sin and wicked pleasure. He was a notorious drunkard, a gambler, and some said a whoremonger. But, still, when Clayburn walked past Maudie's house on a Sunday afternoon, tipping his hat and smiling as he passed, she could not help but smile back and return his attentions, despite her father's stern disapproval.

Then came the night that changed it all. Clay and his buddies, Clint Devane and Joey Lee Tidwell, were drinking and cutting up at the Bloody Bucket. Joey insulted a fellow at the far end of the bar and a fight broke out. Clay and Clint parted the two drunkards before blows could be traded, but as each man took one of Tidwell's arms, intending to escort him to the door, the other man pulled a .22 revolver from his coat pocket and put a slug right between Joey Lee's eyes. Their friend died in their arms, a look of great surprise in his bloodshot eyes, the stench of hard liquor heavy on his last breath.

That night, well after midnight, Maudie Darrow awakened to find a dark form outside her bedroom window. She hurriedly dressed and found Clayburn Biggs on the porch swing, crying his eyes out. Although the two did not know each other very well, Clay told her of the horrid incident at the Bloody Bucket that night. The sobbing words she heard almost seemed like a confession in her compassionate ears, and afterward, the two knelt and prayed. A brief courtship followed, and eight months later, with the grudging permission of her father, the two were married.

Since their wedding day, Clay had proven to be a fine example of a family man. He accompanied Maudie and the children to church every Sunday, and his only vices were tobacco and swearing, two things Maudie figured she could put up with. He had not had a swallow of hard liquor or looked lustfully at a woman other than Maudie since that bleak night at the Bloody Bucket.

"What's troubling you so, Clay?" she asked now. Her hand

caressed one stubbled cheek, moving up his sideburn to smooth out a cowlick of tousled black hair. He did not refrain from her affection, but rather reached up and took her hand in his. His grasp was strong, yet gentle, as he brought her hand to his lips and kissed her knuckles.

"Oh, just the same old thing, Maudie," he sighed.

She pulled up her late mother's straight-backed rocker and sat there on the dark porch beside him. "There ain't no need to worry yourself sick over the land. It's been sold and that's all there is to it. Me and the children, we're doing all right. We're all eating well enough and we have no bad needs. Besides, you're making money doing automotive work for half the price Sonny Martin charges at his garage in town."

"Yeah." Clay nodded glumly. "But there are only so many cars and trucks that need fixing in Bedloe County. After that, I've got no place to turn." He centered his worried eyes on Maudie. "If I could only put back enough money to buy back that land . . . Maudie, I know I could put us back on track. It just hurts me so damned bad to see my papa's land wasted, growing over with weeds. And if he knew that Ransom Potts had the deed to it now . . . well, he'd likely roll over in his grave!"

Maudie saw raw fear and frustration in her husband's blue eyes and it scared her. "Don't ever lose hope, darling. Maybe someday you'll get back that land and raise tobacco like you were meant to do. But until then, we'll get by. We're all healthy; that's more than most folks can say these days."

Thunder boomed from across the woods out back, and for a moment, Clay nearly mistook it for gunfire. But lightning crashed, illuminating the countryside for a split second, and the thunder rolled again, this time with a more natural tone.

"We just ain't making it, Maudie," he told her flatly. "Every day we're having to do without something we took for granted the day before. Little things, but I can see the strain on you and the kids. That's why I've gotta find steady work and find it fast."

The woman did not like how her husband was sounding. "What have you got in your mind, Clayburn Biggs?" Her tone was demanding, but he could detect a hint of panic in her voice.

Clay regretted telling her straight out, but he knew he had

to. He returned his tobacco sack to his pocket and lit his smoke with a sulfur match. "I came across Clara Jones in town the other morning. She told me Norman was still working that steel mill in Detroit, making fair wages, fixing to send for her and the kids. I . . . well, Maudie, I asked her to write Norman and see if they've got any jobs open there."

His wife was shocked. "I don't want to hear you talking of such things, Clayburn. We ain't hurting so bad for you to consider breaking up this family and going north. I already gave up my boy Johnny today. I ain't about to give you up to the road, too."

Clay was about to argue the point, when their conversation was cut short. A shrill, girlish scream sounded from inside the house. Maudie and Clay exchanged glances, and they both left their chairs. They found the source of the screaming in the girls' bedroom. Clay lit a kerosene lamp on the nightstand, and he and Maudie stared breathlessly at the wailing child.

Cynthia Ann stood there in the center of the bed that she and Polly shared. She screamed again and again, her hazel eyes wide in sheer horror.

"Will you shut her up, Mama?" complained Polly. She rolled over on her side and crammed a goose down pillow over her ears.

Maudie stepped to the bed and grabbed Cindy's heaving shoulders. She shook the child gently. "Wake up, honey, wake up. You're having a bad dream."

The red-haired girl ceased her screaming and stared at her mother, her eyes still glazed with sleep. "They killed him, Mama." There were tears rolling down her freckled cheeks. "They killed him."

"Who, baby? Killed who?"

Cindy's eyes suddenly regained their normal intensity, and she stared around the shadowy room in growing confusion. "I . . . I don't know. I can't remember."

"What's going on?" asked Josh. He and his little brother stuck their heads curiously out the door of the adjoining room.

"Nothing, boys," Clay told them. He stared at Cindy Ann as if she were crazy, then turned and walked into the kitchen.

"Your sister just had a bad dream, that's all."

Maudie helped the frightened girl off the bed and took her hand. "Come on, baby. I'll warm you up some milk. It'll help you get back to sleep."

She sat the child down in a kitchen chair, then went to building a fire in the iron cook stove. She gave Clay an annoyed glance, but he did not notice. He stood engrossed at the window, watching the thunderstorm grow in its fury. "It's raining pitchforks and nigger babies out there," he said to no one in particular.

A few minutes later Cindy had drank her milk and was sent back to bed. Maudie watched her shut the bedroom door and shook her head. "I'm worried, Clay."

"About what?"

"About Cindy," she replied. "I can't figure whether she only had a bad dream . . . or a vision."

Clay turned, incredulous. "What the hell are you talking about, woman?"

Maudie hesitated, then answered. "I put off telling you, Clay, 'cause I know you don't hold truck with such things, but now I think you oughta know. Our Cindy has the power of second sight. She has the gift."

"Hogwash!" said Clay. He dropped his half-smoked cigarette to the floor and ground it under his heel. "Ever since that Holt woman lost her baby, I've been hearing a bunch of bull about Cindy Ann being some kinda witch or jinx. Dammit, half of Coleman thinks she's some sort of evil-eyed monster! And here you are, of all people, telling me that she's some kinda freaking fortune teller!"

"Please, Clay, don't carry on such. It ain't nothing to be ashamed of. My mother, she had the gift, as did my great-grandmother. We should be glad the Lord chose to bestow little Cindy with such a divine power."

Clayburn Biggs paced the kitchen, shaking his head in disgust. "Well, you can believe in all that mumbo-jumbo if you want to, Maudie, but it'll be a cold day in hell before I do. I ain't about to put no faith in conjuring and soothsaying, just like I don't believe in haunts and spirits. There's nothing wrong with

Cindy Ann . . . excepting maybe she's a little strange."

"Strange?"

"You know what I mean. A little touched in the head. Don't deny she's acted differently since her stay in the hospital. I believe that fever did something bad to her brain."

Maudie stared at her husband as if she did not know the man. "Clay Biggs, I don't want to ever — *ever* — hear you say such a thing about one of your young'uns again!" Then she stormed down the cramped hallway and slammed their bedroom door behind her.

Clay grumbled an obscenity and stared morosely out the kitchen window. She was right of course. He was acting foolishly. But he simply did not believe in such things as second sight and the foretelling of futures. He thought of the nine-year-old girl and knew right then that that was not what bothered him most. It was the awful resentment he felt toward Cindy Ann. He knew it was terribly wrong, but every time he laid eyes on the child, all he could think of was the generous acreage of prime tobacco land that he had signed over to Ransom Potts and the Coleman Citizens Bank. He had sold that land to pay off the hospital bills that had added up during Cindy's long sickness. In turn, the loss of the land had crippled Clay financially in an already disabling depression. Perhaps he would never fully forgive her for his bad luck, though it truly happened through no fault of her own.

"Confound this rain," he growled to the empty kitchen. He stood at the open window for a long while that night, breathing in the earthy freshness of the downpour and listening to its steady, drumming fall.

Chapter Nine

Harvey Brewer lay in total darkness, his ears clutching for every little noise. Soon, a sound echoed over the pounding swish of the downpour. It was the deep-throated roar of an engine, a truck from the sound of it. The old man remained in his bed, stone still, his muscles tense and restless, his pulse beating swiftly with the adrenaline of pure fear.

The elderly man had turned in early that night. He had devoured a tasteless supper of cold beans and taters at seven, and listened to the state news and evening farm report on the radio, more out of habit than anything else. Then he had fallen asleep on the big feather bed that he and Norma had shared during their long and loving marriage. His sleep had been one without dreams, without physical tossing and turning. It had been the motionless slumber of the dead, or of a man who had simply stopped living a very long time ago.

Harvey had slept for only an hour or so, the only intruding sounds being the faint ticking of the parlor clock and the rumble of distant thunder. Then his peaceful slumber had been jolted asunder by the harsh roar of a vehicle pulling off the main road and onto his property. He had lain there and listened to the rickety truck drive past his house and head down the rutted track into the fields. He knew exactly where their destination lay. The old tobacco barn.

Many had trespassed into the dark security of that abandoned structure before, searching out privacy to commit their individual vices away from the reach of prying and disapproving eyes. All manner of sin, had passed unnoticed in Brewer's back pasture; drinking, gambling, adultery, and God knew what else. But the old man had chosen to look the other way, for confronting the perpetrators would only cause him trouble. It had gotten to the point lately where Harvey Brewer simply did not care who sneaked onto his land anymore.

That stormy, spring night, however, Harvey had been unable to drift back into unconcerned slumber. He had lain there in his shadowy bedroom, ears straining for sounds. They came faintly to him through the open window in the form of incoherent voices, laughter, and the slamming of heavy truck doors. Thunder rumbled overhead, and the elderly man rolled over, attempting to fall asleep; but he could not. His rheumy eyes stared blankly at the dark cracks of the plaster ceiling, an inexplicable dread pressing on his age-sunken chest like some unbearable weight.

The next thing he heard was the violent boom of a gun. There were screams . . . long, horrified screams. Whether they were those of a man or a woman, Harvey couldn't tell for sure. His heart pounded painfully in the hollow of his ribcage as he lay there and listened to the terrible sounds. The screaming ended abruptly, and Brewer knew that only death could have ended the hysteria that swiftly. *What is happening down there?* wondered Harvey, but he made no move to get up.

A second shot rolled across the dense pastureland, surpassing the storm in its violent resonance. Harvey's ancient ears strained against the growing rush of the rainfall, but for a long time he heard nothing. Then, just as he began to think it was all over, a third and final shot was heard, this time at a distance.

Someone's been killed, realized Brewer. *Something awful has happened down there.* Then a sobering thought occurred to him. *What if they come for me next?* He could lie there no longer. He sat up and, with trembling hands, reached blindly for his overalls.

Harvey Brewer went to a closet and rummaged through a clutter of old boxes and mildewed clothing. He found his father's old Remington rolling-block rifle in a far corner, along with a box of tarnished brass cartridges. He fed a round into the breech and snapped back the hammer. Swallowing dryly, he went to the back door and turned on the porch light, his house being the only one on the outskirts of Coleman with electricity.

The night was black and sodden. He could see nothing past the two-seat privy at the edge of the yard. The thick growth of brush and the massive structure beyond were engulfed in dank darkness. *Are they still out there or have they cut and run?* He dreaded the possibility of the first and hoped for the latter. He tightened his grip on the pitted stock of the antique rifle.

The sound of an engine suddenly came from near the barn, and headlights sliced through the driving rain. A gray Ford pickup churned up the dirt road toward his house. Harvey did not step out onto the porch, but stayed well inside the screen door. The vehicle slowed and then stopped just past the outhouse. The driver had noticed the porch light where none had burned before. The truck sat idling in the roadway for a long moment. Then it surged forward and braked to a halt thirty feet from Harvey Brewer's back porch.

The window of the driver's side was rolled down, but the elderly man could only make out a shadowy form in the dark cab. "Who is that out there?" Brewer demanded. "What'd you fellas go and do down there? Thought I heard shooting."

Silence met his questions, then a deep, gravelly voice came from the truck window. "Shut off that porch light, old man."

"Who is that?" Harvey asked. He recognized that voice from somewhere, but could not place it right off.

"I said to shut it off . . . *right now*!"

The threat raised the old man's dander. "I've got a gun here."

He watched as the driver slid a short-barreled scattergun across the sill of the truck window. To emphasize the point, a beefy hand thumbed back the shotgun's twin hammers. "I ain't gonna tell you again."

The sight of those two black muzzles directed squarely at the flimsy screen door dampened Harvey's bravado. Reluctantly he reached over and shut off the light. The labored throbbing of his heart increased, sending a strange tingling numbness down his left arm and the upper side of his chest.

"Who are you?" he asked once again. This time there was less defiance in his feeble voice.

"That ain't no concern of yours," gritted the unseen driver. "Now you just listen to me and listen good. Nothing went on here tonight. You didn't hear or see a thing. Understand?"

"But what'd you do? You were down at the barn—"

One of the shotgun's barrels discharged loudly. Harvey tensed himself, bracing for the force of deadly pellets. But the buckshot hit the porch instead, splintering a wooden post three feet from the door.

"You ain't listening, old man" came the voice again, after the roar of the shot had subsided. "You got absolutely no business down at that barn. You go messing around down there and I'll know about it. And, rest assured, I'll come back and put a round through that sickly, bald head of yours."

The death threat sank into Harvey Brewer's frightened mind, sending him into a palsy of trembling. The rifle dropped from his liver-spotted hands as a sharp pain coursed the length of his arm. He fell back against the dingy wallpaper of the kitchen, gasping for breath and enduring the searing agony in his chest.

"You get my meaning?"

"Yes," rasped the old man.

"Let's get the hell outta here," insisted a different voice within the darkened truck. Then the Ford was shifted into gear and driven up the pathway toward the two-lane blacktop of the main road.

Old Man Brewer groaned. His left side felt heavy, as if he could no longer stand without falling. He staggered to the iron pump at the kitchen sink and, with some effort, pumped enough water to wet his feverish face. Then he stumbled to the security of his bedroom.

My confounded heart, Harvey thought, *that's what's wrong with me.* For years he had flatly ignored the nagging sensation in his chest, ignored Doc Hubbard's warnings of a bad heart problem. Now he would die and he had nothing but his mule-headed stubbornness to blame.

He finally reached his bed and collapsed there in a clenching fit of terrible agony. It felt as if his heart were in the squeezing jaws of a vice. For a few minutes he lay there on his side, his breath heaving from his lungs, sweat trickling down his neck and the pits of his arms. When, at last, the pain diminished into a dull ache, Harvey turned over on his back and shut his eyes.

Just forget about it. His mind whirled, spinning in a dizzying maelstrom of fear and panic. *Just forget about tonight. You ain't gonna fetch Sheriff White in the morning, and you ain't about to go looking around that barn. Just put it clean out of your mind. The fella was right. It ain't no concern of yours.*

Harvey Brewer lay on his feather bed for a long time that night before he finally fell to sleep.. He listened to the sound of rain drumming on the tin roof above. He remembered how he had enjoyed the sound in his youth. Back then it had seemed strangely comforting, lulling one into a sense of placid security beneath the warmth and safety of patchwork quilts.

But that night it conjured an entirely different feeling. It rang dreadfully sinister in his aged ears, like the constant tapping of skeletal fingers on the lid of a casket.

Chapter Ten

A gusty May wind pushed the raging storm clouds farther eastward, and by morning, spring once again reigned across Bedloe County. The dawn began wet and dreary, but as the sun climbed higher into the endless blue canvas of the Tennessee sky, a lazy climate of sticky heat and humidity hung over the hollows and fields of the bottomland; promises of the burning summer to come.

Raindrops dribbled slowly from the leaves of the spreading chestnut tree, striking the open hood of Clint Devane's old Chevy roadster, sometimes finding the brim of Clay's brown felt hat. Between the annoying drips and the elusive problem with the Chevrolet's inner workings, he had no great loss of things to swear about in the oily shade of the automobile's open chassis.

"Want these pliers, Pappy?" questioned Polly. The girl dangled the greasy tool before his eyes. Clay cast a baleful glance at his eldest daughter and shook his head. Along with all the other annoyances that bugged him that Saturday morn, Polly was the icing on the cake. Since well after breakfast, the pigtailed girl had scrutinized her father's handiwork, offering advice and tools that had no logical bearing on the Chevy's mechanics. Now, as the morning drew on, she was beginning to grate on his nerves a mite.

"You sure?" Polly worked the jaws of the pliers, nibbling hungrily on the sleeve of her daddy's gray cotton shirt.

Clayburn Biggs wiped his grease-slickened hands on a bandanna and gave his eldest daughter a warning look. "You just can't help but pester a body to death, can you? Now git . . .

before I take it upon myself to blister your prissy behind."

Polly took her father's threat at face value. She looked around the backyard, perhaps to find someone else to bother. She spotted Cindy Ann sitting near the hickory stump that Clay used for splitting kindling in the fall. Her little sister played quietly with paper dolls she had clipped from the Sears & Roebuck catalogue with a pair of her mama's sewing scissors.

Clay went back to work. Since having words with Maudie last night, he had felt uneasy and on edge. It did not seem to be their money problems or the thought of leaving Tennessee to seek steady employment that lay heavy on his mind. No, it was Cindy Ann and her nightmare that nagged at him. Like he had told his wife, he did not hold faith in such nonsense as seeing visions or foretelling futures. But he had stood there in the bedroom doorway and had seen her horror. The screams, the shock of awful terror ... both had been genuine and disturbing to witness.

Old Tippy launched into a fit of hoarse barking as a rickety truck rumbled up the road from town. It braked to a screeching halt at the shoulder of the road. Hearing the crackle of gravel and the slam of the truck door, Clay peeped over the lip of the hood, hoping to greet someone with automotive problems. The out-of-work tobacco farmer sure could use the extra business.

But that certainly was not the case that morning. Sonny Martin, the town grease-monkey and owner of Coleman's only 'Texaco station, was storming up the driveway. A look of dark fury shadowed Sonny's broad face, and it appeared to Clay that the man might be suffering from a bad hangover.

Tippy snapped playfully at the mechanic's heels, receiving a forceful kick in his direction. The hound dodged the angry foot. Growling, the dog sauntered to the cool shade beneath the foundation of the single-story farmhouse.

Clay sighed. He was sure Sonny had driven his wrecker all the way from town for the sole purpose of bitching and moaning about his loss of work. It was true that Clay had been offering his mechanical expertise to the residents of Bedloe County for half the price Sonny charged his customers. From what Clay had gathered, the station owner spent most of his time idly these days, patching flats and pumping Fire-Chief.

Reluctant to get into a shouting match, Clayburn wiped his hands and stepped around the bumper of the Chevy. "What can I do for you, Sonny?"

Sonny stood there and fumed for a moment. He was a large, heavyset man with ugly features and oily, black hair. He was an ignorant man, considered by his neighbors to be a cruel bigot, perhaps even a member of the local Klan. What few friends he did have usually congregated at the Bloody Bucket.

"I wanna know what you're gonna do about what happened at the school yesterday," demanded Sonny.

Clay studied the man for a long second. "I don't believe I know what you're talking about."

"The hell you say!" boomed Martin. His big fists doubled threateningly. "My boy, Chester, came home from school looking like a damned freight train had run over him. Had two black eyes, bloody nose, a couple of loose teeth. He was bawling around all night about seeing snakes or something."

"What does that have to do with me?"

"I've heard the talk, Biggs. I ain't no damned fool!" Sonny pointed at the red-haired child who played by the stump. "It was that young'un of yours who done it! That Cindy Ann!"

"It ain't so, Pappy!" Polly spoke out. "I saw the whole thing, and Cindy didn't lay a finger on dumb old Chester!"

"Maybe not . . . but she went and put some kinda hex on the boy. Gave him the evil eye and made him see snakes and such."

Clayburn felt the heat of anger begin to prickle the back of his neck. "Now, that's gotta be the biggest crock of bull I've ever heard you utter, Sonny."

"You know about them Martins, Pappy!" proclaimed Polly from atop the hickory stump. "They're all a bunch of bald-faced liars!"

Sonny glared at the spunky girl and took a couple of steps toward her. "Why, you little—"

Clay blocked his path, his eyes cold and humorless. "Polly . . . get on into the house."

"But, Pappy—"

"You mind me, young lady."

Indignantly, Polly stomped across the yard and disappeared into the house. Cindy was left behind at the stump, alone and forgotten for the moment.

Sonny Martin crossed his hairy forearms in a show of dangerous bravado. "Like I asked before, Biggs, I wanna know what you're gonna do about this."

Clay's impatience with the man's ignorance and superstition was beginning to bleed through. "I'll tell you what I'm fixing to do, Sonny. I'm fixing to toss your butt in the road if you don't get off my property right now."

Sonny's dark eyes measured Clay's lanky frame and he laughed. "You sure you can manage it, Clay? I mean, you being such a fine, upstanding gentleman these days. I can remember the time you were right down there in the mud wallow with the rest of us drunkards and bums. You weren't too hesitant about busting your share of heads back then. I don't think you have near enough gut for it now."

Clay's lean face became a hard mask. "I have no beef with you, Martin, but if you insist on talking nonsense and putting down my young'uns, well, I just can't stand for it. If you came here looking for a fight, I reckon I still have the backbone to oblige you."

"Then let's get to it." Sonny grinned. The man grabbed a heavy monkey wrench from off the Chevy's fender. He brandished its hefty weight, intending to lay a forceful blow alongside Clayburn's skull.

He was bringing the greasy wrench around with a powerful swing when an odd thing took place. The weight of the tool had somehow changed. It felt wrong. The hardness of steel had strangely lost its rigid content and now felt peculiarly limp and rubbery. There was the sensation of holding something dry and scaly to the touch. A cold shiver reverberated through him as he hazarded a glance at the thing in his hand.

Sonny's eyes widened and he yelped in sudden horror. There was a snake in his fist, a thick length of slithering, thrashing rattlesnake pulsating between his fingers. The serpent's body began to coil around his wrist, around the muscular bulge of his forearm. He stared, transfixed, at the rattler's head, the depthless pits of the beady eyes, the flickering pink fork of the reptile's tongue. The snake's head arched back, preparing for the strike, and Sonny lost his nerve. He screamed loudly, tossing the cursed thing into the balmy morning air.

But, as the object spun in the spring sunlight, something strange and inexplicable happened. He no longer saw the writhing length of a poisonous snake hurling skyward, but another item entirely, glinting silver like a sunburst in the heavenly blueness. He watched, dazed, as the monkey wrench landed in a patch of young clover, striking the earth with a dull, clanking thud.

Sonny stood there for a long moment, not knowing what to say or do. He stared dumbly at the wrench, then at Clay. The tobacco farmer regarded him as if he were crazy. Then Sonny turned his eyes to Cindy Ann and he knew. The little girl with the fire-red hair sat on the stump, a cheerful grin on her freckled face that by no means matched the cold malice in her hazel eyes.

"Damn you, girl!" croaked Sonny. He stormed back to his tow truck and sped back down the dirt road for town, as if the devil himself were fast on his tail.

Clayburn Biggs scratched his head in complete puzzlement. He looked over at Cindy. His daughter met his attention with a shy, engaging smile. "What . . . what did you just do to him, Cindy?"

The child shrank back from her daddy's question, expecting a scolding or a spanking. "I don't know, Pappy. I just made him see something, I reckon."

"Made him see something," repeated Clay, trying to comprehend the girl's meaning.

"Just like Chester," she confessed timidly. "His daddy doesn't much cotton to snakes, either."

"And you made Sonny see something —a snake — just now?"

Cindy said that she did.

Clayburn crouched on his haunches before the wrench. He stared at it lying there in the thick clover. Then he stared up at the girl. "Do you think you could make me see it? Just like you did Sonny?"

"I don't know," The youngster frowned. There was reluctance in her voice. "I could try."

"Then do it, honey."

Cindy's brow creased in concentration, as if she was putting a great effort into what she was about to do. Her probing mind was not centered on the inanimate object, but on her father. She stared at him for a while, then ceased her mental strain. "I can't."

"How come?"

"You're stronger than they were," she explained. "Chester and Mr. Martin . . . they're kinda dumb. It's easier to fool them."

Clayburn stood and regarded his fourth child with concern. "You go on and play with your paper dollies, pumpkin. I'm gonna fetch me a dipper of water."

As Cindy Ann settled once again at the base of the stump, her collection of cutouts and her imagination her only playmates, Clay ducked inside the house. He went to the sink in the kitchen where the old iron pump drew drinking water from an underground well. Absently, he took a tin dipper from a bent nail on the wall. Working the lever a couple of times, Clay filled the cup with cool water.

He stood at the kitchen window, sipping from the dipper and watching the little girl play. Despite what Cindy thought, her efforts had not been wasted on her father. For a moment, for a mere fraction of a second, Clay had seen something. He had been staring at the monkey wrench when the steel handle seemed to thicken and round, changing in size and texture. He had caught a fleeting glimpse of the rattler's brown diamond pattern just before the vision had faded and there was only the wrench once again.

He thought back to Maudie's ravings again, the foolish nonsense about Cindy having the gift of second sight. He had dismissed her words as the ignorance of old wives tales as he always did when he encountered something he could not understand. But now he had seen the child's power, seen what it had done to a man who would back down from no fight. A nine-year-old girl had twisted that man's way of thinking, made him see things that were not there, and made him scream like a hysterical woman.

Clay stared at his daughter through the open sash of the kitchen window. Before that day, he had regarded Cindy with an emotion akin to resentment. But now, the cold contempt had melted away, and in its place lurked a tense uneasiness, a tangible fear deep down inside. Clay could not figure which feeling he despised more, especially when it was directed toward one of his own offspring.

He stood there for a long while that morning before finally going back out to finish his work on the Chevrolet.

Part Two

Mournful Summer

Chapter Eleven

The thicket stretched like the walls of some dark labyrinth across the open field. Choking barriers of honeysuckle, thistle, and prickly blackberry bramble entwined narrow passageways, converging, then spreading once again into the openness of cool twilight. There was no source of nocturnal light, no moon or scattering of stars overhead ... only an oppressive covering of dense storm clouds pouring their drenching fury earthward.

Someone made their way through the twisted tangle, haltingly, cautiously. The form was shadowy, blending with surrounding patches of blackness, then emerging to continue its agonizingly slow progress. Whether the form was that of a man or a woman could not be determined in the obscurity of the driving rain. The person walked with a limp, however; the shuffling, stiff-limbed gait of the wounded. Rain mingled with warm blood, merging, diluting, then splattering the sodden earth in random droplets.

The crashing turbulence of the surrounding storm was overshadowed by a much more powerful presence. It was one that had existed since creation itself, one that lurked in the shadows of the mind when man first took weapon in hand and pursued the beast of the field. That was what took place that dank night in an abandoned tobacco field… pursuit. And the terrifying force that now tracked the limping form, the hunted, was fear—an emotion so very devastating and unpredictable that multitudes had been stricken down and entire fortresses had toppled beneath the oppressive weight of that single ogre.

The drama that unfolded that night was horror on a much

smaller scale, but horror just the same. The dark, drenched form staggered through heavy thicket, exhaustion and agony winning against faltering endurance. Hysterical thoughts flashed through the victim's panicked mind, harrowing memories of gunfire, blood, and the dead left behind. Death stalked the Tennessee countryside that furious night, a hulking Grim Reaper with a sawed-down length of cold blued steel clutched in his desperate hand.

The figure limped onward. A few more feet of choking thicket was left behind. Through the pouring rain lay the dark folds of woodline, a promise of deliverance from the one who followed. Suddenly a form loomed nearby. The stalker! Quickly dropping to the wet ground, refuge was found beneath a thick growth of wild tobacco. There was the swish of advancing footsteps, growing nearer, then, finding no sign of the hunted, moving on.

A ragged sigh of relief escaped trembling lips. Only a few feet more and then home free. Struggling from beneath the shadowy growth, the figure stood and took a few shuffling steps forward.

"Gotcha . . ." a voice rasped from behind, cruel and triumphant. And, with it, the throaty roar Death.

Cindy Ann pushed up from the depths of the big feather bed and sat there in darkness, a scream trapped in her throat. This time she had not yelled out. She had contained the awful terror and now sat there in the back bedroom, staring into the shadows until most of the disturbing dream had been driven from her mind.

She breathed deeply, sucking in great gulps of humid, summer air which hung uncomfortably in the room, despite the open window. She sank back into the folds of the goose down bed. Polly lay on her side, black pigtails draped askew over a fluffy pillow, sleeping the slumber of the unconcerned. Cindy lay there for a long time, trying to forget the details of her haunting dream, but failing to fully obliterate the dreadful images that lingered.

It was a Thursday night in mid-July. The house was dark,

except for the kitchen where her mother washed the supper dishes by lamplight. The front porch was dark, but occupied. Pappy was out there with a couple of friends from town, Buster Cole and Woody Sadler, who ran Coleman's general store down near the forks.

Cynthia Ann lay there listening to their idle conversation as it traveled from one point of interest to another. They talked of the weather, Roosevelt and his New Deal programs, which team was likely to win the World Series that year, and the speculation of war in Europe in the near future. Locally, the news ranged from Zeke Simpson's prized Black Angus bull getting its privates hung up in a barbed wire fence to Ransom Potts' foreclosure on the Givens farm. There was some talk of a Negro getting lynched in neighboring Trenton County. The young black man had been hung from the under beams of a railroad trestle, and suspicions were that the local faction of the Ku Klux Klan had been the ones responsible.

The red-haired girl grew weary of the talk after a while. She lay there and contemplated the dream. The nightmare had invaded her sleep ever since school let out. It was always the same, the ones involved always obscured and cast in shadow. She was never able to identify them or the place where the grueling chase took place. Several times she felt she had been on the verge of recognizing the hunted one, but it had always eluded her.

After listening to the sounds of men's strong voices and the nocturnal chirping of crickets in the dewy grass outside, Cindy swung down off the bed. The hardwood boards of the floor felt cool against the soles of her bare feet as she padded quietly to the door of the adjoining bedroom.

The quiet sounds of her brothers' slumber whispered through the dark room as she slipped inside. Moonlight shone through a high-paned window, splashing across furniture and sleeping forms. She ignored Josh and Sammy, her eyes settling on Johnny's vacant bed in the far corner. Without hesitation, she turned down a corner of the upper sheet and nestled into the comforting depths of the mattress. For a long while she lay there, staring up at the dark outline of her brother's old Winchester hanging on the wall over a twelve-point deer rack, and also at the spot near the door where his flat-top guitar had stood for so many years.

It had been a month since Johnny and his pals had left for the CCC camp, and still they had received no word from him, not even a postcard. Clay put it down as youthful forgetfulness, but it was clear to see that everyone in the household was concerned over the lack of correspondence. It just was not like Johnny to go so long without writing his family, even if he was working halfway across the state.

Why couldn't you have stayed, Johnny? Cindy wondered as night sounds lulled her into a light slumber. *Why couldn't you be here when I need you the most? You're the only one who would understand, Johnny. The only one I could really talk to.*

She fell back into a deep sleep, this time unhindered by the stalking terror of her nightmare. She breathed steadily, the faint scent of tobacco lingering in her nostrils. But it was not the smoke of her father's hand-rolled cigarette that she smelled. It was a much more ancient intrusion, the musky scent of tobacco leaves, molded and rotten, in the dusty shadows of someplace long since forgotten.

Chapter Twelve

"Mama, here comes that old nigger Jonesy and his junk wagon."

The Biggs children had spent that morning playing on the front lawn, tying sewing thread onto the back legs of June bugs and laughing as they flew them like miniature kites around the persimmon trees at the south side of the house. Polly's sudden exclamation brought Cindy and Sam running. Their mother came from where she had been shelling beans on the front porch. Her face held a scolding look as she regarded the pig-tailed girl.

"Now, what'd I tell you about using that word, young lady?"

Polly shrugged. "Pappy calls them niggers."

"Well, your pappy's too set in his ways to learn any better," said her mother. "You're not. So just hold your tongue."

They stood by the roadside and watched as Old Jonesy ambled up the dirt road toward town. A mangy, sway-backed mule decked out in blinders and a harness pulled the Negro's rattletrap wagon. Its rickety bed was filled with all types of patent medicines, condiments, tobacco, and hardware. There was a shabby canopy over the flatbed from which all manner of pots, pans, and cast-iron skillets hung. As the mule sauntered farther, they clattered and rang like the maddened crescendo of some insane church bell ringer.

The black gentleman who led the mule-drawn wagon was nearly as worse for wear as his source of income. He wore a sweat-stained derby hat over a black head as slick as an eight ball, and his toothless mouth was framed by a scraggly wreath of kinky white whiskers. Although his clothes were old and patched and his shoes were mere scraps of leather, the old man's eyes beamed proudly, brimming with good-natured humor.

"Howdy do, Mrs. Biggs?" he asked with a smile.

"Oh, just getting by, I reckon." She returned the man's warmth. "How are things with you and yours, Jonesy?"

A shadow threatened to rob the merchant of his smile, but it swiftly passed. "I ain't got no complaints," Jonesy replied. "Can I do you for something this fine morn, Mrs. Biggs? Maybe an iron kettle for your stove or some sugar or flour for your baking?"

It was at that moment that Polly spied a cluster of lollipops amid a collection of rock candy and peppermint sticks. The suckers were chocolate and fashioned like faces, the eyes candy buttons, the mouth protruding in rosy wax lips.

"Can we have one, Mama?" chirped Polly excitedly. "Can we?"

"Have what?"

"Those suckers with the big nigger lips! Can we? Can we have one?"

Maudie's face reddened in embarrassment. "I thought I told you to quit saying that, young lady. Can't you even muster a little respect for Mr. Jonesy here?"

She looked apologetically toward the old Negro, but saw no anger or resentment in his aged eyes. The only emotion she could detect was a tired acceptance of things that his people had endured for countless years. "No need to scold the girl, Mrs. Biggs. That's what they look like to me ... nigger suckers."

Blushing, Maudie delved into her apron pocket and produced a twenty-five-cent piece. "I'll take a quarter's worth of flour," she said, aware that Jonesy's merchandise was usually a tad less expensive than the groceries offered by Woody's store down the road.

The old man eagerly pocketed the coin. Lifting the lid off a wooden keg, he scooped flour into a paper sack. He handed the five-pound bag to Maudie, then gave each child one of the wide-eyed suckers. "There you go, children. Enjoy yourselves now."

"You needn't do that," Maudie told him.

Old Jonesy tipped his hat courteously. "Mrs. Biggs, you good people on Newsome Road are the only white folks in Coleman who'll buy my wares. Your kindness and generosity have fed my family many a hungry night, and for that I'm mighty grateful. Besides, young 'uns need a sweet or two, every now and then."

"Well, we're sure obliged," Maudie thanked him and started back for the house, the flour sack cradled in the crook of her arm.

Polly grabbed her sucker and immediately pulled the wax lips from the cocoa brown face. "Look at me! I'm a movie star!" she proclaimed. She placed the garish red lips over her own, prancing prissily around Old Tippy. The coonhound regarded her with dumb fascination, not knowing quite what to think.

Sammy took a hearty bite from his lollipop and ran after his older sister, leaving Cindy standing at the gate with the old man. "Mind if I walk with you a piece, Mr. Jonesy?"

The old man smiled. "Why, I'd surely enjoy the company, Miss Cindy."

They started down the rutted dirt stretch of Old Newsome Road, feet kicking up dust as they walked. The warm breeze of morning was dying down now, and in its place, a sticky heat began to settle in. It would hang over the little farming community until sunset dampened its intensity later on in the evening.

"I reckon you're pretty happy about school being out, ain't you?" Jonesy asked, fishing for a little conversation from the quiet youngster.

"Yes, I reckon," Cindy answered. She nibbled on her chocolate sucker. "Don't have much to do, though. Ain't got many friends to play with, and Polly ... she's always picking on me."

"What about your brothers? You got three of 'em, I recall."

Cindy frowned. "Aw, Josh's always off fishing or traipsing through the woods, and Sam's just a baby. My brother Johnny, he's gone off to the Conservation Corps to work."

Old Jonesy's face abruptly lost its shine, and he appeared to be much older than his sixty-eight years. "Yeah, the CCC. My boy Luther went east to see about one of them government jobs, but they turned him away. Said they didn't want no niggers lazing about and hindering their work."

Cindy looked up at the elderly gentleman. Suddenly, she felt a heavy sadness creep across her mind. "I'm awful sorry about your son, Mr. Jonesy. It was a terrible thing ... them hanging him like that."

The black man's eyes grew moist with tears, and behind those tears lurked a dark anger. "They just didn't have no call to kill my boy like that," he muttered to himself. "Just wasn't no reason for it, a'tall."

Cynthia Ann tugged gently on the man's dark-skinned hand and, catching his attention, looked up into the Negro's haggard face. "But why? Why'd they do such a terrible thing?"

His eyes softened at the girl's concern. "Well, I'll tell you why, Miss Cindy. 'Cause Luther was a proud boy, that's why, and most white folks, well, they just can't tolerate a proud nigger. When a nigger gets too uppity and bold, that kinda scares those redneck crackers. That's what those Klansmen are, girl. Just a bunch of damned fool rednecks!"

"But what did Luther do that was so bad?"

Old Jonesy produced a threadbare hanky from his coat pocket and wiped his eyes. "The way I hear it, Luther got off the bus at Perryville over in Trenton County after being turned down for the CCC job. His pride was hurt and he was angry, and I reckon he just lost his head for a moment. You know that big drinking fountain in the middle of the square out front of the Perryville courthouse? The one where only white folks are allowed to drink? Well, Luther marched right up to that fountain and drank his fill. Seems like the whole town saw him do it, too, from hearing folks talk.

"Well, someone got the word to the wrong people. We found him later on that night. Somebody had done strung poor Luther up. . . hung him from the old trestle south of Elder's Junction. They'd done him awful cruel before they finished. Beat him and striped his back with a bullwhip. It was the Klan who done it. Damned cowards in bed sheets!"

The wagon merchant grew moody and silent. Cindy lapsed into a silence of her own. She had known of bigotry and hard feelings toward blacks all her life, but had not yet grasped the reasons that generated the hatred. And to horribly kill a man for the crime of quenching his thirst, well, it was more than her youthful mind could comprehend.

As they walked along, approaching the fork in the road, Old Jonesy turned curious eyes on his red-headed companion. "Miss Cindy?"

"Yeah?"

"How'd you know that it was my boy who was hung?"

Cindy stopped in mid-stride, confusion creeping into her freckled face. Exactly how had she known that the unfortunate victim had been Old Jonesy's son, Luther? Sure, she had overheard her father's conversation the night before, but no mention had been made of the lynched man's identity.

"I . . . I can't figure it out," she replied shakily. "I just knew."

"Just like you knew that Mrs. Holt's baby was dead?"

The haunting memory of the little white casket and Vera Mae's hateful rage came to mind. *It's happening again,* she thought grimly.

The merchant sensed Cindy's change of mood. "It ain't nothing to be ashamed of, girl. If the good Lord has seen fit to give you that power, then you oughta learn to accept it."

"That's what Mama says. But it feels so wrong sometimes. It seems like I'm the cause of all the trouble I see."

"Naw, that ain't the right way to think," explained Jonesy. "I know this old granny woman up in the hills. She's been birthing babies and foretelling things since she was knee-high to a grasshopper. And, you know, she be the most sensible and caring woman there is. The reason why is because she's proud of what she can do. If you get to fearing and mistrusting your own self over something like that, well, you surely ain't gonna trust no one else. And that's a mighty sorry way to be."

Cindy stood there on the hot dust of the country road and stared up in amazement at the old black man. It was the first time since she had discovered her newfound gift that anyone had explained to her so clearly what she had been feeling and why. And, although the underlying fear still remained, deep-seated and unshakable, she saw for the first time that the power she possessed was not something evil, not something to be cast away and forgotten. No, it was something to be tolerated and controlled . . . and she aimed to do just that, if she could find the courage within herself to do so.

Chapter Thirteen

The subtle art of hand-rolling a cigarette requires a combination of skill and patience. Some master the process rather easily, while others sputter and curse over tobacco and paper, never quite getting the hang of it. Youngsters building their first smoke from the basic ingredients more than often find themselves embarrassed and intimidated by the tedious operation, drawing guffaws and catcalls from nearby veterans. However, few have ever been known to roll their own using only one hand. The sole performer of that small feat in Bedloe County was one Clayburn Biggs.

Josh, Clay's fourteen-year-old son, watched mystified from the passenger side of the old Ford pickup as his daddy winked knowingly and fished in the pocket of his chambray shirt for his pouch of Bull Durham. Letting the truck coast down the busy avenues of Nashville, Clay kept one hand steady on the steering wheel while the other deftly went into action. Two fingers separated the drawstrings, while the farmer brought the cloth bag to his lips, extracting a single rolling paper from the pack. The paper he laid in his palm, cradling it like a small trough. His eyes continued to stare intently through the truck windshield, watching out for sudden red lights and fast city drivers.

With the flair of an expert, Clay looped the drawstrings over two fingers, letting the tobacco sack perch atop the nail of his middle finger. Curling his fingers inward, toward the palm, a generous amount of grainy tobacco was dumped into the paper furrow. Flipping the Durham sack back over his knuckles, it dangled by the strings, out of the way. Now came the tricky part. Any sudden motion—the slamming of brakes or the jarring of an unseen pothole—could very well spell disaster.

Bringing the palm of his hand up to his lips, Clayburn licked an edge of the stiff white paper, his tongue avoiding the mound of tobacco in the center. After the paper had been properly moistened, fingers snaked in under the opposite edge, curling the paper inward in a single, smooth roll. A second later, the task was completed. Clay held the finished product proudly between thumb and forefinger, a perfect paper cylinder packed tightly with an inner core of rich, brown tobacco.

Josh chuckled appreciatively, marveling at the saloon trick as he always did. Clay flashed his sandy-haired son a wide grin and, finding a book of sulfur matches in the bib of his overalls, lit the fresh cigarette. Josh had always had a special place in Clay's heart. Perhaps it was the boy's naive innocence and good nature that always softened the farmer's hard exterior. Josh had never been a truly smart lad. In fact, he was considered rather simpleminded, having failed school several times over, mainly because his attention wandered in the drab confines of the classroom. Josh Biggs was much more happy in the lush timberland of the Tennessee hills; hunting, fishing, and living off the land.

After lighting the hand-rolled smoke and taking a few puffs, he handed the cigarette to his middle son. "Wanna drag?" he offered.

Josh was surprised. All he had ever smoked in his young life was corn silk and rabbit tobacco. He had never been offered the real thing before. "Mama... she'll tan my hide something good if she finds out."

"Don't I know it," admitted Clay. "And she'd have me sleeping on the back porch with Old Tippy if she knew I allowed it. But she ain't gonna find out. Go on, boy, and take a try at it."

The teenager accepted the cigarette and slowly drew a long drag into his lungs. A fit of ragged coughing shook the illusions of grandeur from his mind as blue smoke curled through his nasal passages. He handed the cigarette back to his daddy, his freckled ears reddening at his father's hearty laughter.

The Ford swung off the avenue they had been traveling, detouring to the fast-paced stretch of lower Broadway. Along the way, they passed the huge brick structure that Clay had regretfully come to know so well. Clay spat bitterly out the window as they drove past the city hospital. It was there that little Cindy had spent the better part of last year in the feverish throes of typhoid. It had been a very costly stay as far as Clayburn Biggs was concerned.

Five minutes later they passed the bustling terminal of Union Station and were rolling down the steep grade to lower Broadway, with its collection of stores, restaurants, and night clubs. Upon reaching Second Avenue, Clay parked his truck beneath the Shelby Street Bridge. This was the riverfront section of town, facing the broad channel of the Cumberland River, a gathering of ancient warehouses and commodity businesses.

Clay had driven to Nashville that morning for two reasons. The first was to sell a couple of pounds of wild ginseng that he had dug from the woods behind his house. After being thoroughly washed, dried in the sun on sheet tin, and carefully weighed, the medicinal root sold for a tidy sum of five dollars a pound. The digging had been long and grueling work, but he and the young'uns had collected a couple pounds' worth. And that extra ten bucks would hopefully keep them in beans and taters till the week after next, when Clay began working temporarily at L.J. Pike's sawmill in neighboring Galbreth County.

The second reason for coming to Nashville was to check up on Johnny. Although Clay would just as soon not admit it, he was starting to worry over Johnny's failure to write or contact his family. It just was not like the boy, and besides, Johnny's two buddies, C.J. and Billy, had also been strangely silent as far as correspondence was concerned. Clay had talked with Stella Longcreek at the post office the other day, and he had promised to check on the boys' departure at the bus station the next time he made a trip to Nashville.

A few minutes later, Clay left the business of Brock Brothers' Ginseng, Furs, and Walnuts with ten dollars tucked into a pocket of his faded overalls. He walked to where Josh sat on the rear fender of the truck. "Kinda hot out of the shade today. How's about taking a walk with me downtown? I'll treat you to a Nehi soda."

The boy grinned. "I could sure go for that."

Together, they strolled up the crowded walks of lower Broadway, in no real hurry to get to the corner of Fifth Avenue where the bus station stood. They passed pawn shops, furniture stores, finally stopping at a small market. Clay tossed the clerk a couple of Indian-head nickels, opened the squat cold drink box, and reappeared on the sidewalk with two frosty Nehi Oranges. The man and his son continued their leisurely stroll, savoring the tangy orange sodas and the feel of the cold bottles in their hands.

When they reached the bus station, Clay stopped. "Wait for me out here, Josh. I got some business to take care of."

"All right," agreed Josh. He leaned against the steel post of a street lamp and took another gulp of his soda.

Clay knocked the loose road dust from his bib overalls, straightened the brim of his hat, and started toward the ticket booth near the entrance. He hoped that the questions he had come to town to ask that day would be answered and that he could go home and tell everyone that Johnny and the others had left for the mountains safely and on time.

But, somehow, he had a gut feeling that things were only bound to get worse.

Josh upended his Nehi bottle and swallowed the last of the cold orange soda. He gave his father a puzzled glance, studying the troubled look on the man's hangdog face. His dad was acting differently since leaving the Nashville bus station. The walk up the street had been brimming with hearty talk and joking, while the stroll back down was strangely leaden with silence.

Josh had been on the verge of asking Clay of his troubles, when they passed an establishment by the name of Fogerty's Pawn Shop. Josh caught a glimpse of something out of the corner of his eye. It was something inexplicable, something that just shouldn't have been there in the first place. He stared at the object hanging there in the window above a collection of gaudy jewelry and secondhand items, his simple mind trying to sort out the reasons for why it might possibly be displayed there.

"Pappy," he said, motioning for his father to join him. "Am I wrong or does that look like Johnny's guitar hanging there?"

Clayburn Biggs walked to the plate glass window. His breath hung dryly in his throat as he surveyed the gathering of fiddles, banjoes, and mandolins.

There, in the center, hung an old flat-top guitar. It would have looked like any other time-worn instrument to Clay if it had not been for the telltale marks of something hauntingly familiar to him, as well as anyone else in the Biggs family: the worn wood near the sound hole from years of diligent finger picking, the sliver of wood missing on the left side of the neck where Old Tippy had accidentally knocked the guitar down the porch steps last August, and there, almost invisible between the second and third frets of the fingerboard, was where Johnny had carved his initials with his pocket knife. All the earmarks were undeniable. It was Johnny's guitar, all right.

"I'm gonna have a talk with the man inside," Clay said.

He walked into the shady interior of the little street-side pawn shop. The walls of the shop were lined with a fair collection of bluegrass instruments, household appliances, and a few rifles and shotguns. The glass counter boasted a sparkling sea of wedding rings, pocket watches, and other jewelry. A fat, moon-faced man sat behind the counter, the sleeves of his pinstriped shirt rolled up over large forearms. He eyed Clay with a mixture of contempt and suspicion when the farmer walked in, frowning humorlessly at the faded overalls and the rawboned, rural appearance of the man.

"Help you with something, buster?" he asked, then returned his eyes to the newspaper he had laid out on the countertop.

"Yeah," answered Clay. "That old flat-top guitar in the window. Where'd you get it?"

The shop owner, Fogerty, shrugged his massive shoulders. "I dunno. I bought it off someone, I reckon. Why? You wanna buy it? It's a real steal for fifteen bucks."

"No. All I want to know is who sold it to you. Was it a young fella, maybe eighteen? Tall and lanky with dark brown hair?"

Small, pig-like eyes regarded Clay wearily. "Listen, mister. I buy and sell merchandise from perfect strangers six days a week. I don't remember their faces. I just give 'em a few bucks for their junk, then forget 'em."

The man's indifference was starting to get under Clay's skin. "I know that guitar hanging there, 'cause I bought it for my son a few years back. All I wanna find out is who sold it to you. Don't you have records on such things? A pawn ticket or something?"

Fogerty sighed and pulled a Tampa Nugget cigar box from beneath the counter. He took out a stack of yellowed tickets until he came to the bottom of the pile. "Here it is. Dated the first of last month. Gave the guy five bucks for the guitar. His name was John Brown. That your boy's name?"

"No. I don't know anyone by that name."

The pawn shop owner was tired of fooling with Clay. "Listen, buddy. Most of the guitars and fiddles I buy are off kids who show up in this town looking to get on the Grand Ole Opry. More than often, they find out their chances aren't worth a spit in hell, and by then, they're down to their last dime. They pawn off their guitars, and I give 'em enough cash for a decent meal and a bus ticket back to Hicksville. Maybe that's what happened to your kid."

Clayburn shook his head. "Never. Johnny wouldn't have sold that guitar to anyone and especially not for a lousy five dollars. I'm thinking maybe it was stolen."

Fogerty didn't like what the man was insinuating. "I figure you'd best get yourself outta here before I call the cops, buster."

The lanky farmer glared at the fat man, wanting nothing more than to jerk him over the counter and give his skull a bruising. But it was not trouble he had come to Nashville to find. His objective had been to check up on Johnny and his pals, not get in a bare-knuckle brawl with a local businessman and get thrown into the hoosegow for his hotheadedness.

Without saying another word, Clay turned and left the pawn shop. Fogerty shook his head and fished through the paper for the sports section. "Damned ridge-runner," he grumbled, then went about his reading.

"It was Johnny's guitar, wasn't it?" asked Josh as he and his father started back down the street for Second Avenue.

"Yeah, it was his. But he didn't sell it. Someone else did."

Josh eyed his papa with an expression of slow dawning. "And Johnny and Billy and C.J.? They didn't even get on that eastbound bus, did they? That's why you went into the station . . . to check on whether they did or not."

Clay regarded his son with raised eyebrows. "You ain't half as dumb as I thought you were."

When they had gotten back to the truck and were sitting quietly in the cab, Clay turned to Josh. "Boy, I want you to promise me that you won't mention nary a word of this to your ma and the others. It probably ain't nothing to be concerned over, but you know how worried they get over the least little thing."

"I won't, Pappy. Nary a word. I promise."

Clay started the truck and pulled back onto Broadway, heading southward for the outskirts of town and Bedloe County. The tobacco farmer drove the fifty miles home in total silence, his thoughts on Johnny and that guitar hanging in the pawn shop window. He found himself thinking of little things he had never really thought of before: Johnny's easygoing smile and the way he wore the gray fedora cocked jauntily on his head; and then there was the last time they had been really close, the firm handshake they had shared the day of Johnny's departure.

Johnny's not one to get himself into trouble, thought Clay, a cold dread lying like a well stone in the pit of his stomach. *He's such a fine boy, that son of mine. Such a damned fine boy.*

Chapter Fourteen

It was a steamy hot day in late July, one that was saturated with humidity and unbearable heat. The single, burning eye of the sun shone relentlessly in a cloudless sky, cooking the concrete walkways of Coleman and baking the dusty dry fields of the surrounding area. The day held a lazy creeping of time. Morning stretched past lunchtime into the brilliant shadeless oven of afternoon. Children who regularly spent their free time playing hopscotch or shooting marbles now chose to avoid those sidewalk games, fleeing to the coolness of the rural woods and waterholes.

It was a day that would haunt Cynthia Biggs for the rest of her life.

The eight weeks following the end of school had healed old wounds and vanquished a dark prejudice between Cindy and her playmates. The cruel catcalls of "witch" had petered out. The children of Coleman chose to forget the rumors and suspicions that had circulated following the death of Vera Mae's firstborn child. Even the adults in town had lost their peculiar avoidance of the red-haired girl. Their attention seemed more engrossed in topics like the scorching weather, the coming county elections in November, and the unstable price of tobacco that year.

Even Chester Martin, the school bully, had made amends with Cindy in his own way. He no longer chanted intimidations or threatened her, letting her tag along with him and a few other children their age. In fact, Chester showed a remarkable change in attitude toward Cindy Ann. He almost seemed to hold a grudging respect for the girl. Whether it had grown out of genuine repentance or an underlying fear, Cindy could only hazard a guess.

That day they roamed the dense woods that bordered Green Creek, searching for signs of buried treasure. "It's here, I swear to God it is," boasted Chester. "My grandpa told me there's gold buried all in these here woods. Said back during the War Between the States, folks used to stick their money in a kettle and bury it deep in the woods on account of bushwhackers and those damned Yankees. Grandpa says that a lot of that gold was never dug up, either, 'cause some folks got killed in the fighting or just plain forgot where they planted it."

Cindy, Benny Arnett, and Sally and Susan, the Osborne twins, followed the braggart along the wooded banks of the creek. They, too, had heard the tales of lost Confederate gold from their own grandparents. Some would have labeled the stories as pure nonsense if not for an incident that happened years ago in southern Bedloe County. It took place back in 1921. Roscoe Jobson, a poor dirt farmer, had been plowing his fields one day when the plowshares hit metal. The object uncovered had been an old dutch oven of cast iron, the type used for cooking back in the olden days. No one ever saw the contents of that cache, but it had been gold and plenty of it. Soon afterward, Jobson quit his farming, moved to Coleman, and opened his own feed store in town. He bought a large house, a new automobile, and folks said he still had enough money in the local bank to last him till his dying day.

Tiring of roaming aimlessly in the forest, Chester headed up a steep hollow toward sunlight. "Come on, you slowpokes. I have a good idea where we might find some of that lost treasure."

They followed their leader up the steep ivy-covered grade, the twin girls squealing as a black snake chanced across their path. Cindy tagged along reluctantly, wishing to remain in the cool shade of the forest. It was peaceful there, the only audible sounds being the scurrying of small animals, the chorus of songbirds, and the trickling of spring water over smooth stones.

"You coming, peckerwood?" growled Chester, waiting until Cindy had reached the plateau of hot, dry farmland. The moment she reached the choking growth of heavy thicket, Cindy felt a strange chill shudder throughout her. She crossed her arms, feeling gooseflesh prickle along the surface of her freckled skin.

They stood there on the edge of the old Brewer place. Cindy looked across the great expanse of weedy thicket that covered a good two hundred acres, once rich bottomland brimming with row upon row of lush green tobacco. Harvey Brewer's single-story farmhouse sat close to the main highway. Its clapboard frame showed evidence of rotten wood and peeling paint, long neglected by its reclusive owner. But the heavy growth of thicket and the little house were secondary compared to the huge structure that dominated the center of the Brewer property.

The old tobacco barn. A towering cathedral of weathered lumber topped with wide, rusty sheets of corrugated tin. Eighty feet long and forty wide, it had been the largest curing barn in Bedloe County during the turn of the century. For nearly fifty years, Brewer's barn had been the site of many a tobacco auction and community gathering. In its better days, it had even hosted a few floor-stomping square dances, the steep rafters thrumming with hoots and hollers and the rapid-fire picking of rowdy bluegrass music. But that had been years ago in an entirely different time.

"There's gold in that old barn," stated Chester Martin as the five youngsters crouched in the dense concealment of a patch of pink-headed thistle.

"How do you figure that?" asked Benny Arnett.

Chester glared at the towheaded boy as if he were a born imbecile. "'Cause where else would Old Man Brewer have stashed his money? Not in no bank, that's for sure. My daddy says that he was one of the richest men in the county before his old woman croaked and he went soft in the head. The old coot probably stashed his money somewhere in that barn and forgot all about it."

"You mean we're gonna go in there?" Susan Osborne frowned. Her twin sister also wrinkled her nose in distaste, the thought of dank earth and cobwebs coming to mind.

"Me and Benny are," said Chester. "You sissies can just hightail it on home if you're gonna squawk around like a bunch of wet hens."

The two boys dodged through the narrow passages of the encompassing thicket, leaving the fairer sex behind. "Aw, come on, Susan," urged Sally. "You coming too, Cindy?"

The nine-year-old stood there for a long moment, her eyes centered on the building a hundred yards away. An odd queasiness sat heavy in her stomach, the same feeling she got before a pop quiz in school or the threat of punishment for some great wrong done. "I don't know if we should."

Sally shrugged. "Suit yourself."

The two girls vanished into the growth, and not wanting to be left there alone, Cindy followed.

They all joined Chester beside a clump of wild tobacco, watching the barn as if it were some medieval fortress in a bygone age.

"What about Old Man Brewer?" Benny asked. "What if he takes a potshot at us with that old rifle of his?"

Chester scoffed. "He ain't even home, you idiot! Everybody in town knows he goes into Coleman for groceries every Thursday like clockwork. We could scream our fool heads off out here and no one would be the wiser."

In the sparse shadows of the wild tobacco plant, Cindy crouched, her thoughts clashing in a strange combination of conflicting images. Darkness seemed to close in on her mind, boiling with thunderous fury. Her skin felt as if it were being pelted with the cold splatter of a sudden rain, and there was the swishing of footsteps in high weeds . . . behind her. She felt frozen to the spot, her heart beating wildly, the copper taste of fear coating her mouth.

"Gotcha . . ."

The rough voice seemed to sound directly behind her ear, and she fought to stifle a cry of alarm. Swallowing dryly, Cindy turned sharply and found... nothing. There was only an empty thicket there. No darkness, no cold dampness, only the hot, dry brilliance of the Tennessee summer.

"What's the matter with you?" Chester asked her with growing irritation.

"I thought I heard something."

The twins' eyes grew large. "Maybe we oughta get outta here, Chester."

"Aw, she's just trying to spook us."

As one, they moved toward the very edge of the thicket. "How're we gonna get in? The doors are locked and chained."

Chester grinned mischievously. "I know a way in. Come on."

He lead the others to the western wall of the gray-wood barn. Cindy was the last one out of the bramble, and for a second, another image intruded upon her thoughts: again the cold and rain and, this time, a dull aching pain and the warmth of trickling blood. *I'm shot! Oh, God help me, I've been shot!* Cindy cringed at the voice, for it was somehow frighteningly familiar to her. Try as she may, though, Cindy was unable to identify the one who had gasped those horrified words. The sounds that rushed in on her thoughts at that moment —the heavy rush of a downpour, the brittle crack of lightning — distorted the desperate exclamation, causing the words to echo dully in her head.

"Get the lead out of your butt, carrot-top!" Chester called harshly. The girl blinked, forcing the images from her mind. Chester stood at the weathered wall of the big barn, holding a loose board to one side, allowing for a narrow opening between planks. Benny and the Osborne sisters had already squeezed through into the musky darkness within.

Cindy stared at the black opening, an awful dread gripping her. She could not explain the terrible sensation, the feeling that some heinous act had been committed there, but she knew that she should not go in. *It's happening again,* she warned herself. *You've got to get away from this place. Get back home before you see something you'll regret for a long, long time.*

She heard her thoughts screaming at her to abandon Chester's childish treasure hunt, but still she moved forward, closing the gap between thicket and weathered barn. Despite the oppressive feeling of fear and trepidation, another emotion bled through, smothering the warnings of her mind. Curiosity. That was what propelled her to the opening in the planked wall...that enticing snare that had trapped countless victims in the inescapable grasp of disaster.

As she squeezed through, Cindy peered into dusty blackness, the only light appearing as dust motes drifting through the slits between each unleveled board. Then, gradually, she spotted forms around the massive cavern of wood and tin. There were the three who had entered before her and Chester, as well as objects that had been there indefinitely: shallow ditches full of burnt charcoal and a long, casket-like box that had once served as a chest for tools, farming implements, and the like.

"It's in here," declared Chester, letting the loose board slide back into place. "I can feel it in my bones!"

Sally wrinkled her nose and shifted her bare feet on the cool earth of the barn's natural floor. "Sure is creepy in here. I bet the place is crawling with spiders and snakes."

Her sister echoed her concern. "And it stinks in here, too. Smells like an old dog done crawled in here and died."

Cindy also detected the distinct stench of decay. The putrid odor permeated the barn's stagnant air. It was the same smell that had seeped into the Biggs house when a sickly possum had crawled up under the foundation and died one summer a few years ago.

"Aw, you're a bunch of danged crybabies!" said Chester. He strutted through the vast interior of the old curing barn, eyeing the dark corners and the cobwebbed rafters with great interest.

"There ain't no gold here," voiced Benny, putting in his two-cents' worth despite the possibility of retribution from Chester. "I think we oughta get outta here. We're trespassing. And, besides, this joint gives me the willies."

"Sissies," grumbled the bully. "The whole lot of you." He studied the shadowy confines of the ancient structure, his dark eyes finally settling on the dusty frame of the big tool box. "There . . . there's where I'd stash my gold if I was Old Man Brewer. And, see, it's padlocked. Why would he lock the danged box up just to protect a few rusty tools?"

"What're you gonna do?"

"I'm gonna bust that lock and take a look inside."

Cindy watched silently as the other children followed Chester to the wooden chest. Suddenly, thoughts began to flood her mind again, thoughts that strangely were not her own. They came like the spewing of a great dam, a jumble of dark, shimmering images and voices that rang oddly familiar to her young mind.

Five shadowy forms standing in the muted light of a coal oil lamp, three standing apart from the other two.

"What the hell's going on here?"

The soft rustle of coarse burlap. The glow of yellow light on the barrels of a sawed-off shotgun. *"You've been suckered."*

One of the forms, a tall one, stepping forward. *"Now, wait a minute—"*

"Just shut up!" A gawky scarecrow setting the lantern on the lid of the tool box.

Cindy strained to pull away from the confusing rush of visions. On another plane of consciousness, she could see Chester kneeling before the wooden chest, examining the rusty lock. "Hand me that old hammer there, Benny."

The murky images continued to invade her mind. *"We want what money you're toting,"* demanded the big man with the scattergun.

"I'm getting outta here." This from a little fellow among the three. *"I ain't gonna take this anymore."*

"No, not anymore."

Then the throaty explosion of a shotgun blast boomed in Cindy's ears, causing her heart to skip in mid-beat. The flash of burnt powder and a gorge of blood splattered the earthen floor as the little fellow was thrown back by the shot. She watched in horror the shimmering mirror image of a dying man. He stared dumbly at his friends — at her—his blood-dripping hands attempting to keep his innards from spilling out.

Someone began to scream shrilly. Cindy began to back away from the horrible images that assaulted her. She backed into the far wall of the barn with a thud and, instinctively, laid her hand on one of the crude rungs of the ladder to steady herself.

"Stop him ..." gritted someone behind her. Cindy whirled at the tone of cold cruelty, facing the roughly boarded wall and its makeshift ladder leading to the rafters above. But it was not her hand that now clutched the rung of rotten wood. It was the strongly sinewed hand of a man, dark skinned and calloused, that hovered before her puzzled eyes. The muscles tightened and flexed as if the hand's owner was about to pull himself up the ladder.

She stood transfixed by the strange hand until, abruptly, another object entered the picture. It whistled through the stale air, a rusted mass of steel on a pitted handle of rock-hard hickory. She watched in gruesome fascination as the axe struck the veined wrist with the force of its powerful swing. The girl stumbled backward and sat down hard on the packed earth as the hand separated from its arm in a sickening burst of blood and splintered bone.

Cynthia Ann sat there for a tense moment, her eyes screwed shut, desperately trying to cleanse her mind of the awful images. The moans and screams of the injured man echoed shrilly, then faded into silence. The frightened girl breathed in deeply, a palsy of shaking and nausea threatening to overcome her.

There was a rattle and a curse from the far side of the barn. She struggled to her feet and saw Chester hunched over the padlock with a rusted ball-peen hammer in hand. With a grimace of stubborn determination, the boy began to assault the lock with a number of sharp, well-placed blows.

The pounding of the hammer matched the frantic pulse that thrummed dully in Cindy's ears. *I've got to get out of here, she told herself. Get out before it's too late.* She turned and ran for the loose board at the far wall.

"Where are you going, Cindy?" called Susan.

"Let the peckerwood go," growled Chester. He took a firmer hold on the hammer's handle. "That'll just mean a bigger share of the loot for all of us."

Cindy reached the wall. She began to search for the loose board, her fingers gripping the rough planks, trying to discover the one that would allow her access to the outer world. A world full of sunshine and green trees and life.

"Where is it? Where the hell is the loose one?"

The thought was not her own. Again, the images of another had intruded on her thoughts. The sensation that filled her at that instant was one of pure horror and overpowering panic. And the voice, again it was painfully familiar. It repeated itself over and over again until, at last, she had it pinpointed. A sinking fear pressed in on Cindy as she finally knew who the one in the thicket, the one who had been mercilessly hunted in her dreams, actually was.

The cold realization reaffirmed itself when she caught sight of something out of the corner of her eye. It was a dark object tucked away in the dank shadows near an old plow. She forgot the loose board for the time being and walked apprehensively toward the source of her interest.

It was a hat —a grey fedora long since misshapen and waterlogged by dampness.

She picked up the hat and turned it over in her hands.

"Gotcha . . . Johnny!" rasped the same gravelly voice in her ears, the same voice that preceded the deafening discharge of a twelve gauge shotgun.

Cindy whirled, her heart pounding and tears welling in her eyes, just as the padlock burst apart under a mighty swing of the ball-peen hammer. Chester grinned, freed the clasp from the rest of the broken lock, and lifted up the lid.

"DON'T OPEN THAT BOX!"

Her frantic plea was ignored. The tool chest was thrown open with a squeal of rusty hinges and the clatter of ancient tools falling onto the earthen floor.

Cynthia Ann Biggs ducked through the narrow opening of the wall just as the frightened screams of children filled the old tobacco barn, echoing sharply off the bowed rafters, off each uneven board held in place with ten-penny nails. Cindy's terror matched their own as she burst into the sweltering afternoon sun, away from the stench of decay and the sight of horrible death.

Chapter Fifteen

A rickety, flatbed truck stacked high with freshly cut lumber slowed on the main highway, then pulled down the rutted dirt road that spanned the length of the old Brewer place. Hot summer dust boiled dryly beneath the truck's tires as L.J. Pike drove past the farmhouse, toward the huge structure beyond.

The Galbreth County lumberman sent a spritz of tobacco juice out the side window and cast a glance at his quiet passenger. Clayburn Biggs had not said a single word since they left Ollie Simpkins' farm, ten miles north of Coleman. Sheriff White had left word there that Clay was to get out to Harvey Brewer's place as soon as possible. The only thing they knew was that it had something to do with one of Clayburn's children. "I've told them young'uns a million times they could get hurt bad messing around that old barn." That had been the only statement the lanky man had uttered during the long ride across Bedloe County.

"You want me to stick around, Clay?" Pike asked when he had braked to a halt.

Clay shook his head. He climbed out of the truck and slammed the door shut. "I reckon you'd best get that lumber back to Simpkins. We lit outta there like hell on wheels. Thanks anyhow."

Pike shifted the old lumber truck into reverse and backed up the long stretch of dirt track to the highway. Clay took a dirty bandanna from his back pocket and wiped the sweat and grit from the nape of his neck as he surveyed the activity around Brewer's curing barn. There were three cars parked nearby; two belonging to the Bedloe County Sheriff's department, the other, a dark sedan, he recognized as belonging to Anson Hubbard, Coleman's only practicing physician. A small crowd of people stood a distance from the barn, all friends and neighbors who lived along Old Newsome Road. As he started up the road, a heaviness settling in the pit of his belly, Clayburn stared at the huge building. The tall, double doors of the old barn stood open, the heavy logging chain that had sealed them for years having been removed. Somehow it appeared obscenely sinister, like the gaping, toothless maw of an old geezer who had died in his sleep.

He felt eyes upon him as he reached the gathering that stood close to the edge of the thicket. Tension hung like electricity in the air. *Something's wrong,* Clay thought. *Something's awful damned wrong.* He spotted Maudie and the children and started toward them. His wife's eyes were red and puffy from crying. All of his offspring were there, their faces stricken in sick masks of numb grief. Even young Josh, whose features had been burnt bronze by the summer sun, stared palely at him, a sobering expression of sad confusion replacing his carefree air.

"Maudie?" Clay began, but the question he was about to ask hung dryly in his throat. His puzzled, blue eyes left his wife's colorless face, drifting downward to regard little Cindy. She stood before her mother's flour-speckled apron, seemingly detached from her surroundings. She held a dirty fedora hat in her small hands. It was a hat that Clay recognized immediately.

Clay heard himself being called from the direction of the barn. He turned to see Sheriff Taylor White standing in the open doorway, motioning for him to join him. Reluctantly, the farmer left his bewildered family and started up the twin ruts of the dirt track to the towering entrance of Brewer's rundown barn. An awful dread pressed in on Clay. He felt as if he wanted to turn and run... run until he dropped from sheer exhaustion. At that moment, Clayburn Biggs wished that he were a thousand distant miles from the ominous structure.

"What's going on here, Taylor?" he asked the portly sheriff. The constable was uniformed in a plain khaki shirt and trousers, a polished brass badge over his left pocket and a holstered Smith & Wesson .38 Special on his hip.

Taylor White avoided Clay's eyes, turning toward the murky shadows of the barn's interior. "We'd best talk in here," he suggested, his voice cracking.

Clay knew then that something terrible had taken place. The sheriff was a man who looked you straight in the eye when he spoke and wasted no time in getting to the point of what he needed to say. The big man was acting mighty spooked that afternoon, as if something had shaken his iron constitution to the point of breaking. Clay followed him into the cavernous building, his heart feeling as if it had been replaced by a stone.

Harvey Brewer, Doc Hubbard, and Bedloe County's two deputies, Fred Ezell and Pauly Bishop, stood back in the depths of the old barn, near a long wooden box of a tool chest. They watched silently as Clay entered, then they too averted their attention from him.

"I don't know how I'm gonna tell you this, Clay." Taylor shook his massive head and stared up at the cobweb-shrouded rafters, as if hoping for some divine assistance from the heavens.

Clay half suspected the horrible news that the sheriff was so reluctant in giving. "It's Johnny, ain't it?" he asked straight out. "He's dead."

The lawman turned, his small gray eyes as sad as a hound's. "Yes."

Clayburn closed his eyes and felt a sick quiver run through his lanky frame. After seeing the battered fedora in his daughter's hands, he had expected that awful suspicion to be confirmed. But another part of him had hoped and prayed that the news would concern something else entirely. He stood there for a long moment, a spell of nausea washing over him, then slowly passing.

Taylor White laid a supportive hand on Clay's shoulder. "You all right? You want I should get the doctor over here?"

"No," breathed Clay. "I'll make it." After a long moment of silence, he turned tortured eyes to his friend. "How did it happen, Taylor? And what about his pals, C.J. and Billy?"

"They're all dead. We're still trying to put all the pieces together, but from what we've gathered, someone lured the boys here to Mr. Brewer's barn and killed them. Then they dismembered the bodies and, covering them with lime, stashed them in the bottom of that old tool box over yonder."

Clay looked toward the wooden chest and saw three blanketed forms lying in the shadows. The forms were lumpy and shapeless, not at all resembling those of human beings. "Oh, God Almighty!" rasped Clay. He turned away and put a hand on a support beam to steady himself.

"I'm sorry, Clay," apologized the sheriff. "I didn't mean to sound so ghoulish."

"No, I want to know about it. All of it." He regarded Harvey Brewer. "What about this, Harve? Are you the one who found them out here?"

The old man, looking deathly sick himself, shook his balding head. "Naw, it was a bunch of young'uns. Sonny Martin's boy and some children from town. They were messing around in here and found the bodies."

"Your girl, Cindy, was with them, Clay," Deputy Ezell put in. "Must've been awful her coming across her brother like that."

The sheriff stared at Brewer, trying to read behind the pained expression on the elderly man's face. "Now, you're sure you don't know nothing about this, Harve? Didn't hear no shooting or anything like that recently?"

"Like I told you before, I don't know a thing about this. You know as well as I do that all manner of trash sneaks on my land, trespassing, doing God knows what in this old barn. Sure I hear things sometimes, but I don't come down here snooping around. That's a damned good way to get your head blown off!"

A tense silence filled the barn. Each man stood, involved in his own private thoughts, not knowing exactly what to say to one another. All eyes turned to the open doors as the rumble of an automobile roared faintly in their ears. It was a shiny, tan LaSalle, chrome sparkling in the afternoon sun. They all recognized the roadster as that of Bedloe County's heartless banker, Ransom Potts. In a cloud of dust, the businessman braked to a halt and, leaving the vehicle, stormed in their direction. No one in Coleman cared much for Potts, the sheriff included, but that desolate moment shrouded in the gloomy shadow of death, they could not help but feel pity for the man.

Taylor White sighed. "This sure ain't gonna be easy," he said, more to himself than anyone else. He walked to the entrance to meet the banker when he got there.

Absently, Clay pulled the makings from his shirt pocket, intending to roll himself a smoke. However, his hands shook so much out of frazzled nerves that he had to abort the attempt. He shoved the tobacco sack back into his pocket and stared blankly at the covered forms twenty feet away.

"How are you holding up, Clayburn?" asked Doc Hubbard. The gray-haired physician stepped in front of the man, perhaps trying to block his view.

"I don't know," admitted Clay. "Just can't believe he's really dead. It's so damned hard to get it through my head that he's lying under one of those blankets. Is there any chance that a mistake's been made? That it ain't really Johnny and the others?"

"Afraid not," said Deputy Bishop. "Fred, show him what we found on the boy."

The other deputy took a bundled handkerchief from where it lay atop the wooden box. He opened its folds, revealing a handful of meager possessions. Clay studied the items, a dull ache of emotion growing in his chest. A few cents in change — a silver dime and a few wheat pennies — a buckeye for good luck, and a coil of spare guitar string in a stained pasteboard packet. The last object among the others was the three-bladed Case pocket knife that Johnny had won in a talent contest at the local high school three years ago.

"I'm sorry, Clay, but we're gonna have to keep this stuff for evidence."

The farmer nodded grimly and handed the articles back.

Sheriff White and Ransom Potts moved farther into the barn, their voices growing in intensity as the conversation reached its peak. As usual, Potts had not reacted with shock or grief, but with instinctive anger. His eyes burned with indignation, almost as if he had been cheated out of a substantial sum of money, rather than the life of his only son.

"How did it happen?" demanded the banker. "Why would

C.J. come to this godforsaken place?" Ransom Potts quaked and sputtered in his fury, a huge man in a gray double-breasted suit. The man was soft and vastly overweight, the sign of a pampered and well-fed man.

Sheriff White shrugged. "Mr. Potts, I've told you our suspicions of what happened. The boys must have gotten sidetracked on their way to Nashville. Doc figures they've been buried there for going on two months now."

Ransom's moon face lost a bit of its angry color, the pallid cast of shock creeping into the slack flesh of his jowls and the pits of his piggish eyes. He turned his attention to the doctor, his words less harsh in their tone.

"How were they killed?"

Anson Hubbard looked uncomfortably at the sheriff, then regarded both Clay and Ransom. "I'd rather not get into that till I've had time to do an autopsy. But from just looking at the wounds, I'd say two of them were shot, while the other was murdered with an axe or some such object."

A long stretch of silence followed Doc's brief explanation. Clayburn sat heavily on the frame of the ancient plow, while Ransom Potts paced the floor. The banker dabbed at his massive face with a monogrammed handkerchief, the red flush of anger once again crawling up the nape of his neck into his beefy features.

"I should have known it would come to this, letting my boy associate with all manner of scoundrels and white trash!" Potts proclaimed, staring Clay in the face. "I wanted C.J. to make something of his life. I even offered him an important position at the bank, making a decent wage. But, no, he wanted to defy me and put me to shame. And he did it, too, running off to join that degrading work camp to toil the earth like a common laborer. And I know who was the cause of his defiance and, eventually, his death. It was a damned half-breed and the no-account son of an ignorant tobacco planter!"

Clayburn was on his feet in an instant, his blue eyes steely and his work-hardened fists doubled. Everyone in the barn thought that Potts' insulting words might fire Clay into violence and rightly so. But the lanky man surprised them all. He stood his ground, pinning Ransom stone still with hard words of his own.

"If anyone got these boys killed, it was C.J. who done it. Maybe you never did notice it, Potts, him being your son and all, but folks didn't take to the boy very well. He was a smart-ass and a troublemaker and as stubborn as an old mule, just like his old man."

Fearing that the hostile exchange might lead to blows, Taylor White stepped between the two, laying a firm hand on each man's shoulder. "Fellas, blaming one another just ain't gonna do no good. I know you two have no great love for one another, but you've gotta be civil just this once. I don't have much of a chance in solving this crime without your cooperation. And I want you both to know I am gonna find the lousy bastards who done this. I swear to God I will. And when I do, they'll pay dearly for this terrible act."

The lawman's vow calmed the men. Clay scratched his chin and, eyes on the raw earth of the barn floor, nodded in quiet agreement. Ransom Potts, however, puffed up like a bullfrog, pulling away from Taylor's comforting grasp.

"Well, you'd better just do that, Sheriff," he said, poking a meaty finger in the constable's face. "If you don't bring that murdering trash to justice soon, I'll damned well see that this year's election will be your last. Maybe it's about time this county elected a man who suits the job better, instead of one who spends half his time down at Woody's store, gorging himself on idle conversation, sodas, and moon pies!"

Then, stomping out of the barn, Potts got into his car and headed back for town.

"Don't pay him no mind, boss," said Deputy Ezell. "It was just the grief talking."

White stared hard at the retreating bumper of a car that would have cost him a good three years' pay. "No, that wasn't grief talking," he simply said. "That was just plain, old Ransom Potts raising the usual stink. And, though it may not be the most Christian observation I've ever made, I still think he's one genuine pain in the ass!"

The Biggs family watched as Clay and the sheriff emerged

into the sweltering summer sun, followed by Harvey Brewer. They walked over to where the brood stood in a tight and inseparable group.

Maudie watched her spouse approach with a growing sense of cold dread imbedded in her soul. "Clay . . . was it him?"

The rawboned farmer nodded. His long face had never seemed so colorless and old.

The woman collapsed into the strong comfort of his arms, sobbing wildly over the loss of her firstborn. The children began to vent their grief also, clutching at each other, seeking some small comfort in the midst of their brother's painful memory. The only child who did not cry was Cindy. She stood quietly, her full attention on the misshapen clump of water-stained felt in her small fingers. Her hazel eyes studied each water-spot, each seam and stitch, as if searching for some curious piece of a puzzle that she could not quite assemble fully in her youthful mind.

Sheriff White stooped down to the child's level, running a pudgy finger absently along the crease of the fedora's crown. "Cindy, honey, I'm gonna need this for evidence. Without it, I might not be able to find the bad men who did this."

The nine-year-old's freckled face was leaden with confusion. She continued to stare at the hat, unwilling to give in to the sheriff's gentle request.

With Maudie still sobbing on his shoulder, Clay reached down and ran a hand through Cindy's shock of orange-red hair. "Let him have it, pumpkin."

The child reluctantly released her hold on the fedora. As the fabric of the hat left her fingertips, Cindy lost hold of something more than just the material object. Clutching her brother's hat had sent a peaceful flow of good memories through her mind, memories of Johnny as she last remembered him: his easy grin, smiling eyes, his boyish recklessness. A myriad of songs had danced through Cindy's thoughts, the strumming of the flat-top guitar and the crystal harmony of the young man's cheerful voice. The memories had calmed the girl after her mad dash home from that den of violent death, serving as a pacifier might soften the turbulent mood of an infant.

But now, as Johnny's dirty gray hat left her possession, the darker images returned, the oppressive images of darkness and rain and the thunderous reports of shotguns expelling swarms of pellets, aiming to find their mark and spill life's precious blood upon the rich Tennessee earth.

Her defenses torn down, Cindy suddenly felt the onslaught of raw emotions overcome her. Like the others, she began to cry. Cynthia Ann Biggs wept bitterly for her lost brother, feeling terribly lonesome despite the closeness of her family. And there was a burning anger deep down in her young soul, as if she had been coldly wronged by someone she could not quite place. For a moment, she felt as if the faces of the culprits would emerge from the depths of obscurity, exposed and leering hatefully in the pleasure of the evil committed that rainy night months ago. But the identity of the murderers did not come. While every other horror expressed itself clearly in her mind, the ones responsible still eluded her.

Sheriff White turned from the Biggs family, embarrassed in the face of their grief. He tucked the fedora beneath his arm, then walked back over to where Old Man Brewer stood. "Harvey, are you sure you didn't hear any shots down at that barn? It's kinda hard for me to swallow that something like this took place without you knowing something about it."

Harvey Brewer seemed irritated at the sheriff's suspicions. "Like I told you before, I don't know nothing. I don't know how many times I've gotta tell you that before you believe me, Taylor."

Cynthia Ann heard the old man's gruff denial. She glared up at him through her tears. *You're lying!* she wanted to scream at him, for she knew deep in her heart that Brewer was concealing the truth. She sensed a great fear behind the old man's lies, the cold fear of promised retribution. Someone had put a bad scare into Harvey Brewer, a deep and lasting fright that suppressed every shred of honor and wisdom that the old-timer had accumulated during seventy-eight years of living in the Tennessee bottomland.

Harvey was turning from the sheriff's interrogation when he caught a glimpse of the girl's accusing stare. He opened his mouth, perhaps intending to scold her for showing disrespect to her elders, but his words froze in his throat. He looked into those tearful eyes, and what he saw there shook him to his very bones. Images came to him, rapidly replacing one with the next, each more frightening than the last. The pelting staccato of rain on the tin roof, combined with the boom of distant gunfire and the horrid banshee wail of death screams. The splash of headlights' arching through the darkness of his field, finally settling on the back porch of the little clapboard house. Gruff voices came to mind, threatening and strangely familiar. *Nothing went on here tonight. You understand?* A feeble protest on his part, followed by the thunderous explosion of a shotgun blowing a chunk from a porch post nearby. Then, when they had left, the cold trembling fear and the pain ... oh, that terrible searing pain deep inside his chest!

The sheriff studied Brewer's agonized expression with sudden concern. "Are you all right, Harve? If your heart's acting up again, I can fetch the doctor."

"Just forget it." Brewer shrugged it off. He turned toward the security of his ramshackle house. "It ain't nothing but a touch of heartburn. I don't need that old quack to tell me that."

Without another word, he ambled away from the small gathering. He was mounting the low porch when he again cast a curious glance at the weeping huddle of the Biggs family. The red-haired child still held him in her sights, those innocent eyes blazing angrily in his direction. Harvey wasted no time in locking the kitchen door behind him. He stood, steadying himself at the kitchen table, until the tightness and drumming ache began to fade from his chest. But, even after slumping into a cane-backed chair, the old man found himself unable to rid himself of Cindy's damning stare.

She knows! he realized, burying his face in his hands. A shuddering tremble gripped his feeble body like a palsy, and he sat there waiting, waiting for the heavy knock on the back door and Taylor White's angry demands for information withheld. But his door remained silent and his house unapproached, and he sat there a very long time, until the shadows of evening crossed his floor, wrapping him in a dark shroud of fear and lonesome despair.

Chapter Sixteen

The funerals of Johnny Biggs and Billy Longcreek were held at the Coleman Church of Christ. It was a simple, solemn service conducted by the Reverend Powell. The pews were packed during the comforting eulogies of the two boys, and there was much weeping and the flickering of paper fans. After the brief service, pallbearers carried the two caskets to the graveyard that bordered the church grounds. The somber weather matched the darkened moods of those gathered at the double burial. Mostly neighboring farmers and their families surrounded the gravesites, along with a few sympathetic townsfolk who had thought well of the two young men who were to be committed to earth.

The funeral of the other victim, C.J. Potts, was held separately in the town cemetery near the county courthouse. The gathering there was much smaller than the one in the country. Ransom Potts and his frail wife, Betsy, a minister, and a group of reluctant bank employees were all who attended.

At the rural graveyard, only a few yards from where Vera Mae Holt's stillborn child had been buried a few months earlier, the unseen remains of Johnny and Billy were laid to rest. There was much sobbing and praying as the pinewood caskets were lowered and covered with rich, Tennessee clay dirt. The only one of the Biggs clan who did not shed a tear was Clayburn. The farmer stood beside his grievous wife, his lean face as rigid and cold as sculptured stone. His neighbors were respectful of the courage he showed in the face of such a dark day in his life. But, if they had looked closer, if they could have read the emotion behind those sharp blue eyes, they might have sensed that sturdy rock on the verge of crumbling; for the eyes are a mere extension of the soul, and that man's tortured soul was raging with a turbulent mixture of grief, bitterness, and rage.

After all had been said and done, the gathering dispersed. Clay Biggs and his quiet family drove home in the beat-up Ford pickup. When they had reached the house, the truck parked in the driveway, they all sat there for one silent moment, no one anxious to move from his spot, each one submerged in their own private thoughts of Johnny. Finally, Clay climbed out of the truck and, without a word, marched past the house to the outbuildings out back, shedding the dark jacket of his Sunday suit as he went.

"I've got to get ready for the neighbors," Maudie said aloud, herding the children into the house ahead of her. "You young 'uns change into your old clothes, you hear me?"

"Yes, Mama," they all answered.

Maudie hurriedly set her black veiled hat and purse atop the hallway chifforobe and headed for the kitchen. Once there, she began clearing the eating table, making room for the offerings to come. In the South it was a long-standing custom at times of death to bring food instead of flowers and other condolences. It was a thoughtful and well-appreciated gesture, for the bereaved family was most often too upset to prepare supper after the burial. Soon there would be knocks upon the door, and the neighbors would enter, staying only long enough to share their sorrow and leave their covered dish on the kitchen table. Fried chicken, deviled eggs, and bowls of fresh vegetables from the garden, the offerings were meant as much more than a free meal to the grieving family, but as an offering of friendship and understanding.

Maudie was passing the kitchen window when she stopped in her tracks. She stared at her husband through the dirty panes. Clay was standing beside the woodpile, shirt sleeves rolled to the elbows, a long-handled axe balanced in his right hand. She watched as he took a section of maple from the woodpile and set it upright on the hickory stump. The man stared at the cylinder of rough timber for a moment, his eyes seeming to flash angrily at the very sight of it. Then, with a mighty heave of the axe and an ugly grimace of pure rage, he swung the blade downward, splitting the wood cleanly in half.

Little Sam walked in from the boys' bedroom, slipping an overall strap over his left shoulder. He stopped at the back door and peered through the rusty screen as his father cleaved another stick in half. "Why's Pappy splitting wood?" he asked his mother. "It's only the middle of summer."

Maudie did not answer. She merely watched her man as he swiftly reached for another slab of wood, positioned it atop the stump, and angrily swung the axe downward. Her heart ached for Clayburn, for she knew the hurt he was experiencing and the great anger over their son's senseless death. If Johnny had died in a natural way, if he had drowned in a swimming hole or fallen out of an apple tree and broken his neck, then maybe Clay could have accepted it better. But Johnny and his friends had been purposely lured to Brewer's barn and horribly murdered for the few greenbacks they carried. The act itself was unbearable to them all, but not knowing who the killers were, knowing that they still walked free and unpunished, that was what made it so very hard for Clay to accept. And the only way he knew to vent his emotion was through physical labor, perhaps the only true thing that Clayburn Biggs understood in life.

She sensed eyes peering over her shoulder and turned to find Polly and Josh staring in disbelief. "What's Pappy doing?"

Maudie turned Polly around and, holding her ebony pigtails aloft, buttoned the back of her pink cotton dress. "He's chopping wood," she replied.

"But it's July," Josh said.

"Don't you go questioning your pappy's doings," she snapped at the two. "If he wants to cut down every tree in sight, well, he's surely got the right to do so. Now wash up. Won't be long before the neighbors get here."

Polly and Josh exchanged puzzled glances. They went to the kitchen sink and began pumping water into the basin. Cynthia Ann craned her thin arms around her neck to fasten the collar button of her own flower print dress. She wandered to the screen door. Standing beside her little brother, she too watched as Clay continued his mad fit of wood splitting. But where the others only regarded him with frightened curiosity, the red-haired child sensed the true nature of the beast that had him in its grasp.

White hot emotion washed across the backyard toward her, assaulting her mind. The raw heat of rage was what wielded that axe, not her father. A great anger, forged from grief and despair, possessed the farmer, driving from him all the wisdom and common sense that had governed the Biggs clan since its conception.

Cindy saw her father's face, flushed red with fury, twisted into an ugly mask of mental anguish. She saw the tanned forearms bunch and jerk with flexed sinew, the big hands clutching the axe handle as if it were forever joined to the flesh of his palms. She witnessed the unbridled force of each blow, splitting wood like a hot knife through butter. The broad axe hit with a powerful *thunk,* scattering the splintered remains of the firewood over flowered clover and brittle summer grass.

Words came to her, words that she never thought would echo in that gentle farmer's mind. *You bastards!* his thoughts spat like venom as he replaced a halved stick with a fresh one. *Lousy . . . no-account . . . sons of bitches . . . killed my boy! Killed my Johnny! Stinking murderers . . . lousy, stinking bastards!* Again, the leanly muscled arms would heft the axe, cocked over the right shoulder, then bring it hurling downward with awful force — a killing force — as if the sharply honed edge had been intended for a human skull rather than a lifeless chunk of wood.

A horrible feeling began to creep into Cindy, the feeling that her father's senseless rage was gaining in momentum, gripping his mind in its uncontrollable fury, rather than burning itself out. Somehow she felt as though her father might hurt himself or someone else if it was not ended right then and there. Without thinking, the girl burst through the back door, leaped off the low porch, and ran toward the smokehouse.

"Cynthia Ann!" screamed Maudie, a great fear welling up inside her. "Get back here! Get back here this very instant, young lady!" Her eyes were frantic, her attention torn between two points. One was her red-haired daughter sprinting barefootedly across the grass, while the other was an axe-toting madman who swung his deadly tool again and again into the hickory stump, no longer bothering to vent his rage on maple slabs.

Tearfully, Cindy stopped a careful distance from the stump, flinching under a hail of splinters and fragments of wood. "Stop it, Pappy! Stop it!" she screamed, the nearness of the terrible hate so close now that it frightened her to the point of hysteria.

Maudie came out on the back porch. "Get away from him, Cindy!"

The man's eyes lifted from the scarred surface of the stump, eyes that blazed feverishly with a hatred that bordered insanity. The axe was cocked back for one final swing. Clayburn's attention settled on the little girl, and for a frightening second, Cindy was sure that her father was going to bring the heavy, steel wedge whistling down upon her head with killing force.

"STOP!" she screamed and felt something boil up within her, as if some ferocious animal had awakened from a deep slumber. Clay felt it, too, for some great force wrenched at the axe in his hands, tearing the pitted handle from his fingers. The force seemed like some violent wind — no, it appeared much more solid than any gust the farmer had ever encountered. Clay was knocked backward, falling hard on his back amid crab grass and maple chips. The long-handled axe spun end over end, knocking a jagged hole in the south wall of the gray-wood smokehouse, disappearing from view into the murky confines of the shed.

Horrified, Cindy ran. She did not run to the safety of her mother's arms, but rather for the heavy growth of the woods that lined the Biggs' back acre. Clay got shakily to his feet, his face now pale and strained, having lost every trace of the insane rage that had commanded him moments before.

"Cindy!" he called hoarsely. "Cindy . . . I'm . . . sorry!"

The child was gone though, having fled into the shadows of the dense forest where Green Creek wound like a flowing quicksilver snake across half of Bedloe County. The farmer stared down at his hands, blistered from the mad assault on the woodpile. They shook nervously, like leaves on a blustery autumn day. He studied the huge crater in the planked wall of the smokehouse. "Dear Lord!" breathed Clay. "Dear sweet Lord!"

Maudie and the children stood on the back porch. They watched silently as their provider and protector, the strongest and steadiest man they had ever known, sat down on the chopping stump and, placing his head in his hands, began to cry.

Herding the three children inside, Maudie closed the porch door, sealing her husband's grief from prying eyes. Polly, Josh, and Sam . . . none of the three said another word. They lingered around the kitchen table, stunned, trying to digest the events, of the last few minutes. Maudie felt on the verge of tears herself; but a sudden knock on the front door steeled her spirit, and she knew she must be strong.

"Polly, answer the door," she said, attempting a pleasant smile. When the girl had left the room, Maudie closed the kitchen curtains. She did not want any of the visitors to see Clay in his time of weakness.

Quickly, she whispered a silent prayer before turning to greet the neighbors who had arrived bearing gifts of food and sorrow.

Cindy crouched in the sparse shade of a wild tobacco plant. It seemed as if she had been there for hours, clinging to that single spot in Harvey Brewer's thicket. It was where she felt Johnny the strongest. There, in that choking patch of brambled overgrowth, the girl experienced her brother's lingering presence. Like with the abandoned hat, she concentrated on the more pleasant essence and tried hard to ignore the terror and hopelessness that hung around her like an ominous shadow that could never be driven away.

The sky was darkening with evening when a sound drew her attention. Noisy footsteps and the swishing of thick weeds parting around denim trouser legs could be heard clearly near the edge of the thicket. The progress of the intruder grew louder, nearer, as Cynthia Ann withdrew farther into the shadows beneath the leafy stalk. The approaching sounds conjured harsh memories not her own. They were Johnny's, those lonely panicked emotions that raced through her mind. The cold pelting of rain, the warm even flow of blood and pain, and fear. Most of all fear.

She held her breath as the man stopped only a few feet from the clump of wild tobacco. She peered past the yellowed, sun-withered leaves and stared at the scuffed leather and rawhide laces of a pair of old work boots. Her anxiety eased, for she knew the footwear by sight. Her father had worn those old boots as far back as she could possibly remember.

"Pappy," she said softly.

Clayburn Biggs squatted down on his haunches, no longer dressed in his Sunday best, but wearing overalls and a faded chambray shirt. Cindy had half expected anger to flare in his long face, the type that preceded a good, sound spanking. But his features did not hold that fire at all. Relief softened her daddy's homely face. "Lordy Mercy, girl. I've been looking all over for you."

Rather than pulling her from under the leafy shade of the wild plant, Clay joined her there, pushing aside a clump of sticky cocklebur to make room for his lanky bulk. He removed his brown felt hat and set it atop his knobby knees.

Cindy started to apologize for running away at the family's time of sorrow, but her daddy beat her to it.

"Cindy Ann . . ." he began hesitantly. "I wanna say I'm sorry for what happened today. Well, doggone it, I reckon I just lost my head after coming back from your brother's funeral and all. You oughtn't have come up on me unexpected like that, pumpkin. I was so danged mad I could've ended up hurting you bad." Clay said nothing about the axe flying through the smokehouse wall. He could not rightly say for sure whether it had merely slipped from his grasp or if some inexplicable force had plucked it from his hands at just the right moment.

The girl took her father's work-calloused hand, and it closed around her own. Thick fingers which could crack walnuts cradled her diminutive hand gently, comfortingly. For the first time in a very long time, she felt truly close to her father. Cindy snuggled nearer to the warmth of his lean body, sensing none of the resentment or cold alienation that had kept them apart since her lengthy stay in the Nashville hospital.

She did not want to ruin the moment. She wanted to bask forever in the undeniable love of her father. But there was something she knew she must tell him, something that he had a right to know. "Pappy . . . this is where it happened. This is where they killed Johnny."

Clay stiffened at her knowing words, and at first, she was afraid she had turned a wonderful moment into just another ugly instant in an already dismal day. But her father's reaction soon eased, and he wrapped a protective arm around her, as if to assure her that he understood. The angry scolding words of disbelief, like those he had uttered in the kitchen that stormy night in May, never came. They continued to sit there in silence, until Clay's deep voice, cracking with emotion, asked a question of her. A question she had been waiting for him to ask.

"Cindy ... do you know who did this? Do you know who killed your brother and his pals?"

The child's brow creased, and she slowly shook her head. "I just see shadows of them, only hear their voices. I never see their faces, though. Sometimes I think I'm going to, but, no matter how hard I try, I just can't."

Clay squeezed his daughter's shoulder. "That's all right, pumpkin. I reckon those things come to you by chance. I reckon you can't just pluck thoughts outta thin air at random, can you?"

"No, I can't." Cindy stared up at her father with sudden wonder. "Pappy, you do believe that I can sense these things, don't you? You do believe that I have the gift?"

The tobacco farmer ran a hand playfully through her crop of red hair, while his eyes met hers, dead serious, and full of honesty. "Cindy Ann, from now on I'll believe any damned thing you tell me."

A feeling of such profound adoration filled the youngster's heart that she practically threw herself into her father's arms. She hugged his neck tightly. "I love you, Pappy."

She could feel the nervous bob of his Adam's apple as he returned her affection. "I love you, too, baby," he croaked. And, although it was hard for her to grasp at first, Cindy felt her father's tears soak through the threadbare material of her cotton dress. Never before had she known her father to cry openly.

In the young girl's opinion however, his tears were not those of weakness, but those steeled from an inner strength born out of love.

They embraced for a moment longer, then, hand in hand, father and daughter began the long walk home.

Part Three

Vengeful Autumn

Chapter Seventeen

The triple homicide at Brewer's barn served as the main point of conversation during the long, hazy days that led into August. Everyone had his own opinion of who the murderers were and why they had not yet been apprehended. Most of the citizens in town figured the culprits to be drifters who had wandered into Bedloe County, performed their heinous act, and then rambled on. Surely, they all voiced, the killers were several states away by now. On the other hand, those who lived on the rural stretch of Old Newsome Road and the surrounding countryside reckoned differently. Those who gathered on the porch of Woody's General Store for cold drinks and conversation traded their own thoughts on the killings. Most had a gut feeling that the ones involved were local people, the kind you would least expect of such a terrible crime. Why, one farmer countered, it might very well be your dearest friend or your next-door neighbor who done it. And it could happen again, too. Maybe next time to someone's wife or daughter. The thought was disturbing, but one that certainly could not be ruled out.

The ones most affected by the grisly incident were, of course, the families. Stella Longcreek had taken to bed sick after her son's funeral. She lay day after day in a dark room, her spirit broken some said. After all, Billy had been the only solid thing in her life, her very pride and joy, since the trouble she had had with the boy's boozing father before his abrupt departure. Ransom Potts had changed little in the face of his own son's death. His insolence and impatience toward those he met on the street had increased, and he wore a constant frown of grudging bitterness across his pudgy face. Most of the residents of Coleman chose to avoid him altogether. However, those who chanced to cross the banker's path noticed a subtle touch of melancholy in his hard eyes. Although he did not let it show, grief over C.J.'s violent death gnawed at him from the inside like a hungry rat trying to chew itself free of a corn crib.

The Biggs family went about their daily activities, constantly aware of that single vacancy in the household; the empty chair at the supper table, the absence of guitar picking on a warm summer evening . . . little things that continuously hammered home the painful realization that Johnny was forever gone from their midst. The children spent their days around the weathered farmhouse, biding their time working the garden or roaming the woods out back, rather than playing with the neighboring kids. Maudie kept busy, doing her daily chores and praying to the Lord to give her the strength to make it through one more day.

Clayburn had run out of odd jobs and mechanic work, and the temporary job at Pike's lumber mill had run its course weeks ago. He spent long hours sitting out back of the smokehouse, staring glumly at the weedy acres of lost tobacco land, so very near, but legally out of reach. He avoided going to town, mainly because of the stares of silent sympathy generated toward him. And there was the problem of money. Storekeepers whom he was once friendly with gave him the cold shoulder. They all knew of his dwindling finances and figured that he would come asking for credit eventually. But they should have known the man better. Clayburn Biggs was a proud man, one who shunned the thought of accepting charity, even in the oppressive shadow of such hard times. Clay was again considering seeking work in the mills and factories up north, but he had not mentioned this to Maudie. He knew she would strongly disapprove of him leaving the family, especially during their difficult time of grief and misfortune.

Besides the kin of the victims, one other resident of Bedloe County was receiving his share of unwanted scrutiny, and that was Sheriff Taylor White. Since the discovery of the triple murder, his skills as a lawman had been pushed farther than ever been before. For twenty years the constable had spent his time locking up drunkards, soothing domestic squabbles, and discouraging the theft of watermelons from Ernest Leslie's half-acre patch. Now he had been forced from the comfortable position of peacekeeper into an area of law enforcement that was totally strange to him. He had to walk in the ill-fitting shoes of an investigator now, an ability that Taylor was not quite sure he was up to.

He had given the murder case all he had, that was for sure. He had talked to that pawn shop owner in Nashville and tried to determine the identity of the man who had sold Johnny's guitar, but he had gotten about as much useless information as Clay had. Then there had been half dozen free-talking souls who had claimed to have seen the three boys at the Bloody Bucket one Friday night in late May. The tavern owner, Otis Schofield, even admitted that they had been there; that he had nearly gotten into a scrape with C.J. Potts after serving him one his infamous "Golden Mule" specials, but that was all there was to it.

As July drew on into August and gradually approached the coming of autumn, Sheriff White began to realize that he had come to a standstill in his investigation. There had been precious few leads to begin with, for very little incriminating evidence had actually been found at the scene of the murders. Sure, they knew that a shotgun had been used in the crime, but then nearly every man in Bedloe County had some sort of scattergun in his possession. That gave him about two thousand suspects to consider. There was also no description of the culprits' vehicle or even that of one of the killers that he could go on.

Recently, a number of citizens and old acquaintances had approached him asking — some demanding—to know what progress had been made in the case. It finally got to the point where White avoided his own friends and neighbors, tired of having to admit defeat time and time again, weary of seeing the same expressions of disappointment and, perhaps, suspicious doubt, in their eyes. Rumors had begun to circulate about the sheriff's competence, pointing out his feet-dragging failure to bring any suspects to light. After a while, Taylor began to wonder about his abilities as a lawman, too. The county elections would be held that November, and that had him worried. Maybe Ransom Potts' threat would prove true. Perhaps the majority of Coleman's citizens would take a long, hard look at him that election and, for the first time in years, seriously wonder whether or not he deserved another term in office.

Chapter Eighteen

All the suspicions, all the painful grief and hard feelings came to a head one blustery day in late September.

The sudden realization of who had actually murdered the teenaged boys occurred, rather strangely, during a simple visit to Woody's General Store. If anything good had bloomed from the tragedy of Johnny's death, it was the renewed affection between Cindy and her father. It was a noticeable contrast to the indifference and downright hateful behavior that Clay had shown toward the child following her long sickness. Before, a barrier of tense silence had separated the two, but now their conversations were sprinkled with jokes, good-natured kidding, and a quiet understanding. To a surprised Maudie, they seemed like long-lost pals, and she was delighted to see Cindy tag along when her daddy did his chores. Clay seemed pleased as well. He appeared to genuinely enjoy his daughter's company.

That Saturday afternoon, Clay pulled his Ford pickup off the main road and onto the dirt shoulder that fronted the old country store. Woody's mercantile looked like a picture postcard that day, its roughly hewn structure and corrugated tin eaves wreathed by the forthcoming promise of newly turned leaves. Reds, golds, and yellows peeked discreetly from the fading greenery of oak and maple that grew in the V-shaped fork which separated the highway from the rutted dirt avenue of Old Newsome Road. Along with a cloudless sky of rich azure blue, the entire scene was a far cry from the brittle dry heat that had parched the land only a few short weeks ago.

Cindy Ann jumped down from the cab of the truck, landing awkwardly on the slick leather soles of her new winter shoes.

Clay chuckled, and together, they passed the rusty gas pumps outside. As they reached the two-by-four steps of the store's lengthy porch, Cindy breathed in deeply. She always loved the autumn air, for the nippy breezes always seemed to possess some invigorating quality, forever spiced with the tart tang of wood smoke and the damp freshness of fallen leaves after a drenching rain.

An elderly man, whipcord lean and gray, met them halfway on the steps. Clay shook the man's spidery hand as the gentleman peered at him through thick-lensed spectacles. "Well, how are you doing today, Mr. Loftis?" Clay asked of him.

"I'm doing fine, Clayburn Biggs," Jasper Loftis replied, finally recognizing the farmer's hangdog face. "Fit as a fiddle in fact. And you and yours?"

"We're getting by" was Clay's reply. "I was sorry to hear that Miss Alice was feeling poorly. Hope she's doing a mite better today."

Mr. Loftis scowled sourly. "Aw, she ain't sick one bit. That old woman's been ailing of one thing or another since the day we wed. I reckon the day she stops her bitching and moaning is the day I'll really start worrying about her."

Clay nudged his daughter, and Cindy turned shy eyes on the wrinkled parchment face of the elderly man. "Afternoon, Mr. Loftis."

Jasper looked down as if he had not seen the child until that moment. "Now, which one do we have here? Is this little Cynthia Ann?"

"Yes, sir."

Mr. Loftis grinned broadly, exposing toothless gums. "Well, now, ain't you growing into a fine, young lady." He fished in a vest pocket until he found a shiny, new wheat penny. "There you go, child. Buy yourself a penny candy on me."

The red-haired girl accepted the coin with bright hazel eyes. "Thank you!"

"You're surely welcome," the old man replied.

"I reckon we'll be seeing you and the missus at bible study tomorrow morning," Clay put in as Jasper ambled, walking stick in hand, toward an immaculately polished Model T.

"We'll be there, Clayburn Biggs, if we can pry our old bones from beneath the quilts that early in the A.M. The mornings have been getting down-right chilly here lately. My arthritis might give me hell, but I'll be there."

They reached the summit of the store porch. It's floorboards were loaded with feed bags, wagon wheels, and empty whiskey kegs with JACK DANIELS OLD NO.7 stenciled across the lids. The walls were decorated with all manner of advertisements, some new, some anciently old. Tin signs praising Coca Cola, Lucky Strikes, and Martha White's Self-Rising Flour hung around the screen door, their borders edged with spotty traces of rust and corrosion.

"Howdy, Clay!" called Woody Sadler from where he smoked a pipe behind the counter. "Pull up a chair and sit a spell."

Clay waved to a gathering of familiar faces around the potbelly stove at the rear of the store. Andy Grissom, Buster Cole, and Dusty Ballard sat perched on cane-backed chairs in a semicircle around the radiant heat of the woodstove. A single chair stood empty, one usually reserved for Taylor White during the weekend. Come to think of it, thought Clay, that chair had been unoccupied during most of the past two months.

"Don't have time for jawing today, fellas," Clay admitted. "Been patching a roof for Pastor Phillips in town, and I gotta get on home to do some chores of my own. Just stopped by to fetch a few necessities." He handed Woody a list scribbled by Maudie. The storekeeper sucked on the stem of his pipe and went to gather the items wanted.

"Mr. Sadler, I got a penny here," Cindy chirped over the edge of the counter. "I'd like some jawbreakers, if you please."

"Jawbreakers?" he snorted, taking her money and placing three red-hot Fireballs in her tiny hand. "Once was the time when young ladies nibbled on lollipops and peppermint sticks. What do they ask for now? Jawbreakers, horehound, and hard rock candy!"

Cindy Ann crammed the cinnamon candies in her mouth, pocketing two of them in one cheek and one in the other. She went directly to a shelf at the far wall where a sparse collection of toys stood among cans of split-pea soup and tins of Dr.

Bartholomew's Miracle Mange Ointment.

"You'd best have a seat, Clayburn," Dusty suggested. "The way old Woody moves, you might be standing there till Thanksgiving."

The store's proprietor ignored the snide remark. He shook out some paper sacks and began to fill them with cornmeal, flour, and white cane sugar.

"Don't mind if I do," Clay said. The farmer had always enjoyed the homey surroundings of Woody's store. The rich smells of tobacco and leather goods, the crackling heat of the woodstove, the hearty conversation of men he had known all his life . . . it was an oasis of sorts, a refuge from the hardships that pressed on all their minds during lean times like these.

They all watched in amusement as Clay produced the makings and constructed one of his single-handed cigarettes. Buster Cole offered him a light, and he accepted it with a curt nod.

"How's work, Clayburn?"

Biggs shook his head. "Scarce. There's just so many odds and ends a man can do in this county.

"I know what you mean," Dusty agreed. A veil of gloom shaded his robust face. "I just ain't making it selling milk and eggs to the folks in town. Been thinking of going over to Clarksville, maybe Nashville, and finding steady work of some sort."

"The work is up north," put in Buster, who was no better off than his friends. "Detroit, Chicago, Philadelphia. I hear they're always looking for able-bodied men who ain't afraid of hard work. Offering fair wages, too."

"Too damned far for a steady paycheck, I'd say," said Clay.

They all sat there for a long moment, in silence, the only sounds coming from the iron stove and Woody Sadler. After a while, Andy Grissom spoke up, pausing first to send a spritz of tobacco juice into a brass cuspidor nearby. "Boys, hog killing time is coming up, and I've got seven to be butchered. I'm gonna need a hand in doing it, so I'd be obliged if you three could help me out. Afraid I can't offer you cash money, but I'll give you all the pork you can carry."

"We'd sure appreciate that, Andy," replied Clay, his eyes

grateful. Buster and Dusty echoed the sentiment.

The copper cow bell over the front door jangled with the entrance of two new customers. The men at the stove nodded in quiet greeting, although none of them were overly familiar with the pair. Woody Sadler glanced up as he scratched another item off the grocery list. "Well, if it ain't Hanson and Darnell. What have you boys been up to lately? Haven't seen hide nor hair of you two in a good long while."

"We've been up to Kentucky helping some kin of mine with a little personal business," answered the bigger of the two men.

"The shotgun shells still on that top shelf over yonder?" inquired the other, as lanky as a vineless beanpole. "We're gonna get in some squirrel hunting this evening."

Woody turned back to his work. "Yep. Top shelf, far aisle."

As they headed down the aisle for the ammunition shelf, the hefty fellow in the plaid wool coat and hunting cap brushed past the little girl who had her attention glued to a china doll in a blue calico dress. Cindy would have paid the two no mind, except that something strange happened—something that she could not fully explain at first.

A peculiar feeling washed over her, an abrupt sensation of cold contempt and fear combined. She stared up at the big man, a noticeable shiver running throughout her thin body.

"What's the matter, girl?" remarked Hanson. "Did a possum walk over your grave just now?"

The men continued on, the skinny one cackling loudly as if his partner had cracked a good one. The sounds of their voices as they discussed the correct load for squirrel echoed dully in her ears. She backed away from them and down the aisle toward the door. "Pappy," she called. "I'm going back out to the truck."

Clay took a drag on his cigarette. "I'll be out directly, pumpkin." He gave her a quick wink, then returned to a conversation concerning the coming deer season.

Cynthia Ann let the door slam behind her, then ran to the passenger side of her father's pickup truck. She sat on the running board, her arms crossed and her eyes staring absently at flattened bottle caps on the hard-packed earth. She tried to shake the awful feeling that had gripped her in the store, but was unsuccessful. The broad, ugly face of the big man lingered in her mind's eye: the sandy blond crewcut, the nose that had been twice broken, and those eyes . . . those cold, gray eyes as cunning and humorless as those of a wolf. She had seen something bad in those eyes, heard something evil in that gravelly voice. Exactly why she felt that way, Cindy Ann could not understand. It was not something she could easily put her finger on, just something that she knew about the man.

The slap of the screen door and the heavy clump of boots on the porch steps roused the child from her thoughts. She sat perfectly still on the running board, hoping the two would not notice her as they passed. But Hanson caught her out of the corner of his eye and, nudging his friend, just could not resist walking over to tease the nine-year-old.

"Now, I hope I didn't go and scare you none back there in the store," he rumbled loudly, stooping to her level. "Surely wouldn't want you to fear me, girl. It's plumb bad luck to have a red-haired woman peeved at you, you know."

"Yeah," put in the one called Darnell. "You oughta know, as many redheads that have jilted you."

Hanson gave his partner a withering glare that shut him up instantly. He turned his attention back to Cindy. "You're a cute little heifer, all fire-red hair and freckles. And that nose . . . why, I believe I'll just steal that for myself." And, with that, he brought his massive hand close to her face, then drew it away with a snap.

"Gotcha!" He laughed, his thumb protruding between the index and middle finger, giving the illusion of a captured nose.

Cindy could only stare in sudden horror, so much so that she swallowed her dwindling jawbreakers in one gulp. But it was not the childish prank that disturbed her. Rather, it was the man's voice grating in the far reaches of her subconscious. *Gotcha* . . . it reverberated over and over again, until finally another image accompanied the word: a murky figure of a man in the driving rain, the brittle click of a shotgun's hammer being cocked and a skeletal grin unseen in the darkness.

Gotcha . . . Johnny!

The child gasped in sudden shock, her eyes widening, her

face growing starkly pale. In terror, her head craned back and hit the cool surface of the truck door with a rattling thud.

"Now look what you did, Bully," said the lanky one. "You done gone and frightened the young'un."

Hanson roared with laughter, opening his massive paw to expose his reddened thumb. "I was just funning you… see?"

Cindy could only stare at the big man. Her lips quivered as she looked Bully in his cold gray eyes. "You're the one," she breathed. "You're the one who done it."

"Done what, little missy?" He chuckled at the girl's startled expression.

"You're ... the one ... who killed ... Johnny."

Bully's laughter choked off into silence. He craned his beefy neck around to regard his sidekick. Claude stood there with the frightened eyes of a rabbit, looking as if he had seen a ghost. "Let's get the hell outta here, Bully!"

"Hush up," the big man growled. Then, with softer eyes, he turned back to the girl. "What kinda foolishness are you talking, girl? You know we ain't the ones who done that terrible thing."

"Yes, you did," said Cindy, the flame of defiance suddenly flaring in those hazel green eyes. "You killed them all in that old tobacco barn, then buried them there. You both had a hand in it!"

Bully and Claude stood there in stunned silence, not knowing exactly what to think or do. Darnell watched his buddy closely, for he knew Bully well. The big man had a bad temper, not the hot-headed impulsive kind, but the scheming slow-fused type. He could see that temper burning now behind those small gray eyes. Claude waited breathlessly for Hanson's reaction to the girl's accusation. You never could tell with Bully. The big man might laugh it off as a joke or suddenly reach out and snap the youngster's neck like it was nothing more than a stick of dry kindling.

Whatever Bully had in mind, it was lost to the sudden slam of the mercantile door as Clay Biggs crossed the porch with his meager purchase.

"Come on, Bully!" hissed Claude, digging his fingernails

into his pal's broad shoulder. "Let's get outta here!"

Bully nodded, but remained face to face with Cindy for a final, lingering moment. An evil hatefulness exuded from the man as his eyes bored deeply into her own. "You tell your folks — you tell *anyone*—and I'll surely kill you."

Then the two were gone, walking swiftly past the double gas pumps to a primer gray truck which sat parked under a towering oak. Cindy watched as Bully gave her one last threatening glare. Then he stashed the box of shells under the truck seat and, climbing inside, headed the vehicle north toward town, churning a billow of dust and gravel in its wake.

"Let's get on home, Cindy," Clay said from around the front fender. Numbly, the child obeyed her father and climbed into the truck. She sat there quietly as her father set the groceries in the back and fumbled for his keys.

On the short drive home, Clay eyed his daughter with concern. Her bubbling happiness had faded into silent despair during their visit to Woody's store. He figured he knew what it was; the fancy china doll on the toy shelf. Surrounded by cast-iron fire engines and ball and jack sets, the doll was the only thing that mattered to Cindy during their weekly visits. Clay knew that she wanted Santa to bring it on Christmas morning, but the doll was just too expensive for the farmer's budget that year. He would even have trouble scraping up enough for the traditional orange and candy stick that blessed each child's stocking on that holiest of winter days.

But he suddenly realized that that was not what bothered her when Cindy abruptly broke down and cried. Clay pulled the truck to the side of the road and leaned over the seat, resting one work-calloused hand on the child's quivering shoulder. "What's wrong, baby?"

Tearful eyes lifted upward. She had to try several times before coherent words could break the force of her weeping. "Those two men… back at the store. They ... they scared me."

A tightness clenched in Clay's narrow chest. He recalled Bully Hanson and Claude Darnell standing near the truck when he came out. "What did they do, pumpkin? What did they say that frightened you so?"

"They said they'd kill me, Pappy ... if I told you."

"Told me what?"

Cindy wiped her eyes with the sleeve of her patched sweater. "They were the ones. They were the ones who killed Johnny."

An electric thrill sparked through Clay's lanky frame, and he sat there for a long moment, unable to speak. He listened as she told him of Bully and Claude's part in the murdering of the three young men. She also told him, after a silence of nearly three months, of the knowledge concealed by Harvey Brewer.

When her tale had been told and her weeping calmed by Clay's soothing words, they continued on their way home. Each one, father and daughter, wrestled with the conflict of their own private thoughts. Cindy's were full of horror and shock at the frightening discovery, while Clay's were forged from a much more primitive emotion.

Cindy sensed the feelings and suddenly knew what he had in mind. "Don't do it, Pappy," she pleaded, tears resurfacing. "Please . . . don't do it."

Clayburn Biggs said nothing. He continued his steady pace down the rutted dirt road, his knuckles white with strain as he clutched the steering wheel, his piercing blue eyes glaring furiously through the dust-speckled windshield, as if searching out some secretive and unsavory destination that lay out of sight on the darkening horizon. A destination that would find Clay ready and willing to do what needed to be done.

Chapter Nineteen

That night after supper, Clay slipped, unnoticed, into his and Maudie's bedroom. Feeling his way through the darkness, he reached the heavy chest of drawers. For a moment he stood there. He listened to the muffled sounds of activity in the rear rooms of the house; the clatter of his wife washing the evening dishes, the laughter of Polly and Sam as they warmed up the radio for that night's listening.

Satisfied that no one would intrude, Clay located the third of five drawers. He rummaged through his meager assemblage of long-handle underwear and woolen socks, until he found what he was looking for. He brought a paper sack out and, sitting on the feather bed, withdrew its contents from the brown paper wrapper.

Moonlight shone through the front window, trickling coldly down the length of blued steel and checkered walnut. The gun was a Colt .45 semi-automatic pistol, one that he had won off Gary Lee Horne in a poker game back during his gambling days. Horne had sneaked it back from Germany after the World War, and he claimed to have killed a dozen Krauts with the sidearm. Knowing the drunkard well, Clay figured his boast to be pure bull, but he certainly knew a good firearm when he held it in his hand. Pressing the magazine release, the slender clip slid smoothly from the butt. Clay checked the magazine. It was fully loaded with seven rounds of .45-caliber ammunition. He slapped the magazine back into place, worked the slide, and jacked a cartridge into the breech. The action was as smooth as silk, and frankly, he was surprised. After all, the handgun had lain dormant in the underwear drawer for nearly twenty years.

Clayburn breathed in deeply, the muscles of his face and neck tensing at the very thought of what might take place that autumn night. He could still recall his youngest daughter's eyes staring across the table at him during their quiet meal. He had purposely avoided her gaze, for she was the only one there who knew what he intended to do. Cindy knew he would hunt out two men that night, and if he had the chance, gun them down. She also knew, as he did, that his planned vendetta might very well backfire. The consequences of his drastic action could prove fatal. After all, these were cold-blooded murderers he was dealing with.

Driving the disturbing thoughts from his mind, he tucked the .45 into the back of his waistband and slipped on a denim jacket to conceal the bulk of the weapon. "Maudie," he called from the hallway. "I'm going out for a while." He took his hat from the coat rack near the door and started to leave.

His wife's puzzled stare stopped him in his tracks. "Now, where in heaven's name do you think you're off to on a Saturday night?" she demanded, water-soaked hands planted on wide hips. She knew her husband's routine well enough to be suspicious. Since they were first married, Clay had spent his Saturday nights at home. He would eat, then listen to the Grand Ole Opry and, after smoking a leisurely cigarette or two, retire for the evening.

"I'm going to talk to a man about work," he lied.

Maudie's disbelief was evident in the lines of her face. "You sure now? Nothing ain't wrong, is it?"

Clay forced a grin. "Of course not. You go on and finish your dishes. I'll be back before you know it."

"All right," Maudie replied. She did not return the smile as she turned back to the sink.

Cynthia Ann still sat at her place at the supper table, doodling on an envelope with a stubby lead pencil. She watched as her father opened the door and unfastened the hook on the screen. Desperately, she lashed out with her thoughts, hoping the warning would ring true. *Please, Pappy, don't go!* Clay froze for a fleeting second, and at first, Cindy thought that maybe she had succeeded. But then he was gone, closing the door behind him in a scraping of warped wood against the doorjamb.

The nine-year-old listened. Her alert ears picked out the slamming of the truck door and the rumble of its engine as the vehicle headed in the direction of town.

The rapid-fire melody of bluegrass music drifted in from the parlor as the Nashville show began on the radio. "Ain't you gonna listen to the Opry, Cindy?" asked her mother.

I must tell her, thought the red-haired girl. *Pappy told me not to, but I've just got to, for his own sake.* She could imagine attending the funeral of her father, burying him there beside Johnny, wreathed in the grievous weeping of a widow and four surviving youngsters. And, also, she could imagine walking down Coleman's main street one afternoon. Bully Hanson would be standing there in front of Jenson's Drugstore, and when no one else was looking, he would give her a devilish wink, his eyes as cold and gray as the granite of a tombstone. The mere thought horrified Cindy. Was it a sliver of prophecy that had come to her or only her vivid imagination?

She knew that she dared not take any chances. "Mama . . . something terrible is gonna happen tonight."

At the grim tone of the child's voice, Maudie whirled. A china saucer slipped from her soapy hands, shattering on the boards of the kitchen floor. She paid it no mind and hurriedly sat in the chair opposite her daughter. "Does it have anything to do with your father?"

Cindy nodded and, tearfully, recounted the day's harrowing events. She told her of the awful discovery of Johnny's murderers and of Clay's reaction to the news.

"But why didn't you tell me before he left?" asked Maudie.

Cindy shrugged, her freckled cheeks streaked with fresh tears. "He told me not to tell," she finally said. "Besides . . . I figured he wouldn't like me anymore if I said anything."

Quickly, the woman went to the bedroom. A prayer on her lips, Maudie tossed Clay's underwear onto the floor; looking for the gun she knew he kept hidden there. Panic nearly seized her when she found it missing. "Lord in Heaven have mercy!" she exclaimed.

She stood there for a long moment, thinking it over, knowing that with each tick of the clock, Clay was a fraction closer to the ones he sought. "Cindy Ann… do you have any idea where he might be going?"

The nine-year-old closed her eyes and breathed deeply. At first, she sensed nothing. Then the odor of cigarette smoke curled through her nostrils and an unfamiliar taste crossed her tongue… as bitter as medicine, with a burning bite to it. "Mama… what does whiskey taste like?"

Instantly, Maudie knew. "Josh!" she yelled. "Josh, get in here this minute!"

The lanky teenager ambled out of the parlor, followed by Polly and Sam. Josh was slow-witted in some ways, but he was a shrewd judge of character. He could tell with one glance that Maudie was close to hysteria. "What's wrong, Mama?"

"Josh," she began, closing her eyes to calm herself. "I want you to run down to Woody's store as fast as you can. Woody closes early on Saturday night, but you knock on that door till he lets you in. Now listen to me, Josh, and remember what I say. I want you to call Sheriff White and tell him there's gonna be bad trouble over at the Bloody Bucket and that he should get over there as quick as possible. You got that?"

An expression of serious determination could be seen in Josh's normally dreamy eyes. "I'm on my way, Mama. Don't you worry none." He grabbed his hat and coat and was out the door and across the yard in a flash.

Suddenly, Maudie felt herself engulfed in a family hug, flanked on all sides by the frightened faces of Polly, Sam, and Cynthia Ann. She hugged them back with all her might, seeking comfort from their closeness. "You've gotta stop him, Lord," she whispered as warm tears overcame her. "Stop him from what he wants to do and bring him back home where he belongs."

Clay stood in the darkness outside the Bloody Bucket's front window. He stared through the dirty pane, keeping well enough back in the shadows so that the multi-colored neon beer signs would not illuminate his grim features.

He leaned against a sweet gum tree, the late September air cool on his flesh, the hardness of the gun a constant reminder in the small of his back. The only sounds that reached his ears were the boisterous noises that echoed from within; the faint music of the Opry on Schofield's tube radio behind the bar, the clinking of beer bottles, and the uproarious laughter of drunken men following the punch line of some filthy joke. The sounds that Clayburn once relished now assaulted his ears, mocking him. He longed for the nocturnal symphony of nature's creatures, but there was only frigid silence beyond the saloon. The song of the cricket and the croak of the bullfrog had left with the heat of summer.

He stood there under the turning branches that night, the only outside light originating from a handful of stars and a sliver of silvery moon. His hard blue eyes studied the gathering inside. The place was packed, as it usually was on a Saturday night, but only one man at one particular table interested him. He watched through a choking pall of cigarette smoke as Bully Hanson beat his fifth opponent at arm wrestling, slamming the poor sucker's wrist down on the hardwood table with such unbridled force that it was a wonder every bone in his hand was not broken. The defeat brought a booming laugh from Bully as the loser laid down his money and, with injured pride, hobbled off to the bar to get even more plastered than he already was.

Claude Darnell was not there, but Clay knew where the man was. After their afternoon's squirrel hunting, Claude had checked into Miss McSharron's boardinghouse on Dogwood Drive, while his buddy had headed straight for the seedy nightlife that Schofield's Bloody Bucket provided in full. Claude didn't worry him much anyway. He was like some kind of trained carnival monkey who was only dangerous when his buddy was around to command him. It was Bully Hanson whom Clayburn had his worries about. The man was deadly. In the short time Bully had been in Coleman, he had been heralded by the Bucket's patrons for his roughhousing and his ruthless need to emerge the victor, whether it be a simple bet or a hellacious fight with fists or knives.

And it was not only apprehension that plagued Clay, but a nagging doubt in the back of his mind. What if Cindy was wrong this time? True, her visions were frightening as far as predictions coming to life was concerned. But what if her imagination was stepping in where intuition had reigned before? He could be waiting there in the darkness to kill an innocent man. He knew he had to find out for sure. He had to know without a shadow of a doubt that the blowhard drunkard inside was actually the cold-blooded slayer of his eldest son.

Leaving his post, he moved through the gravel lot, skirting the dark hulks of the cars and trucks parked there. He reached Bully's pickup truck sitting under a black walnut tree, a ghostly splash of primer gray in the night. Surveying the lot and finding no prying eyes cast his way, Clay moved to the passenger door of the cab. He found it unlocked.

Slipping inside the cab, he was hit with the sour stench of corn liquor and bodily sweat. The floor of the truck was cluttered with bits of paper and trash. He started there, rummaging through the mess, searching for a single shred of evidence that might link him to the heinous murders of three innocent boys.

The noise from the beer joint grew louder as someone left to stagger home to his loved ones. Clay hunkered down farther onto the floorboard, figuring he would go unnoticed. His fingers groped through the trash, sorting the rubble, discarding bottle caps and cigarette butts. Then, as he fished deeper beneath the seat, his fingernails located a thin, flat object there in the dank shadows. He turned it over in his hand, a cold chill running through him. Holding it up to the sparse glow of the quarter moon, he found that he held a guitar pick. It was a smooth brown oval crafted from tortoiseshell, the type used widely in the South. But one feature set it apart from all the others. A couple of initials had been scratched into one side of the pick. The letters J.B. . . . Johnny Biggs.

The terrible rage renewed itself, boiling like a fireball in the pit of his gut. He pocketed the guitar pick and started to lift himself from the floorboard. He had found enough to ease his doubt, and now he would settle things with Bully.

That time came faster than he could have imagined. The door to the driver side of the truck was suddenly wrenched open. Bully Hanson stood there, glaring at him in a haze of intoxicated confusion. "What's going on here?" he snarled. Then he saw that it was Clay, and the realization struck him. "So, that little redheaded bitch told you, did she? Well, her snitching just got her old man blown all to hell!" And, with that, he reached under the seat and found his shotgun. Shucking the burlap from its sawed-down length and snapping back both hammers with the heel of his free hand.

Clay tumbled out the opposite door, landing heavily on the hard-packed gravel. He slammed the door shut just as Bully unleashed a single load. The bee swarm of double-aught pellets obliterated the truck's side window, showering fragments of glass across Clay's neck and back.

Bully let loose a bellow of triumph, heading around the front of his truck, the stubby length of gunmetal fisted in his meaty hand. His enthusiasm choked off into a fit of cursing when he found no bloodstained body to gloat over. There was only the glitter of broken glass on crushed stone.

"Damn it, Biggs!" he cursed, starting toward the shadows beyond the parking lot. "You get your ass on out here and die like a man!"

His staggering progress was interrupted when Clay kicked out from beneath the truck's greasy undercarriage. The toe of his boot cracked the back of Bully's ankles, sweeping him off his feet. Hanson crashed on his back in the hard gravel, an expression of surprise replacing the leering grin. The twelve gauge spun from his hand, landing with a clatter atop the truck's sloping hood, out of reach.

"Of all the filthy tricks!" sputtered the big man. He sat up to find Clay standing over him, the .45 pistol held firmly in both hands. "Now, just wait a second, buddy," croaked Bully, the gun's muzzle staring him in the face like a dark, unseeing eye. "You got it all wrong. I didn't do it. I didn't kill your boy ... honest!"

Clay's lean face was rigid and uncompromising. "You're a damned liar, Hanson." He thumbed the safety off and began to squeeze back on the trigger. "And a dead one, as of now. This is for Johnny, you lousy bastard!"

A loud voice from across the lot drew their attention. "Hey, what's going on over there?" demanded Otis Schofield, his bulky silhouette filling the door frame.

Clay twisted his head instinctively toward the sound. That was when Bully made his move. Powering to his feet, he closed a massive paw around the barrel of the pistol. The two men struggled for a tense moment, the gun's muzzle lifting skyward. Clay squeezed off a couple of deafening shots before the big man backhanded him hard across the mouth. Bully uttered a low chuckle as he wrenched the firearm from Clay's weakened grasp. He slung it off into the darkness, where it bounced several times in the gravel before skidding to a halt.

"No guns now," said Bully. Grabbing a handful of Clay's shirtfront, he tossed the man up against the hard trunk of the black walnut. "You so all-fired anxious to get at me now, farmer?"

Clay's eyes flashed. "It don't matter to me whether I do it with guns or fists, you sonofabitch. One way or another, I'm gonna kill you tonight."

The big drunk laughed as the tobacco farmer stepped out swinging. Despite his intoxication, Bully ducked the first two punches, the third glancing ineffectively off his broad shoulder. He delivered a single solid jab of his own, nearly caving in his opponent's rib cage. Clay fell back, the breath expelling harshly from his lungs. He felt himself back against the tree, Hanson barreling in on him, his fists flailing.

Otis Schofield stood with a crowd of curious patrons at the honky-tonk door. The saloon owner peered intently into the murky twilight, trying to figure out who was fighting whom. "You need any help out there, Bully?" He held the baseball bat in one hand.

"No thanks, Otis." Bully continued jabbing at the farmer's lean frame, dividing the blows between body and face. "I've got this sucker on the ropes. Won't be long before he's down for the count."

Through the sporadic bursts of pain, Clayburn knew that his adversary was right. Hanson had an advantage on him, for it had been nearly twenty years since Clay had been in a brawl. It looked as though Bully was only beginning to warm up. He knew he had to get away from those merciless blows as soon as he found a letup in Bully's barrage.

It came as the big man brought his right hand rearing back, wanting to savor the sight of the final punch that would shatter the farmer's jaw. Clay slid to a squat as the fist loomed near. Bully bellowed as his ham-like fist smashed forcefully into the tree. Hanson stumbled back in agony, clutching his injured hand. That was when Clay eyed the man's protruding stomach. Coming out of the crouch, he began to hammer away at Bully's midsection, driving him out of the dense shadows into the sparse light of the parking lot.

Unbeknown to the brawlers or their group of boozed spectators, a couple of dark sedans eased up the road from town, their headlights doused. There was the faint crackle of tires on gravel as the vehicles pulled off onto the shoulder and braked to a stop.

White hot anger having possessed him, Clay lit into the man like wildfire on dry prairie grass. Work-hardened fists pummeled Bully, leaving his torso for the ample target of his face. Despite the hoots and hollers for Hanson's benefit, the big man stumbled blindly backward, blood coursing freely from cuts, his cheekbones swelling with ugly bruises.

The primer gray pickup bounced on worn springs as a wicked blow threw Bully up against the bug-speckled grill. Clay was getting ready to continue his assault, when he noticed a confusing gleam of inspiration spark in his enemy's small eyes. Bully's good hand reached behind him, grasping across the hood, and suddenly Clay knew that he had made a grave mistake.

The drunkard lashed around in a sweeping arch, a bulky length of blued steel fisted in his left hand. The barrels of the scattergun struck Clay across the bridge of the nose. A sharp pain traveled through his battered face and a spurt of warm blood splashed across the front of his rumpled chambray shirt. Through the red haze of pain, Clay heard the man's triumphant laugh once again before a heavy blow in the gut doubled him over. He slumped to his knees in the gravel.

Clay looked up to see the twin muzzles of the twelve gauge, like the eyeless sockets of a skull, staring him full in the face.

"You know, your boy Johnny was a real bitch to kill, too. Had to chase him halfway around Brewer's back pasture before I caught up to him," Bully said in a coarse whisper. "But, eventually, he lost out . . . got a load of buck through the back of his head. Doesn't look like his old man is gonna fair much better."

Clayburn wanted to curse the man, but a lump of silence constricted his throat. He continued to glare into the depthless pits of those shotgun barrels as Bully thumbed back the left breech hammer with a resounding click.

Bully Hanson was about to lay his finger upon the hair trigger, when a chill traveled the length of his spine. He felt the cold muzzle of a revolver press against the base of his skull, nuzzling into the short blond hairs on the back of his neck.

"You twitch a muscle, Bully, and I'll put a .38 slug right in your brain," hissed Sheriff Taylor White in his ear.

Suddenly, Deputies Ezell and Bishop were standing before him. One eased the shotgun carefully from his grasp, while the other positioned his hands behind his back and snapped a pair of handcuffs around his thick wrists.

"You heard him, didn't you, 'Taylor?" asked Clay, accepting a handkerchief from the portly lawman. He dabbed at the free flow of blood from his busted nose. "He admitted it. He admitted he killed my boy Johnny."

White nodded and holstered his Smith & Wesson. "I heard everything." He turned to Bully and regarded the man coldly. "Ezell, take this murdering trash to the car."

After the deputy had herded the felon across the lot to the waiting sedan, White turned to Pauly Bishop. "I want you to go over yonder and get a statement from every man in that beer joint. I want to know exactly what each man heard or saw out here. After that, I want you and Ezell to go over to the boardinghouse and take Claude Darnell into custody. And you fellas be careful, too. Without Bully there to control him, he might lose his head and do something crazy."

"We'll bring him in," promised Deputy Bishop. He started for the curious gathering at the tavern door.

Taylor helped Clay to his feet. "You okay?"

"Yeah. A little worse for wear, but I'll be all right."

The sheriff walked a few paces and retrieved Clay's .45 from where it lay. He shucked the clip and stuck the pistol in his belt. "I'll hang on to this for a while," he told him.

Clay nodded. All his anger had drained for the time being, his soul purged of the poisonous need for revenge. He slumped against the bumper of Hanson's truck, feeling exhausted and miserable. He and Taylor stood there in silence for a long moment, then the lawman propped his foot on a muddy fender. "How'd you know it was him, Clay? I mean, hell, I didn't even suspect him myself."

"I didn't either at first." He wondered if he should confide in his friend about the true nature of his discovery, then decided that it would be for the best. "Taylor ... it was Cindy Ann who told me. She's the one who knew it was Bully and Claude who killed those three boys."

The big constable stood there, somewhat skeptical at the farmer's statement. "Come on now, Clay. I've heard the gossip about Cindy just like everyone else, but I didn't pay it no mind. I figured all that talk about her having second sight was just a lot of bunk."

"Well, it ain't," confirmed Clay. "It's all true, every last word of it. Cindy does have the gift. And it ain't no small thing either. She can pick up on folks feelings long after something's done happened and can come close to reading a man's mind. Dammit, Taylor, sometimes her power is so spooky it scares me half to death."

The sheriff could see his friend was dead serious. He nodded and clapped a supportive hand on the farmer's shoulder. "All right, so why don't you tell me what she had to say."

Taylor White stood there in the September twilight, listening to the man's story. As Clay told of Hanson and Darnell's murderous act in the shelter of the old curing barn, as well as the knowledge concealed by Harvey Brewer, White felt a mixture of amazement and revelation come over him. Between Clay's rendition and the frustrating aspects of the murder case, things began to become clearer. The evidence began to interlock with criminal motive like missing pieces to a jigsaw puzzle. When all had been said, the constable knew that his investigation had just been given new life. As it now stood, he had more than enough evidence to convict both Bully and Claude; but he knew he had to place both men at the Brewer barn that stormy night in May, and there was only one man in Bedloe County who could do that for certain.

"Clay . . . do you feel up to riding out to Harvey Brewer's place? I figure we oughta have a good long talk with that man."

"I'm with you, Taylor," agreed the farmer. "But could we stop by my house first?"

"What for?"

Clayburn felt a little foolish, but his desperate need to see justice done was much stronger than his pride. "I want us to pick up Cindy. I want her to go along."

The sheriff wanted to protest. He wanted to argue how the interrogation of a witness in a brutal murder case was no place for a child to be. But strangely enough, he knew that Clay was right in asking. In the back of his mind, he knew that Cindy might possibly be the only one who could pry a confession from that stubborn old man, the only one who might be able to transcend Brewer's fear and reach the honesty they all knew lay hidden somewhere beneath the surface.

Chapter Twenty

In spite of the chill of the evening, Harvey Brewer sat on his back porch, the old hickory rocker creaking beneath his weight. The hundred-watt bulb burned overhead, unhindered by the swirling swarm of candle flies and gallynippers that had congregated there during the warmer months. Brewer's porch stood out as an island of pale yellow light amid a sea of dense inky blackness.

He had been rocking and dozing when the rumble of an automobile caught his attention. Instantly, his feeble heart began to race. He had reacted that way to the sound of passing motorists ever since that haunting night last spring. He half expected to see that familiar gray truck roaring into sight, the ugly muzzle of a sawed-off shotgun perched over the lip of the open window.

But, no, he did not want to dwell on that sordid memory again. It had gnawed at his insides ever since those poor lads had been discovered in the barn, invading his dreams like some dark beast with an insatiable hunger. It was over and done with now, and no one could do one damned thing to bring those boys back. *There's no need to torture yourself so,* he tried to convince himself. *Just lay that awful guilt to rest!*

That night, however, he would not be able to shrug it off so easily, for the vehicle that pulled around back and halted a few yards from the porch was the sheriff's navy blue patrol car.

"How do, Harve?" called Taylor White, walking over to the porch. Brewer was caught between confusion and deep-seated fear as Clayburn Biggs and his daughter followed the hefty lawman.

"Kinda late for a social call, ain't it, Sheriff?" barked Harvey, dispensing with formalities. He eyed Clay's battered face, the eyes and nose swollen with splotches of violet blue. "What in tarnation got hold of you, boy?" he asked.

Clay stared at the elderly man, unsmiling. "Bully Hanson."

Harvey tried to hide his sudden panic. His heart fluttered in his chest, and for a moment, he thought he might faint. *Why are they here?* His mind raced at a feverish pace. *Could they possibly know?* He noticed the little red-haired girl standing beside her father and suddenly knew that they did.

But he would not let on. He mustn't. It was for his own welfare. It was the age old instinct of self-preservation that overruled his common sense, that and pure and simple fear.

"That's what we came out here to talk to you about, Harvey," Taylor began. "We arrested Hanson and his buddy Claude Darnell tonight for the murders of those three boys. We just wanted to make double sure that you didn't see nor hear anything that might connect them with the killings."

Harvey shook his head firmly. "I told you before, Sheriff, I don't know nothing about what happened out there. I'm just an old man who wants to be left alone. So why don't you just leave me be? It's nearly nine o'clock, about time for me to turn in."

Taylor traded a glance with Clay. "You know very well what we want to know," stated Clay, irritated at the man's stubborn front. "How long are you gonna lie through your teeth for those murdering bastards?"

"Now, see here, Clayburn Biggs! I'll not sit here and be talked to like that!"

"Okay, let's just calm down now," suggested Sheriff White. He regarded the old man wearily. "Harvey, if you're concerned about Bully, don't worry. He's in the county jail now with no chance of bail. You're perfectly safe, if you feel like giving us a statement about what happened."

Harvey was unshakable. "I still don't know what the hell you're talking about. Now, I told you before I can't help you none. When are you gonna believe me and get off my back?" Out of the corner of his eye he watched Cindy Ann. She had left her father's side and now stood near the center porch post. The other two men were oblivious to her activity, but Harvey was painfully aware of every move she made.

"We've gotta have a witness, Brewer!" Clay said, his voice half plea and half demand. "They killed my son, for heaven's sake! We gotta put them away for good."

"I'm sorry about your loss, Clay," grumbled Harvey. "I truly am. But I just can't be any help to you." He watched in mounting agitation as Cindy picked at the splintered post. Her nimble fingers found something there, and abruptly, her eyes grew hard and serious. In the porch light, the elderly man could see the tiny object cradled in her palm. It was a single pellet of double-aught buckshot.

"Come on, Clay," urged Taylor, his voice heavy with disgust. "We're wasting our time here." The constable was starting toward his car, when Clay reached for his arm and stopped him. "Wait a second, Taylor." He followed the farmer's eyes and studied Cindy and Old Man Brewer for a tense moment.

Something was happening. The youthful hazel eyes of the child were glued to the rheumy gray orbs of the elderly gentleman. Harvey had stopped his steady rocking. He simply sat there, stiff as a board, his face taut with gaping fear. The two were engaged in some strange game of mental tug-of-war. Taylor could somehow sense the tension between them. It almost had the invigorating feel of raw power, like the disruption of the ozone when lightning strikes too close to home.

Harvey Brewer was unaware of the two men, for in his mind they no longer existed. He was still at his home, but was no longer surrounded by a cool cloudless night in late September. Heavy sheets of spring rain swept down from a turbulent sky, thunder rumbling in the distance. *Oh, no, please!* his thoughts pleaded. *I can't live through this horrible night again!*

A voice answered him. The voice of a child. *Then tell the truth.*

No.. . I can't do that. They'd kill me for sure if I told them anything. His heart pounded like a trip hammer in his shallow chest.

All right, if you don't think you can . . . The nightmare continued. Strangely enough he was no longer sitting in his rocking chair. Instead, he stood in the kitchen, staring through the pane of the back door. The heavy length of the Remington rifle was once again in his hands. *I don't want to be here!* cried his thoughts, but he was unable to pull away from the awful scene of déjà vu.

Headlights arched through the driving downpour, heading from the direction of the barn, turning sharply into the backyard. The truck halted just past the outhouse, the engine idling loudly. Shadowy forms watched him from the depths of the cab. *Shut off that porch light, old man,* grated an all too familiar voice.

Who is it? he yelled, although he knew exactly who it was.

I said to shut it off . . . right now. The cavernous muzzles of the scattergun slid through the window, a beefy hand thumbing back twin hammers.

He did not waste any time. Reaching over, he worked the switch. But something was wrong. Nothing happened. The porch light continued to burn.

I ain't gonna tell you again, you old geezer!

I'm trying! he croaked, frantically snapping the light switch on and off. *Something's the matter with it!*

Then, from nearby, the voice of the child again. *Will you tell now?*

No, I can't.... He stared out the window and saw the shotgun directed not at the porch post, but straight at him. And behind that gun glared the evil face of Bully Hanson. *I warned you, didn't I, old man?*

Harvey tried to reply, but it was too late. The twelve gauge discharged, the boiling of gun smoke and the boom of the shot stretching out, needlessly prolonging his awful terror. He watched, dumbfounded, as a swarm of tiny lead pellets winged their way toward him in slow motion. He tried to pull away, tried to duck to the side, but he could not. His feet were rooted to the spot. Agony gripped his heart as he saw the silver-gray pellets part the dirty screen and shatter the glass pane in a burst of tiny explosions.

"I'll tell!" Brewer screamed, lurching from his rocker and slumping to the dirty boards of the porch. "I'll tell you everything ... just stop it!"

Clay and Taylor rushed up the steps and helped him back

into his chair. "Are you all right, Harve?" asked the county sheriff.

The old man ignored the frantic beating of his heart. "You were right, Sheriff. It was Hanson who did it. Claude Darnell was in the truck with him. I heard the shots, the screams, and they pulled up to the house afterward ... threatened to kill me if I told a soul about it. I'm sorry I lied, but I was scared they'd come back for me."

"Then, you'll agree to be a witness for the prosecution?" New hope sparkled in Taylor White's eyes.

"Yes, anything you want."

After making sure the old man was all right, they bid him good night and walked to the car. "You know" grinned Clay, "I believe I'm gonna have me a good night's sleep for the first time in months."

Taylor breathed a sigh of relief. "You ain't the only one."

Cindy Ann lingered by the porch post a moment longer; staring at the feeble man who sat slumped in the hardwood rocker. "I'm sorry I did it, Mr. Brewer," she said in a low voice. "I'm awful sorry."

Harvey's ancient eyes held no malice for the youngster. He smiled tiredly. "Don't be, young lady. It was just something you had to do. And you know something? I'm real glad you did. This thing's been hanging over me for a mighty long time."

"Come on, Cindy," called Clay from the automobile. "Let's get on home."

A look of mutual understanding passed between the girl and the elderly man, then she was running to join her father. Harvey leaned back and rocked for a while longer. All the fear, all the agitation, had been flushed from his system, along with the constriction in his chest. *Perhaps,* he thought, getting up to go into the house, *I might also have a good night's sleep.*

And that was what he experienced for the first night in three and a half months: a deep, dreamless slumber ... the sleep of a man finally at peace with himself.

Chapter Twenty-One

The case of the State of Tennessee versus James "Bully" Hanson and Claude Darnell took place the final week of October. "The Coleman Triple Murder Trial" was the label pinned on the proceedings by reporters from neighboring areas. The Nashville Banner, the Tennessean, and even newspapers as far away as Memphis and Chattanooga had presented substantial coverage of the heinous crime committed in Harvey Brewer's curing barn. Although there were plenty of other stories more worthy of column space, most of the local press simply could not resist the gruesome sensationalism sparked by violent death in an otherwise peaceful farming community.

The trial was held two days before Halloween, and it looked as though the entire county had turned out. Most of the shops that lined the main street were closed that day, as well as the elementary and high schools. All manner of spit-and-polish sedans and rattletrap pickup trucks lined Coleman's narrow avenues. There was an air of festivity that lingered in the town square, one enhanced by the invigorating coolness of the autumn weather and the russet hues of October leaves. A few jack-o'-lanterns sat perched on residential porches. Their jaggedly carved faces leered insanely at passersby while they patiently awaited the twilight hours of All Hallows Eve.

Inside the red brick courthouse the main chamber was packed with spectators. The hardwood pews located behind the restraining banister were occupied by a swell of townsfolk, dirt farmers, and the curious from a half-dozen adjoining counties. The gathering rumbled and roared with good-natured talk and gossip. Women traded recipes for chess pie and peach preserves, while the men swapped jokes and political opinions. A group of pipe smokers at the courtroom doors listened with amusement as Jake Winters told, for the umpteenth time, how his prized heifer, Maybelle, had been sucked through the cone of a tornado and hurled clear into Galbreth County. There she had been found the following day, sprawled atop the Andersonville water tower, dead, but with nary a broken bone in her lifeless body.

The pews at the foremost end of the gallery were the quietest. No conversation buzzed among their occupants, no idle chatter, only silent waiting. On the right side sat Clayburn Biggs and his family. Clay was decked out in his Sunday finest, as were Maudie and the children. Stella Longcreek sat there with them. She was a pale, shrunken shadow of the feisty woman she had been before the horrible discovery in Brewer's barn.

On the front pew to the left sat Ransom Potts and his wife, Betsy. The banker, too, had experienced the weathering effects of grief. His normally full suit coat now hung on him loosely, for he had lost nearly fifty pounds that summer. His face seemed older and paler, the robust fire of arrogance having left his features, and his hairline had receded dramatically. Physically, Potts had deteriorated more than any other member of the three sorrowful families.

It was nearing nine o'clock that morning when Taylor White introduced the Bedloe County district attorney to the Biggs family. "Folks, this here's Willard Shaw from Nashville. He'll be the man prosecuting this case."

Clay shook the man's hand and was pleased by the firm grasp. The tobacco farmer usually disliked lawyers about as much as he did bankers and politicians, but Willard Shaw was different. He was a large man with a rawboned ruggedness that transcended his double-breasted suit and brown wingtips. There was a genuine touch of Will Rogers in Shaw's wry smile and the haphazard cowlick that protruded past his neatly cut hair.

Shaw shook hands with each and every member of the Biggs clan, then with Mrs. Longcreek. Afterward, Clay asked a question of the attorney. "What are our chances of seeing those two get the electric chair, Mr. Shaw?"

The prosecutor cast an appraising glance at Bully and Claude, who sat with their lawyer, A.J. Branchworth, at the opposite table. Both defendants were dressed in ill-fitting suits, starched white shirts, and ties. Darnell sat stiff and uneasy, his tight collar making his Adam's apple stand out even more. Bully on the other hand seemed more at ease. He reared back in his chair, hands clasped across his beer belly. He looked more like a man relaxing at a church picnic than one on trial for the brutal slayings of three young men.

"I think we have an excellent chance," replied Shaw. His voice had the crisp, resounding quality of an auctioneer. "Considering the amount of evidence Sheriff White has compiled and the valuable testimony of our witnesses, Mr. Brewer in particular, I'm fairly sure we've got it in the bag. And you've got my assurance that I will do everything in my power to see justice done."

His promise lifted their spirits and gave them new hope. "God bless you, Mr. Shaw," said Stella, placing a frail hand on the man's arm. He clasped the woman's hand warmly and then returned to the prosecutor's table with the sheriff.

At nine-fifteen, Fred Ezell, who was acting as bailiff, took his place beside the judge's oaken bench. "Will you all please rise," he requested loudly. All idle chatter broke off, and the gathering stood as one. The last to get to his feet was Bully Hanson, who grunted lazily and acted as if the whole thing was one big joke.

"The Honorable Lester T. Mullen presiding," announced Deputy Ezell as the chamber door opened and a small, black-robed man approached the bench. Mullen was a balding man in his early sixties, his eyes pleasantly neutral and his upper lip sporting an enormous handlebar mustache of iron gray.

He took his time mounting the platform and taking his place at the huge podium that sat between the American and Tennessee flags. Gavel in hand, he rapped sharply, calling the court to order. "You may be seated."

A great rumbling of folks taking their places, along with a few stray coughs and throat clearings, filled the courtroom, then faded into expectant silence. The men in the back put away their pipes and ground their cigarette butts underfoot, settling against the ancient wallpaper of the back wall for the duration of the trial.

Judge Mullen turned his attention toward the twelve man jury. They sat on cane-backed chairs at the right side of the courtroom, having been selected earlier that morning. All were well-known men in the community, businessmen and farmers mostly. Out of the twelve, Clay knew only two personally. One was Woody Sadler from the general store. The other was Andy Grissom, the man Clay had helped butcher hogs only a couple of weeks earlier.

"Gentlemen," began the judge. "You have been selected for the duty of jurors in this session of the Bedloe County criminal court. For the next few days you will be presented with a great amount of evidence and testimony relating to the case at hand. Two men are being tried for the murders of three teenaged boys. I want you to absorb the evidence carefully, listen to what each witness has to say, and, at the proper time, discuss the case with your fellow jurors. After a sufficient amount of deliberation, you will return to this courtroom with a verdict of guilty or not guilty. In the former case, you will also provide an appropriate sentence pertaining to the severity of the crime these men are charged with. Now, are there any questions before we proceed?"

The jury indicated that they fully understood all that had been said. "Very well," Mullen said with a nod. "Bailiff, we shall flip a coin to see who starts the opening statements."

Fred Ezell dug a quarter from his trouser pocket. "Gentlemen?"

"Heads," requested the public defender.

"Then its tails for me," District attorney Shaw accepted graciously.

The coin was tossed. It came up on the Washington side. "You may begin, Mr. Branchworth."

"Thank you, Your Honor." The defense attorney was of average build, with wavy brown hair and droopy eyes that seemed to regard everything with an expression of weary disdain and suspicion. If Willard Shaw had the crisp report of an auctioneer, then Branchworth's delivery was more like the boisterous callings of a sideshow barker. He began his statement in a rolling baritone voice that caught the attention of everyone within earshot.

"Gentlemen of the jury, we have in this court today a case that should never have been brought before you. At this table here we have two men—two innocent men who have been wrongfully charged with the horrid murders of three young men. Why do I believe they have been wrongfully accused? Well, I shall, during the course of this trial, show you irrefutable evidence, as well as solid testimony that will, beyond a shadow of a doubt, prove my clients innocent. These two men, James Hanson and Claude Darnell, are indeed newcomers to this fine community. But just because they are strangers to you all should not cast them as instant suspects in your eyes. True, they are prone to drink and fisticuffs occasionally, but for the most part they are hard working and trustworthy gentlemen who have never had the slightest intention of doing grave harm to their fellow man." That remark brought a few low chuckles from somewhere in the back. The attorney directed a withering glare in that general direction, then turned his eyes back on the twelve jurors.

"You gentlemen may very well have come to this court today with your minds already set on the final outcome. But all I ask of you is a little objectivity, a little unbiased understanding on the part of my clients. Remember that sometimes things are not quite what they appear to be. During the course of this trial, I shall prove this to be the rule, rather than the exception."

After A.J. Branchworth had had his say, it was Willard Shaw's turn to present his case.

"How are you gentlemen doing today?" he greeted with an easygoing smile. After receiving a few nods, he went on. "You know, Mr. Branchworth over there, he has a mighty eloquent way of speaking. I heard tell he studied law up in Boston, and I reckon that's commendable enough. These Harvard fellows, they like to use those ten-dollar words out of the Webster dictionary and make their statements awful flowery. Kind of spellbounds you just to listen to them sometimes.

"But, you know, no matter how much poetry and polish they

put into it, no matter how many big words they use to throw you off course, they just can't hide the truth of the matter. It just sticks right out like a sore thumb. And that's the case here today. The truth, plain and simple."

Willard Shaw stood before the attentive jurors, his easy smile suddenly giving way to a solemn frown. "You've got a hard job ahead of you. But don't despair, because I'm going to do my best to make your task easier. I am going to present enough evidence to you, along with testimony from several men you have come to respect in this community. Enough cold hard facts to erase any lingering doubt about these two men on trial. Before this is all over, every one of you will know deep down in his soul that Bully Hanson and Claude Darnell did, in fact, brutally murder and dismember three fine young men. Johnny Biggs, William Longcreek, and Clarence Judson Potts were led to an abandoned barn on the property of Harvey Brewer, lured there by the promise of a simple drink of moonshine whiskey. But upon arriving there, they were horribly murdered, all because of greed—all because of a handful of greenback dollars, a little pocket money for a weekend of drinking and carousing in Nashville.

"Are we going to turn our thoughts away from the fate of those poor boys? Are we going to let their murderers walk the streets, thinking they have gotten off scot free? No, I don't believe any man, woman, or child here today could comprehend such a thought. And I am confident that you, gentlemen of the jury, will end up doing the right thing. I am sure that you will listen to the evidence presented, weigh the words spoken today, and come to the correct decision. For your sake and, most of all, for the sake of those poor boys who are not here today to plead their own case."

All in all, the case of Tennessee versus Hanson and Darnell seemed to be off to a spirited start.

Chapter Twenty-Two

The first thing that Willard Shaw did before calling his first witness was to identify each and every piece of physical evidence. The items lay on a broad table, each labeled and positioned in correct order.

There were three small piles of meager belongings that had been discovered in the pockets of the unfortunate victims and the single tortoiseshell guitar pick that Clay had found on the floorboard of Bully's truck. Johnny's gray fedora, water-stained and earthy, sat in the center of the table. Shaw took each item and turned it over in his nimble fingers, explaining which possession belonged to whom.

Then he moved on to the more destructive articles. There was a small tin partially full of lead pellets: double-aught buckshot extracted from both the bodies of the murdered boys and the splintered post of Brewer's back porch. Beside the pellets was Bully Hanson's sawed-down L.C. Smith shotgun. The breech was cracked open, revealing the dark chamber of each shortened barrel. The last item on the table was an old hand axe. Its heavy blade was crusted with flakes of rust, its foot-long handle pitted and tacky with old varnish. The hatchet had been found in the thicket beside the tobacco barn and was believed to be the weapon used to split Billy Longcreek's skull in half.

As the district attorney left the table, he knew in his heart that one other item should have been there and that was Johnny Biggs' flat-top guitar.

During his investigation of the case, Shaw had gone to the Nashville pawn shop and had done his level best to convince the owner of the seriousness of the case at hand. But the man had stubbornly denied knowing exactly who had brought the guitar in. After all, he claimed, it had been nearly five months. The lawyer had left the pawn shop feeling that he had been lied to. The last time he saw that simple flat-top, it hung foremost in the cluttered window where it had hung since last May, its fifteen-dollar price much too rich for passing musicians.

"Doctor Anson Hubbard, please approach the witness stand."

After taking the oath, the silver-haired physician settled into the chair to the right of the judge's bench. Willard Shaw flipped through a few sheets of paper, studied a typewritten page for a moment, then leaned against the edge of the prosecution table.

"Dr. Hubbard, you are the only practicing physician here in the town of Coleman?" he asked for the record.

"Yes, sir. Matter of fact, I'm the only one in Bedloe County."

The district attorney nodded. "Did you receive a phone call from Sheriff White on July twenty-second of this year?"

"Yes, I did."

"Could you please tell us the extent of that conversation?"

"Well about two o'clock that afternoon the sheriff called me at my office in town. Told me to meet him over at the Brewer place. Said they'd found some bodies hidden there."

"And you arrived at Mr. Brewer's property shortly thereafter?"

"Yes," agreed Doc Hubbard. "I accompanied Taylor into Mr. Brewer's tobacco barn, where the bodies had been discovered."

"And, as acting coroner of Bedloe County, did you examine those remains?"

The elderly physician hesitated, remembering that stifling summer day. "Yes sir, I did."

"There were three bodies?"

"Yes, but it was difficult to tell at first."

"And why was that?"

The doctor looked uncomfortable. "Well, the victims had been . . . *dismembered* before burial. Also they were badly decomposed. Someone had dumped a bag of lime over the remains, perhaps hoping to dispose of them faster. But they didn't use enough to do much good."

A rush of excited discussion swept the courtroom. Judge Mullen had to rap his gavel several times to regain order.

The prosecutor continued. "But you finally separated the remains and determined them as belonging to three individuals?"

"Yes." Hubbard's face paled slightly at the memory of what they had found inside that tool chest.

Willard Shaw approached the bench and quietly conversed with Judge Mullen for a moment. The judge faced the gallery of curious spectators. "Ladies and gentlemen, I have been informed that the next series of questions may be quite graphic and somewhat disturbing. If there are any women or children who wish to leave, please do so now."

A couple of elderly spinsters left their pew, as did a young mother who dragged her children, whining and complaining, from the courtroom.

"All right, you may proceed."

Shaw nodded politely. "Now, Doctor, would you please describe in detail the extent of these individuals' wounds?"

Again the physician hesitated, then went on. "One body had been assaulted with a heavy, sharpened instrument, probably an axe or hatchet of some sort."

The prosecutor lifted the hand axe from the evidence table. "An instrument similar to this one?"

"Yes. That may very well have been the same one. Anyway, there was a devastating wound on the victim's head. The axe had been swung with great force, for it made a deep opening in the cavity of the man's skull from the top of the scalp, clear down to the bridge of the nose."

"And the cause of death for this individual was . . . ?"

"Severe trauma to the frontal lobe of the brain. I would say that he died instantaneously."

"This individual was later identified as William Longcreek, is that correct?"

"Yes." Anson Hubbard shifted his eyes to the first pew behind the banister. Maudie Biggs was helping a sobbing Stella Longcreek down the center aisle toward the back. The doctor suddenly felt like a callous, unfeeling ghoul sitting there on the witness stand.

"Could you please tell us of the second body?"

The doctor continued. "The second individual had been killed by a severe gunshot wound to the lower abdomen, just below the rib cage. The wound measured six inches in diameter and extended throughout the trunk of the torso. The stomach and intestines were badly damaged, and the spine had been severed by the force of the blast."

"And you determined the wound to be made by what sort of weapon?"

"By a shotgun. A twelve gauge using a double-aught hunting load."

"Could the wound have been inflicted by this gun?" Shaw asked, lifting the sawed-off scattergun from the table.

"From the spread of the buckshot, yes, it certainly could have."

"The second victim was later identified as Clarence Judson Potts," the attorney stated for the record. "Now, Doctor Hubbard, would you describe the wounds of the third and final victim."

"The third boy had been shot twice, but only one was a fatal wound. He had been shot once in the upper thigh and buttock of the left leg. The pellets penetrated muscle tissue, but did not damage any bones or major arteries. The second shot had caused a severe wound to the victim's head. The blast entered the back of the skull, traveling through the mass of the brain, and exited from the right maxillary or upper jaw. Because of the force and closeness of the gunshot, most of the right side of the face was totally obliterated."

Doc Hubbard finished his grisly diagnosis, his mouth as dry as cotton wadding. He avoided looking toward Clay and his family.

"And the third individual was ...?"

"Johnny Biggs," he sighed.

"Your witness, counselor," called Shaw, returning to his table.

A.J. Branchworth left his seat and eyed the elderly physician. "Doctor Hubbard, you are absolutely sure that the gunshot wounds were made by a twelve gauge shotgun?"

"Yes sir, I am."

"And the double-aught buckshot? How did you come to that conclusion?"

"A number of pellets were found in the victims' bodies. They were all double-aught. Approximately .330 of an inch in diameter."

Branchworth took the shortened gun from among the evidence. He studied it carefully, handling it as though he had never held a firearm in his life. "You say the wounds were made by a sawed-down shotgun. How did you determine that? Couldn't they have been inflicted by a standard shotgun with barrels longer than this one right here?"

"I don't believe so," pointed out Hubbard. "The size and severity of the wounds suggest a gun with shortened barrels. You see, the shorter the barrel, the greater the spread of the shot pattern. A shotgun with, say, twenty-eight-inch barrels would have made a much smaller, concentrated wound. Perhaps one or two inches in diameter, compared to six."

Branchworth frowned at the stubby length of gunmetal, opening and closing the breech several times. "Are you absolutely positive that this is the exact shotgun that killed two of those three young men?"

"They were killed by a sawed-off twelve gauge," the doctor replied. "Other than that, I couldn't say for sure."

A gleam flickered in the lawyer's droopy eyes for a second. "So what you are saying is that this shotgun found in Mr. Hanson's possession can not be positively identified as the same weapon that killed those boys? That, in fact, those wounds could have been made by an entirely different make and model of shotgun? Perhaps a single-shot or a pump shotgun, rather than one with side-by-side barrels?"

"I suppose so."

The public defender walked back to the evidence table. "One more question, Doctor." He took the rusty hatchet and hefted it gingerly in one hand. "Is this the axe that was found on the Brewer property at the time the bodies were discovered?"

"It is."

"Then could you tell us if this hatchet was tested for blood samples?"

The physician replied affirmatively.

"Did you discover any traces of blood on this item?"

Hubbard's face clouded. "No, the tests were negative." Privately, the doctor knew that the absence of blood was perfectly understandable. After all, the hatchet had been lying out there in the open thicket for nearly two months after the time the murders had actually taken place. Bad weather and pouring rain could very well have obliterated any traces of Billy Longcreek's blood from the blade of the short axe.

However, A.J. Branchworth did not give him sufficient chance to explain that particular point. He returned the hatchet to its correct place, a smug grin on his clean-shaven face. "No further questions, Your Honor."

Chapter Twenty-Three

"Do you swear to tell the truth, the whole truth, and nothing but the truth . . . so help you God?"

"I do," declared Taylor White. He lumbered up to the witness stand and had a seat. The hardwood chair creaked noticeably beneath his vast weight.

"Mr. White, you are the acting constable of Bedloe County?" asked the prosecutor, laying the groundwork for the following bout of questioning.

"Yes sir, I've been the sheriff hereabouts for nearly twenty years."

"And when did you first become involved in this murder case?"

Taylor cleared his throat nervously. He felt the curious eyes of the twelve jurors on him, as well as those from the gallery, watching him closely. "It was on the twenty-second of July. I happened upon Harvey Brewer in town. He'd bought himself some groceries and was about to walk home. I offered him a lift on account I was going that way anyhow. Besides, Harvey has a bad heart and I just didn't like the idea of him walking that far in the hot sun. He's on in his seventies, you know."

The lawman was introspective for a brief moment, as if sorting out the events of that sweltering July day. But he had no trouble in doing so. The discovery of horrible death was ever present, forever tattooed into the flesh of his brain. "When we pulled up outside Harvey's place, we heard the most godawful commotion down there at the old tobacco barn out back of his house. We heard young'uns screaming, not out of fun . . . they were scared half outta their wits. I saw the Biggs girl run off across the thicket into the woods, and I ran down there to the barn to see what was going on. When I got there, a few other kids from town were piling out of a hole in a side wall. They were crying, screaming, and carrying on. I asked them what the matter was, but couldn't get a clear answer from any of them."

"Did you then enter the tobacco barn?" asked Willard Shaw.

"Yes." Taylor White nearly shuddered in reply.

"What did you find there?"

"I squeezed through that opening, and a smell like some dead animal hit me. It was dark in there, so I couldn't see very well at first. I drew my service revolver and went on inside. It was then that I noticed the tool chest a few feet away. Its lid had been opened, and I figured that's what those kids had been up to. They'd been messing with that old tool box, and whatever they'd found in it had thrown a scare into them."

"And could you tell us all exactly what you found in that chest?"

Taylor's moon face began to grow pallid around the eyes and mouth. "At first I thought the remains of a single person were in there. Then I saw that there was more than one. Two, maybe three, bodies had been chopped up and stacked in there neat as cord wood. A coating of lime had been dumped over the remains to help quicken decomposition and keep down the smell."

"And after that you contacted your deputies and Doctor Hubbard?"

"Yes. After the doc had made his examination and we had identified the three boys, we contacted the families as well."

The prosecutor walked over to the evidence table and indicated the dirty fedora hat and the three piles of assorted possessions. "Did you find these items on the victims?"

"Yes, in their pockets. All that seemed to have been taken was money. The hat there was found by Cynthia Ann Biggs in a corner of the barn. It belonged to her brother."

"What motive do you believe led to this heinous crime?"

"Simple robbery to begin with, then maybe one of the boys made a wrong move and triggered the killings. We've about decided now that they were lured to the barn by the promise of bootleg whiskey. It's a fact that the three boys were seen on the night of May twenty-ninth at the Bloody Bucket, a beer joint across the railroad tracks. They tried to buy some drinks, but were run off by Otis Schofield, the owner. From the way we see it, they happened across someone in the parking lot, were promised moonshine, then driven to the old barn and murdered."

Shaw paced the floor for a few moments, moving to the conclusion of his questioning. "Did your investigation of this case go smoothly after the initial discovery was made in late July?"

"No, sir, on the contrary. There was very little physical evidence to be found at the scene of the crime and no witnesses that we knew of . . . at the time. We had no description of the murderers, no description of the vehicle they had been driving, nothing concrete to go on. Whatever leads we came upon just didn't pan out. Toward the end of September I figured those killers had done gotten away scot free."

"Then, on the night of September twenty-sixth, something happened to turn the case around," the prosecutor pointed out. "Would you please tell us of the events of that evening?"

The warm morning sun beamed through the courthouse window. It glistened like golden fire on the brass star pinned above Taylor's breast pocket. "I received a call that night from Clayburn Biggs' son, Josh. He told me that there was gonna be bad trouble at the Bloody Bucket and that I should get over there fast. I rounded up my deputies and drove over to the tavern to check it out."

"And what was taking place when you arrived?"

"There was a fight going on between Clay Biggs and Bully Hanson. Or I should say, it was done over with. I got there just as Bully was about to shoot Clay with that sawed-off shotgun of his. Had it aimed square at Clay's head. He was on the verge of pulling the trigger when we showed up and arrested him for the murders of those three boys."

"What gave you reason to suspect Bully Hanson and Claude Darnell of killing those young men?"

"'Cause Bully admitted to it right then and there."

"What were Mr. Hanson's exact words?"

"He said that Johnny Biggs was a real bitch to kill; that he'd had to chase him halfway across Brewer's field before he finally caught him and put a load of buckshot through his head."

"Your witness, Mr. Branchworth," extended Shaw.

"Sheriff White," began the counselor, approaching the stand. "During the lengthy and sometimes fruitless investigation of this particular case, did you ever get the impression that the citizens of Coleman were getting somewhat restless as far as your lack of progress was concerned? Did you ever feel as if they had lost confidence in your ability as a lawman?"

Taylor White felt a cold weight in the pit of his ample stomach. He knew that he was under oath, that he must answer truthfully. "Yes ... yes, I did get that impression a few times."

"In fact, did you not begin to believe that their concerns were genuine? That, perhaps, your skills as a county sheriff were not up to handling a complex case of triple homicide?"

The constable was beginning to resent the tone of the questions being directed at him. He shifted uncomfortably in the witness chair, a pink flush of embarrassment slowly creeping into his thick neck and jowls. "Maybe so;" he finally said. "I reckon I might've had some doubts after a while."

A thin grin possessed Branchworth's dull features, and a devilish twinkle could be detected in those droopy-lidded eyes. "And then, on that September night, you came upon a drunken brawl in the parking area of a local roadhouse. My client made an off-color remark as to the killing of his opponent's son, perhaps merely to goad him into further fisticuffs, and you, Sheriff White, suddenly found a solution to a lot of nagging problems that were making you into, shall we say, a picture of incompetence?"

"What the hell are you trying to say, mister?" snapped the lawman. His knuckles whitened with growing anger as he gripped the arms of the chair he sat in.

"What I am saying, Sheriff, is that you wrongfully arrested my clients, James Hanson and Claude Darnell, without any physical evidence, without any confession other than the hazy mutterings of an intoxicated mind. Did you not, in fact, find the opportunity to jail these two men and use them as scapegoats in an irresistible chance of closing the whole grisly case and making yourself look good to your fellow constituents? It being only a few months until the county election, the idea must have seemed like a godsend to save your own hide!"

"Objection!" called Willard Shaw, rising from his table. "Your Honor, I must object strongly to the insinuations that Mr. Branchworth is making. Sheriff White has been a respectable citizen and exemplary law officer in Bedloe County for nearly two decades. For the defender to even allude to Taylor White in such light is nothing more than pure slander!"

Judge Mullen agreed. "Objection sustained." He directed a baleful look at the public defender. "You will kindly refrain from any further remarks of a libelous nature, Mr. Branchworth."

The attorney took the scolding with a grain of salt. After all, he had accomplished what he had set out to do. The murmur of the spectators and the thoughtful expressions that crossed the faces of the jurors told him that he had successfully planted the first seeds of doubt in the backs of their minds.

Chapter Twenty-Four

"Mr. Biggs, did you go to the Bloody Bucket on the night of September twenty-sixth?"

"Yes, I did," replied Clay. He sat on the witness stand, work-calloused hands clasped idly in his lap. He looked out of place there, like some actor who had been miscast in a stage play. Neither the dark Sunday suit, shiny patent leather shoes, nor any amount of Wildroot Creme Oil could conceal the rural homeliness of the man. He could very well have approached the stand decked out in Duckhead overalls and a red flannel shirt, and no one there would have thought any less of him.

"What were your intentions that night?" continued Willard Shaw.

Clay cast his eyes nervously around the crowded courtroom. "Well, I reckon I was out to kill Bully Hanson."

An excited murmur spread like wildfire across the gallery. Judge Mullen quickly put a lid on it, striking sharply upon the bench top with his gavel. "I will have order in this court," he stated gravely. The conversation ebbed back into silence.

The prosecutor went on. "Why would you take such drastic action? Everyone I've talked to has made you out to be a fine, level-headed family man, not one who would go off half-cocked."

"I had a strong suspicion that Hanson and Darnell were the men who killed my boy Johnny."

Shaw absently scratched his cowlick. "And did you confront Bully Hanson with your suspicions?"

"Not right off," admitted Clay. "First I had to get it straight in my head that they really did it. I went to Bully's truck and searched for some shred of evidence that might link them to the killing."

"And did you find anything?"

"I did. A guitar pick that belonged to my son."

The district attorney took the tortoiseshell pick from the evidence and held it aloft. "Is this the item you discovered? A guitar pick with the initials J.B. scratched on one side?"

"It is. I found it on the floorboard of Bully's truck."

"Objection!" called A.J. Branchworth from the table where Claude and Bully sat. "The evidence in question was obtained by illegal search. Furthermore, it was obtained by a civilian acting on a whim of utter desperation and not by a law officer with the proper warrant to conduct a legitimate search of my client's vehicle. I ask that this particular piece of evidence be stricken from the record."

The judge was reluctant to give in to the attorney's demand, but he knew his grievance rang true. "I'm afraid he's right, Mr. Shaw," Mullen pointed out. "Bailiff, please remove item Number Four from the list of evidence."

Willard Shaw was disheartened by the exclusion of the guitar pick, but did not let it show. He went on, business as usual. "What happened then?"

"Bully found me rooting around in his truck. He was pretty liquored up, and he pulled a sawed-off shotgun from under the seat."

"Did he discharge the shotgun?"

"Yes . . . once. He blew out the side window of his own truck trying to shoot me."

"What happened after that?"

"Bully lost hold of his gun, and we went at it, tooth and nail, for a while. After just about getting the tar whomped outta me, I finally got Bully backed up against his truck. He found his shotgun and was on the verge of shooting me when the sheriff showed up."

"Mr. Biggs, did Bully Hanson say anything to you when he had that gun pointed at your head?"

Clay's hangdog face grew sullen with dark emotion. "Yes. He admitted to killing my son at Harvey Brewer's place."

"Your witness, Mr. Branchworth," offered Shaw, this time with less enthusiasm than before. He was beginning to dread the defender's cross-examination of his star witnesses. Branchworth was like a turkey buzzard, circling his prey until a weak spot appeared in their testimony, one that might take away from the prosecution's case and give more substance to his own.

A.J. Branchworth approached the stand with a polite smile on his face, a smile that Clay could see right through. "Mr. Biggs, when you confronted Mr. Hanson, did you not also have a firearm in your possession?"

Clay could not lie. "I did."

"And did you not fire two shots at him, whereas he only fired once?"

"The muzzle was aimed upward when we were wrestling. It fired twice into the air."

Branchworth shook his head solemnly, as if he were about to scold a naughty child. "Mr. Biggs, in my opinion those are not the actions of a man in his right frame of mind. If you suspected Mr. Hanson of this crime, why did you not go to Sheriff White with your suspicions? Why did you choose to take the law into your own hands?"

Clay stumbled over his words, suddenly angered by the questions fired at him. "Well, I had to be sure before I did anything like that. I had to be certain that what I'd been told was true."

A new light sparked in the lawyer's eyes. "Did you say that someone told you? Well, please tell us all exactly who told you that Mr. Hanson and Mr. Darnell had killed those three boys."

Clay knew then that he had made a bad mistake. He clammed up, reluctant to reply. "I'd just as soon not say."

Lawyer Branchworth planted his fists on his narrow hips. "Need I remind you that you are under oath, Mr. Biggs?"

Clay knew that he was jeopardizing the validity of his own testimony, but there was nothing else he could say. He was caught between a rock and a hard place. "It was my daughter who told me. My youngest daughter."

The attorney's eyes widened incredulously. "Your daughter?

Are you saying that you went out to that roadhouse with the intention of killing a man, simply because a child told you to?"

"She didn't tell me to!" gritted Clay. "She just had a feeling that Bully and Claude were the ones who done it, and I believed her."

"She had a *feeling*?" roared Branchworth. He looked as if he would have burst out laughing if he could have gotten away with it. "Exactly what does that mean ... she had a *feeling*?"

Clay felt cold anger well up inside him. "My daughter, Cindy Ann, has the gift of second sight."

More excited talk from the spectators. More banging of the gavel and threats to clear the courtroom from the judge.

A.J. Branchworth strutted around the witness stand like a bantam rooster. The fire of pure meanness sparkled in his muddy brown eyes. "What are you trying to tell us, Mr. Biggs?" he asked loudly. "That your daughter is something of a soothsayer? A fortune teller of sorts?"

"Nah, it ain't like that. She just has feelings. She sees things that other folks don't have the gift to see."

"Sees things?" bellowed Branchworth. He relished the fool he was making Clay out to be. "Do you mean she sees things that aren't really there? Hallucinations perhaps?"

"No, that ain't what I meant...." Clay sputtered.

"Isn't it true that your daughter, Cynthia Ann, was in a Nashville hospital with typhoid for nearly six months? Could it be that she might have suffered some irreparable damage during that long illness? Perhaps she is really a little touched in the head; could that be a possibility, Mr. Biggs?"

"Objection, your Honor!" bellowed Willard Shaw, standing in protest.

But the public defender was on a roll. He totally ignored the prosecutor's motion. "Do you usually make a habit of believing everything your daughter tells you? I think not. I believe the grief over your son's death has impaired your own stable judgment."

Clay could only stare at him in shocked silence. The spectators of the gallery reacted similarly.

A.J. Branchworth was about to launch into another barrage

of character assault, when a strange feeling overcame him. He broke out into a fit of sweating, perspiration coursing down his forehead and the nape of his neck. Blood pounded dully in his temples. He felt as if he were strangling, as if his breathing were somehow constricted. He tugged at the knot of his tie, but it only seemed to tighten even more.

Leave my daddy alone.

The voice seemed to resound from somewhere inside his head, not from any external source. He whirled and swept his eyes across the gathering of spectators. A sea of puzzled faces regarded him. They all stared at him as if he had suddenly gone mad. He was turning back when he caught a glimpse of a small red-haired child sitting in the front pew. She glared at him venomously. He quickly turned back to the witness before him.

"Perhaps, Mr. Biggs, it is *you* who are suffering from a mental breakdown," he rasped, his voice suddenly hoarse. "Maybe the death of your son and the troubles you've been having finding work have finally caught up with you and—"

I said to . . . leave . . . him . . . ALONE!

Branchworth's eyes nearly bulged from their sockets. The starched white collar of his dress shirt was constricting, tightening little by little against the lump of his windpipe. It seemed to be shrinking, much like a strip of wet rawhide does when exposed to a blazing sun.

Judge Mullen regarded the attorney with raised eyebrows. "Counselor, do you have any further questions for this witness?"

The tension around his throat was so great that he could hardly speak. "No, your Honor. That is all."

Abruptly, the paralyzing constriction eased, returning his breath to normal. For a moment, he had felt as if his throat would be crushed like a field mouse trapped in the tightening coils of a king snake.

A wall clock in the outer hallway struck the hour of noon, prompting Judge Mullen to call an hour lunch break. As the courtroom began to empty, Branchworth slumped into his chair. A palsy of shaking trembled through his nimble hands as he shuffled a stack of legal papers and stuck them into his briefcase.

"What did you stop for?" asked Bully before being escorted back to his cell. "You had him right where you wanted him and you just let him slip away!"

The lawyer did not answer. He watched as the Biggs family left the courtroom. Cindy Ann flashed an innocent, girlish smile that made his blood run cold. He sat there quietly for the next hour, a look of bewilderment on his ashen face, and tried to regain his faltering composure.

Chapter Twenty-Five

"Mind if I join you folks?" Willard Shaw approached the Biggs family at the base of the courthouse steps, his dark brown jacket draped over one arm. He held a brown paper bag in one hand.

"We'd be pleased for the company," invited Clayburn. Maudie was handing out ham sandwiches to the members of her brood. She reached to the bottom of the pail and found a spare. "You're more than welcome to share our lunch, Mr. Shaw."

"No thank you, dear lady." The lawyer smiled graciously. "I brought my own." He swept aside the shriveled husks of a few dead leaves and sat down. He dumped the contents of his sack onto the flat of the step: a shiny red apple and a bologna sandwich wrapped in waxed paper.

Noticing a couple of boys playing nearby, Shaw called them over. "Why don't you fine fellows run across the street to the store and bring us all a Coca-Cola." He dug a fifty-cent piece from his vest pocket and flipped it to them. "And buy a couple for yourselves, too."

"Gee, thanks a lot, mister!" They grinned in unison, then headed off for Flander's Grocery.

"You needn't do that," said Clay.

Shaw flashed his Will Roger's smile. "My treat. I insist."

It was not long until the boys returned with seven frosty bottles of pop. They commenced eating, the bright noonday sun warming the concrete beneath them, taking a little of the chill from the brisk, October breeze.

"I kinda feel bad about what happened up there on the

witness stand," apologized Clay after a few moments of awkward silence.

"Well, don't," assured the prosecutor. "I've known A.J. Branchworth for years, and he has a mean streak in him a mile wide. Hates to lose a case more than any man I've ever known. He has an uncanny knack for turning a man's testimony inside out. Believe me, he could have done far more damage than he did. Just can't figure out why he backed off when he did."

Cindy hid a mischievous grin behind the crust of her sandwich.

"So you still think we've got a good chance of winning this case?"

Shaw nodded. "Branchworth didn't do that much damage. Besides, my next witness will be Harvey Brewer. If anything makes this trial, it'll be his testimony."

They ate in silence for a while, a rural farming family and a big city lawyer enjoying a simple meal. When Willard Shaw finished his sandwich, he started on the apple. He sat quietly on his step, studying the members of Clay Biggs' fine family. His attention, however, lingered on the red-haired child who sat between her mother and father. There was no question about it. There was something different about her. Shaw could tell that just by looking at her.

"Mr. Biggs, what you said on the stand today about your girl Cindy ... is it true?" he inquired, not knowing whether he was stepping out of line in asking. "Does she really have the gift of second sight?"

Clay's blue eyes hardened in defensiveness, then softened just as quickly. "Yes, sir, what I said was true." He watched the city slicker carefully, trying to detect some trace of skepticism in his face. He found none.

"Must be pretty scary to you sometimes, young lady," Shaw said sympathetically. "Knowing about things you don't understand."

Cindy nodded shyly. *You couldn't know just how scary it can be,* she thought.

"So you believe in such things?" asked Maudie with interest.

"Indeed I do, ma'am," assured the prosecuting attorney.

"I believe there are a good many things in this world that are beyond man's comprehension. Powers of the mind may seem bewildering and unnatural to some folks, but they are little to scoff at compared to other phenomena. Why, take the Bell Witch up in Adams, Tennessee for instance. Back in the early 1800's, the John Bell family was supposedly terrorized by a spirit from out of nowhere. It disrupted the Bell household, torturing the elder Bell and his daughter Betsy to no end. It vowed to drive John Bell to his death and prevent Betsy from marrying her childhood beau, and over the course of many years, it did just that. Then it bid farewell to Mrs. Bell — Luce as it referred to her—and to the Bell sons and stopped its persistent haunting for seven years. It reappeared later on, but without the activity it had exhibited before, and then vanished from the lives of the Bell family forever.

"Plenty of God-fearing folks in Robertson County claim that the spirit still dwells in the cave on the Bell property, raising all kinds of ruckus. A good friend of mine, a college professor by trade, once spent a night in the Bell Witch cave. He went up there with all manner of scientific equipment, intending to disprove the existence of such an entity. Well, the following morning, those of the Bell descendants who still lived on the farm went down to the cave to see why the professor had not come to the house for breakfast. They found him crouched in a far corner of the barren cave, gibbering like an idiot. His eyes were wild and his hair was snow white, where it had been pitch black the day before. His equipment had been smashed against the walls of the cave, thrown there by some great force. He has spent the remainder of his days in an asylum for the insane, talking nonsense about a great pounding upon the walls and mocking voices surrounding him from all sides. I can't say for sure whether there are indeed such beings as spirits and demons, but I will say this; something up there in that cave turned an educated man into a babbling lunatic in the span of a single night."

The Biggs children giggled nervously and shivered in spite of themselves, as most youngsters do when told an especially creepy ghost story.

The big clock above the double doors struck one. They were about to file back inside with the other spectators when Sheriff White's patrol car pulled up at the curb. Taylor had left immediately after his degrading cross-examination, partly to get away from the questioning eyes of the townspeople, but most surely to pick up Harvey Brewer.

As the constable and the star witness approached the courthouse steps, they all noticed how haggard and unwell Harvey appeared that afternoon. The elderly man was dressed in a dark suit and bow tie, but other than the crispness of his attire, he frankly looked like death warmed over. His wrinkled skin held none of the robust color it usually did. The skin of his face hung like pale parchment ravaged by time. His rheumy eyes had an unhealthy yellow cast to them, and they held an emotion beyond that of simple fear. The man was utterly terrified; that was clear for everyone to see.

"Are you feeling all right today, Mr. Brewer?" Shaw asked, not liking the way the man looked.

"Well enough, I reckon," Harvey replied curtly. There was a tremble in the man's voice. Something had him spooked.

The sheriff noted everyone's puzzled faces and turned to the elderly man. "Harvey, why don't you go on in and have a seat. I'll be in directly."

"You won't be long, will you?" There was something akin to panic in Brewer's ancient eyes.

"I'll be right in, I promise."

When the old man had crept up the courthouse steps and disappeared through the double doors, Clay turned to his friend with concern in his voice. "Harvey looks pretty shaken today."

"He has good reason to be," said the lawman. "He had a little visit from some of Bully's pals last night. From what Harvey told me, they were stinking drunk, cussing to beat the devil, threatening to kill him if he dared testify today. They shot out every window in his house, too. He'd surely have gotten hurt himself if he hadn't hidden in the root cellar till they left."

"That's awful!" exclaimed Maudie. "Do you know who was behind it?"

"I've got a pretty good idea it was Otis Schofield and his

bunch. But I ain't got a lick of proof to pin it on them, though."

Willard Shaw's eyes were serious. "Do you think he'll testify truthfully, Sheriff? You don't think he would change his story just to save his hide, do you?"

"He's plenty scared, but he'll tell the truth when the time comes. He feels mighty guilty for covering up what he did, and I believe he wants to make amends. But that ain't what's bothering me. Did you see how rundown the man looks? I believe his heart has been acting up on him again."

The district attorney was thoughtful for a moment. "I suppose I could motion for a recess, give him time to calm down a little and have Doc Hubbard check him out."

"I suggested that to him," said Taylor. "But he just wants to get it over and done with. Can't say I blame him none either."

"Well, all we can do is keep our fingers crossed," said Clay. He herded his clan up the steps, and they joined the growing swell of spectators who had returned for the second session of questioning.

Willard Shaw stood on the sidewalk awhile longer, relishing the pleasant mixture of warm sunshine and cool autumn air as it ruffled his hair. Turning back to the job at hand, he was not at all sure that Harvey Brewer's testimony would have the impact he had once hoped it would. He almost felt as if his ace in the hole had been hopelessly lost the night before, swallowed up by the shattering of broken glass and the sound of drunken threats in the darkness.

Chapter Twenty-Six

Harvey Brewer sat in the witness chair before the eyes of Coleman, appearing old and shrunken, a sad shell of the "influential citizen" he had once been. At the turn of the century, he had been one of the wealthiest tobacco growers in Bedloe County. He had reaped over two hundred acres of prime Burley and Pryor a year, but after his wife's tragic passing, he had let all of that slip from his grasp. Now he was known only as a recluse, an unsociable hermit who lived on the edge of choking thicket that had once been known as the richest tobacco land in Tennessee.

The elderly gentleman had taken the oath, and before the prosecuting attorney began with his questioning, Harvey sat there, his nerves worn to a frazzle. His mind raced back to the night before. It had started around midnight, wrenching him from a sound sleep. The roar of trucks and automobiles had washed across his property like a wave of foreboding doom. He had lain there beneath the patchwork quilt that Norma had made forty years ago, listening intently as the rough idling of engines ceased and doors slammed loudly. Then the drunken yells, the hoots and hollers, the barrage of obscenities began.

You'd best forget about testifying against Bully Hanson tomorrow, you crazy old bastard. You'd best keep your damned mouth shut or you'll be sorry! You hear us, Methuselah? You utter one word against either Bully or Claude and you'll be laid out on the undertaker's slab, drilled and dried, before the following morn!

He had left his bed, clad only in a dingy nightshirt, and approached the bedroom closet. He had intended to get the rifle and fire a few rounds over the drunkards' heads, hoping to scare them away. But the shooting started before he could get there. Windows shattered inward, rifle slugs and buckshot tearing through wooden studs and yellowed wallpaper. Harvey fled like a frightened child down the hallway to the small trapdoor at the rear of the kitchen pantry — the door that led down into the musky depths of the root cellar. He hurried down into the pitch black of the hole, locking the door against the crash of wanton destruction. Curled up in the far corner, he lay there. An awful lance of agony twisted through the center of his shallow chest like a sharpened spike of red-hot iron. There he writhed in horrendous pain until he finally passed out. He had awakened with the dawn, feeling sick and feeble, the pain in his heart only a dull, lingering ache. He had lain there for a long time, listening to the morning birds. The cellar that had once housed a store of canned preserves and potatoes was now an earthy dungeon laced with forgotten spider webs and dank mold.

Now, perched upon the witness stand, Harvey swept his gaze over the milling gallery of spectators. On a pew near the back he spotted them, the culprits of his night of terror: Otis Schofield, his bartender Jasper Berle, and three of the Lynch brothers, a bunch of hooligans who spent their free time boozing and gambling at the Bloody Bucket. They all wore sullen expressions, their bloodshot eyes promising death for his bold disregard of their nocturnal warnings. He ignored them, but the awful fear remained deeply set.

The source of that paralyzing emotion sat no more than fifteen feet away. Bully Hanson reared back in his chair behind the defense table, a crooked grin splitting his broad face like the skeletal leer of a death's head. Bully's gray eyes had a flatness to them. They were dead eyes, the eyes of a mounted bass on some fisherman's lodge wall. But somewhere beneath that glazed expression lurked a consuming hatred born of pure evil.

"You are Harvey Brewer?"

The old man jumped at Shaw's voice. He had not even noticed the lawyer as he approached the stand. "Yes, I am."

"And you own property along Highway 81, approximately three miles south of Coleman?"

"That's right." Harvey cast a fleeting glance back at Bully. The big man was toying with a lead pencil, caressing its wooden length like a bone in the jaws of some prehistoric beast. *I told you to keep your freaking mouth shut, didn't I?* Bully's eyes seemed to taunt. *But, no, you gotta spill your guts and finger me for the murderer. Well, that's your mistake, old man. A very bad mistake.*

"On your property there is a small house and a barn used for curing tobacco leaves after they are harvested. Is that correct?"

Harvey's eyes pulled away from Bully's bitter grin and regarded Willard Shaw. "That's correct. I used the barn up until 1928. My wife, Norma, died then, and I got outta the business."

"This barn . . . I have heard that it has been used by numerous trespassers as some sort of hideaway. Is that true?"

"Yes," agreed Harvey. "It sets a far piece back from the road, and it's been locked and chained for years. I reckon there are a few people in this town who sneak down there to find some privacy. Kids mostly, smoking and drinking and necking with the gals. Once a band of hoboes stayed the night, but soon they moved on."

"And you do not alert the sheriff during any of these trespassings?"

The elderly man shrugged. "Never really saw no need to. Nobody ever made no trouble for me, so I just left them alone."

Bully was still glaring straight at him, the sinews of his thick wrists working as he continued to fool with the pencil. *If I ever get my hands on you, old geezer, I'll surely kill you. I'll take hold of you and snap your freaking neck like this here pencil. I'll squeeze the very life outta those brittle old bones of yours!*

The pain hit him then. The familiar, searing pain from deep within his chest. It seemed to flare throughout his body much faster than the other times before, arching up his swayed spine, numbing the muscles of his left shoulder with a thousand tiny pinpricks.

"On the evening of May twenty-ninth, the evening that the three boys were seen at the Bloody Bucket, you were awakened from your sleep," the prosecutor pointed out. "Would you please tell us about that night?"

The pain grew worse, a new agony blossoming with every

beat of his heart. But he went on with his testimony, trying to conceal the extent of his suffering. "I heard a truck turn off the highway and head down the road toward the barn. I didn't think anything of it, till I heard the shots."

"Shots coming from the vicinity of the barn?"

"Yes. Sounded deep, like a shotgun."

"Did you hear anything after that?"

Harvey nearly collapsed. The crushing pain in his chest was unbearable. "Yes, a scream," he managed. "Then, after that stopped, more shooting."

Willard Shaw eyed his witness cautiously, noticing the strained expression on the old man's face. He decided to continue. "What happened after you heard the last shot?"

"Nothing for a while. Then the truck drove back up from the barn. I'd done gone to the back door and turned on the porch light. The truck pulled up to the porch and someone pointed a shotgun at me from the open window."

"Did you see who occupied the truck?"

"No, it was too dark." Harvey had to struggle to keep his mind on the questions being asked. His left arm was numb and heavy, feeling as if it had fallen asleep.

"Did you recognize the voice of the man driving the truck?"

"Yes. I certainly did."

"Then, could you tell the gentlemen of the jury and everyone else in this courtroom exactly who that voice belonged to?"

The elderly man opened his mouth, his eyes growing wide and glassy. The words of final accusation froze solid in his throat. He had made the grave mistake of looking toward Hanson again. Bully had lost his cruel grin. An expression of seething hatred now gripped his ugly features, turning his coarse skin a fiery red. The killer's eyes bored into Harvey's soul, tearing away the armor of his stubborn bravado, exposing the soft underbelly of his fear. *I warned you what I'd do, dammit! I warned you!* And, with that, in a trembling fit of rage, Bully snapped the yellow pencil cleanly in half.

The brittle snap rang throughout the courtroom, turning heads toward the source of the sound. It echoed in Harvey Brewer's aged ears like a gunshot, and at that very moment, he felt something snap inside his chest. He let out a grunt, then lurched from the witness chair. His body hit the boarded floor with a resounding thud.

For a moment, no one made a move. All eyes stared at the prone form of Harvey Brewer, uncomprehending, as if perhaps the old planter were pulling some bizarre practical joke on his neighbors. One of the Lynch brothers snickered loudly from the back row, but received a stiff nudge in the ribs from Otis Schofield. The displaced mirth seemed to break the spell of inactivity, and suddenly the courtroom roared back into life. The rafters of the chamber almost seemed to expand with gasps of surprise and cries of concern.

Willard Shaw and Deputy Ezell were the first to reach the elderly man. They were soon joined by the judge and Taylor White. "Doctor!" the sheriff called into the crowd. Anson Hubbard was already past the restraining banister, toting the black leather bag that accompanied him everywhere he went.

The curious multitude began to strain forward, some genuinely anxious to lend a hand, but most just herding closer to get a better glimpse of the shocking turn of events. Lester T. Mullen stepped in front of the gateway before his court could be overrun with gaping spectators. "Please return to your seats," he demanded more than requested. "You have no business up here. We have more than enough people looking after this gentleman. Please, just bear with us." The crowd grumbled and groaned in protest, but returned to their places on the hardwood pews.

Carefully, at the request of Doc Hubbard, they turned the old man over on his back. Harvey's nose was bloodied, and the upper bridge of his dentures hung haphazardly over his lower lip. The physician tenderly removed the ivory and laid it aside. He delved into his bag and found a stethoscope. Hubbard pressed the rounded piece to several places, attempting to detect a pulse. He found none. Lastly, he positioned the flat of the instrument on the center of Harvey's chest. He could hear liquid filling the elderly man's torso and knew suddenly what had happened. The snap Harvey had felt had been the wall of a weakened artery giving way, flooding the upper cavity with life's blood.

"I told the man to take better care of himself," said Doc Hubbard almost bitterly. "Told him he had a bum heart. But, no, he wouldn't listen. He was too damned stubborn!"

The realization of Harvey Brewer's sudden death swept through the courtroom, softening the roar to a respectable whisper. There being nothing more to be done for the man, Ezell and White carried his body out the back way to the meeting room where the town council gathered monthly. They laid him on the long table to await the short trip across the square to Platt's Funeral Home.

Regaining his seat and rapping his gavel for order, Judge Mullen called the prosecutor and public defender to the bench for a conference. "Mr. Shaw, I don't want to appear callous; but this is a court of law, and the proceedings must go on, no matter what. Do you have any further witnesses to present for the prosecution?"

The district attorney felt a sinking feeling tug at the pit of his stomach. "No, Your Honor, I don't," he sighed in resignation. "I reckon the State of Tennessee rests."

Mullen nodded sternly. "Very well. Please return to your seats, gentlemen." After the two had obeyed the judge's request, the balding man with the handlebar mustache regarded the twelve-man jury. "Gentlemen, the prosecution has informed me that its deliberation has concluded. In light of the grave tragedy that has happened this afternoon, I shall postpone further proceedings until tomorrow morning, when the defense will present its witnesses. I will ask that each of you refrain from discussing the aspects of this case with each other or with anyone else, be it family or friend." The gavel rang loudly. "This court is adjourned until nine o'clock tomorrow morning."

As the citizens of Bedloe County filed from the courtroom, armed with sufficient fodder for the Coleman gossip mill for some time to come, Willard Shaw tucked his law books and typed briefs back into his satchel. He watched as Bully Hanson and Claude Darnell were handcuffed. As they were readied for the journey back to the county lockup downstairs, he studied the faces of the accused. Claude was skittish, as jittery as a squirrel. He seemed bewildered by the incident on the witness stand, looking as though he didn't know exactly what had happened.

On the other hand, Bully knew exactly what had taken place. The attorney could see it in his eyes, in the smug set of his lopsided grin. Murder had been committed that afternoon, cold-blooded homicide plain and simple. Many would label it as a natural demise; the old man's heart had finally done him in. But Willard Shaw saw it quite differently. Schofield and his drunken cronies had primed the pump, so to speak, but it had been Bully Hanson who had performed the execution. His overbearing presence in the courtroom had been just as deadly for Harvey Brewer as his sawed-off shotgun had been for those three boys in the dark dankness of the old curing barn.

Chapter Twenty-Seven

Surprisingly enough, the first witness for the defense the next morning was Otis Schofield.

"Do you own a drinking establishment outside of Coleman, Mr. Schofield?"

"Yeah," replied Otis. "The Bloody Bucket across the tracks on Willow Spring Road." The saloon owner was massive, close to three hundred pounds. He had gone to great pains to make himself as presentable as possible. He wore a crisp white shirt buttoned at the neck and cuffs, concealing the bristly mat of chest hair and the bulging forearms with their bawdy tattoos. He had his hair slicked back and his beard trimmed, but there was still the puffy redness of his face and the bloodshot eyes —both signs of a raging hangover. Obviously, Schofield was a heavy drinker and practiced what he preached.

"Did you have a conversation with James Hanson around the second week of May?"

"May the twelfth, I believe it was," Schofield agreed. "He told me he and Claude Darnell were going up to Kentucky for the summer. Said his uncle Zeke needed some help with his crops and they were gonna go to Muhlenberg County and give the old man a hand."

"Are you absolutely sure that this conversation took place on the twelfth?"

"I'm pretty sure." Schofield glanced over at Bully and was relieved to see a pleased look on the big man's face. "I remember it was my bartender's birthday and Bully bought him a shot of rye whiskey to celebrate. Yeah, it was the twelfth."

An expression of budding confidence bloomed on the face of

Lawyer Branchworth. "Well, then, that casts a new light on the situation. If both James Hanson and Claude Darnell left Bedloe County on the twelfth of May and arrived in Kentucky shortly thereafter, then they certainly could not have been responsible for the heinous slayings of three teenaged boys, which, according to Dr. Hubbard himself, were committed on or around the date of May twenty-ninth. Does that sound like a logical assumption to you, Mr. Schofield?"

"Yes sir, it certainly does." The honky-tonk owner seemed almost too eager in his answer. He grinned with tobacco-stained teeth, glad to have done a good turn for his friend Bully.

After Branchworth had finished, the prosecution had its chance to cross-examine. Schofield detected a trace of devilishness in Willard Shaw's good-natured smile. It made him uneasy, for he knew the man was up to no good.

"Mr. Schofield did the three young men—C.J. Potts, Johnny Biggs, and Billy Longcreek —enter your establishment on the night of May the twenty-ninth?"

"I don't know if that was the exact date or not, but, yes, they came into my place one night in May."

"Did they come there to buy liquor?"

"I reckon. They said they were off to the CCC camps, and that Potts boy, he wanted to buy his buddies a beer."

"Did you sell them the beer?"

A nasty grin flickered across the man's bearded face. "Well, I sorta played a little joke on them. C.J. came strutting in there like he owned the joint, so I figured to take some of the wind outta his sails. I gave him one of my special brews."

"Special brews?"

"Yeah." Schofield grinned maliciously. "A mug full of horse piss."

The prosecutor looked disgusted. "Horse urine? That seems like quite a sick prank to pull on someone to me."

Otis shrugged. "The guys down at the bar sure seemed to think it was funny." That drew a few stray chuckles from Schofield's cronies in the back row.

Willard Shaw continued his questioning. "Exactly how did C. J. Potts react to such a crude joke?"

"He got mad as hell. Tried to come over the bar at me," recalled the roadhouse proprietor. "I had to ward him off with a baseball bat. His buddies dragged him outta there. If they hadn't, he'd have gotten himself hurt."

"And that was the last you ever saw of C.J. Potts?"

"Yeah, I reckon so."

The prosecuting attorney regarded him coldly. "The way I gather it, that was the last time anyone saw C.J. Potts or any of the other boys."

"Hey, it was only a joke, okay?" stammered Otis Schofield, attempting to defend himself from the lawyer's insinuations. "I just wanted teach the boy not to act like he owned the whole damned town, like his old man does."

"Practical jokes backfire sometimes," Shaw told him. "Sometimes they can lead to misunderstanding and hard feelings . . . sometimes to violence. That has happened more than a few times at the Bloody Bucket, has it not, Mr. Schofield?"

The saloon owner felt his gut grow tight with apprehension. "Just what are you trying to say, fella?"

"What I am saying is that perhaps you should be sitting over there at that table with Hanson and Darnell."

Otis gaped. All the blood drained from his face, and his temples drummed with the rapid course of his pulse. "Now, wait just a minute—" he gulped.

But abruptly, the prosecutor withdrew. "No further questions, Your Honor." He returned to his seat, a look of deep satisfaction on his face. He had done what he had set out to do: make Otis Schofield sweat a little for the night of terror inflicted on poor Harvey Brewer. He did not want him feeling that he had gotten away, unscathed, with his drunken harassment of the elderly farmer.

"You may step down, Mr. Schofield."

The owner of the Bloody Bucket took the judge's words as a narrow escape in itself, and he nearly ran down the center aisle for the back door. His wild bunch followed, as bewildered by the turn of events as he was. None of them returned for the conclusion of the proceedings that day.

A.J. Branchworth's final witness was a man whom no one in Bedloe County had any knowledge of. He was a stern man with eyes as cold and gray as granite, his lower face obscured by a full beard of scraggly white whiskers. He sat upon the stand contemptuously, like a man who had more important things to do with his precious time.

"Would you please tell the court your name, sir."

The old man glared at the crowd in the spacious room. "Ezekiel Hanson."

"And what relation are you to the defendant, James Hanson?"

"I'm his uncle."

Lawyer Branchworth studied a yellow legal pad for a moment, more for dramatic effect than anything else, then continued. "Where do you live, Mr. Hanson, and what do you do for a living?"

"I live in Muhlenberg County, Kentucky, sir," declared the bearded man. "As for my livelihood, I am a farmer."

"Did both James Hanson and Claude Darnell come to your residence about the middle of May? And, if so, why?"

"Yes, they showed up at my place," said Zeke Hanson. "I'd talked to Bully a few months earlier, told him I'd need a hand with my crops come summertime. Both Bully and his friend Claude were right considerate, offered to come up and help me out for room and board."

"So, from the date of May the fourteenth till roughly the last of September, both defendants were in Kentucky, helping you on your farm."

"They were indeed."

A.J. Branchworth nodded, satisfied with his witness's testimony. "Your turn, Mr. Shaw."

Willard Shaw removed his reading glasses and laid them on the table. He approached the stand with a few sheets of official-looking papers in one hand. "You say you are a farmer, Mr. Hanson," the attorney countered. "What sort of crops did you plant this year?"

"Corn and beans, a little tobacco." Zeke regarded his interrogator with suspicion. "Why do you ask?"

"Oh, it just seems peculiar, is all," Shaw told him, holding up one of the typewritten sheets. "This is a copy of the deed to your property, Mr. Hanson. I had the Muhlenberg County clerk send it down to me, in anticipation of your testimony today. What this document tells me is that the hundred and fifty acre property you own has no pastureland to speak of. It mostly consists of woods and hills and hollows, doesn't it? Not exactly prime land for corn and tobacco."

"You calling me a liar?" growled Ezekiel Hanson.

"Oh, no. I couldn't do that in a court of law. I'm just presenting facts, that is all. Such as this criminal record sheet from the Kentucky Board of Correction."

"Objection, Your Honor!" called out Branchworth. "It is not my witness who is on trial here. His occupation and past history have nothing whatsoever to do with this case."

Judge Mullen would not be bullied however.

"No, but the credibility of this man's testimony does have a great bearing on the proceedings at hand. Objection overruled!"

The prosecutor continued his onslaught of damaging material. "You have quite a rap sheet here. Known as Ezekiel "Red-Dog" Hanson, you've made yourself quite a name as a moonshiner in western Kentucky. Three convictions during Prohibition, served a total of seven years in the state penitentiary for manufacturing and selling bootleg whiskey, transporting it across state lines, assaulting a revenue agent with intent to do bodily harm..."

"All right!" snapped Zeke Hanson. "Everyone gets the picture. No need to drag all my dirty laundry out into the open!"

"Then you do not deny the facts that I've just presented?" Shaw asked him. "You do not deny that you are not a farmer, but rather a known bootlegger in three Kentucky counties?"

Hanson said nothing. He just sat there, red-faced with fuming anger.

"No further questions."

On his way back to his table, Willard Shaw gave his opponent Branchworth a big grin of triumph. The defense lawyer pretended not to notice, but he did. Just as Branchworth had sabotaged the testimony of the prosecution's witnesses, Shaw had thrown a legal monkey wrench into the defense's game plan, destroying the credibility of both their witnesses.

"Payback is hell in the legal profession," Hamilton Shaw had always told his son. Willard agreed with his father's wisdom. But he only fought dirty when circumstances demanded it, like the chance of cold-blooded murderers being set free.

Chapter Twenty-Eight

At the end of every trial there is a time of waiting. Sometimes the period is brief, sometimes horrendously long. As the hands of the big wall clock neared two-thirty in the afternoon, the Bedloe County jury had been in the deliberation chamber for nearly three hours. It was a promising sign for both prosecution and defense alike, for it showed that the twelve men were going over the testimony carefully, making sure they came up with the right verdict, one that they would be able to live with for the rest of their lives.

The gallery was a mass of milling conversation and opinion. Children ran up and down the aisles, screaming and laughing, until their mothers made them stop their shenanigans. Some folks sat quietly during the wait, like the families of C.J., Johnny, and Billy. Lester Mullen and Sheriff White played checkers, trading moves across the broad oaken top of the judge's bench.

The attorneys, Willard Shaw and A.J. Branchworth, also sat silently, each one immersed in his own private thoughts. Each man experienced the strain of the past two days, feeling both mentally and physically exhausted and, yes, even spiritually so. Their final arguments had both been powerful; both had summed up the merits and inconsistencies of the testimony presented. But in the end, both men knew that only one factor would eventually determine the fates of Bully Hanson and Claude Darnell. That factor was the plain old, common horse sense of those twelve men in the jury box.

It was shortly after three o'clock when the bailiff led the twelve back into the courtroom. Judge Mullen quickly stashed the checkerboard beneath the bench and rapped his gavel, calling the court back to order.

"Gentlemen, have you reached a verdict?" he asked gravely.

"Yes, Your Honor," confirmed the jury foreman, Garret Gentry, who ran Gentry's Hardware & Farm Implement on Jefferson Street. "We find the defendants, James Hanson and Claude Darnell, guilty of three counts of murder in the first degree."

A tremendous rush of excitement overcame the spectators. A great relief seemed to spread throughout the courtroom, for the majority had figured the men to be guilty all along. However, no group was more relieved at the outcome than Clayburn Biggs and his clan. Maudie wept openly, thanking the good Lord for the justice bestowed on the ones who murdered her firstborn. Clay closed his eyes, mouthing a silent prayer of his own, devoid of tears, but choked with emotion nevertheless.

Judge Mullen allowed for the sudden outburst, then called for order. When some semblance of calm had returned, he centered his attention back to the jury. "Mr. Foreman, have you come to a decision as to the sentence for these two men?"

"Yes, sir, we have. We have voted the death penalty for both defendants."

More excited talk. More banging of the hardwood gavel.

Judge Mullen regarded the men at the defense table with his usual attitude of neutrality. "Please stand and accept your sentence." When the two had done so, the judge continued. "James Hanson and Claude Darnell, this court has found you both guilty of three counts of first degree murder. For these heinous and unforgivable crimes, you will receive the death penalty. You will be incarcerated in the state penitentiary in Nashville until January the first, the scheduled date of your execution. At twelve o'clock midnight you will be strapped into the electric chair and electrocuted until you are pronounced dead."

Claude slumped back into his chair, pale and trembling with a palsy of bad nerves, his eyes glazed in disbelief. Bully seemed to take it better, but not by much. His huge face grew beet-red with sudden rage, but he said nothing, made no outburst. He turned his eyes on the Biggs family and glared murderously at little Cindy. The red-haired child shrank from the man's awful hatred, glad that she would soon never have to lay eyes on either man again.

Lester Mullen thanked the jury for doing their civic duty, then adjourned that session of the Bedloe County Court.

Taylor White shook the prosecutor's hand in congratulation, then went over to help his deputies prepare Bully and Claude for custody. He clapped his own nickeled handcuffs over Bully's thick wrists. "You boys have got a nice long ride to the state pen. In fact, we're gonna make sure you get there tonight."

Hanson grinned hatefully. "To hell with you, fat boy," he growled over his shoulder.

The sheriff lifted upon the chain sharply, purposely digging the steel of the bracelets into the murderer's flesh. "Move it, you sonofabitch."

In the front pew, Clay wiped away his wife's tears with a calloused finger. "You all right, Maudie?"

She smiled up at him, then gave him a quick hug around the waist, something she rarely did in public. "I'm just happy, that's all. For a while I was afraid they were gonna go free."

"God was on our side all the way," he told her. "Maudie, why don't you take the young'uns on out to the truck. I wanna go out back and watch them take that trash to their just reward."

"Can I come with you, Pappy?"

Clay looked down at his youngest daughter. Cindy stared up at him with those soulful, hazel eyes — eyes that possessed the sweet innocence of a nine-year-old, yet also held an underlying maturity brought about by things that no adult should ever have to experience, let alone a child. He considered telling her no, but knew he did not have the right. In a way, she was just as much a part of this whole horrible event as was Bully Hanson or her brother Johnny. Perhaps even more so, in some disturbing way.

When they got to the rear door of the brick courthouse, it appeared as though a lot of people had the same idea as Clay. Dozens of citizens stood along the sidewalk, some spectators, some of them jurors. There were young boys who loitered in hopes of seeing two murderers being escorted to the cars that would take them to the "big house" in Nashville. Reporters from some of the state's biggest newspapers stood nearby, wearing PRESS cards in their hatbands and toting big flashbulb cameras.

There was small talk during the brief wait, concerning everything from who was the better lawyer to the mechanics of the electric chair. Clay and Cindy found a spot midway down the concrete sidewalk. The farmer shook hands with old acquaintances, then grew quiet. The girl leaned against her father's leg, surveying the growing crowd of onlookers. She picked out familiar faces, dismissing the ones strange to her. One in particular caught her attention and held it.

Ransom Potts stood down near the very end of the pathway. His three-piece suit of gray material hung off him in wrinkled folds. Above the wilted collar hung a slack and pallid face with sad, hound dog eyes. Cindy was intrigued by the great change in the banker's appearance. She remembered him as a huge, foreboding man, a man frightening in the power he had over other people's lives. She recalled playing over at Elsa Collins' house two summers ago, when Potts came rolling up in that big tan LaSalle of his. There had been some heated talk on the front porch with Elsa's parents, the flash of paper with small print. Then havoc broke out. Mrs. Collins began to cry, and her husband followed Potts to the car, cussing him for all he was worth. But the banker had simply ignored the man as if he weren't even there. Potts had climbed calmly into his auto, a smug little grin on his face. The Collins had moved to Georgia only a few days afterward, the bank having foreclosed on the property that Mr. Collins had owned for thirty years.

The Ransom Potts that Cindy had witnessed that distant June morning, the pompous miser with the life-shattering slip of paper, no longer existed. He had been swallowed up, digested, and then spit out by a devastating emotion known as grief. The death of his only son, C.J., had hit him incredibly hard. He now seemed like a shallow ghost, his hollow eyes glued to the steel door that led from the basement of the courthouse.

She watched as his pudgy hand shifted in his jacket pocket, as if getting a firmer hold on some object. It hit her then. There was a rush of motion before Cindy's confused eyes, much like the dizzying rides they had at the county fair. Suddenly, she was looking at Potts from a different perspective. It was as if she were watching from overhead, perhaps sitting on the limb of that big oak nearby. With a strange mixture of fascination and horror, she once again became the lone spectator of sights and sensations that no normal person could experience.

The sheriff was there, escorting Bully and Claude down the sidewalk. Flashbulbs popped; catcalls followed the convicted felons on their brief walk to the patrol cars. Then, when they neared Ransom Potts, there was an abrupt flurry of movement. The banker fumbled with something in his pocket. He withdrew his hand. It held a gun, one of those little snub-nosed revolvers, barking flame and belching smoke. Claude Darnell dropped in his tracks, a neat hole in his forehead. Bully turned to run and took two in the lower back. But Potts did not stop there. Like some lunatic out of control, he continued firing. A bullet found the massive belly of Sheriff White. Blood spurted down the front of the lawman's khaki shirt. Then the gun was lifted, away from the three blood-splattered men. The muzzle was directed toward the dispersing crowd. It shifted from a mortified reporter, to Amos Foster the school janitor, and then settled on a lone, lanky tobacco farmer in a crisp Sunday suit.

Her father!

Then the awful vision was gone. She stood where she had before, The sidewalk was bare except for a few dead leaves and cigarette butts. The courthouse door was still closed and locked. Trembling, she slumped against her father's leg.

Clay noticed her sudden agitation. Crouching, he turned her to him, concern on his lean face. "Cindy . . . is something wrong?"

It took her a moment before she could answer. "It's Mr. Potts . . . he has a gun."

Clay surveyed the gathering until he spotted Potts on the far side of the walkway. "Come on, Cindy." He took the girl's hand and headed in that direction.

A few minutes later, the heavy door opened. Out stepped Claude and Bully, followed by the sheriff and his deputies. Reporters readied their cameras, while towheaded boys squeezed through to get a look-see. And Ransom Potts stood waiting, his heart pounding wildly, his hand sunk deep into his side pocket.

"You don't wanna do that, Ransom." It was Clayburn Biggs' baritone voice in his ear. The banker struggled to pull the gun from his pocket, but the farmer's strong hand held his wrist secure.

"What the hell are you doing?" he huffed. "Let go of me this instant!"

"I won't let you do it." Clay's voice was calm, almost soothing. "I don't like you one damned bit, but I won't let you throw your life away. Bully and Claude, they've already been sentenced to death. If you do this, you'll only be destroying yourself."

But they killed my son! he wanted to plead. *They murdered my Clarence ... my poor, poor boy!* But his stubborn pride would not allow him to show such weakness. "I don't know what you're talking about!" he spat, then stormed off across the courtyard, his fancy French loafers swishing through the dead leaves.

With a sigh of relief, Clay ruffled his daughter's fiery red hair. "Thanks a lot, pumpkin." He smiled gratefully.

Hard soles clacked on concrete as the men advanced down the sidewalk. Insults were hurled at the two felons. A boy with a slingshot sent a shard of rock at Claude with dead-eye accuracy, cracking him across the shin. The gawky man howled with pain, but soon forgot his agony as they neared the sedans that would carry them to the state pen.

Then, abruptly, there was Bully, halting long enough to confront Clay, face to face. "I'm gonna kill you, farmer. Somehow, I'll get out and then you're all dead meat!" The murderer displayed an extra evil grin for Cindy. "Especially you, little bitch!"

Cindy shrank back from the big man, but her father quelled her fears, his hand settling comfortingly on her narrow shoulder. "Don't pay him any mind, darling. He's finished."

Onward the two men were herded, like cattle driven to the slaughter. Pushing them into the backseat of separate cars, Taylor White and his men waved to the crowd gathered there. "I'll be over to the store for some hot coffee and a moon pie when I get back," the sheriff called to Woody Sadler as he climbed into a car himself.

"And it'll be on the house, too," the storekeeper promised. The citizens of Coleman complimented his generosity and knew that the lawman deserved it. Some folks had had their doubts about Taylor White in the past months, but now that uncertainty was forgotten.

"Let's go home, pumpkin," Clay said.

As they walked toward the blue Ford pickup, Willard Shaw met them in the parking lot. He stood there as if he had been waiting for them. Clay shook the lawyer's hand vigorously. "I want to thank you for all you've done. You did a fine job of seeing justice done."

The attorney smiled that wry grin of his. "My only regret in this case was that I never got to know Johnny. From all I gathered, he was a talented boy."

"He would've liked you, too, Mr. Shaw. You remind me of him in a lot of ways."

Willard shifted his satchel to his left hand and dug into his vest pocket for his keys. "Come on over to the car for a moment. I've got something for you."

Clay and Cindy followed the man to a black Chevrolet. Shaw fiddled with the lock to his trunk for a moment, then withdrew an object and handed it to the lean farmer. "Here, I wanted you to have this."

Clay could not believe his eyes. It was Johnny's flat-top guitar, the one he had last seen hanging in the window of a Nashville pawn shop. He took the musical instrument in his work-hardened hands, running his fingers gently along the smooth varnished surfaces of the contoured wood. He looked at the big city lawyer with wonder. "You shouldn't have done this."

"I had to," Willard Shaw told him flatly. "It really griped me knowing your boy's pride and joy was gathering dust in some sleazy hock shop downtown. I ran over there yesterday evening and made a deal with the slob who owns the place."

"But, I can't pay you for this," Clay admitted shamefully. "I barely have enough to feed my family, let alone fifteen dollars for the guitar."

"Don't give it a second thought," Willard assured him. "I

jewed the guy down to five bucks. Besides, I really wanted you to have it. You already lost your son. At least you'll have this as a keepsake."

Clay felt all choked up. "Much obliged," he said. Again they shook hands, and then Clay and his daughter started for the truck.

Halfway there, the red-haired child stared up at her father and saw the glint of tears in his eyes. "Pappy, are you crying?" she asked.

"Yes, pumpkin." He nodded, unashamed of the emotion. He squeezed her hand tightly, reassuringly. "But it's all right. Everything's all right now."

Chapter Twenty-Nine

Ransom Potts entered the Coleman Citizens Bank, walked through the lobby, and headed straight for his office. The tellers who stood idly at their stations suddenly began to shuffle papers and turn their attention elsewhere; anything to give the impression of being busy. But the bank president did not give his employees a second thought. He seemed to have much more somber matters on his mind.

Rose Baxter, the head cashier, approached him before he reached the frosted glass door of the rear office. She spoke to him reluctantly, but knew that someone should mention the result of that day's trial. Rose had worked for Potts for nearly thirty years and had grown to truly loathe the man and his arrogance. But ever since his son had died in such a grisly fashion, she had almost found herself pitying her penny-pinching boss. C.J.'s death had hit the man hard, devastating him physically and softening his snobbish attitude. It just went to show that the banker was not quite as heartless as everyone thought.

"We heard about the verdict, Mr. Potts," said Rose. "We would all just like to say how glad we are that things turned out for the best."

Ransom regarded her absently and nodded, his eyes glassy and distant. "Thank you, Mrs. Baxter." He took a couple of steps, then stopped. "Oh, you and the others may have the rest of the day off. Just lock up after you leave. I'll be in my office until late."

The cashier couldn't believe her ears. Ransom Potts giving time off? She thought she would never see the day. "Thank you, sir," she blurted, then went to inform the others before he could change his mind.

Ransom went into his cramped office, shutting the door behind him. He plopped down into a great leather chair. His wait was brief, and soon, he heard Mrs. Baxter locking the front door. The banker sat motionless for a few minutes more, then reached into the bottom drawer of his desk. He withdrew a crystal decanter of bourbon and a shot glass.

The sun hung high in the cloudless Tennessee sky and then gradually dropped toward the western horizon. The brilliance of a glowing sunset seeped through the slats of the venetian blinds, splashing an eerie crimson hue across his desktop. The bottle was half empty now. He poured himself another shot and sipped it slowly. The liquor no longer burned his innards. He felt nothing in the way of physical sensation anymore. Only the awful, searing pangs of mental anguish remained.

His bloodshot eyes stared straight ahead, past the leather desk blotter and the engraved box of Cuban cigars. They focused on one single point of interest, a framed photograph of a cocky young man in a tweed jacket and knickers, his hair slick with pomade, his face clean-shaven, void of the scraggly, pencil-thin mustache the boy had grown the previous winter.

Ransom took another swallow of the amber liquor. He reached for the golden frame, gripping it so intensely that the scalloped edges dug into his fatty palms. It had been the only photograph that C.J. had ever agreed to sit still for, the only lingering image of a lost son. The banker's small eyes grew shiny as he continued to stare, studying each line, the texture of his clothing, the jaunty set of his face. Ransom Potts had contemplated the photo many times since C.J.'s tragic death, perhaps to make up for all the attention he had neglected to show over the last eighteen years.

In a fit of despair, the businessman slammed the frame down on his desktop with such force that the glass shattered. Bitterly, he poured himself another drink. He could not figure it out. He had given the boy everything money could buy, had provided him with opportunities that any other young man would have jumped at. But would he listen to his old man? No, he only shunned his advice, going out of his way to show contempt for his father. Running off with that hayseed trash and getting himself killed! That was what you got for associating with bad company like that.

But who was he to determine exactly who was bad company or not? After all, he himself was not exactly the most loved and respected of Coleman's citizens. No wonder C.J. had grown up hating him. He had forever been surrounded by greed, prejudice, and utter disdain for those his father did business with. C.J.'s world had been assaulted by talk of foreclosure, tax evasion, and illegal banking practices since birth. Had Ransom ever taken his boy to a baseball game or read him a bedtime story when he was little? Had he ever taken the time or inclination to even tell his son that he loved him?

Tears came swiftly and without warning. With a shuddering sigh, Ransom took the gun from his jacket pocket. It was a snub-nosed .38, nickel plated with grips of polished ivory. *I should have shot those bastards,* he thought. *I should have shot someone. Bully, Claude, even that meddling Clayburn Biggs! I should have shot—who? Who should I have really killed?*

The last rays of sunlight glinted off the empty liquor bottle, and he saw his haggard, pathetic image reflected in the chiseled glass. He began to laugh and cry at the same time. *I see it now. The answer is so very simple. So damned simple to see!*

The following morning Rose Baxter would find her boss slumped over his desk, the gun in his hand and the ugly wound of a .38 caliber slug in his right temple.

Part Four

Deadly Winter

Chapter Thirty

Percy Evans sat by the window of his motel office in the late of the evening. He supped on a modest meal of white beans and cornbread, his attention focused on the steady drift of virgin snow. It sifted down from the heavens in a swirling, frantic flurry. Snowflakes the size of goose down lit on the frigid ground and froze instantly, creating huge drifts that measured a foot deep in some spots.

Halfway into December and it's starting already, thought Percy glumly, for his rheumatoid arthritis scorned the cold and complained feistily with pain. *Why, I can hardly see past the mailbox out yonder! Dadblamed winter sure is getting off to a dreadful start!*

Most everyone in Tennessee had voiced similar opinions of the weather in the past twenty-four hours, for it was the heaviest snowfall that had hit the state so early in December since 1889. Usually the really rough weather held off until January or February at the latest, but not this year. The bitter frost of late November had served as a subtle omen of the brutal season to come.

Percy's radio became so hindered by static that he finally turned it off. He continued to sit there in silence, eating his supper and watching the darkness set in for the night as it cast an eerie blue sheen upon the crust of pure white snow. For a while all he could hear was the minute ticking of ice crystals collecting on the tin roof of his cabin. Then the faint roaring of an engine reached his ears, muffled at first, then growing in depth and resonance as the automobile churned its way up the snow-clogged highway.

The motel owner stepped to the window as the blinding flash of headlights arched across the small parking area out front. Percy nodded in approval as a sedan marked with the insignia of the Tennessee State Troopers pulled up and two men waded through the drifts for the office. At least he would make a little cash that night, if nothing else became of it. The five cabins that Evans owned were empty now. His busy season was summer, when travelers took the long route from Nashville to Memphis. Oh, there were a few cabins occupied during hunting season, when those city fellows came down hoping to bag a deer or two, but between December and April, business at the roadside motel was few and far between.

A draft of unbearably cold air slapped his wrinkled face as he held the door open in cheerful welcome. "Come on in, boys, and warm yourselves by the stove. Ain't fit weather for man or beast out there tonight."

The two men, clad in long overcoats and hard-billed caps bearing brass badges, accepted his hospitality without reply. They tracked slush across the hardwood floor and stood, shivering, before the cast-iron woodburner. As they passed cold-numbed hands over the comforting warmth, Percy Evans appraised the two officers. One was a big, stocky fellow, while the other was whipcord lean. He could not see their faces clearly. The troopers had their collars pulled up and their hat brims down against the bitter bite of the storm.

"Cold enough for you gentlemen?" he ventured in a chipper tone of voice.

The big one turned and regarded him with humorless eyes. "Yeah. Cold as a witch's tit."

Percy didn't know whether he should laugh or not, so he dispensed with formalities and came right down to business. "I reckon you fellas want to wait out this storm for the night. I usually charge a dollar a person, but you being officers of the law and all, I'll knock it down to seventy-five cents a head. That includes fresh linen, hot water, and there's a hot plate, too. All the conveniences of home, wouldn't you say?"

The trooper stared at Percy wearily, then dug into his pocket. He came out with a crumpled dollar bill and a Franklin fifty-cent piece and tossed them on the old man's supper table. "Which one?"

Percy handed him a key from off a hook on the wall. "Cabin Two. Checkout time is eight o'clock tomorrow morn . . . but if you'd like to sleep longer, I won't charge you extra."

"We ain't figuring to stay that long," piped the thinner of the two. His face was gaunt and strangely pale in the shadows of his collar. "Just gonna get a couple hours' shut-eye, then be on our way."

"Oh, I see."

The pair reached the door and stood there for a moment, letting frigid air and snow blow inside. "You got any tools around here we could borrow?" asked the big fellow.

"There's a tool shed out back, officer," volunteered the old man. "Ain't locked. Y'all just help yourselves to anything you need in there."

Cold eyes raked Percy. "Much obliged."

Then they were gone, the door slamming loudly behind them. Percy shuddered in the chill that now occupied the small room. Hesitantly, he walked to the window and watched as they went back to the patrol car. Percy's heart skipped a beat when the big fellow reached into the backseat and withdrew a pump shotgun, a Winchester Model 97 from the looks of it. After delivering a withering glare toward the office, the two shuffled off toward the tool shed around back. Absently, Percy locked his door and immediately felt foolish. *What the hell are you getting so jittery about?* he lambasted himself irritably. *They're officers of the law, state troopers. They mean you no harm.*

Angry at his underlying suspicions, Percy went back to his supper of beans and cornbread. Both dishes were cold, so he bitterly pushed them aside. His appetite seemed to have been dampened considerably by the disturbing twilight visit.

"Hold that door open," said the hefty police officer. The smaller man obeyed. As his partner rummaged through the clutter of rusted tools and accumulated junk, he watched in growing agitation, knowing what he was looking for and for exactly what purpose. He trembled, not from the cold, but from sheer nervousness.

"Found it," roared the burly man with a grin of triumph. He held a hacksaw. Its frame was speckled with the rust of neglect, but its blade was clean and missing only a few teeth.

As he tossed more clutter aside, another grin replaced the previous one, a grin brimming with cruelty and, yes, even bloodlust. He held an object out to his compatriot. "Here, you'd best hang on to this. You might need it." He chuckled deep in his throat, as if relishing the lurid humor of some obscene joke.

The skinny trooper could only gawk at the object. It was a hatchet. Its short handle was turned of seasoned hickory, its heavy, edged blade forged from a wedge of thick steel. "I don't want it," he gulped in little more than a whisper. He vividly recalled what had happened the last time he had held one of those things in his hand, and he quaked at the very thought.

"I said take it!" the other grated angrily. "You're sure as hell gonna need it."

Dumbly, more out of fear than anything else, he accepted the hand axe. He quickly slipped it into his coat pocket, where he would not have to look at it or think of the violent implications that its possession might eventually lead to.

Hiking back through the snowdrifts, they locked themselves into the small cabin. After stoking the woodstove with dry kindling, they shed their coats and hats. Instead of the snappy, navy blue uniforms of state troopers, the two wore drab coveralls of faded gray, the standard issue clothing of the Tennessee penal system. The leader of the two, who had twin revolvers stuck in his waistband, immediately went to work on the twelve gauge. First sawing the flare of the walnut stock down to the wristpiece, he then hacked a good-sized piece from the barrel. With a smile of grim satisfaction, he worked the pump a couple of times, then deftly loaded the gun with double-aught shells.

The lanky fellow paced the floor nervously, wringing his hands and glancing at his partner worriedly. Finally, he gathered the courage to stand his ground. "I've got something to say to you, and I want you to hear me out. Okay?"

The big guy shrugged and sat down on the single bed, an amused expression on his broad face. "All right. Say what you want."

Surprised by his friend's graciousness, he went on. "I don't think we're going about this right. I mean, we're heading in the wrong direction. We oughta be heading up to Kentucky to your Uncle Zeke's place. Not back there! For heaven's sake, not back to Bedloe County!"

The stocky man with the blond crewcut approached him with a warm smile, his hand outstretched, as if offering reassurance. But suddenly, anger flashed in his small gray eyes, emerging swiftly and without warning. The hand of warm understanding lashed out savag It was the first time ely, knocking him off his feet. He stumbled backward and crashed into the far corner.

Gasping in shock, the slight fellow put a hand to his nose. His fingertips came away red with blood. IIt was the first time since they had begun traveling together that his buddy had ever struck him. All he could utter was a silent sob as he stared up in terror at the man he had chosen to follow blindly for the better part of a year.

"You ain't got no say in this, you idiot," said Bully Hanson, brandishing his sawed-off shotgun. "We got us a score to settle back in Coleman, so you'd best get your head straight. You chicken out on me and I swear I'll kill you where you stand."

And he meant it. Claude could sense the truth of Bully's deadly warning. He struggled to his feet and eyed the cabin door, before slumping on the bed in near exhaustion. They slept for the next two hours or, rather, Bully did. Claude lay there and listened to the other's snoring. He continued to stare at the door almost forlornly, weighing the possibility of slipping out unnoticed. All he wanted to do at that moment was to make it outside that cabin and run like hell. But he knew that his effort would be wasted. He would hear the click-clack of the shotgun action, and then Bully would put a round of buckshot squarely between his shoulder blades.

Claude Darnell forgot about escape for the time being and thought about Bully's vengeful plans. The horror returned in full force... the horror of what had taken place that rainy night last May. In a couple of hours, they would be back in Bedloe County and it would start all over again; the gunfire, the blood, and the screams of the dying. Lying there, he wondered if facing the electric chair could be any worse than facing the senseless bloodletting that he would participate in later on that dark, winter night.

Chapter Thirty-One

"I've been looking for you all over, Clayburn Biggs." Sheriff Taylor White closed the door of Woody's General Store and made his way carefully down the cluttered aisles of merchandise. A few power lines east of Coleman had snapped beneath the weight of snow and ice, plunging the rural community into darkness. A faint orange glow lit the rear of the store, the result of two kerosene lanterns and the fiery slats of the cast-iron stove door.

"Me and Josh, we've been out delivering firewood most of the day," Clay told him. He and his son sat around the potbellied stove, mugs of hot coffee cradled in their frostbitten hands. "Thought we'd stop by the store here and bum a cup off Woody before we headed home."

Woody poured the sheriff a mug full, and the lawman accepted it eagerly. He removed his hat, setting it on the front counter. His huge face was pinched with the pink flush of bitter cold, and his eyes were troubled. "Clay... I've got some bad news for you, and I don't know exactly how to say it."

"No need to hold out, Taylor," Clay assured him. "Tell me what's on your mind." The tobacco farmer felt a cold dread creep into him, the same sensation he had felt upon the news of Johnny's death. *What's happened now?* his mind raced. *Is it Maudie and the kids? Has something happened to them?* He prepared himself for the worst, but even then he was not entirely prepared for what the constable had to say next.

"Bully Hanson and Claude Darnell are on the loose. They're out there right now somewhere, running from the law."

Clay was stunned. "But how? I thought they were in custody

in Nashville. Their execution is only a couple of weeks from now. How'd they get out of the state pen?"

"They were never there," Sheriff White growled in disgust. He settled into a cane-backed chair, knowing he had a long explanation to give. "You see, due to overcrowding in the state penitentiary, they stuck Bully and Claude over in Brushy Mountain Prison for safekeeping. I reckon I should've told you that from the very start, but I didn't see any need to. Anyway, early this morning two state troopers took them into custody and started for Nashville. They were to deliver them to the state pen this evening to wait out their stay till the first of January. But something happened along the way. They never showed up.

"Nobody knew anything was wrong until a motorist spotted two men lying facedown in the snow an hour or so ago. It was the troopers. The way we figure it, the patrol car slid off the highway into a snow bank. The troopers were a couple of green rookies, shouldn't have ever been put in charge of men as desperate as convicted killers in the first place. Well, they got the bright idea of putting Bully and Claude to good use. They removed their cuffs and leg irons and had them out there pushing the car out of the ditch. You can imagine what happened next. Once they got the thing back on the road, Bully and Claude overpowered the two, killed them with their own weapons, and dumped their bodies in a gully. We figure those bastards have been on the road for nearly six hours now... a helluva head start in this nasty weather."

"Surely you don't think they'll head back to Bedloe County," Woody Sadler scoffed. "They'd be damned fools to come back here again."

The sheriff shrugged. "We gotta be ready for that possibility. Frankly, I think they're well over the Kentucky line by now. But you never know. Bully had such a hate in him, no telling what he might do."

Clay sat near the stove, quietly listening to the discussion between shopkeeper and lawman. The awful dread that had gripped him before still had a hold on him, even more now. He also experienced an underlying fear, one that strangely enough did not seem to be wholly his own. It was as if he were feeling someone else's mortal terror as well ... someone very close to him.

Abruptly, he was out of his chair, the coffee cup slipping from his grasp, spilling hot java upon the dusty floorboards. Josh stared at his father in sudden surprise, as did Sheriff White and Woody Sadler.

"What's the matter, Pappy?"

Clay grabbed his hat. His face was pale and rigid. "We've gotta get out to the house right fast. I got a bad feeling something's wrong there. Oh, Lord, I *know* that something's wrong!"

"I'll follow you over there," the Bedloe County constable offered. He had not seen his friend so shaken since that sweltering summer day in Brewer's curing barn.

"I'm coming, too." Woody took a shotgun from beneath the counter, checked its loads, and then extinguished the kerosene lamps.

They all moved into the frigid darkness as one; Clay and Josh headed for their Ford pickup, while the other two climbed into White's patrol car. The ominous clouds and their snowfall had moved eastward, leaving a clear, moonlit sky. Clayburn looked over his shoulder as he backed the truck out onto the snowy stretch of Old Newsome Road. His Parker ten gauge was hanging in a rack in the truck's rear window.

Lord, let it be a wild goose chase! he prayed beneath his breath. But deep down inside, he knew that it wasn't. He could still hear Bully's threat of vengeance, could still see the murderous fury in his cold, gray eyes.

By the light of a coal oil lamp, Maudie busied herself with her sewing. She glanced up every so often to eye the cuckoo clock in the outer hallway. The ornamental hands showed the time was well past eight o'clock. Worry creased her face, but she tried not to let it show. Polly was spending the night with one of her girlfriends in town, leaving her alone with Cindy and little Sam.

The children were leafing through the toy pages of the Sears & Roebuck catalogue, picking out which gifts they wished Santa to bring. It was all in fun, of course. Both youngsters knew that things were hard and that there would be no red fire engines or china dolls with frilly lace skirts beneath the tree that year. It hurt Maudie to know that she and Clay could not provide for the wants of their children like some of the folks in town could. The Depression had hit the rural families the hardest, and she knew that some parents would purposely tell their children that Santa was not coming that year, so as not to get their hopes up. Maudie and Clay would not do that, however. They refused to dash their youngsters' Christmas spirit with the harsh reality of poverty. Santa Claus would come that winter as he had the year before, even if only to leave a navel orange and a peppermint stick in each child's stocking.

The veil of uneasiness passed over the woman again like a tangible shadow. She laid her sewing aside on the kitchen table and sat in the glow of the lamp. It was true that Clayburn and Josh had promised to be back home in time for supper, and it was more than two hours past, but she knew that was not what pressed on her mind so heavily. She had felt a strange sensation of foreboding all day, and she had not been the only one either. Cynthia Ann had shown signs of anxiety since awakening that morning. Saying nothing, she had simply stared at the sweeping blanket of snow as it cascaded silently earthward. Maudie had questioned the girl once, asking if there was anything wrong. "I don't know, Mama," the nine-year-old had said quietly. "I don't know yet."

Maudie was getting up from her chair when the rumble of an engine echoed down the road. It grew louder, then sputtered into silence as it stopped out in front of the house. Doors slammed, accompanied by the faint crunch of fresh snow being trodden underfoot.

"It's Pappy and Josh!" piped four-year-old Sam. He jumped from his chair and started for the front door. Maudie grabbed him by the arm, pulling the boy to her before he could reach the hallway.

Cindy also knew that something was wrong. She calmly closed the catalogue and turned the wick of the lamp until the room grew dark. The three waited there in pitch blackness, their labored breathing the only sounds to be heard. That and the steady click of the hall clock's pendulum swinging to and fro.

For a long moment only frigid silence encircled the little farmhouse. Then heavy footfalls sounded on the front porch. They clumped across the breadth of the boarded floor, slowly and purposefully. They were the footsteps of two men, but not the ones of their loved ones. Maudie had listened to Clay's footsteps upon the floor for twenty years, and that was long enough to determine that these sounds belonged to strangers.

A heavy rapping came upon the front door. It rattled the very door in its frame, such was the force of the man's knocking. Maudie backed toward the rear door of the kitchen, the one that led to the enclosed back porch and the yard beyond. Sam accompanied her easily, but Cindy stood frozen to the spot. A great shudder of realization shook her thin body like a spasm, and she gasped in shock.

"I know, Mama," she whispered softly. "I know who it is now."

The glass pane of the front door exploded inward as the caller's impatience reached its limit. A gloved hand groped over the jagged sash, locating the skeleton key in the lock. The door swung open with the creak of unoiled hinges. Moonlight flooded the narrow hallway, revealing two dark forms in the garb of policemen. But there was no one there to witness their abrupt entrance. The house was empty.

Maudie and the children moved sluggishly through the heavy snow, twenty-degree weather stinging their exposed skin, cutting through their thin clothing as if they wore nothing. The woman started for the rear of the house, toward the double doors that led down into the root cellar, but Cindy tugged at her hand, stopping her. "That's one of the first places they'll look," she whispered, then led the way across the snowy yard in the direction of the smokehouse.

They could hear the men going through the house, turning things over, searching for frightened souls cowering in the dark. Then the shooting began. Windows winked with the thundering flash of lightning as a shotgun fired a half-dozen times. Buckshot pelted blindly through darkened rooms, rupturing glass panes and tearing faded wallpaper.

But no blood was drawn by the angry assault; no painful screams were uttered.

At least not yet.

"They must be outside," one muttered. The two stalkers stepped out into the backyard, their eyes searching for signs in the moonlit snow. The skinny one turned toward the door of the cellar. However, the big man was cleverer in his tracking. Spotting the profusion of deep tracks leading toward the grey-wood smokehouse, he laughed loudly. "This is gonna be like shooting quail," Bully said. He dug shells from his coat pocket and began to reload.

"They're coming for us, Mama," Cindy gasped, her breath escaping in small white clouds. "We've gotta get away."

"Where to?" her mother asked. Her voice seemed distant and without emotion. "We've no place to run to. They're gonna kill us, baby. Just like they killed your brother."

"No!" said Cindy. "It won't be that way. Not if we run. We've gotta get to the woods. Do you hear me, Mama?"

"Yes," Maudie answered. "To the woods." They all three left the rear of the old shack and quickly descended into the wooded hollow. They slid down the steep slope, skirting the leafless trees that lined Green Creek.

When they reached the frozen channel of the small branch, they paused and listened. A great fit of growling and barking erupted from near the henhouse. The protective attack of the family's bluetick hound ended in the deafening boom of a shot-gun blast.

"Old Tippy!" cried Sam, tears rolling down his face. "They got Old Tippy!"

Crossing the creek at its narrowest point, they moved onward. "Where are we going, Cindy?" Maudie asked several times. Receiving no answer, she and the boy followed nevertheless.

Cynthia Ann trudged onward through the snow, silently contemplating the murderous nature of the men who hunted them. There was only one place to run to now. And, although Cindy had vowed never to set foot there again, she somehow had known all along that the killing must end where it had first begun.

Chapter Thirty-Two

Clay pulled his truck into the driveway, then doused the headlights. Sheriff White braked to a halt close behind. As they left their vehicles, they paused to study the dark sedan parked at the edge of the road. The constable eyed the license plate in the glow of his flashlight. "Yep, it's that state patrol car, all right."

"Damn!" grated the farmer. He looked toward the house. From where he stood by the mailbox, he could clearly see that the front door stood open, the glass of the pane shattered. "We're too late," he groaned hopelessly. The shotgun sagged heavily in his trembling hands as he proceeded toward the porch with caution.

"Be careful now, Clay," warned the sheriff, starting around the side of the front porch. He held the big flashlight in one hand, his service revolver cocked and ready in the other. "I'll take the back way."

Expecting the worst, Clayburn mounted the low porch and ducked through the open door. The muzzles of the old Parker probed the darkness ahead. He stood there for a moment in the hallway vestibule, letting his eyes grow accustomed to the murky shadows. He could see the moonlit windows of the parlor and his bedroom from where he stood. The glass of the panes had been blown away, the curtains shredded by buckshot. The big chifforobe had been viciously overturned in some horrible fit of rage. The signs of violence chilled Clay to the bone, increasing the awful dread tenfold.

"Stay here for a moment," he told Josh and Woody. He felt his way through the darkened bedroom. Reaching the chest of drawers, Clay rooted through his underwear and found the .45 in the paper sack. Taylor had returned it to him shortly after the murder trial, and there it had remained, hidden and forgotten amid threadbare long johns and woolen socks.

He checked the magazine, then rejoined the others. The Parker was handed to Josh. "I trust you to do the right thing with this, if the need arises."

The boy was flattered by his father's confidence. "You can count on me, Pappy."

There came the crackle of broken glass beneath footsteps farther down the hallway, from where the kitchen was. Their attention and their guns were drawn to the source of the noise. Clay called out, "Who's there?"

"Just me," said Sheriff White. He appeared in the doorway, his gun held muzzle up. "There's something back here you oughta see."

Clay prepared himself for the shock of bad news. "Did you find . . . Maudie and the young'uns?"

"No, I haven't found anyone yet," replied the lawman. "But I have a good idea where they went."

The three joined Taylor on the back porch. A wide rut of deep footprints stretched across the snowy backyard, past the shadowy hulls of the weathered outbuildings. Clay spotted something and ran out to find the still body of Old Tippy. He laid a hand on the dog's bloody carcass and found it lukewarm to the touch. The hound had not been dead for very long. He stared at the profusion of tracks. They faded into the dense darkness of the heavy forest beyond.

"We'll never find 'em out in them woods," voiced Woody Sadler. He peered into the close-grown trees with a scowl on his face.

Suddenly, it came to Clay. He almost grinned at the sheer irony of it all. "I know where they're going," he told them. "Come on. We can get there faster if we drive. I just pray to the good Lord that we get there before they do."

Like frightened animals, Maudie and her children tore through the snow-laden thicket of the old Brewer place. The overgrowth of dead vines and blackberry bramble was like a maze, opening to dark passageways and just as swiftly choking away into dead-end blinds. But Cindy seemed to remember the best way through the thicket, and soon they had broken through, exhausted and breathing great plumes of frozen air.

Maudie caught her wind and stared in horror up at the towering structure of weathered wood before them. It was the old tobacco barn. It appeared even more menacing in the frozen twilight than it had on that hot July day last summer. "I can't go in there, Cindy," she said. "Not in there of all places!"

"We have to, Mama." Cindy tugged on her mother's pudgy hand, but could not budge her. "Listen! They're coming for us."

The sounds of men crashing through the underbrush, cussing in anger, grew nearer with each passing moment.

"Hurry up, Mama!" pleaded the red-haired child. "We've gotta find some place to hide. We gotta go inside the barn!"

"But the door is locked and chained."

"I know a place we can get in," assured her daughter. Finally, Maudie consented and, lifting Sam in her arms, followed Cindy to the western wall of the curing barn. A loose board was swung aside on its nail, and they slipped easily inside.

At first only cold, murky darkness greeted them. But soon their vision adjusted. Narrow spears of moonlight shone through the cracks of the boarded walls, stitching across the earthen floor in zigzag patterns. They could make out the shallow trenches of dark charcoal, the ancient mule plow, and at the far end of the barn, the casket-shaped tool box that had once served as a makeshift tomb for three unfortunate souls.

Maudie was about to speak when they heard voices directly outside.

"We got 'em cornered now. Just as well. I like a good coon hunt, but this damned cold is getting to me." There was a brief hesitation, then Bully's voice sounded again, gruff with irritation. "Well, come on. What're you waiting for?"

Claude's voice was shaky, almost feeble in its reply. "If we're gonna do this, Bully, I don't wanna use this confounded axe again. It's too damned messy. At least give me one of them pistols you took off the state troopers."

Bully laughed mockingly. "Hell, you'd more than likely shoot your own foot off. Let me handle the firearms. You got what you need, so let's go in and do it. You hear me?"

If Claude made any reply, it was much too low for them to detect. There was the crunch of heavy boots in the snow, then the coarse rasping of wood against wood as the two men began to shoulder their way through the narrow opening.

"Over there!" hissed Cindy. They fled as quietly as possible toward the dense shadows at the far end of the barn. Crouching behind the tool chest, they waited. Maudie clamped her hand over Sammy's mouth, stifling the whimper of stark terror that nearly escaped from his lips.

The rustle of clothing sounded in pitch blackness, then the voices resumed. "They're over there."

"Where?"

"Behind the tool box." Bully's voice was almost joyous in its tone. "I can hear them breathing."

"How do you wanna do this?"

Bully thought for a second. "You take the flashlight and flush them out for me." The brittle click-clack of the shotgun pump rang throughout the barn with a crisp note of finality. "I'll be ready to do my part."

Reluctantly, Claude advanced toward the dark hump of the tool box. The beam of the battery-powered light cut a pale yellow swath into dense obscurity. His other hand clutched the hatchet tightly, ready to take a lethal swipe at anyone who started his way.

Cindy peered over the edge of the tool chest lid. She saw the weaving circle of light and the gawky scarecrow of a man behind it. She wanted nothing more than to do as her mother and little brother did, to cower tearfully in numbing fear and await horrible death, perhaps praying to the Lord for salvation at the final moment of life. But she knew that she could not. Cindy knew that she had to do something, had to stop them some way. She certainly had the power to, if only she had the chance to conjure it up in time.

You killed Johnny! Her mind suddenly bristled in white-hot anger. She could feel a strange sensation welling up inside her now, a hatred so great and unrelenting that it both amazed and frightened her. *You killed my brother Johnny and his friends and thought you could get away with it. Well, your murdering will end right here and now! I swear to God it will!*

She focused her influence on Claude. She did not even try for Bully, for she knew the brutish man was much too stubborn and strong of will to be fooled. But Darnell ... he was different. The lanky fellow with the oily hair and buckteeth was mentally unstable, weak in terms of the mind. His consciousness would be simple to manipulate, easy to twist toward any illusion she wished to conjure.

And the image she created that night was the most horrible one she herself could imagine.

Claude advanced on the tool box. He hefted the hatchet in his hand, ready to use it if necessary. "I can see em, Bully," he called over his shoulder. A dark form stirred behind the meager shelter of the chest.

"Good. Now flush 'em out." Bully's eyes gleamed cruelly in the sparse moonlight. *I'm gonna get that little redheaded bitch first. I'm gonna blow her freaking head off!*

Claude took a couple of steps, then stopped in mid-stride. The beam of the flashlight trembled as his body shuddered in a great spasm of uncontained horror. His eyes grew wide and glassy. His knobby throat gurgled in constriction, and he nearly fainted dead away at the sight of what he had figured was Maudie and her two children.

What rose from the chill darkness behind the oblong box was the lean frame of a young man; a lanky boy of perhaps eighteen, his drab clothing streaked and stained dark with fresh rivulets of blood. Claude tried to pull his gaze from the apparition, but he could not. He found himself staring straight into the brutalized face of violent death, a pale, blood-streaked half of a face, a youthful handsome face that had once winked at the pretty girls and smiled that wry, good-natured smile.

It was Johnny . . . and he was coming for him.

A low moan expelled from Claude, growing in volume and intensity. Soon he was backing away, screaming at the top of his lungs. The hatchet swung blindly from side to side, frantically attempting to ward off the horrid thing that shuffled sluggishly toward him.

"What the hell's wrong with you?" growled Bully from behind.

But, as far as Claude was concerned, his friend no longer existed. The only thing that filled his consciousness, the only point of concern that pressed his childlike mind, was the gory specter that advanced on him. At least he figured it to be a ghost. It looked so solid, so very real, that it might be able to reach out and grab him at any moment.

That was when he stopped in his tracks, but not by his own choice. Something had halted him, had taken hold of his left shoulder and physically ended his horrified retreat. He shuddered at the touch of something on his shoulder, the limp cold weight of something long-since dead. He struggled to break free from its hold, but he could not. Claude was frozen to the spot. With a sniveling whimper, he began to turn his head. His skinny neck swiveled in small jerking motions, his huge eyes craning downward, ever downward toward the awful thing on his shoulder. He did not want to, but he had to look. Something *made* him look.

It was a hand... a pale, almost skeletal hand, speckled with fresh droplets of blood and bits of throbbing tissue. Slowly, almost imperceptively, the gruesome appendage began to change. It began to decompose before his very eyes, rotting away, the outer tissue giving way to stringy sinew, the festering meat budding with the pulsating bodies of a hundred maggots. When the flesh had finally putrefied and slid away, only bones remained. Stark white bones clutched at his shoulder, the joints crackling, the fingers digging painfully into his collarbone, drawing warm red blood. His blood!

Claude Darnell let out a scream... the awful tortured screech of a banshee. With a sudden surge of strength, he pulled away from the skeleton's hold. Grasping the hickory handle of the hatchet in both hands, he whirled. There was no stopping him. He brought the axe around in a mighty swing, intent on bringing its heavy blade crashing down upon the horrendous wraith who held him, the dead who had somehow returned to life, searching for retribution for ghastly crimes committed there so many months ago.

But it was not Johnny who received the brunt of Claude's desperate blow.

The thunderous report of a twelve gauge rolled across the frozen countryside. Clay heard it as he turned off the main highway onto the Brewer property and his heart leaped into his throat. With a curse, he looked over at his teenaged son and gunned the engine of the old truck. "Hang on, Josh. We're going right through those barn doors!"

The Ford gathered speed on the icy pathway that led from the boarded house to the barn. Out of control, it hurled toward the double doors. Clay and Josh ducked as the pickup crashed through weathered lumber, snapping the rusty logging chain cleanly in half and knocking both doors from their hinges.

Once the truck's tires found a grip on the earthen floor, Clay slammed on his brakes. The vehicle lurched to a stop in the center of the cavernous structure. The farmer leaped from the cab, leveling the pistol in both hands. Josh followed suit. The double-barreled Parker swept the musky interior, both hammers cocked.

Taylor White and Woody Sadler came running, their own firearms drawn, prepared to gun down the escaped felons. "Freeze, you two!" growled the sheriff. But when he rounded the fender of Clay's truck, he gaped in sudden shock. He let the muzzle of his revolver droop, then absently returned it to his holster.

No one fired a single shot. It was far too late for that. The twin lamps of the truck revealed a scene so unexpected that the four could only stare in bewilderment. It was the last thing any of them would have expected to find in the empty confines of the old barn.

Claude Darnell and Bully Hanson lay prone on the cold earthen floor. Both were dead. The ways of their demise were ghoulishly violent. Claude had nearly been cut in half by a shotgun blast. His midsection glistened where a huge, ugly wound replaced his abdomen. Chewed entrails and the stark white column of Claude's fractured spine could be seen, and they all looked away.

They then focused their attention on the other man. Bully Hanson had taken the full force of Claude's frantic swing through the top of his head. The big man's skull had been split open from bristled crewcut clear down to the bridge of his nose. Bully's eyes stared through a gory curtain of blood. They held not a look of puzzlement, but an expression of panicked realization. Perhaps the evil murderer had known what was taking place in that final moment when he grabbed Claude roughly by the shoulder. Perhaps he had seen the madness in his partner's eyes that fleeting second the hatchet had descended and had known precisely who was responsible for Claude's fit of terror. As the sharpened blade had crashed through his skull, his fingers had jerked spasmodically on the shotgun's trigger, thus ending the lives of both men in an instant of violent retribution.

Clayburn Biggs tucked the .45 in his belt and started past the ugly tangle of bodies. He walked toward the tool chest, toward his family who stood there tearfully. A great surge of relief filled him. Soon he was running. He embraced them, never wanting to let go. After the outpouring of emotion had settled, Clay turned to Cindy, who stood apart from the others.

"Are you all right, pumpkin?" Clay asked gently. The girl did not answer. She just stared, frightened and confused, at the bloodstained bodies of the men who had meant to do them harm. The child trembled uncontrollably, her hazel eyes suddenly brimming with tears.

Wrapping his coat around her shivering form, Clay pulled his daughter close. The tears came freely, as well as the muffled cries of her remorse. "I'm sorry, Pappy! I didn't want to do it . . . but I had to. They would have killed us!"

"I know, baby," her father assured tenderly. "You did the only thing you could have done. Everything's all right now. You're safe."

Clay lifted his daughter into his arms and started for the truck, Maudie and Sam following silently. He halted before the Bedloe County sheriff, who still stood over the two bodies, not knowing exactly what to think. Clay looked Taylor White square in the eyes. "They killed each other, right?"

Both Taylor and Woody exchanged knowing glances. They looked at the victims of the double homicide, then eyed the sobbing child in Clay's arms. They decided to do the right thing, the decent thing, for if they had voiced their true suspicions beyond the drafty confines of that old barn, no one would have believed their story anyway.

"Certainly they killed each other," agreed the constable. "There's no two ways about it."

"They did themselves in, all right," echoed the storekeeper.

Silently, the two men watched as the Biggs family began to climb into the blue pickup truck and, with a clashing of gears, leave the horrid place. They stared into the night long after the truck's lights had faded. The grisly murder of a woman and her two children could have very well taken place that night, but the horrible evil had been thwarted. Something had turned killer against killer in the frigid shelter of the old tobacco barn. And, although it was difficult for either man to swallow, they knew exactly what had served as the catalyst.

The fatal weapon had been the simple mind of a child… a mind blessed with a precious gift from God.

Epilogue

Cynthia Ann returned home in November of 1956, as she did every Thanksgiving.

Usually the reunion was a time of festivity, a remembrance of the rural heritage she had known as a child. At noon there would be a spread of country cooking laid out on the dinner table: turkey, dressing, corn on the cob, and hot pumpkin pie for dessert. Later on, after an evening of hearty conversation, they would all ride into town. The rapid-fire pace of backwoods bluegrass music would drift invitingly from the high school gymnasium, and soon the square dance would begin. The varnished boards of the basketball court would thrum with activity until midnight and, on some occasions, clear into the early hours of the morning.

But on that Thanksgiving Day, however, the air of celebration was missing, and for good reason.

Cindy was going home to visit her father, perhaps for the last time in her life.

Much had happened since those latter days of the Great Depression. Clayburn Biggs had never found the chance to buy back his precious tobacco land, but he had found steady work at Pike's lumber mill in neighboring Galbreth County. Shortly afterward, Clay was offered the position of foreman, which he eagerly accepted. The money was good, what with military contracts being so plentiful during the Second World War. He worked there up until a few years ago, when his health began to fail him.

Cindy was a beautiful young woman of twenty-nine. She still possessed the freckles, the fiery red hair, and the eyes of hazel green. She was happily married to Richard Garrison, a service station mechanic. They had a comfortable life: a mortgaged home in Nashville, a '56 Chevy, and two boys, Rick and Kenny, ages eight and six.

Stormy autumn clouds hung low across the Tennessee sky like mats of filthy cotton, and a chilly breeze ruffled the dry brown grass as the Garrison family mounted the creaky front porch of the old Biggs homestead. Cindy gave her husband a little smile, a nervous smile that smacked of an underlying dread. Richard squeezed her arm gently in reassurance. Herding the kids ahead of her, they opened the front door and entered the dimly lit hallway. "You boys be quiet now," she told them firmly. "Your Grandpa is resting in the next room."

At the sound of the door closing, Maudie appeared from the kitchen, wiping flour from her hands with a dishcloth. "I'm so glad you could make it," she said. Her sad eyes, heavy with bags of age and worry, settled lovingly on her daughter. Maudie was still the stout woman she had been twenty years ago, but the erosion of time had taken its toll. Deep lines and crow's feet marked her face, and her hair, pulled tightly into a bun, was snow white in hue.

"How are you doing, big sister?" Sam smiled from over his mother's shoulder. Her baby brother was now a strapping young man decked out in the khaki uniform of a Bedloe County deputy.

"Just fine, Sam. How do you like the new job so far?"

"Oh, I'm getting the hang of it," said her brother. "It's pretty tame compared to Korea, but that's the way I like it."

Standing there in the musky hallway, they were gripped by an awkward silence. Two of the Biggs clan were not present. Polly had married a lawyer and moved to California. Their brother Josh had caught a German bullet during the D-Day invasion and died on Normandy Beach.

"Come on into the kitchen, boys," Sam called to his nephews. "I've got a new card trick that'll knock your socks off."

"Come on, Daddy." Rick and Kenny tugged on their father's hands, pulling him toward the bright and cheery kitchen.

"Go ahead, Richard." Maudie smiled. "I've got a pot of coffee on the stove."

"Never could resist a cup of your java, Maudie." The handsome mechanic winked. Then he was dragged from view by his anxious sons.

Mother and daughter looked at each other, then embraced. They clung to one another for a long moment, then Cindy studied her mother's melancholy eyes. "How's Pappy doing?"

"He's worse," Maudie told her truthfully. "The coughing spells are getting more frequent, more violent. I've worried myself sick trying to get him to go to the hospital, but you know your daddy's opinion of hospitals." The woman rummaged through her apron pocket and brought out a clean handkerchief. She handed it to her daughter. "He told me he wanted to see you as soon as you got here."

Cindy took the cloth offered her and nodded grimly. After her mother had left her alone in the hallway, she lifted the floral handkerchief to her nose and mouth, then went in, closing the door behind her.

The room was dark and stuffy. It smelled of sickness and medicine, of stale sheets and mildewed wallpaper. She stood, there in the shadows until a ragged fit of coughing drew her attention to the far side of the room. Her father lay in the big four-poster bed that he and Maudie had shared for over forty years. Quietly, Cindy crossed the room, pressing the handkerchief to her lower face. She fished beneath the drapes of a side window for the drawstrings that would open them.

"Leave them closed," rasped a feeble voice, hoarse with phlegm. "The light hurts my eyes."

"All right, Pappy." Cindy pulled up her mother's rocking chair and sat close to the bedside.

Eventually, the coughing spell ran its course. Clay hacked thickly into his own handkerchief, expelling bloody spittle into its folds. "Help me sit up, pumpkin," he requested.

She did as he asked. It took little effort to move him and arrange two feather pillows to support his gaunt frame. It hurt Cindy to see her father that way. Tuberculosis had hit him unexpectedly and without prior warning, taking his body by storm. As the disease progressed, he had lost much weight and most of his iron gray hair. The skin of his face, wrinkled beyond his years, seemed transparent and yellowed like parchment paper. His eyes, which once blazed a piercing blue, were now bloodshot and sunken in shadow.

They merely sat there in silence for a while, neither one knowing what to say. Both knew that the power of words had lost its importance long ago. Both knew that there were other things, other means of communication, that made the art of verbal conversation seem lackluster and trivial in comparison.

Cindy waited, seeing in her father's eyes the wish that had become so familiar to her. He had asked it of her again and again, especially since his illness, but it was one that she could never bear to grant.

His eyes, muddled and cloudy, settled on her own. "Cindy," he finally said. "Cindy, I want to remember. I want to remember it *all*."

Cynthia Ann felt choked up inside. With all her heart she wanted to deny his simple request. But she knew she could not this time. The time for denying was past. Her father was dying, and she was obliged to fulfill his final wish, even if it caused them both considerable pain.

"All right, Pappy," she said, smiling sadly behind the cloth of her hanky. She took his huge hand, the palms still hard with calluses from decades of back-breaking labor, in her own. Cindy cleared her mind of the clutter of present day thoughts and images. When she had prepared herself emotionally, the memories began to come freely, memories of the year that had hit them all the hardest. Clayburn stiffened, then settled into his pillows, his ravaged face relaxing.

Together they remembered.

1936. The year of her recovery from typhoid, the year that Johnny had left on a sunny May morning and whose body had been revealed by an unwilling act of hindsight on a sweltering July afternoon. They relived Johnny's funeral, Clay's hellacious attack on the woodpile, and Cindy's realization of the murderers' true identities on a blustery September day. The rageful brawl at the Bloody Bucket came next, followed by the October trial of Bully Hanson and Claude Darnell, the jury's verdict of guilty, and the suicide of Ransom Potts.

Then the retrospective grew more ominous and threatening in nature. They revisited that horrifying night in mid-December when there came the pounding of vengeful death upon the door, demanding to be let in. The explosive assault on the farmhouse, the terrifying chase into the snowy woods, and then the last-ditch refuge inside the old tobacco barn. Cornered behind the tool box, with Bully and Claude closing in for the kill, Cindy had worked her magic, as terrible and devastating as it had been, setting the two men against one another and destroying them with their own weapons.

Both father and daughter were in tears when their fingers finally separated. Shakily, Cindy rose from the rocker and tenderly tucked the sheets around her frail father. They exchanged a look of mutual understanding before Clay drifted into exhausted slumber. The year they had just explored had been the worst year of their lives. Yet, then again, in a very peculiar way, it had also been the best. All the tragedy, all the grief and violent anguish, had served a purpose. It had brought a rural tobacco farmer and his shy, nine-year-old daughter closer together. It had cemented the broken bond between them, a bond that would remain forever steadfast, even after the old man's passing.

"I love you, Pappy," she whispered, then left the darkened room.

Sam and Richard noticed the redness of her eyes and the drawn look of her face when she entered the kitchen. "Hey, you fellas want to see my patrol car?" Sam asked in his easygoing way. He began to usher the two boys out the back door. Graciously, knowing that mother and daughter had things to discuss, Richard tagged along.

"I'll even let you flash the lights," added Sam. "But we can't turn on the siren because —"

"Yeah, I know," grumbled Rick in disappointment. "'Cause Grandpa is resting."

"You show some respect, young man," his mother scolded. Then they were out the back door and heading for the black and white Plymouth parked beside the ramshackle smokehouse.

"Boys will be boys," Maudie reminded her from where

she stood over the assortment of simmering pots and pans on the gas stove. She checked the turkey, then poured a couple of mugs of rich black coffee. She brought one over to Cindy, who sat silently at the kitchen table. Fresh cream and sugar was exchanged without comment.

They sat there alone for a long time, saying nothing. Each woman grappled with her own troubled thoughts; Cindy rehashing the last few moments of psychic intimacy with her father, Maudie dealing with the dreadful expectation of losing a man she had loved for most of her lifetime.

"When will he be leaving us, Cindy?" Maudie asked abruptly. Her gaze was not on her daughter, but directed at the coffee cup in her liver-spotted hands.

"It's hard to say," Cindy told her. "I believe sometime after Christmas."

Maudie nodded solemnly, accepting what her daughter told her, but secretly knowing that Cindy did know. In her heart, Maudie Biggs knew that Cynthia Ann knew exactly when her father would die; the day, the hour, perhaps even the moment. But she did not press the matter. Actually, she was grateful for Cindy's restraint. There would be less of a sense of painful expectation if death came quickly and without advance warning.

Early evening was drawing into dusk when the Garrison family started home. As the two-toned Chevy headed down the main highway for Nashville, the car turned off on a desolate stretch of abandoned dirt road. Heavy thicket grew rampant on each side, nearly obscuring the boarded farmhouse and the larger building that stood a hundred yards away.

"I won't be long," Cindy told her husband when the car had braked to a halt.

"Are you sure you don't want me to come along?"

"No." She smiled. "This is something I need to do alone."

Richard kissed his wife and let her go. He knew about this place. When they had first married, Cindy had told him of that horrible time back in '36. He had been compassionate and understanding, even if he could not fully comprehend exactly what had taken place there.

"Be careful now. That old barn looks like it's ready to give up the ghost."

Cindy walked down the rutted pathway, her hands crammed into the pockets of her woolen coat. Her spouse's remark rang ironically in her ears. If any place in Bedloe County possessed ghosts, it was surely the old tobacco barn. Men had died there horribly in the wake of gruesome circumstances. Greed, murder, and even vengeance had played a part in their violent deaths.

She approached the ancient structure, marveling at the changes that had taken place during a span of two decades. The barn itself was a ghost. A section of the great pitched roof had caved in beneath weakened rafters. Large sheets of rusted tin lay across the earthen floor. The weathered boards of the walls had given way to years of termites and rot. The deterioration gave the barn an eerie skeletal appearance in the gray light of the chilly November evening.

Carefully, Cindy entered the belly of the sagging hull. She walked its length, passing the old plow, stepping over scattered boards and the last lingering traces of black charcoal. She reached her destination—the tool chest. A support beam had fallen sometime over the years, caving in the lid, and the rusty collection of tools were gone, taken by kids in search of souvenirs. Strangely enough, the oblong box appeared much smaller than it had at the time of her childhood.

Cindy stood there where she had not been since the winter of 1936, and although the feelings were faint, they still lingered. Maybe, she thought, the old horror would always be there, like a permanent stain that could never be scrubbed clean. Perhaps too much blood had soaked into the dank earth, too much death had rattled the roughly hewn walls that it could never be eradicated by driving rain or howling wind. Yes, it was still there, faded and colorless like an old photograph, but still reminiscent of the same disturbing course of events.

"Excuse me, ma'am?"

Cindy jumped at the sudden voice, the short hairs at the nape of her slender neck tingling. She stared at a gaping hole in the barn wall where loose boards hung like jagged teeth around the opening. Someone stood there, the form obscured into silhouette.

It was a lanky young man with a shotgun slung over one shoulder and a droopy hat snuggled above oversized ears. As he stepped closer into view, the shadows slipped away. He was younger than she had first thought —thirteen or fourteen — and awkward as most boys were at that age. A slack-skinned redbone hound accompanied him. Cindy's sudden startlement evaporated, and she smiled at the young man. At first, the similarity had spooked her, it had been so uncanny.

"Ma'am," the boy said once again. "You oughtn't be walking around in there. This old barn's a real death trap. Been falling apart ever since I can remember. Wouldn't surprise me none if it took a notion to cave in any day now."

"I'll be careful," Cindy assured him.

The boy remained for a moment longer, staring into the shadowy interior with apparent unease. "My pa, he's told me stories about this place. Said some awful bad things happened here . . . back a long time before I was born."

"Your pa was right," she said. "Some awful bad things."

The boy shrugged. "Just figured I oughta warn you, ma'am."

The youthful hunter and his hound disappeared from the dark frame of the opening. She saw him pick his way through the thicket, searching for small game for that night's supper table.

Cindy was turning to leave the barn herself, when something metallic drew her attention. She knelt beside the tool box, catching the object between her fingernails. It was a tarnished silver dime with the year 1936 stamped at the bottom edge. The memento brought back unpleasant thoughts, but she kept it anyway, dropping it into the side pocket of her winter coat.

She was rising when a small sound came from the ruptured barn wall. Someone stood there, staring at her.

"I told you before, I'll be all right," she began, but suddenly her breath caught in her throat.

The silhouette that stood there was different now. She had thought it was the boy at first, but it wasn't. The person who now filled the aperture was heavier in frame and older, perhaps eighteen years of age. Something brought a welling of fear from Cindy's soul—or, rather, it was two things. Both were characteristics she had not known since that long-ago summer. One was the young man's hat, a crisp fedora perched at a cocky angle on his head. The other was the distinctive hourglass shape of a flat-top guitar held firmly in one hand.

The barking of the coonhound drew her attention to the opposite wall of the barn. Through the missing boards, she could see the young hunter crashing through the bramble behind his dog, his shotgun ready for an airborne covey of quail.

Cindy's heart pounded. *There are ghosts here,* echoed her thoughts. She was afraid, but even more, she was anxious. Anxious to look upon her brother's smiling face once again.

"Johnny ..." she whispered.

But when she turned around, there was no one there.

BONUS NOVELLA

POTTER'S FIELD

Author's Note

I love writing about Cindy Ann Biggs because, in a comforting way, it brings my mother back to life.

To both me and the members of my family – particularly those on my mother's side – there is no doubt whatsoever that Cynthia Ann is, in reality, Earline "Nean" Kelly, who succumbed to lung cancer in 1989. After all, the character is based on her life as a child in Depression-era Tennessee. She holds the same bright red hair, hazel eyes, and sprinkling of freckles as my mother did at that age, as well as similar physical and emotional characteristics. From the many stories she told me of her childhood exploits and her disturbing bouts of "psychic revelation", I'm 99.9% sure that the shy, fever-frail youngster that lives in the pages of *Hindsight* was the same one who grew up on the rural outskirts of White Bluff, Tennessee, riddled with hardship, but surviving in the face of adversity and extremely poor odds.

Following the writing of *Hindsight* in 1986 and its eventual publication in 1990 (two scant months following Mama's passing), I would often wonder how Cindy Ann turned out following those awful months that spanned 1936. Did she live in dread for the remainder of her life – as my mother did – wondering what disaster, or whose death, would be revealed at any given moment? Or did she learn to accept her "gift" and view it as something to be cherished and put to good use, instead of something to be feared and reviled?

In the following novella, *Potter's Field,* you will find that Cindy – now sixteen years of age – has taken the latter path. She has taken control of her wondrous talent (rather than allowing *it* to take control of *her)* and decided to use it in a beneficial manner. And, as *Restless Shadows,* the sequel to *Hindsight* reveals, Cindy has turned her unique gift of second sight and her need to help those in need of closure into a peculiar – yet helpful – career of sorts.

But sometimes doing the right thing has its share of pitfalls; pitfalls so dark and treacherous, that it is possible that one might lose their way amid the journey and find themselves totally and utterly lost.

Thus is the tale of *Potter's Field* and the dangers that lay in plain sight above level ground... as well as those concealed deep beneath it.

RK

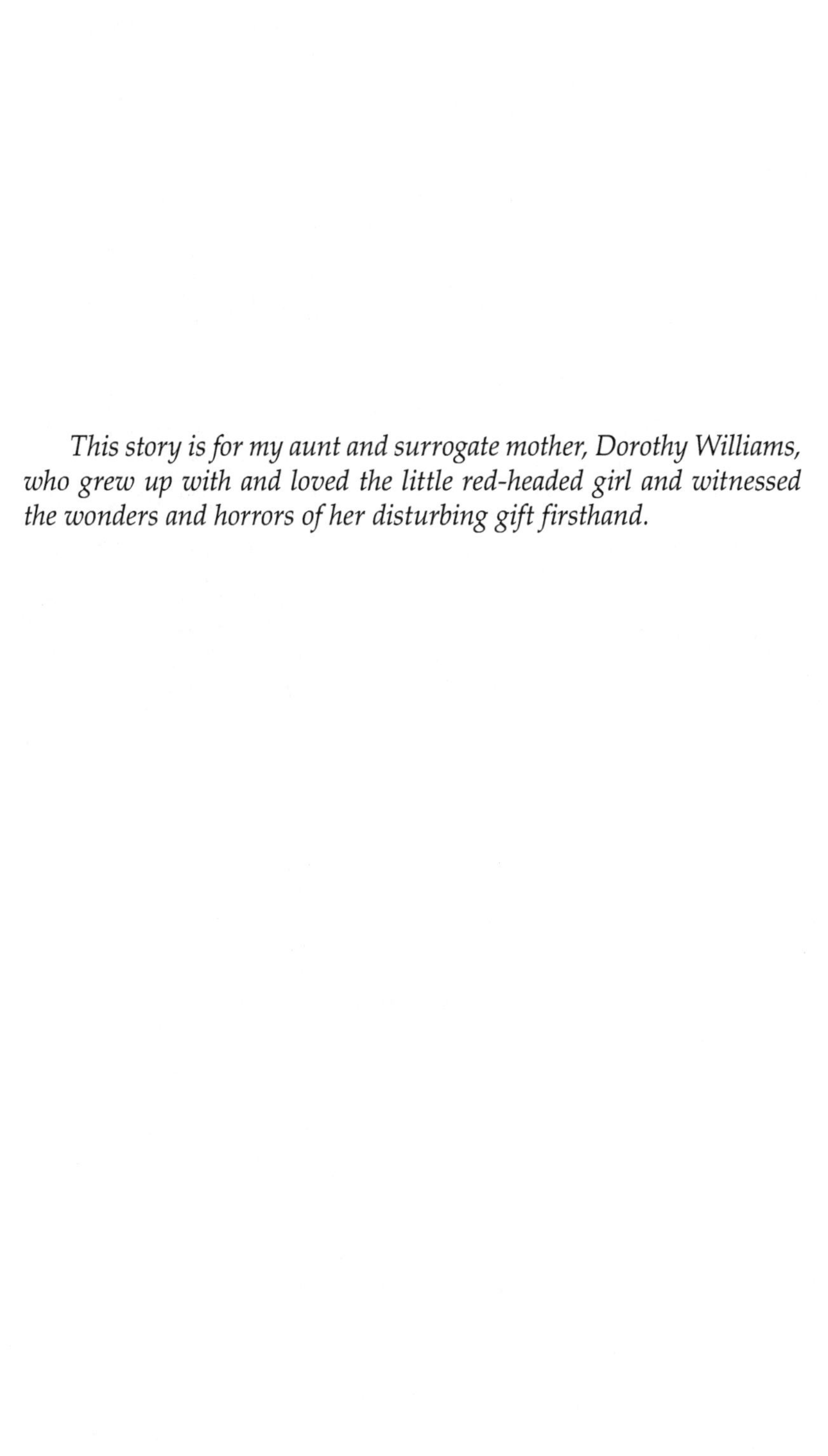

This story is for my aunt and surrogate mother, Dorothy Williams, who grew up with and loved the little red-headed girl and witnessed the wonders and horrors of her disturbing gift firsthand.

It was a muggy Sunday afternoon in the summer of 1943 when the black sedan appeared at the far end of Old Newsome Road. From where they sat on the front porch, they could see it heading their way, leaving a billowing cloud of red clay dust in its wake.

"Think they're lost?" Clayburn Biggs asked his wife, Maudie. His eyes studied the approaching automobile while he absently constructed one of his one-handed cigarettes.

"I don't know," the woman said with a shrug. She fanned herself with a funeral home fan with a painting of Jesus holding a lamb printed on one side of the cardboard. "We rarely see a nice car like that way out here."

"They're not lost," said the girl who sat, reading, on the hanging swing at the far end of the porch. "It's *us* they're coming to see."

Clay and Maudie looked at one another. If their daughter said that it was so, there was no point in denying the matter.

Soon, the car pulled to the side of the road in front of the Biggs' farmhouse. The engine idled for a long moment and then grew silent. Two men climbed out and stretched in the blazing August sun. One was tall and lanky with sandy blond hair, while the other was big and burly and dark-haired, almost bear-like. They wore dark suit pants, long-sleeved starched white shirts, and thin black ties, while their jackets had been discarded and left in the sedan. At first Maudie thought they might be Jehovah's Witnesses, but their clothing was not Sunday-go-to-preaching attire, but apparently what they wore on the job every day of the week.

Leisurely, the two started across the front yard toward the porch. "Hello," the tall one called out with a boyish smile. He held a stack of manila folders in his right hand.

"Howdy," replied Clay with a nod. "What can we do for you, fellas?"

"We're hoping that we've finally found the Biggs residence. We've gotten lost several times, driving up and down these back roads looking for it."

"Well, you found it." Clay eyed them both with suspicion. "The question is, why would you *want* to?"

The big fellow took a black wallet from his pants pocket and flipped it open, displaying a badge and a card with an official stamp across its face. "We're federal agents, Mr. Biggs."

Sammy Biggs sat up straight from where he had previously lain slumped in a chair next to his mother. The ten-year-old's eyes widened with sudden interest. "The FBI? Honest to goodness?"

The tall agent chuckled and mopped at the nape of his neck with a handkerchief. "That's right, son. Believe it or not, we are. I'm agent Robert Upchurch and this is my partner, Nathan Moore."

The big fellow nodded curtly. He didn't seem nearly as friendly as the other man was.

"You boys look hot enough to fry eggs on the toes of those shiny black shoes of yours," Maudie told them. She got up out of her rocking chair and started for the front door. "Ya'll get on up here in the shade and I'll fetch you some cold iced tea."

"Thank you, ma'am," said Upchurch gratefully. "That would sure hit the spot."

After Maudie had gone inside and the men had sat down in a couple of straight-backed chairs on the porch, Sammy hopped up and studied the two men without a hint of shyness. "So you really are G-men? Sent down here to Coleman by Mr. Hoover himself? Do you have handcuffs and guns and all that?"

"Stop pestering the fire out of these gentlemen, Sammy," Clay said, giving his son a warning look. After the boy had returned to his seat, the former tobacco farmer studied the two government men cautiously. "What I wanna know is why boys like you would have cause to come all the way down here to see me."

The two men glanced at one another and then looked toward the far end of the porch. "Uh, we didn't come to see you, Mr. Biggs," Agent Upchurch replied. "To tell the truth, we came to see *her.*"

Clay lit his homemade cigarette with a sulfur match and took a long drag. "Who? Cindy Ann?"

Before they could answer, the girl on the swing looked up from the copy of *Little Women* she had been reading. "They want me to help them, Pappy."

Clayburn Biggs turned and regarded his daughter. It was hard to believe that the tall, willowy sixteen-year-old with the long red hair and lightly freckled complexion was the same little girl who had once played with paper dollies while he did mechanic work amid the shade of the persimmon grove. She possessed none of the painful shyness and flighty behavior she had back then. Now she was quiet and patiently calm, possessing a maturity beyond that of a normal teenager. Clay figured – considering all the trouble she had been involved in seven years ago – Cindy had been forced to grow up a bit faster than was customary.

"What in tarnation do you need her to help you with?" Clay asked them point-blank.

Agent Upchurch took a folder off the top of the stack he had brought with him. "According to our file on Miss Cynthia Ann…"

Maudie reappeared with two tall glasses of sweet tea in her pudgy hands. "The Federal Bureau of Investigation actually has a file on our Cindy Ann? Pardon me for saying so, Mr. Upchurch, but that's downright disturbing!"

The tall man smiled gently. "No need to be alarmed, ma'am. Mr. Hoover keeps open files on all manner of U.S. citizens… some who might be threats to our nation's security and some who might be beneficial to the Bureau and its various investigations. Miss Cynthia Ann is one of the latter."

Agent Moore took a long swig of the iced tea and regarded the barefoot girl in the swing with an undisguised smirk on his broad, clean-shaven face. "According to our sources, your daughter allegedly possesses the power of second sight."

Clay cracked an amused smile. "I take it you don't cotton to such things, Agent Moore."

"No," the man told him truthfully. "I can't say that I do. It just seems like a bunch of hoo-doo and fancy parlor tricks to me." A sly expression gleamed in his small eyes that could have been mistaken for pure meanness. He took the pile of folders from his partner and shucked one from off the bottom.

"Nate, I don't believe that is necessary..." Upchurch began to protest.

"Well, I do!" He walked over and thrust the file, almost a little too forcefully, into the face of the red-headed girl. "Here. Let's see if you can give us a *reading* on this file. Or do you need to break out the tea leaves and tarot cards?"

Cindy Ann ignored the man's sarcasm and, laying her book aside, took the file that was handed to her. She opened the folder. Inside, were several sheets of paper bearing a few paragraphs of information. Attached at the upper left-hand corner of the first page with a paper clip was a black and white photograph of a girl around Cindy's age. She had curly blonde hair and a defiant expression on her pretty face.

The teenager stared at the photo for a long moment and then shrugged her narrow shoulders. "Sorry."

Moore huffed impatiently and shook his huge head. "So you can't tell us a single helpful thing about this missing girl, can you?"

Cindy's eyes were steady as she looked in him full in the face. "No, I can't tell you anything about the girl in this photograph. But I can tell you about the woman who typed this report. That she is in her mid-thirties, has a nervous habit of biting her fingernails, and has miscarried two times."

A nerve beneath Nathan Moore's left eye twitched. He jerked the folder, almost angrily, from her grasp. "So what does it take for you to put on your fortune teller act, little sister?" he asked, his voice harsh and demanding in its tone.

"Usually she has to touch something that they touched," Maudie said, not at all pleased with how the bigger FBI agent was acting toward her daughter. "Or touch the person themselves."

Moore grinned. "Okay. I'm game." He held out his right

hand. "Here, grab hold of me and read my mind."

Clay Biggs frowned around his cigarette, looking ready to stand up and intervene. "Hey now! This is getting outright ridiculous!"

Cindy Ann smiled gently. "It's alright, Pappy." Then she reached out and took the man's meaty hand.

For a moment, Agent Moore stood there, tapping his foot, a look of utter disbelief on his face. Then, abruptly, he felt a bout of dizziness hit him. As he began to grow a little sick to his stomach, a thought crossed his mind. Or, rather, someone *else's* thought.

Do you really want me to tell everyone what I see inside you? the voice of Cindy Ann Biggs echoed through his brain. *Like, perhaps, how you like to burn your wife with cigarette butts?*

The man jerked his hand from her grasp like a man flinching from contact with a live wire.

Clay chuckled. "Hit a nerve, did she?"

Nathan Moore said nothing. Frowning, he sat back down in his chair and, taking a swallow of the cold tea, grew quiet.

Cindy looked at the other man. "Exactly what would you like me to help you with, Agent Upchurch?"

The lean man took a drink to wet his whistle and then began to speak. "Between the spring of 1928 and the autumn of 1933, a dozen young women between the ages of fourteen and twenty-two, were reported missing in the states of Kentucky, Ohio, and West Virginia. Some of them were troubled teenagers and considered to be runaways. But at least eight of them were good girls from good homes. They were almost certainly abducted, walking home from school, the store, or their local library.

"After several years of investigation, following every little lead that came our way, we discovered that the disappearances were connected. A couple of weeks ago, we finally pinpointed a suspect in the abductions, as well as a possible burial ground for the victims."

A cold sensation suddenly filled Cindy, canceling out the stifling summer heat around her. "You're talking about *him,* aren't you?"

Maudie stared at her daughter, uneasy at the haunted

expression in the girl's hazel eyes. "Who are you talking about, baby?"

Clay's long face hardened as he realized who she referred to. "You can't possibly mean…"

"Yes," she said in scarcely a whisper. "Bully Hanson."

"Lordy have mercy!" moaned Maudie. If she had been Catholic instead of a dyed-in-the-wool Baptist she would have likely crossed herself.

Sammy suddenly looked frightened. "Was that the same guy who chased us into that barn when I was little?"

Clay and Maudie traded worried glances. "Sammy, why don't you go on out in the back yard and play?" his mother suggested.

"Aw, I want to stay and…"

"Take your BB gun with you," his father told him. "Shoot a blue jay or two."

"Really? Yes, sir!" Sammy hopped off his chair and headed into the house to fetch his Red Ryder. Allowed to shoot his gun on the Sabbath and live birds at that! He wasn't about to pass up such a golden opportunity.

When the boy was out of earshot, Moore spoke again, ending his brooding silence. "That's correct. The man responsible for Johnny Biggs' death is the one we believe is responsible for the disappearance and murders of those twelve missing girls. Maybe even a few that we aren't aware of yet."

"He was certainly capable of doing such a horrible thing," Maudie said. "He was pure evil, plain and simple."

Clay took a drag on his cigarette and looked over at Upchurch. "What about Claude Darnell? Do you think he was involved, too?"

"No. Hanson didn't cross paths with Darnell until 1935. We believe he acted alone." The agent regarded Cindy, who sat pensively in the swing, her feet tucked beneath her. "We were hoping that you would accompany us to the farm that Hanson rented from a man named Alex Potter in Millersville, Kentucky, and help us pinpoint the locations of the buried girls. I know this seems grisly and a tad insensitive on our part, but we would really like to close these cases and move on. Also, the families desire closure. The discovery of the remains would go far in giving these poor people some much-needed peace of mind."

"I'm not sure I'm ready to allow such a thing," Clay declared firmly. "Cindy's had her share of dealing with death; enough to last her a lifetime. Don't you have other people with similar abilities in your dadblamed files that could help you with this?"

"Yes, in fact, we do," Upchurch told him. "But Cindy has something that they lack. She has a personal connection. I believe she would be more receptive to the site of the murders for the mere fact that they were committed by Hanson. She knew the man firsthand, which gives her an advantage over a psychic who has no connection whatsoever."

"So that's what you call them?" asked Cindy. "Psychics?"

Upchurch nodded. "Yes. And there are more of them out there than you can imagine."

That fact both comforted and disturbed the sixteen-year-old. In sincere hands, the gift of second sight and the quirky little talents that went with it, was a good thing; a blessing from God. But in a person of questionable character, capable of deception and spite, it might be downright dangerous… as lethal as a gun or a knife.

"Well, what do you say, Miss Cindy? Will you assist us in this investigation?"

She hesitated for a long moment. In her mind, she weighed the bad with the good. On one hand she dreaded having anything to do with Bully Hanson and his darkness again, especially if it brought back old memories of that deadly summer of 1936. But on the other hand, it would be well worth it to bring some lasting peace to a grieving mother or father somewhere.

"Mama?" she asked. "Pappy?"

"I believe it's up to you, baby," her mother said, although she looked terribly unsure about it all.

"You're old enough to make up your mind, sweetheart," her father told her. "It's been slow at the sawmill lately, so I'll be happy to take off a few days and go with you, if you don't mind your old man tagging along, that is."

That seemed to be the deciding factor that helped her make up her mind. "Alright," she said. "I'll do it."

Early the following Wednesday morning, Cindy and her father stepped off the train at the Millersville depot. The sixteen-year-old was clad in a modest summer dress that her mother had sewn by hand, worn shoes, and Maudie's oversized straw hat that she wore while working in the garden. According to the two FBI agents, the forty acre spread of the old Potter farm was utterly shadeless. She would need something substantial to shield her from the intense August sun.

Clay wore khaki pants, a blue chambray shirt, and a light jacket. The tan fedora atop his head reminded Cindy of how her brother Johnny once wore his; tilted slightly in a cocky manner. His clothing was much better than the pair of red long handle underwear and threadbare Duckhead overalls that he had jokingly threatened to embarrass his daughter with. In his hand was a battered, old suitcase he had bought at a thrift store in Coleman, just for this occasion. Both his and Cindy's spare clothing and toiletries were packed together in the satchel and, hopefully, were enough for the duration of their stay.

"You know, this town ain't much bigger than Coleman," Clay told her. "So how come I feel like some country bumpkin fresh off the turnip truck?"

Cindy self-consciously tugged at the brim of the floppy sun hat. "I feel like Anne of Green Gables."

Her daddy raised an eyebrow. "Who?"

"Just a book I read once," she said smiling.

Clay nodded. His daughter had spent a lot of time with her books lately. He had known her to walk the long stretch to town and back just to trade in one book for another. In his opinion, she would likely grow up to be a writer or a librarian.

They stood awkwardly on the train platform, until a familiar voice called out from behind them. "Mr. Biggs! Cindy Ann!"

They turned to find Agent Upchurch heading from the direction of the train station. Behind him were Nathan Moore and a pretty woman with dark auburn hair.

"How was your trip?" he asked, taking the battered suitcase as they started through the depot, toward the black sedan parked out front.

"The Nashville-Louisville Railroad needs to fix a few uneven tracks, but other than that, it was tolerable," Clay told him.

Cindy studied the woman curiously. Her hair was styled like the USO girls she had seen on some of the recruitment posters in the Bedloe County courthouse; rolled into broad curls on top and hanging long and luxuriant in the back and sides. Her face was pretty and embellished with only a touch of lipstick and rouge. Her eyes were brilliant blue – the color of her mother's Blue Willow dishes at home – but they held a sadness that seemed unflattering and wrong on such a beautiful person. She wore a dark gray jacket with skirt with a delicate white silk blouse underneath.

"Oh, pardon my lack of manners," Upchurch said. "This is Sandra. She will be transcribing and photographing every step of this investigation, as well as anything we uncover."

"Mr. Biggs," she greeted with a respectful nod. Her eyes brightened somewhat when she regarded the red-headed girl. "Hi, Cindy Ann. I'm glad to finally meet you."

"It's nice meeting you, too, Miss Sandra," Cindy replied. Something nagged at her – a peculiar sense of déjà vu – but she simply couldn't figure it out.

The woman laid a delicate hand on Cindy's shoulder. "Are you nervous, dear? About what we want you to do?"

The girl nodded. "A little, I reckon."

Agent Moore looked sternly at his wristwatch. "We had better get on to the farm and get to work. Uncle Sam isn't paying us to stand around and chew the fat."

As the burly agent climbed into the driver's seat of the sedan, Upchurch rolled his eyes and opened the rear door for Clay, Cindy, and Sandra.

"I take it he's one of them 'by-the-book' fellas," Clay said, loud enough for Moore to hear.

"That's something of an understatement, Mr. Biggs," the lanky agent replied with an apologetic grin.

In several ways, the Potter farm ten miles north of Millersville was eerily similar to the tobacco farm of Harvey Brewer back in Coleman.

An acre from the road stood a lone, two-story farmhouse. It had seen better days. Its white coat of paint had pretty much flaked away due to harsh weather and its roof sagged visibly in the middle, with more than a few shingles missing or damaged. There was a long front porch and a screened in back porch. Around the house stood a cluster of outbuildings; a chicken coop, a tool shed, and an outhouse – a two-seater from the size of it. The thought of someone sitting next to you while you did your business both disgusted and amused Cindy.

To the far left of the house stood the ruins of a barn that had burnt down long ago and had never been rebuilt. Behind that stretched thirty-nine acres of open land. The only trees in sight were a stand of tall pines and cedars at the rear of the property. One thing about the earth that was nothing like Brewer's farm, was the absence of vegetation. No weeds, no bramble… nothing. Just acres of uneven soil, textured with clods of earth and exposed rock.

It's almost like everything on top died because of what's buried underneath, she thought to herself and shivered.

"What's the matter, Cindy?" her father asked at her apparent unease. "Did a possum walk over your grave?"

She said nothing in reply; simply stared at the sunbaked stretch of unmarked graveyard.

Standing several yards from the eastern wall of the house was an Airstream travel trailer, gleaming in the sun like a silvery egg. Lounging in the shade of that corner of the porch was a short, bearded man with thick spectacles. He wasn't particularly old – about the same age as her father – but the way he carried himself and his general expression told of hardships far beyond those experienced by a man approaching fifty. He wore a crumpled shirt with its sleeves rolled up to the elbows, and dark trousers held up with suspenders. With him were three younger men in work clothes; common working men in comparison to his grizzled college professor.

"That's Dr. Abraham Polyak," Upchurch told them as they strolled toward the house. "He recently came to the United States from Europe. He's a forensic anthropologist and will be helping us confirm the identities of the remains we find."

As they reached the porch, Polyak stepped down, smiling. He shook hands with Clay and then turned to Cindy Ann. "Ah, Fräulein! It is so good to finally meet you!" he said enthusiastically.

As he extended his hand, the girl noticed a long line of blue numbers tattooed along the skin on inside of his forearm. She had no idea what they were… until his hand met hers.

Sezierraum! Leichen-Raum! Exekutions Statte! Gaskammer! Ziereis! Kommandeur Ziereis!!

The next thing Cindy knew, she was sitting on the edge of the porch with everyone huddled around her. Miss Sandra crouched in front of her. The woman's pretty face was full of concern. "Are you alright, Cindy? What happened? You gave us quite a fright."

Agent Moore eyed her suspiciously. "Were you speaking… *German?*"

Dr. Polyak nodded grimly. "Yes, she was." He sat down next to the sixteen-year-old, careful not to make contact with her again. His bearded face was pale and shaken. "You were speaking of Mauthausen, were you not?"

Cindy nodded as she turned to him. "How did you escape such a horrible place?"

Polyak shrugged his shoulders. "It was a fluke… one chance in a million that presented itself and I took it. I was laboring at the edge of the rock quarry and, when the guards were busy beating a fellow inmate, I fled into the forest. I feared that the SS soldiers would hunt me down, but they did not." He chuckled humorlessly. "I suppose they thought I was too weak to survive in the wilderness, but I fooled them with my tenacity."

"All those poor people." Tears bloomed in the girl's eyes. "And your family."

"Long dead before my escape," the Hungarian said, wiping a few tears of his own away with a handkerchief. "Boundless evil exists upon this earth, Fräulein… and it goes on still."

She looked at him, questioning. "Who is Ziereis?"

Polyak's hands clenched in rage, the knuckles whitening, as he remembered the arrogant commander of the Austrian concentration camp, but his face remained gentle. "The Devil,

Cindy Ann… like your Bully Hanson. Yet a thousand times worse."

For the first time, Cindy noticed a flatbed trailer parked a short distance from the silver trailer. There were a dozen long, pinewood boxes stacked upon it.

"What are those?" she asked.

"Receptacles for the remains once they are located and exhumed," Polyak explained.

"They look like coffins to me."

The Hungarian's eyes were sad behind the lenses of his spectacles. "Until their families give them a proper farewell, I suppose that they will serve as such."

The girl seemed embarrassed by all the attention. "Please… I'm okay." She looked up at Agent Upchurch. "Can we go ahead and begin?"

"Are you sure… after what just happened?" he asked with a frown.

"Yes," she said, leaving her seat on the porch. "I feel particularly…" She searched for the right word and then found it. "*Receptive* right now."

"Okay. Then let's get to work."

Cindy wanted to see the house first.

The moment she stepped across the threshold, goose bumps prickled the flesh of her arms. Dirty, snickering laughter echoed distantly in the back of her mind, followed by low, feminine moans of anguish and pain.

"He has been here," she told them.

They didn't have to ask who she was talking about.

Silently, she roamed the bottom floor, past the side parlor, down a narrow hallway to the kitchen at the back of the house. Then she returned to the staircase that faced the front door. Cindy stared at the shadowy landing of the second floor for a long moment, her breath shallow.

"You don't have to go up there, pumpkin," her father told her.

"Yes, I do." Then she mounted the stairs a riser at a time with the others following a yard or so behind her.

The upstairs corridor was dark with only a zigzag pattern of sunlight shining through the cracks of a single boarded window at the far end. Rooms lined the hallway, some open and some closed, and cobwebs dangled from the rafters above. The floorboards creaked beneath their feet. The wood squeaked and squealed as though it were a living thing being trod upon rather than planed and sanded lumber.

Halfway there, Dr. Polyak stopped in his tracks. His breath hitched in his chest and he leaned heavily against a wall to steady himself. "Ó Istenem!"

Cindy turned and looked at him. "So you feel it too?"

"The aura of death?" he answered. "Yes indeed. Not as strong as at Mauthausen… but it is here nonetheless."

The sixteen-year-old nodded grimly and continued onward. There was a bedroom at the end of the hallway on the right-hand side. The door – peeling paint with a tarnished brass knob – was closed.

Cindy shuddered and took a step backward. "I… I can't go in there."

"Why not?" asked Sandra.

"That's where it happened."

"What happened?" Upchurch wanted to know.

"The rape and torture," she said in scarcely a whisper.

"Could you give us specifics?" Agent Moore asked her callously.

Cindy turned and regarded him coldly. "Believe me… you'd rather not know."

"She's right," the lanky FBI man said. "Our main objective right now is locating the bodies of the victims. We can dwell on the cause of their deaths later."

A minute later, they were back outside in the blazing sunlight. "I'm ready to begin," she told them.

Upchurch nodded solemnly. "Then let's go to the field."

The sun cast nine o'clock shadows from the back of the house as they stood between a tool shed and a rickety chicken coop. Cindy placed her mother's straw hat upon her head and kicked off her shoes. She wiggled her toes, letting the powdery earth work between her toes.

"I know it is only morning, but the ground is already scorching hot," protested Sandra. "It will burn her feet." Despite her concern, she wrote steadily in a steno pad, recording the progression of that day's events.

Clay Biggs displayed a lopsided grin. "Cindy Ann's been going barefoot in the summertime since she was able to walk, ma'am," he assured her. "I'd say the soles of her feet are about as tough as the bottoms of those high-heeled shoes of yours."

They watched as she stepped out onto the uneven earth of Potter's north forty. She took several steps, paused, and then walked a few more. That went on for nearly an hour and a half. Sometimes she would turn and walk to the far end of the property line, which was cordoned off by a low stone wall, and then, turning on her heels, stroll slowly to the opposite boundary. Her face was bland and expressionless, but her eyes burned in the shade of the floppy straw hat, as though staring across a great distance, attempting to see something upon an allusive horizon.

Finally, with only an eighth of the acreage covered, Cindy turned and shrugged her freckled shoulders. "I'm sorry... but nothing yet." She stared across the sun-baked earth toward the tree line at the far reaches of the property. "I think he buried them away from the house... some distance away."

"Well, it's almost lunchtime," Agent Upchurch said, consulting a pocket watch. "I suggest we retire to the shade of the front porch and have us a bite to eat before attempting it again."

Everyone agreed, ready to be out of the relentless sun. Cindy stood there for a long moment, her eyes closed. Then with a sigh, she accompanied the others back to the old farmhouse.

They relaxed in the coolness of the shade and lunched on egg salad sandwiches and lukewarm Coca Colas.

The men congregated at the far end of the porch, while Cindy and Sandra sat with their backs to the wall at the opposite end. Upchurch, Moore, and Clay, as well as the workers, smoked and talked, discussing baseball, boxing, and the War overseas. Clayburn Biggs said very little. Cindy knew he was a bit uncomfortable – and untrusting – around city folk. Seeing Abraham Polyak sitting alone in the oval doorway of his Airstream, she knew that he felt the same way, especially concerning men who worked for the government.

Halfway through their meal, Sandra began to look pale and peaked. "Are you alright, Miss Sandra?" Cindy asked her.

"I… I believe I'm going to be sick," the woman said, getting shakily to her feet. She stumbled a couple of feet, then stepped off the edge of the porch and ducked around the corner. Cindy heard the woman begin the retch violently, then throw up.

"What the hell's the matter with her?" Moore asked, taking a long draw on his cigarette.

"I think the heat has been too much for her," Cindy said. Then she left her seat against the front wall of the house and went to see about her.

She rounded the corner and found Sandra leaning against the wall, green around the gills, holding her stomach. The woman saw her standing there and smiled self-consciously. "I'm sorry. I guess I just…"

"How long have you been expecting?" Cindy asked her without hesitation.

Sandra looked startled. "What… what do you mean?"

The girl lowered her voice as she approached. "You're pregnant, aren't you?"

The auburn-haired woman looked both elated and frightened at the same time. "Yes. I didn't want to believe so… but I suppose you're right."

As Cindy took another step forward, something came back to her. *She is in her mid-thirties, has a nervous habit of biting her fingernails, and has miscarried two times.*

"You were the one who typed the reports about the missing girls," she said.

"Yes, and the one on you, too," Sandra admitted. "That's why I was so glad to meet you. I feel like I know you, after all the research I've done on you and your family."

The two stood in awkward silence for a long moment. Then Cindy walked over and reached for the woman's right hand. "Do you mind?"

Sandra was hesitant. "I don't know if you should."

"Please," the girl said gently. "It'll be okay."

Reluctantly, Sandra extended her short-nailed hand and Cindy took it.

A warm smile crossed the teenager's face. "Don't worry. You'll be fine this time."

Sandra looked at her anxiously. "Do you mean…?"

"No miscarriages. The babies will be as healthy as spring colts."

The woman's eyes widened. *"Babies?"*

"Yes." Cindy squeezed her fingers. "Twins. A boy and a girl. Billy and Brenda. One full of mischief and the other sweet and shy."

Gratitude gleamed in Sandra's blue eyes. "Thank you for that."

"You're welcome."

Cindy was about to let go of the woman's hand, when she noticed a circular mark on the underside of her wrist. It was small and pink, about the size of a…

Again, thoughts from several days before came to mind. *Do you really want me to tell everyone what I see inside you? Like, perhaps, how you like to burn your wife with cigarette butts?*

This time it was Cindy Ann's eyes that widened in surprise. "You're married to Agent Moore?"

Sandra nodded silently. She glanced toward the corner of the house as though expecting the man to appear at any moment.

Cindy turned the woman's hand until the ugly butt-shaped burn mark was revealed. "And he did *this* to you?"

Sandra jerked her hand away and pulled the cuff of her blouse down across her wrist until the scar was concealed. "He's a good man," she whispered. "He just has a temper sometimes."

"Pardon me for saying so, Miss Sandra, but he strikes me as a man who would want his wife at home, washing clothes and sweeping floors… not working for the FBI."

Sandra shrugged and attempted a smile. "He just likes for us to be together as much as possible, that's all."

Then, in Cindy's mind, Sandra's voice. *He is a terribly jealous man.*

Suddenly, something seemed to dawn in the woman's eyes and she looked scared half to death. "Please, don't tell him. You know, about the babies. Let me do that... when the time is right."

"Sure," Cindy assured her. Without thinking, she reached out and gave the woman a hug. "It's a secret between the two of us."

Sandra hugged back. Cindy felt her tremble slightly. "Thank you. I appreciate that."

"I reckon we'd better get back... before he comes looking for you."

The woman with the long auburn hair nodded. Together they returned to the porch and quietly finished the last of their lunch.

Around one o'clock, they were back at work again.

Polyak and Sandra Moore followed at a short distance, while Cindy roamed the massive field, heading in one direction and then another. The girl would pause for a long moment and then begin again, her bare feet padding upon the uneven earth of the Potter property.

Agents Upchurch and Moore, as well as Clay Biggs, stood beside the farmhouse's screened-in back porch and watched.

"She seems to be picking up on something," the lanky FBI man stated hopefully. "Her wandering seems to be less erratic... like it has a purpose now."

Moore snorted, blowing cigarette smoke from his nostrils like soot from the stack of a train. "Frankly, I don't think she has a clue. Look how she goes in one direction and then another. Those fellows that Pollock..."

"Polyak," Upchurch corrected him.

"... yeah, Polyak... those fellows he hired, they won't be turning earth with their spades any time today."

"I wouldn't be so sure," Clay told him. "Cindy can't just turn it on and off like a water spigot. She just about has to be right on top of something before the feelings hit her. That's a large piece of pastureland out yonder. She just hasn't come across the right spot yet."

Moore shook his head in disgust. "I was against this from the beginning. Bringing a kid in to do a man's job! You Bible-thumpers might take stock in soothsayers and prophets, but I prefer scientific methods over such nonsense."

"Oh, like taking a shovel and digging up every last inch of this forty acre spread, I suppose?" Clay asked him, irritated.

"Maybe, if need be. If you ask me, we're wasting our precious time and J. Edgar wasted two round-trip train tickets from Hicksville."

Clay was about to give the big government man a piece of his mind, when he looked off across the dusty expanse of field and noticed his daughter standing stone still at a particular spot a quarter of the way across the pasture. "Wait just a second," he said. "Something's happening."

"Why the hell do you say that?" demanded Moore.

Clay was about to answer when Cindy Ann dropped to her knees in the dirt and began to scream.

The thin crescent of a moon hung in the dark autumn sky like a scrap of discarded toenail against black velvet. Earthward, crickets and toads sang an uneasy chorus, while a girl's frightened weeping joined in.

"Oh...oh God! What're you gonna do?" she sobbed, her voice garbled with emotion. She stared at a lopsided rectangle of open earth that lay before her. The coolness of the evening caressed her bare skin, raising gooseflesh and causing her to shudder uncontrollably.

"It's a freaking grave," came a gravelly voice behind her. "What the hell do you think I'm gonna do?"

He had done enough already; with his hands, his mouth, his manhood, and all manner of carpentry tools. She looked down at her left hand and cried even louder at the absence of three fingers there. The hacksaw hadn't been the worse of it, though. "I... I want... my... mama!"

"Your mama would be ashamed to lay eyes upon you, whore. Naked and bleeding, missing part of what God gave you. Miserable little bitch!"

She was screaming hoarsely now. "Mama! I want my mama!"

"Enough of this shit!"

Then she felt her head yanked backward by the bloody strands of her hair and gasped as cold steel was laid across her throat...

Cindy sensed the ones around her closing in, intending to provide support and comfort. "Stay away from me!" she wailed, on her hands and knees in the dirt, her eyes screwed tightly shut.

"Cindy, honey…" her father said, but could say nothing else. He felt utterly helpless as his daughter's lean body was wracked with violent sobs.

"Here!" she shrieked. The index finger of her right hand dug into the bare earth, splitting the nail in the process. "She's here!"

"Who?" Sandra asked softly. She shifted her steno pad and brought the stack of manila folders from where they had laid underneath.

"Melissa," Cindy muttered, her terror bleeding away until it finally subsided. "Curly brown hair, gray eyes, a scar on the tip of her chin where her brother accidently hit her with a garden hoe when she was eight."

The woman found the correct file. "Melissa Jacobson from Galbreath, Ohio." The photo clipped inside showed a fresh-faced girl with dark wavy hair and a tiny scar on her chin, just like Cindy had described.

Clay stepped in and gently helped his daughter to her feet. With tears in her eyes, she embraced him, burying her face in his shoulder. At the same instance, Dr. Polyak approached the spot and placed a red flag where the indention of Cindy's fingertip marred the earth.

Robert Upchurch sighed, as though finally able to breathe again. "Well, that's number one."

Polyak nodded his balding head. "Yes… eleven to go."

Cindy abruptly pulled away from her father and regarded them. "Eleven more? Oh no… there are more than that." She stared at the vast expanse of dusty farmland, her eyes haunted. Then she locked eyes with the bearded Hungarian. "You'll need to bring another wagonload of caskets, Doctor. Maybe more."

Cindy located the remains of three that afternoon. One was Melissa Jacobson and another was a fifteen-year-old girl with long blond hair named Susan Winters. One of the bodies Cindy found wasn't one of the twelve the FBI was searching for; a young Negro woman named Nettie Brown. Cindy's heart had ached for an hour after that discovery. Bully Hanson had been particularly sadistic prior to her death.

Dusk fell as the workers dug the remains from the spots where the tiny red flags had been placed and gently deposited them into three of the narrow pine boxes. Then Agent Upchurch decided that it was time to call it a day.

The FBI men offered to put Cindy and her father up at a local road court for the night, but Cindy preferred to stay and sleep on the screened-in porch. She claimed that she wanted to be there, in case something important came to her. Dr. Polyak offered them the comfort of his trailer, but Clay told him that country folks were accustomed to roughing it. Cindy's daddy wasn't too proud to accept a few pillows and blankets that the Hungarian doctor had on hand, however.

Cindy slept uneasily that night. Her slumber was invaded by horrifying scenes of what the three girls had endured at the hands of Bully Hanson. Finally, she got up at the crack of dawn. As the starry summer sky paled into grayness, she left her father asleep on the porch and quietly walked across the field.

In the gloom, she would stop every now and then, close her eyes, and listen to the sound of a distant freight train or the cooing of a dove in the bordering underbrush. It felt good to be alone for a change. Yesterday had been difficult; she hadn't enjoyed being observed every moment. It seemed like the day's success was solely on her shoulders, which, truthfully, it was. But even though she was the one who had found the bodies of the three missing girls, Cindy still couldn't help but feel like a performing animal, like the unicycle-riding monkey at the county fair.

It wasn't long before the sun began to cast an orange glow across the sky. Cindy was walking along the eastern border of the Potter property, staring at the ground at her feet, when a voice startled her.

"Howdy!"

She glanced up to find a boy sitting on the stone wall that ran along the field line. He was around the same age as her, maybe a little older. He was tall and lanky with dark brown hair and a wry smile on his face which reminded her of her late brother, Johnny. He wore a white t-shirt and jeans held up with suspenders.

"Howdy," she said back. "Where did you come from?"

The boy shrugged. "Here, there, and everywhere. What's your name?"

"Cindy." She had almost said Cindy Ann, but she was afraid adding her middle name would sound childish to him. "What's yours?"

"Tommy," he told her, flashing a smile that made her heart quicken. "Tommy Lang."

She nodded and lowered her eyes a bit, then started walking again.

"What are you up to? I'd say you were divining for water, but you ain't toting a forked stick."

A trace of a smile crossed Cindy's lips. "I *am* divining, in a way. Did you know that some innocent girls were killed and buried on this here property?"

The boy's jaw nearly dropped to his collarbone. "You don't say!"

"That's what I'm helping with. Trying to find them all."

"But how can you do that?" he asked, puzzled.

"It's hard to explain," she replied with a frown. "Some folks can walk the land and find well water. I can find dead folks."

"That sounds downright creepy. In fact, it sort of gives me the Heebie-Jeebies." He grinned and gave her a wink. "I still think you're kind of pretty, though."

The red-haired girl blushed, but returned his smile. "Kind of?"

"Well, heck, you *are* pretty. In fact, I wouldn't mind hopping down off this wall and giving you a kiss. If you'd let me, that is."

Cindy's cheeks blushed even brighter. Her heart hammered in her narrow chest. She had never kissed a boy before. Part of her was scared to death, while the other half sort of hoped that he would find the courage to take the chance.

"Cindy!" her father's voice called from the direction of the house.

Annoyed, she turned to see Clay standing beside a campfire next to the silver Airstream trailer. Abe Polyak was there, too, brewing a fresh pot of coffee. She waved at her pappy, then turned back to the stone wall.

Tommy Lang was gone.

Cindy's heart sank. Her father must have scared him off.

She thought of the boy with the dark hair, brown eyes, and easygoing smile, and felt a twinge of anxiety. A peculiar sensation settled in the pit of her belly; like a swarm of butterflies trying to take flight, but instead careening off the inner walls of her stomach.

He was just a silly old boy, she told herself. *A runaway, more'n likely. Nobody you need to be trifling with.*

But, walking back toward the house, she had a hard time convincing herself that what she was telling herself was the God-honest truth.

By Friday afternoon, they had located nine bodies.

Five were missing girls that the FBI had files on, while four weren't. The victims that they had no information on seemed to bother Agents Upchurch and Moore to no end. *I reckon I'm upsetting their perfectly-balanced investigation,* she thought, not without an underlying smidgen of satisfaction. In her eyes, the girls who hadn't been reported were every bit as important as those who had.

The sun was beginning to drop to the west, when Cindy stepped on a patch of earth halfway across the field and felt a jolt run through her, from the soles of her feet to the top of her head. Then, abruptly, time and place shifted.

"Need a ride home?"

"I…I really shouldn't," she said, still walking along the roadside, trying to ignore the man in the pickup truck. She remembered how her mother always warned her about steering clear of strangers. She walked a little faster, her school books held tightly against her chest. She still had a half mile to go.

"Come on… I ain't gonna hurt you none." The sky rumbled with distant thunder, followed by a few stray raindrops. "Better get in or you'll be soaked to the bone."

The rainfall began to intensify. She knew he was right. Against her better judgment, she opened the passenger door of the old Ford and climbed inside. The second she was inside, the heavens opened and the rural countryside was enveloped in a drenching downpour.

"See? Now accepting my generosity turned out to be a good idea after all."

"Uh, I reckon so." She pointed through the rain-speckled windshield. "I live a half mile up the road. The white house with the picket fence out front."

The man shifted into gear and sent the truck heading up the road. He held a Coca Cola bottle out to her. "Want a drink?"

The girl licked her lips. It had been a month of Sundays since she'd had a cold drink. "I better not."

"Go ahead," he urged. "I haven't drunk from it yet. Just popped the top a minute before I happened upon you."

Timidly, the girl took the bottle of pop. She took a drink and grimaced. "It doesn't taste right. Bitter."

The driver shrugged. "Just went flat, I reckon. Oughta go back to that country store and get my nickel back."

Thirty seconds later, the girl knew that she had made a bad mistake. Her vision began to swim and her arms and legs grew heavy and sluggish. "What… did you do to me? What did you put in that drink?"

She tried to reach out to open the door, perhaps to attempt escape, but she couldn't seem to find the handle. Her heart sank as they passed her house. Her mother was in the side yard, quickly trying to take down the clothes she had pinned to the drying line. She wanted to yell out, to cry for help, but she simply couldn't find the strength.

With some effort, she turned her head toward the driver of the truck. He smiled at her, but it wasn't the good-natured grin he had displayed before. This time there was cruelty to his smile, as well as something dark and dangerous in his stone gray eyes.

She began to cry as his free hand ran up her thigh and disappeared within the folds of her skirt.

"We're gonna have such a good time… just you and me."

Again, Cindy found herself on the earth; this time lying on her side, knees curled toward her chest. "The bastard," she muttered. "The ugly, evil bastard." Her fingers clawed at the earth, as if trying to gouge the eyes of Bully Hanson out of his smug, grinning face.

Sandra knelt beside the teenager. She refrained from reaching out to her. The woman had discovered that it only hampered the girl's readings, or visions, or whatever they were. "Cindy?"

she asked softly, holding her fountain pen expectantly over her steno pad.

The girl looked up at her, tears streaming down her face. "Elsie Baxter. Mount Ansel, North Carolina." She sobbed softly, anguish in her hazel eyes. "She was twelve years old, Miss Sandra. Only twelve!"

"Humph," grumbled Moore beneath his breath. "Another stray cat."

"Cindy," said Agent Upchurch, crouching next to her. "Cindy… do you think you could find some of the girls that we are specifically looking for?"

The sorrow in Cindy's eyes turned into rage. "Does it matter that she wasn't in one of your precious files?" she snapped, climbing weakly to her feet. "She was a poor, defenseless child! She was walking home from school and he took her and violated her!" The sixteen-year-old approached Upchurch, causing him to back up a few steps. "Do you want to know what he did to her once he brought her here? Do you! Because I can! I can tell you every horrible, nasty, hideous thing he did to poor little Elsie!"

The FBI agent swallowed dryly, at a loss of words. "I think we ought to knock off for today. Cindy needs her rest."

"I'd say so," Clay Biggs said. He embraced his daughter and his heart ached as she leaned limply against him, weeping forcefully against his chest. "Let me give you fellas a bit of advice. Start treating every one of these girls that Cindy's finding for you like they were your own long-lost daughters. Each one was as important as the other. If you don't want to do that, then me and my daughter will step back onto that train to Tennessee and you'll still have a field of corpses, with no earthly idea on how to pinpoint their whereabouts."

"I apologize if I sounded insensitive, Mr. Biggs," Upchurch told him. "It's just a little frustrating that most of these girls that are being exhumed aren't the ones we are actually looking for."

"Don't you think it's frustrating for Cindy, as well? Good Lord, man, she's not just finding these girls for you, she's feeling and experiencing everything that they did. Their fears, their despair, their agony. And it sure as hell is taking a toll on her, too. We've only been here a couple of days and it looks like she's already lost a pound or two. Honestly, I don't know how much longer she can do this."

Cindy mumbled something into her father's shirtfront.

"What's that, pumpkin?" Clay asked, pulling away.

"I said, I can do it for as long as it takes," his daughter told him. Her moist eyes were full of determination. "I'm the only strength these poor girls have now. They can't climb out of the grave under their own power, so I have to help them… even if it hurts me in doing so."

Later that evening, after supper, Cindy slipped away from the others and made her way, unseen, across the shadowy pasture, to the stone wall. For some reason, she wasn't at all surprised to see Tommy Lang sitting there in the same spot he had occupied earlier that day.

"Howdy, Miss Cindy," he said. "I've missed you."

I've missed you, too, she wanted to say, but didn't. "Have you been out here all day, hiding? Did you see me at my work?"

The boy's smile faded and he nodded solemnly. "And grim work it is, from the looks of it. I watched them dig the bones out and stick 'em in those wooden crates."

Cindy suddenly felt self-conscious under his gaze. "So, what do you think of me now? After you saw what I can do?"

"I'd say you're mighty special for doing it," he said. "Makes me want to jump down and give you that kiss even more."

"Then why don't you?" she asked boldly. She thought better of her question an instant later and regretted challenging him. If he did make a move toward her, she would likely cut and run like a frightened doe.

But Tommy remained where he was. "I don't know. Honestly, I don't know why I don't come right over there and give you a big ol' smooch on the lips."

Cindy planted her fists on her narrow hips. "Could be that you're just plain lazy."

The boy chuckled and extended the palms of his hands. They were thick with calluses. "Do these look like the hands of a slouch to you?"

"What... have you been working at one of the local farms or something?"

"Naw." His smile grew broader, until it nearly looked too big for his lean face. "I got me a job digging ditches."

"Well, you didn't dig no ditches today, if'n you were in the thicket yonder, spying on me," she told him.

Tommy Lang simply sat there, staring at her. "Yeah, I certainly oughta try to steal a kiss. Or play you a pretty song. I'm right good on the harmonica, if I do say so myself." His smile upended into a frown. "Only I lost mine a while back."

"Well, find it and you can play me that song," she said coyly. "And if I like it, I might just let you have that kiss."

"Hot dog!" he said with a laugh. Then he swung his legs over the stone wall and disappeared into the thicket and the gloom of dusk.

Later that night, after her father had drifted to sleep, Cindy quietly left the back porch, careful not to let the screen door squeal on its rusted hinges. Barefoot, she padded across the earth to the glow of the trailer's campfire. Dr. Polyak sat there, hunched before the flames, watching them listlessly. She could tell, not only by the sadness on his face, but his very thoughts, that his mind was thousands of miles away in a hell called Mauthausen.

"Mind if I join you?" she asked softly.

Polyak jumped. He looked up at her and smiled, embarrassed. "You startled me, Fräulein. But what couldn't startle a man on a parcel of land such as this? One so full of death and lost dreams."

She sat on the ground on the opposite side of the fire from the forensic anthropologist. "You were thinking about..." She closed her eyes for a hesitant second, and then reopened them. "About Ward 7."

A haunted expression shown in the middle-aged man's weary eyes. "Yes. Ward 7. The laboratories of Doctor Frankenstein and Doctor Jekyll all rolled up into one, with the playground of Baal and Beelzebub thrown in for bad measure. It was to be my turn... the day following my escape. They were to open my head and extract a fragment of my frontal lobe, perhaps even more."

His eyes returned to the dancing flames of the fire. "Sometimes I wonder what sort of man I would have become if they had succeeded. Or, rather, what sort of slavering, thoughtless creature."

"Monsters like Ziereis, like Bully Hanson, can tear down one's body and mind," Cindy told him, "but they can't conquer one's soul. That is forever beyond their grasp."

Doctor Polyak removed his eyeglasses and studied the sixteen-year-old. "Such wisdom and bravery in such a young girl. How have you come to possess such gifts in such a short period of time?"

Cindy matched his gaze, sadness showing in her youthful eyes. "By staring death nakedly in the face, Doctor. Time and time and time again."

Polyak shook his head and stirred at the flames with a long stick. "I wish you had never been brought here. You don't deserve the grief that has been foisted upon you… as well as the insolence and disrespect displayed by that pair of buffoons in tailored suits."

"Upchurch and Moore? They're just doing their jobs."

"They're twiddling their thumbs and drawing a nice, fat paycheck," Polyak told her. "You are the one doing all the work. And doing a fine job of it, too."

"Thank you," she said quietly, not quite sure that it was a skill to be particularly proud of.

A minute later, the Hungarian spoke again. "I have been meaning to ask a favor of you."

"Of course," said Cindy. "Anything."

He stood up, ducked inside the oval doorway of the trailer, and emerged with something cupped in the palm of his hand. He held the object out to her. It was a fragment of bone; about four inches long and brown with age.

"Would you mind telling me your impressions of this?" he asked, almost sheepishly. "I know it is silly, but it was one of my first discoveries when I studied anthropology as a young university student. There were fragments of ancient pottery in the same vicinity, as well as stone arrowheads and tools."

Cindy reached out and took the sliver of bone. Instantly, impressions flooded her young mind. "This belonged to a man.

Different from men today… very brutal, very *primitive.* He was in his mid-thirties, I believe, strong and a great hunter. He went upon the plains to find meat for his family, but he met a violent end at the mercy of some great beast. A huge cat with long fangs."

Polyak's eyes twinkled. "A sabertooth tiger!"

Cindy nodded. She handed the relic back to the doctor. "How did I do?"

"Excellently!" He stared at the piece of bone and then reverently stuck it in the pocket of his britches. "I thank you kindly for that, Fräulein. More than you could know."

Again, their conversation lapsed into silence. When it resumed, it was Polyak that spoke. "You know, I have heard you out there, in the pastureland. In the morning and late in the evening… talking to someone."

Alarm shown in the girl's eyes. "It was… just a friend," she stammered nervously. "Please, don't tell Pappy about it. I'm not sure if he would be very understanding. When it comes to me, he's mighty protective, like a grumpy ol' bear protecting its cub."

Polyak smiled and nodded, but the expression in his eyes was peculiar. "I will keep what I have heard to myself," he assured her. "But my advice to you, Cynthia Ann, is to take care. Watch yourself and do not let anything deter you from the work you have been brought here to do. It is extremely important work… much more so than even you realize."

His words made the girl feel a little uncomfortable. She stood up and rubbed her arms, despite the muggy heat of the night. "Well, I'd better get some sleep. I've enjoyed our talk."

"So have I, Fräulein," replied Polyak. "Rest well."

Cindy started back across the short stretch of dark earth that stretched between the silver trailer and the farmhouse. Silently, she crept back through the screen door and settled into her blankets on the oak boards next to her father.

She sighed deeply and closed her eyes. *Heavenly Father, please give me strength,* she prayed, listening to the crickets in the darkness beyond the mesh of the screen.

It wasn't long until an uneasy slumber claimed her… and she began to dream.

She found herself lying not on the boards of the porch floor, but on a bed. A sagging bed in a cramped room. Moonlight shone through the single window. The nocturnal glow revealed dark linens beneath her. She reached down and ran the palms of her hands along the bed sheets. They were coarse and stiff with dried blood.

Cindy wanted to leap up and flee that awful killing place, but she could not. She could only lie there, motionless, staring at the room around her. On a table nearby, stood a long metal tool box. It was open and, scattered around it, were a dozen or more utensils. Hammers, screwdrivers with their flat ends filed to wickedly sharp points, C-vises, hacksaws… all coated with blood and thick clots of flesh and hair.

She heard footsteps beyond the closed door. Footsteps that echoed distantly at first… then grew nearer.

Again, Cindy attempted to pry herself from the gory mattress, but she was held in place. This time she looked at her wrists and ankles. They were bound with thick rope and the heavy leather of old shaving strops. Her breath hung in her chest, afraid to exhale, as the brass knob slowly turned and the mechanism opened with a click.

Slowly, the door swung inward. But it was not the hulking, broad-shouldered form of Bully Hanson that filled the doorway. Rather it was a procession of young girls… dozens of them. The gathering filed into the killing room, one by one, and stood around the walls. They were all naked and mutilated… as they had been in their final frantic moment of life.

"You can not trust him," said a fair-haired girl of fourteen. Empty sockets yawned where her eyes had once been..

"Who?" Cindy asked. "Who are you talking about?"

"You can not trust him." This from a girl with hair as long and red as Cindy's. Her teeth had been yanked free with a pair of pliers, as well as her fingernails.

"Can't trust who?" Cindy demanded. "Agent Moore? Doctor Polyak? Who?"

The girls simply stood there and stared at her… those who still possessed eyes, that was.

Then the moon in the window drifted behind a cloud and the room was choked with pitch darkness.

Cindy awoke to find herself standing in the center of the field.

"What am I doing out here?" she said aloud. Frightened, she turned in the direction of the house and started back.

She had taken only a few steps, when she stubbed her toe on an object partially protruding from the earth. Curiously, she stooped and dug the article from the soil.

Cindy held it in her hand for a long moment, taking in the sensations it conjured, letting it tell the whole sordid story in flashes of darkness and flowing crimson.

"Oh no," she whispered, her lips trembling. "No... it can't be true. It just *can't!*"

Still holding the object, she swiftly ran back to the rear porch of the old farmhouse, crying all the way.

The following morning, at the crack of dawn, Cindy returned to the place where she had discovered the object the night before.

She stood there and faced the stone wall. A moment before, the top of the rock barrier had been empty, but now Tommy Lang sat there, beaming that boy-next-door smile at her.

"Well, you wanted to kiss me," she told him. "Come and do it."

Tommy's smile broadened. "You kidding me?"

"No. I'm willing, if you are."

The boy hopped down off the wall and, with a swagger, made his way across the pasture toward her.

As he approached, Cindy's heart quickened and she felt her spirits sink. The knuckles of her right hand whitened as she clutched the thing she had found half-buried in the earth of the abandoned field.

A moment later, he was standing scarcely two feet in front of her. "Are you sure about this?" he asked.

Cindy's hazel eyes began to moisten. "Just kiss me," she replied, her voice cracking.

"Well, here it goes." Then he leaned forward, directing his lips toward hers.

And, like a mirage, drifted right through her.

Tommy Lang seemed startled. "What... what just happened? I didn't even feel you."

"That's because..." Tears trickled down Cindy's freckled cheeks. "That's because you're dead."

The boy laughed, but there was no humor in the sound. "I don't understand."

"Take a look at what I found buried in this spot and you will." Lifting her right hand, she opened her fingers. Lying across her palm was a rusty, dirt-encrusted harmonica.

Tommy's eyes widened. "Oh God... now I remember."

Cindy closed her eyes and saw it all, exactly how it had happened in October of 1933.

Tommy tossed the last shovelful of dirt out of the rectangular hole, then the tool up afterward. He was preparing to climb out of the grave, when he found Bully Hanson standing at earth level, staring down at him.. He had his latest victim with him; a girl named Laura from West Virginia. Her pretty blond hair had been shaved from her head and she was all bruises and razor cuts from scalp to feet.

"Did you dig it deep enough, Tommy?" Hanson asked him. "Deep enough for two?"

The boy stared at his partner in shock. "What the hell do you mean, Bully?"

"It's time for us to part company," he replied. He gave the girl a shove. With a shriek, she lost her footing at the tip of the grave and fell into the shadowy pit.

"But... but I helped you get them," the boy protested. "We shared them, Bully." An unstable light shown in his brown eyes. "We made them scream, beg for mercy. And you want to turn around and stab me in the back?"

"No stabbing this time, Tommy boy." Bully Hanson grinned as he withdrew a sawed-off twelve gauge shotgun from the folds of a burlap bag and cocked the twin hammers.

Cindy's mind was filled with fear, as well as the flash and thunder of the shotgun discharging. She heard Tommy scream out once... then there was only silence.

An hour later, Clayburn Biggs and Abraham Polyak walked across the field to where Cindy Ann sat in the dead center of Potter's field, her chin resting atop her knees, her eyes dazed and unfocused.

"Baby doll," Clay said, kneeling next to her. "Are you okay?"

She pointed to where an old harmonica lay on the ground at her feet. "You'll find two buried here. A girl named Laura Peterson… and a boy named Tommy Lang."

Cindy Ann and Clayburn Biggs spent two weeks in the little Kentucky town of Millersville. In that fourteen day period, Cindy helped the Federal Bureau of Investigation located thirty-four missing girls; the twelve they had been looking for, plus twenty-two more that they had no idea were even there. They had also discovered the remains of an eighteen-year-old boy by the name of Tommy Lang, which was believed to have been Bully Hanson's accomplice in the abduction, torture, and murder of the unfortunate victims.

Cindy and her father stood on the platform of the Millersville depot, waiting for the afternoon train to arrive. Agent Robert Upchurch was there, as well as Dr. Polyak.

"Cindy, I appreciate your help in closing these cases," Upchurch said, shaking the girl's hand. "And so does the Bureau. You did a great service, especially for the parents of all those poor girls."

"I'd like to say it was my pleasure, Agent Upchurch," she replied, "but, honestly, I can't. There was no pleasure to it at all."

"Of course not," he said. "But like I said, we sincerely thank you for what you did."

Cindy turned and regarded the Hungarian doctor. "Doctor?"

Polyak embraced her tightly, his eyes tearing. "You know how we talked of devils, Fräulein? Well, there are angels as well. I doubted that once, but you made me a believer."

"I'm no angel," she whispered. "I'm just a girl with a gift."

"A gift from God," he assured her, then stepped away.

Clay glanced around. "Where are Miss Sandra and Agent Moore?"

Suddenly, a peculiar expression crossed Cindy's face. "Will you gentlemen excuse me? I've got to go to the bathroom."

Quickly, she left the railroad platform and made her way into the long structure of the train depot. She passed the rest rooms and emerged from the door at the opposite side of the lobby. Cindy stepped onto the boards of the building's long front porch and turned to her right.

There, at the far end, next to some crates and luggage, Nathan Moore had his wife cornered. The look of terror in her pretty face told Cindy that he had found out about her most recent pregnancy.

"So when were you gonna tell me about it, huh?" he demanded, his massive frame dwarfing Sandra's small stature. "Didn't you think I had a right to know?"

"Of course, dear," she said in a timid voice. "I... I just wasn't a hundred percent sure that I actually was, that's all."

Moore's tiny eyes darkened and he blew cigarette smoke from his nostrils. "You know very well that I don't want any kids."

"There's nothing we can do about it now."

He took a lumbering step forward. "I can take care of it... the same way as last time."

Sandra cowered between two stacks of crates. "Please, Nathan... don't hurt me. I want these babies. I really do."

"Babies?" Moore's face reddened in rage. "I told you I didn't want children, Sandra." He took the cigarette from his thin lips and brought it up to her face. "I warned you before, but apparently you didn't get the message."

The woman with the auburn hair flinched, waiting for the sensation of burning pain... but it never came.

Instead, the big man's eyes widened and he shook his hand, sending the cigarette to the floorboards of the depot platform. He stared at the back of his hand and saw the flesh grow pink and pucker. A wisp of blue smoke drifted from the hole in his hand as the circular wound first turned crimson red and then blackened.

"Leave her alone," warned a voice from behind him.

Moore turned to find Cindy standing several yards away. "This ain't none of your damn business, girl!"

The sixteen-year-old's eyes were stone cold. "I'm making it my business."

The FBI agent took a single step toward her and then began to scream. Half a dozen burns surfaced across his body, one after another, each the size and shape of a cigarette butt. He dropped to his knees, his breath hissing between his clenched teeth.

Cindy walked over and knelt before him. "Listen to me and listen good. You will not raise a hand to your wife or your two children. And you'll not take a cigarette to them either. If you do, it will come back to you tenfold. Believe me, it will. I've already planted the seed inside you. If you suffer because of it, you only have yourself to blame."

The girl heard footsteps behind her and then her father's voice rang out. "Cindy… what's going on here?"

"Just having a heart-to-heart talk with Agent Moore here," she said, standing up. "Isn't that right?"

Grudgingly, the big man nodded and, painfully, rose to his feet. He glanced over his shoulder at this frightened wife. Except that she was no longer intimidated by him. Her eyes were stern as she regarded him. He knew then that his hold on her was gone. If anyone needed to watch their step now, it was him.

Fifteen minutes later, the train headed for Tennessee pulled out of the Millersville station. Cindy waved at them all from her window, then settled back in her seat with a sigh.

"Glad to be getting back home?" her father asked her.

"You better believe it," she told him. Cindy sat there quietly for a long moment. "Pappy?"

"Yes, Pumpkin?"

"Do you think I could… you know… keep on doing this?"

"Doing *what*?" he asked, although he knew exactly what she meant.

"You know, helping folks," she said. "Like I did Agent Upchurch and all those families who suffered because of Bully Hanson's evil ways."

Clay was amazed. "And you would actually *want* to do it? I know how hard this was on you."

"Yes… but it was also extremely satisfying. Almost like I was called to do it, the way some men are called to preach."

Clay shrugged and tipped his hat over his eyes, intending to get a little shut-eye on the long trip home. "I reckon the police could use a girl like you every now and then."

Cindy stared out the window at the lush green countryside rushing past her. She smiled at her reflection in the pane of glass, which appeared more woman than child. *If they call me, then I'll come,* she thought to herself. *After all, how can the devils get their just dues if the angels sit on sidelines and do nothing?*

About the Author

Ronald Kelly was born November 20, 1959 in Nashville, Tennessee where he was raised a Southern Baptist. He attended Pegram Elementary School and Cheatham County Central High School (both in Ashland City, Tennessee) before starting his writing career.

Ronald Kelly began his writing career in 1986 and quickly sold his first short story, "Breakfast Serial," to *Terror Time Again* magazine. His first novel, *Hindsight* was released by Zebra Books in 1990. His audiobook collection, *Dark Dixie: Tales of Southern Horror,* was on the nominating ballot of the 1992 Grammy Awards for Best Spoken Word or Non-Musical Album. Zebra published seven of Ronald Kelly's novels from 1990 to 1996. Ronald's short fiction work has been published by *Cemetery Dance, Borderlands 3, Deathrealm, Dark at Heart, Hot Blood: Seeds of Fear,* and many more. After selling hundreds of thousands of books, the bottom dropped out of the horror market in 1996. So, when Zebra dropped their horror line in October 1996, Ronald Kelly stopped writing for almost ten years and worked various jobs including welder, factory worker, production manager, drugstore manager, and custodian.

In 2006, Ronald Kelly started writing again. Since then, he has written and published several new novels (Hell Hollow, Restless Shadows, and The Buzzard Zone), numerous short story collections, and has become an elder statesman of Southern-Fried Horror in his chosen genre. In 2021, his collection of extreme horror tales, The Essential Sick Stuff, won the Splatterpunk Award for Best Collection. He is currently working on The Saga of Dead-Eye, a five-volume horror western series. Book One, Vampires, Zombies, & Mojo Men was recently published by Thunderstorm Books and Silver Shamrock Publishing.

Ronald Kelly currently lives in a backwoods hollow in Brush Creek, Tennessee, with his wife and young'uns.

Curious about other Crossroad Press books?
Stop by our site:
http://store.crossroadpress.com
We offer quality writing
in digital, audio, and print formats.